For G, who hates this sort of thing

DOWN STATION

SIMON MORDEN

First published in Great Britain in 2015 by Gollancz
an imprint of The Orion Publishing Group Ltd
Carmelite House, 50 Victoria Embankment
London EC4Y 0DZ

An Hachette UK Company

3 5 7 9 10 8 6 4 2

A CIP catalogue record for this book is
available from the British Library.

ISBN 978 1 473 21146 9

Printed and bound by CPI Group (UK) Ltd, Croydon, CR0 4YY

www.simonmorden.com
www.orionbooks.co.uk
www.gollancz.co.uk

If you want a map, you must draw it yourself and keep it secret.

1

Mary looked at the watches in the window with an emotion that swung like a metronome between wonder and envy. They were beautiful, glittering bright with polished metal and inset jewels, and they were so very expensive. They shone like the sun, and they belonged on her skinny wrist. The work that had gone into just that one with the silver-steel bevel and the three separate dials must have been incredible, and no matter how many hours she worked, however hard she saved, she'd never be able to afford it in her lifetime.

The price tag was almost incomprehensibly high, as if whoever had written it out in fine, precise figures, had daydreamed away and added too many zeros. It had to be a joke; an obscene joke, even, aimed right at her. She wasn't laughing.

A hand came out from behind the display to snag the stand. As the watches retreated, Mary could see into the shop beyond. Tall glass cabinets with black velvet squares that showed off the clarity and colour of the gems, the coolness of the platinum, the warmth of the gold. Blond wood on the floor. Rich red on the walls. Lights. Lights everywhere.

She was about to turn away into the night when she accidentally caught the eye of the woman dismantling the window display.

For a moment, the immaculately made-up face, powdered and shadowed and lipsticked, froze, taking in Mary's scruffy Puffa jacket and scraped-back coils of black hair, her dark eyes and the acne scars on her cheeks.

And for a moment, rather than scorn or derision, a slight, secret smile and a rise of an artificially arched eyebrow. Neither of them could possibly afford to shop there. Then she turned her head – a voice, calling from somewhere unseen – and she hurried away towards the back room.

Mary imagined the clacking the woman's stiletto heels would make on the floor, the soft smell of a floral perfume, the whisper of material as stockings brushed against a tight pencil skirt. She imagined the woman's boss, paying her a pittance and using her beauty to sell beautiful things.

Her fingers, buried deep in the pockets of her jacket, curled involuntarily into fists. A brick wouldn't break these windows, thick and laminated. And even if it did, and she grabbed a watch in the second before the alarms went off and the street behind her filled with blue flashing lights, and somehow she avoided immediate capture – what would she do with it? She couldn't possibly wear it, and fencing it would leave her with, at best, a few quid in her pocket because the property would be red hot.

She'd be better off lifting something with a plastic strap from a display in a department store. More her style. More in keeping with her budget.

However: she had faithfully promised the magistrate she wouldn't do that again, because she had a job now, and was taking responsibility for her life, just as her solicitor and her probation officer had told her to say. It was a promise that, to everyone's surprise, including hers, she'd kept for nine weeks now, along with the job they'd got her.

She hadn't had to take it. She could have told them to stick it – except that everyone was expecting her to, and that, perversely had made her jut her chin and say she'd do it. It had probably

2

been the deciding factor in keeping her out of Holloway.

Mary turned from the window and the dazzling reflections of light. The street, though busy with black taxis and red buses, late-night theatre goers and rich kids, seemed dark and mean. It didn't help that the sky was so low: bulbous clouds descended almost to the rooftops, pregnant with rain, turning the harsh sodium glare a deeper red.

From away over Richmond, the first growl of thunder reached Leicester Square. For a moment, the sound stilled every other noise. People looked up, realised they were unprepared for a downpour, and contemplated their choices.

By the time Mary finished her shift, it would be morning and the storm would have blown over. She'd walk all the way back, tired and dirty, to her hostel along the freshly washed pavements. But still, inexplicably, despite everything, free. Not exactly free: she had regular meetings with her probation officer, a wispy thing called Anna who didn't seem at all afraid of her, and then there was her Anger Management course, which wasn't a surprise in the slightest, and her supervisor at work who would rat her out in an instant if she didn't turn up on the dot.

But free all the same. There were compensations to working for the Underground. The other – aside from not being banged up for twenty-three hours a day, or whatever the current regime demanded – was the people she worked with.

It was like clocking in with the United Nations every day, but she was a London girl and fine with that, though some of the accents were difficult – not just at first, either. Supervisor aside, and he really was a prime piece of shit, the rest of the crew didn't seem to mind her past, or her future for that matter. All that counted was whether she pulled her weight in the now.

She lugged her heavy bag across the road against the flow of traffic, towards the tube entrance. Another low boom echoed from the west, and the waverers decided against stopping for that last drink, heading for the stairs too.

When they pushed past her, running and talking too loudly for the confines of the concourse, she had her mouth open and an insult balanced on the tip of her tongue.

She checked herself, as she'd been taught: her breathing was fast and shallow, and inside she felt the cold rush of rage. Those that worked with her had lots of fancy names for it, but none of the labels meant anything to her, except a single off-hand comment that she seized on. The Red Queen was the one she recognised and owned: the terrible desire to give orders, to be obeyed, was deep inside her. Yet she knew she'd never be in charge of anything, let alone be a queen.

She counted to ten, and hoisted her bag back on to her shoulder. By then, they were gone, voices muffled in the depths. They were jerks. They probably hadn't even seen her. She was better than to rise at their carelessness. She took a deep breath, and carried on.

She had a pass: a proper pass that she'd had to sign for, that carried her photo – God, she hated it because it made her look like this weird child-thing – that allowed her to access almost everywhere and everything. Losing it would mean instant dismissal. Losing it and not telling anyone she'd lost it would be enough to land her inside. They may as well have printed her details on a gold brick instead of a laminated piece of plastic, for all they went on about 'the integrity of the system'.

The ticket hall was all but empty. A couple of stragglers tripped down the stairs from another entrance, stumbling and looking back the way they'd come, then hurried on to the barriers, wallets already out and in hand.

She followed them, touching in on the pad. The gates banged back, and she twisted to get her bag through.

Then it was the long ride down the escalator, down to the deep levels where it was hot and humid, and ever-so-slightly foetid. The advertising panels flickered their wares at her, five-second looped images, discordant and bright: enough to catch her attention and slam a message into her eyes, but not enough to seduce or explain.

One was for a holiday. How long was it since she'd had a holiday? They'd had day-trips from the home that had been, to quote one of the staff, a logistical nightmare. One of the other members of staff had said it was more like herding cats. It had been Southend, usually, and Eastbourne once.

That'd been a disaster. The M3 had locked solid, and they'd barely had time to eat fish and chips in some formica-countered sea-side shed before piling back in the minibus for the trip home. Eight teenagers with a broad spectrum of emotional and educational problems, four carers. It was a wonder that any of them made it back alive.

Again, the five-second image: a white beach and blue sea, and a lone woman, just about in a bikini, lithe and tanned and happy, running into the waves. Visit Greece, it said.

Mary didn't have a passport. She didn't even know if she had the documents to get a passport. She knew she'd need a birth certificate, and if one existed for her, she'd never seen it.

She imagined it, for a moment. That she was the woman. That the white sand was hot under her feet and between her toes. That the water was clear and bright and broke like diamonds as the wave hit her shins.

She stumbled off the end of the escalator, nearly falling in the process.

It was a dream. A pipe-dream. The woman in the jeweller's would one day meet a rich man who liked her enough to take her on holiday to Greece. And good for her. Nothing wrong in that. If she had the opportunity, she should grasp at it with both hands, and get out while she still could.

Mary took the stairs down to the westbound platform of the Piccadilly line. The last train was still ten minutes away. She was early.

There was nowhere to change. Literally, nowhere. Whatever

she was going to do, she had to do it here on the platform, amongst the drunks and the stoners. She could wait, but then it was always a rush to get kitted out, Mr Nicholls with his clipboard chivvying and tapping and looking at his watch.

So she walked down to the far end of the platform, right to where the jumpers usually positioned themselves for their one final step across the ill-minded gap, and dropped her bag to the ground.

The CCTV could see her, so she turned her back as she shucked her jacket. All she was wearing underneath was a thin tan vest that was a shade lighter than her skin. It got hot, working in the tunnels, and the first day, against all advice, she'd made the mistake of wearing a T-shirt and a pair of sweat pants.

She'd cooked, and she wasn't going to do that again.

From inside her bag, she dragged her thick orange boilersuit. Ironically, it made her look like she was on a chain gang, or she was one of those Guantanamo inmates. She shook it out, kicked off her shoes, and quickly dragged her jeans down to her ankles.

The rumbling she felt through her feet told her that a train was due. Probably eastbound on Piccadilly, as it was too solid a hit to be the nearby Northern line.

Someone wolf-whistled. She ignored them, and sat on the platform, on the boiler suit, to pull her jeans free.

With a few practised moves, she had the bright orange suit up to her waist. Left arm, right arm, and she was covered up, the zip-up front open to her navel but nothing showing.

She had a pair of heavy work boots in the bag too, steel capped, solid, thick rubber soles. She stepped into them and crouched as she laced them up. Now she looked down the platform, at the men where the whistle had come from, and studied their gelled hair and sharply ironed shirts. They could have been anything during the day – brickie, office drone, city trader – but here, at night, together and full of drink, they were all the same.

Now she had the uniform on, the oversized sexless boiler

suit and the big brown boots, perhaps she was a less of a catch, though she knew it wasn't the catching that mattered. For men like that, it was about the chase, a quick fumbling conquest, and move on.

She tied her unruly curls up in a red bandanna and piled her discarded clothes into her bag.

Five minutes until the last train.

The platform should have been filling up, but it was still sparse. She perched herself on one of the inadequate seats to wait, feeling the distant passing of other trains reverberate in her bones.

There should have been others of her shift down on the platform by now. She couldn't explain their absence. She chewed at her already gnawed fingers, hunched over.

The overhead sign ticked down the seconds and the minutes.

And suddenly they were all there, walking in a loud phalanx out of one of the connecting corridors and into her sight.

The meeting. She'd forgotten the meeting.

Her sudden relief was replaced by burning panic. She jumped up as if hearing a shot and took a step forward to explain to the clip-board wielding Nicholls. But what should she say? Some flannel about being late because of ... what? She hadn't been late. She'd just forgotten. Tell him that she'd blown the meeting off as a waste of her time? She was supposed to be avoiding the snark and triggers for confrontation.

She'd have to apologise. God, she hated doing that, especially to little weasel-faced Nicholls and his stupid ratty moustache. Mama was with him, matching him stride for stride, rolling her body like a ship at sea. If Mama was there, it'd be fine.

It was Mama who called to her first.

'Mary! Where've you been, child? Mr Nicholls,' and the way she said 'Mr Nicholls' always managed to convey just how much she'd like to scrape him off the underside of her shoe, 'Mr Nicholls was worried about you.'

'Sorry. Sorry. I was here in plenty of time, and I was just used to the routine.' Mary raised her gaze for a moment, and looked at the reflections of the overhead lights in Nicholls' black-rimmed glasses. 'I missed the meeting and I'm sorry.'

Nicholls stopped in front of her and consulted his clipboard. 'Mary. All staff are required to attend such meetings as management see necessary to facilitate the smooth running—'

He was interrupted by an almighty boom, like someone slamming a heavy steel door. It echoed forever along the tunnel.

When it had faded, he clicked his biro and started again. 'All staff—'

'Oh, let's not worry about that now, Mr Nicholls. Mary's a good girl and a good worker.' Mama was in full flow. 'She's fine and strong, and she was here early. She's always on time and never misses a day. She's one of the best on this team and she said she was sorry and I can tell her what we all talked about while we work, which is what we're not doing now.' She turned to the rest of the shift and shooed them into action with her thick fingers. 'Come on, people. We're keeping Mr Nicholls waiting.'

Nicholls might have the clipboard, but Mama seemed to run the show.

As the others put their bags down and started on suiting up, the last train was called. It seemed to settle matters, and Nicholls found it necessary to consult the top sheet of the sheaf of paper he had in front of him.

'Get changed, Noreen,' was all he said, and went to the locked telephone box on the wall.

Mama waited until their supervisor was otherwise occupied, then took Mary by the elbow.

'What d'you want to do something stupid like that for, girl? You know he's just itching for the chance to report you.'

'I forgot, all right?'

'Well, don't you go forgetting again.' Then she added. 'Help Mama into her finery, girl.'

Mama was short, but wide, and wore nothing under her boiler suit but a pair of hefty knickers and a bra with more cross-bracing than Tower Bridge. Her wide legs filled the trousers, and she held in the rolls of chocolate-coloured flesh while Mary zipped her up.

'You're okay, girl. But you got to pay more attention. Doesn't matter if you do the job nine times out of ten. Folk like Nicholls, he's watching for that one time you don't.'

A waft of hot, steamy air presaged the arrival of the tube train. It rattled and squeaked into view, and the carriages flashed by. Then it slowed, and the blur of windows resolved into discrete images of people mostly standing, even though there were plenty of empty seats.

They looked nervous. Some of them wanted to get off, and did so quickly the moment the doors opened, jumping the gap and hurrying quietly away. Those getting on were frowning, glancing behind them, hesitating before boarding.

The buzzer sounded, the voice intoned. The red lights at the rear of the train receded into the black tunnel, grew faint, winked out. The flurry of litter stopped wafting on the track bed, and was still.

Mama took a pair of cotton gloves from the cleaning cart, and a black bag. She passed them to Mary, then helped herself.

'Aren't you supposed to be telling me what Mr Nicholls was saying?'

'Oh, it's nothing worth wasting your time on, or mine, either. Now you stay out of trouble, girl.'

'Yes, Mama.' Mary pulled on her gloves and flexed her fingers, watching the woman dole out supplies and advice to the rest of the shift. Most of them were women, none of them British except Nicholls, and he didn't really count as part of the team. He didn't do any of the work, just looked occasionally at his watch when he thought they were behind time and cracked the whip a little harder.

The three little tunnel lights winked from white to red. The rails were no longer live, and it was time to get to work.

She wasn't the first to lower herself down into the suicide pit, the deep gap between the running rails, but there was plenty of debris for her to pick up. Scraps of paper, sweet wrappers, more copies of the bloody *Metro* than she could count, buttons, coins domestic and foreign, articles of clothing – the baby socks and shoes she could understand, but the items belonging to adults? Seriously? – empty wallets thrown in by pickpockets, phones dropped by tourists, plastic bags, tin cans, bottles, pairs of glasses, and the thing that had freaked her out at the start but no longer bothered her: hair.

Teased out of passengers' heads by the whirlwind of passing trains, it formed spidery clumps, not just at the stations, but deep into the tunnels where it had to be picked out from the rocky ballast, by hand, by people like her.

Earrings weren't uncommon. Mainly paste with plated fittings, but occasionally something of worth turned up. And rings. Mary often wondered about those. Had they been lost from a cold hand, much lamented and impossible to replace. Or had they been torn off in anger and thrown under the train in an evocation of sympathetic magic that would have the ring-giver similarly cast under the wheels of an oncoming train? It wasn't called a suicide pit because it saved lives; rather, the concrete trough was there because it made it easier to retrieve the broken, scattered bodies afterwards.

They were supposed to turn the expensive stuff – notes, wallets and purses, lost travel cards, jewellery – over to Nicholls. He was, in turn, supposed to log it all and transfer everything to Lost Property in Baker Street. They were each supposed to watch everyone else and make sure the rules stuck. It was a lot of supposing. Mary knew at least a couple of her shift were in the habit of diverting the most saleable items inside their boiler suits. It was risky, but they thought it a perk of the job.

She didn't do that. She couldn't do that. She had to keep her nose clean. She was getting almost nine quid an hour which, when fences were offering somewhere between five and ten pence in the pound, was pretty good money. Some of it was going on paying off her past fines, but it wasn't like she had many outgoings.

But she didn't feel like she was going straight. She still had the same urges as before, to take what she wanted and lash out at those who pissed her off. The fear of what would happen if she gave in kept her partly in check, and recently, some little bit of pride flickered in her heart, sparked from God knew where.

She'd cleared her immediate area, and ducked under the middle rail to collect the debris from the far side of the tracks. Though the power was off, she was still reluctant to touch the rail, despite her rubber-soled boots. Her bin bag started to fill.

The tunnel echoed again to a growl of deep, distant violence. As she looked up, so did everyone else. She caught Mama's eye, and the women stared at each other until Mama shrugged.

'Rail replacement near Hyde Park,' said Nicholls from the platform, tapping at his clipboard. 'Come on, we haven't got all night. Back to work.'

2

The sparks from the angle grinder were intense and alive, as captivating as a firework. The noise was incredible, though; a singing wail that cut through skin and bone as much as it did the ear defenders that Dalip was wearing. He held on to them, in case they fell off and he became deaf. Outside in the marshalling yards, it was just about bearable. Inside the tunnels, conversation was reduced to simple signs and anticipation.

The bullet-headed man lifted the grinder from the broken rail and inspected his cut with a practised eye. He nodded with satisfaction and put the machine aside, holding it easily in one hand where Dalip struggled to use two.

He pulled his own ear defenders off and shoved them down around his neck. He mimed for Dalip to do the same.

See? The man who'd been introduced as Stanislav gestured to the rail, expecting Dalip to bend down and appreciate the skill involved. Dalip dutifully did so, admiring the thin bright slice taken out of the rail. When he straightened up, Stanislav mimed, *Now we lift the failed section and take it away.*

He bent down and scooped up two long metal bars, each with a hook at one end. He passed one to Dalip, and started to twist free the metal keys that held the rail to the sleepers. The top half of his boilersuit was tied around his waist, and his bare arms, slick with grease and sweat, bulged with muscle as he leant into each action. He made it look easy when it was anything but.

The track was replaced when it was necessary – and the keys had been forced into place by big men with big hammers. Releasing the rail again was a matter of leverage and technique, and Dalip had neither, relying instead on brute force that was too often beyond his meagre strength.

They were supposed to work as a team, each side of the rail, and match the other's movements. Stanislav watched the young man struggle and clench his teeth, swinging on his iron bar like it was a piece of gym equipment, before shaking his head and resting a gauntleted hand on the lever. He leaned close and shouted over the din.

'No. Use whole body. Lean out, arms straight, turn from shoulders.' He demonstrated and the key turned smoothly. 'You see. We are tool users, yes? Not brutes. Now you try.'

Dalip did his best to emulate Stanislav's technique, but he jerked at it. The older man frowned, and started to step in.

'No. No, I'll try again.' Dalip could feel the effort, the strain in his forehead where it was tight against his turban. This time, smoothly and cleanly, the bar an extension of his arms.

The key turned, and he felt the rail rise. He grew giddy with delight.

'Very good. Now the other fifteen.'

His smile slipped. This was what it was always like. An achievement made, a skill acquired, an exam passed: always a stepping stone to the next goal, and never a moment to bask in the joy of simply succeeding. And Stanislav was just another man in the role of teacher, to be respected and learned from.

Dalip nodded, and applied himself to the next key. It came out more easily. Perhaps it was easier, perhaps it was the looser rail. Perhaps he was doing it right, but that didn't matter, because there would be another thing along soon enough that he couldn't do, and would have to be taught, there in the dark and the dirt and the noise.

The rail was finally free. Eight men, stripped to the waist, carried it away with pairs of giant pincers, and brought a new one, whole and gleaming under the yellow lights. They lowered it into place with brief, shouted commands and started to knock it in, fixing it back to the sleepers with rhythmic blows of their lump hammers.

Dalip watched them and envied their nonchalant expertise. Oh, it wasn't like he was going to spend his life fixing broken rails – he was going on to make trains that floated above, rather than ran on, rails – and this was just a placement, the first of many, to give him some idea of what engineering was supposed to achieve at the sharp end. How the whole infrastructure of the Underground – tunnels, trains, ventilation, pumps, stations, even the movement of people from above to below and back again – had been designed and built.

There was so much to learn, he despaired sometimes.

Stanislav carried the first part of the rail welder to the site of the join, dumped it by the side of the track and jerked his head to indicate that Dalip should follow him.

He did so, obediently, like he did everything else asked of him. There was a shovel, an oxyacetylene torch, the gas tanks to go with it, and a reaction vessel with an outside so burnt it looked like a cinder. Bags of dust. Wet sand to seal the casting. All of it needed to be moved.

It was hot enough in the tunnel already. It was the hardest work Dalip had ever done, and he was barely an hour through. The thermite reaction they were setting up would fill the tunnel with acrid smoke and thick yellow flames, making the harsh conditions worse, and yet these men, hard-muscled and terse, laboured in it day after day. He couldn't cope. He'd faint and fail. He didn't belong there.

And whether Stanislav had spotted the panic in the boy's eyes

14

and realised he needed reassurance, or whether it was simply well-timed: he clapped Dalip on the back of his orange boiler-suit, hard enough to rock Dalip on his feet, and gave him the thumbs-up.

It was enough to steady his nerves. He was here to learn, not to be humiliated.

The whole tunnel shook as if struck. Dust hazed the air, and the lights flickered. The whole work crew stopped in mid-swing.

'What—'

Stansilav put an oil-smeared finger to his lips, and listened to the noises with wary attention.

They were a long way under London, and there should have been nothing else down with them but other tunnels. If something had happened above, on the surface, it would have had to have been immense to reach them. A bomb? A building falling down? An aircraft crashing? All three?

There was nothing to compare with the initial concussion, though a low groan of pressure creaked through the walls.

Their supervisor walked along the rail bed, making sure he was seen, exchanging words with his crew. No one else moved.

Along the tunnel wall were two bare wires running parallel to its length, suspended on clips at about head height. The supervisor clipped the terminals of his phone to the wires and pressed the call button.

He pressed the earpiece against the side of his head, and waited.

When he had to press the button again, there was a collective shifting of posture, of gently laying down the tools they were still holding, getting ready to move in whichever direction they had to go, and quickly.

He pressed the button for a third time, and stood, head bowed, praying for an answer.

When none came, he swiftly unclipped the phone and pointed east.

'We're evacuating. Green Park. Go.'

Everyone else had trained for this. Dalip had had an hour's talk. Stanislav took a handful of Dalip's boilersuit at the shoulder and didn't let go.

'With me. We walk. Watch your feet.'

'What's happening?'

'We do not know.' Stanislav half-shoved, half-dragged Dalip in the direction of Green Park. 'That is why we are leaving. If it is nothing, we will come back and carry on. If it is something, we can find out what it is. If it is a bad thing, better we are not here, between stations.'

It started off as a low rumble which slowly reached a crescendo, and then it faded away again. Rather than Stanislav holding Dalip up, there was a mutual bracing of each other against the shaking ground.

'Is that a bad thing?' asked Dalip.

Stanislav gave a thin-lipped smile. 'Not good.'

Everyone quickened their pace.

'Does this happen often?'

'No.'

'Are you going to let go of me?'

'No.'

The lights winked out, and it was utterly black for a moment. Torches were already in people's hands, and bright blue beams cut through the dusty air like searchlights. Dalip stumbled, and was held up long enough to find his feet again on the rocky ballast. Stanislav swept his torch across the tunnel roof and floor.

'Get yours and put it on. Put your hand through the strap and tighten it to your wrist.'

Men were walking past them in pairs, keeping an eye on each other, making sure no one was left behind.

Dalip fumbled his torch on, and fitted it around his hand as he'd been told, still with Stanislav maintaining a death-grip on his boilersuit.

'Okay?'

Dalip nodded, realised that he couldn't be seen, so mumbled, 'Yes.'

'Stay with me. Whatever happens, stay with me.'

They moved back up through the column of men and as they turned the slight corner, the green emergency lights on the platform of Green Park came into view.

Dalip remembered to breathe again. He was soaked with sweat, his face slippery, his first attempt at a beard prickling with the heat. Less of a dream, more of a nightmare, but at least the station was ahead. As was a fiery red glow in the distance, beyond the sickly light of the platform, where the tunnel headed east under the centre of the city.

He started to pull back even as Stanislav propelled him on. But he knew that he didn't want to get closer. The red was thickening, growing more real, like looking into the heart of a furnace. He twisted and struggled.

Stanislav picked him up, one handed, and slammed him against the tunnel wall.

'What?' he roared, 'Do you want to die down here? Do not fight me, boy. Do not ever fight me.'

Dalip tried to push the man away, the torch around his wrist dancing as he slapped at Stanislav's chest.

'We don't want to go that way!' he finally managed, just as Green Park's lights failed with a sigh.

It wasn't dark, though. Everything was suffused with red, and as the rest of the work crew reached the edge of the station, the first one burst into flame. His boilersuit caught with spontaneous ignition, starting at the front, rolling around him in a sheet until he was a candlewick, stumbling and tripping, arms holding the fire aloft. And another.

Bulbs popped, tiles cracked, plastic melted, metal warped and started to drip.

Stanislav's clothing was smoking. So was his own.

Now they were going west again, and they ran with no pretence at calm. The air was thick, alive with shadow and rippling with heat, the soles of their boots sizzling on the ballast, the rails cracking like whips as they expanded.

There was a ramp up, like the ones that led to platforms, except that they hadn't gone as far back as Hyde Park. Dalip lifted his torch and saw a brick wall, and that the wall had a door, and that the door had twisted out of its frame and was open just a crack.

He had no idea where he was, just that the infernal heat was behind him and the incredible noises were ahead of him. He turned aside and ran at the door, digging his fingers into the gap and pulling against the warped wood that seared the flesh from his hands even as he brought his foot up to gain leverage against the wall.

Stanislav used his own savage strength, and hinges squealed in protest. The door resisted, then gave, spilling them both to the baking ground. The older man was up first. He took Dalip's collar and dragged him through the doorway, throwing him on to his back in the tiny room.

The red heat outside grew and grew. The paint on the door began to blister. Stanislav pulled his sleeves over his hands, gripped the door handle firmly, and bellowed his defiance.

The door banged against the jambs, and still the paint bloomed and puckered. Dalip thought he was going to die there, watching the door burst into flame, waiting for the wall of heat to ride over him, his clothes igniting, his hair turning to brief, bright lights and his turban a fiery crown. He would wear the same silent expression of sudden, violent death as the rest of the work crew had done, his mouth making momentarily a hollow circle before his flesh scorched and his muscles grew rictus tight.

He scrabbled back as far as he could go, until he realised he was against another door, and it was cold metal.

He leapt up, pulled the handle. The door opened easily and

cleanly. It was dark on the other side, but that didn't matter for the moment.

'In here,' he said, just as the paint blisters burst with blue fire. Stanislav pushed past, and Dalip closed the door smartly behind him.

Stanislav slumped against the wall and coughed until he vomited, turning his head at the last moment to splatter the ground with acid bile.

Dalip's eyes burned from the fumes and the heat. His throat was raw, his head hurt, his skin was sore and he couldn't stop shaking.

The others had died, right in front of him, lighting up and lurching around on the rail track until they fell. He felt his own stomach tighten, and he tried to swallow, but he was parched.

'Where are we?' he managed. He fumbled for his torch and tried to make sense of the discordant images he was seeing. Two more doors. A series of grey cases and switching gear, also grey.

'Down Street.' Stanislav wiped his mouth with his hand. 'Disused station.'

'We must have gone past it the first time.' Dalip tried the door in the long wall; all that lay beyond was a rusted bath tub, no taps.

'There is no one here. No one to get help from. That is why we went to Green Park.'

'The others. They're—'

'Dead. Yes.' Stanislav pulled himself upright on the painted switch-gear. 'You saw them. They could not have lived. We must work hard not to join them.'

Dalip scrubbed at his eyes, which felt like they were full of grit. Work hard, the bullet-headed East European had said. He knew how to do that. He'd done nothing but, even though it was a different sort of work to this. He recognised that he should be curled in a little ball in the corner somewhere, mind numb, but instead, despite being out of breath, in pain, half-roasted, barely able to see or speak, he was unnaturally calm. Presumably, the shock would hit later, when he was back home, sitting at the kitchen table with his mum and dad and a cup of tea.

'Okay,' he said, 'Can we get out of here?' He put the back of his hand on the door they'd come through, and jerked it away. Too hot.

'I believe so. We must find the exit.' Stanislav shone his torch at the remaining door, opened it and peered through.

The next room was dominated by a tall case, also spray-painted in the same grey colour. Beyond that, another door, a narrow corridor, and suddenly the space opened out. Their torch beams picked out a broad junction, and an arrow on the wall – a modern one, with a stylised symbol of a running figure heading through an opening. When they investigated, they found stairs going up.

'Up is good, right?' Dalip stood at the bottom of the steps: at the top, the corridor appeared to turn to go back over the tracks.

'Up is the only way, whether it is good or not. Come.'

Stanislav walked carefully up the broad stairs, torch beam scanning ahead. Dense white smoke curled in the curved roof space and reached tendrils down towards them. He crouched to keep his head out of the worst of it, and Dalip ducked down, too.

The portion of the corridor that bridged the rail track below was melting. The floor seethed and swam, and the tiles that had clung to the walls throughout the Blitz were spalling off, cracking and falling into the slurry below.

'That way is out. It may take our weight, it may not. It may kill us anyway.' Stanislav spat on to the ground, and it hissed. 'Who goes first?'

Dalip wanted to nominate himself. The bridge wasn't going to last. If he didn't go now, he'd not do it at all.

'Together.'

They ran through the molten bitumen, side by side, sending up splashes of black liquid. Their thick overalls helped protect them from the worst, even though the distance was something they might have jumped if they'd had clearer heads and more time.

They were out and through, and in the darkness and smoke, it was easy to miss that the corridor turned sharp left. There was suddenly a wall rearing up at them, and a moment's confusion as they swung their torches to see which way to go.

Stanislav fell, tripping on a raised concrete plinth that jutted out into the corridor. Dalip was past him before he realised, and came back.

Words were impossible. Every breath was like being stabbed. He knew he wasn't strong enough to drag him, let alone lift him. All he could do was tug urgently at the man's sleeve and shine a light in his face.

Stanislav's already flattened nose dripped blood, running over his top lip and into the corners of his mouth. He spat, and spat again, and dragged himself up. Their faces were very close together and, despite their situation, the one thing that struck Dalip at that moment was the look of utter, snarling determination on the other man's face.

Stanislav roared at the fire, giving it his pain and anger and frustration, and it was enough to carry them both to the next door. They threw themselves through, heaving it shut behind them.

A stairwell. They were in a stairwell, with a narrow caged lift running up the middle of a metal spiral staircase. The air was thick with dust, and it was blessedly cool.

Now they were no longer running, no longer living from one heartbeat to the next, they both stopped. Dalip knelt on the ground in amongst the dirt and debris and pressed his turbaned head against the gritty floor. He could still feel the intermittent vibrations, dulled by the thickness of the cloth, and hear the drawn-out groans of tortured rock and iron.

Stanislav patted his shoulder. 'Come. We must make a report. To someone.'

Dalip ached. Everything that wasn't red raw was bruised. 'Okay.'

'You did not need to come back for me.'

'I – I did. You looked after me more than I did you.' Dalip sat up and used the end of the stairs to stand. With their torches dangling from their wrists, expressions were unreadable.

'You are just a boy. You have the rest of your life. And I … I. Ah well. What does it matter?' Stanislav slapped him on the back again. 'Come. We must climb.'

'What do you think's happened?'

'I do not know. It is big, whatever it is.' He started slowly up the stairs, and Dalip's torch caught the other man's boots. The soles were baked black like the bottom of an oven.

3

Mary looked behind her. She could hear the metallic pinging of footsteps on the stairs they'd just climbed themselves.

'There's someone coming.'

There were five of them. Four left from her own group, just one stray from another. How could they have been reduced in number so quickly? The darkness and confusion and, above all, the burning heat simply seemed to have swallowed them up, one by one – this one falling, that one trying to pull them back up, another just faltering to a stop, exhausted, and letting the oncoming tide of destruction take them.

All they had were those little green glow sticks, those and their work-wear. Everything else had been lost. Her bag, her clothes, left back at Leicester Square, had to be nothing but ash by now.

She had no real idea of where she was, either, only that there had been emergency exit signs and that they'd seemed like the only hope of escape. Going back had been out of the question. Going on had been just as unlikely: she'd been on her last legs, and she was used to running.

She hadn't had to persuade the others to follow her. They'd just piled in behind her, fewer than she'd expected, and blundered around in the dark until someone had found the way up.

It had been almost too late: the naked metal grille they'd had to pass, which led back out to the tunnels, had been glowing cherry red, and the heat had been almost too great to bear.

She couldn't remember if there'd been more than five of them at that point. Perhaps they'd lost someone else between then and now, too frightened, too tired to carry on.

There were five. And shortly there'd be more.

She moved to the back of the group, holding her glow stick high. There was a little door in the wall at the end of the short corridor where they were huddling, and just as she reached it, it opened at her.

She shrieked, and that brought a cry of shock from the other side. A bright white light struck her full in the face, and she raised a hand to shield her eyes.

'Point it somewhere else, you fucking idiot.'

'Sorry.'

The torches turned their aim toward the ground: the damage was done, though. Night sight ruined, Mary couldn't see anything.

'How many of you are there?'

'Two. There's two of us.' The voice that spoke seemed very proper, very English, despite the hoarseness. 'How many are you?'

'Five.' There'd been twenty of them when they'd started. How could there be only five left? 'What's happening? Why is everything on fucking fire?'

'Do I look like I know?'

She couldn't tell what he looked like, but someone with that accent ought to know.

'Well, do you?'

A voice behind the first man spoke. 'Miss? Please move out of the way. We would like to come in.'

She shuffled to one side, and two dark shapes edged past. They headed towards the remains of the cleaning crew, leaving her with the door. Noises – bad noises – echoed from below, grinding and groaning and booming, as if a monster was loose in the tunnels.

Perhaps there was a monster loose in the tunnels. It made as much sense as anything.

She pushed the door shut, and leaned on it for a moment's rest. Then she realised that the men would try and leave through the emergency door to street level, and she hurried to stop them.

'Wait, wait.'

Her sight was returning slowly. One of the men, the shorter, wider one, had already turned his torch off, and was indicating to his taller companion that he ought to do the same.

With the bright lights extinguished, and only the steady green glow from the sticks, it became easier to see.

Easier also to tell that the way out, the door that led to the pavement outside, was outlined in an inconstant red.

Stepping over the legs of the other women, the three of them stopped at the heavy fire door with its push-bar mechanism. Bolts secured the door top and bottom, but there was a slight gap at the edge of the frame.

'We can't go this way, and there's no other way out,' she said. 'The whole street's on fire. I mean, where's the fucking fire brigade when you need it?'

The taller man – he had something on his head, a bandage of sorts, that made him look taller – risked putting his eye to the crack and peering out.

'It's burning. Everything's burning.' His shoulders slumped. 'I thought we were—'

The other man checked for himself, taking his time. 'We cannot stay here. All we can do is choose when we leave.'

Mary reached forward and poked the man. 'Oi. We can't go out in that.'

Even in the gloom, she could feel his ire, and she drew her hand back.

'Listen,' he said, and she prepared herself for a lecture.

But he said nothing, and she decided that she would listen.

Over the close-by panting and soft moans, behind the more distant, tortured noises rising up from beneath, she could hear a dull roar, like a static hiss. That was new. And it was getting louder.

When she'd had her fill, she asked him, 'What is that?'

'I do not know,' he said. 'but I do not want to be here, in this tiny corridor, when it finds us. Also, the building above us will be on fire. At some point it will collapse. We have to leave before it falls on us.'

She looked around. Everyone was watching them.

'Do you want to die here?' he growled.

'I don't want to die out there.' She realised that she might not have a choice. 'There must be someone coming for us?'

'London is on fire! If we are going to live, we have to save ourselves, as we already have done, as we will do again.' He spoke past her, to the others. 'On your feet! Up! We must be ready.'

He didn't wait. Before Mary could stop him, he brought up his foot and landed it squarely on the push-bar. The bolts banged back, the door swung open.

The narrow street was burning. Fire poured from the shattered windows in the building opposite. A line of cars, wreathed in thick orange flame and black smoke, were parked along the kerb, sitting on their steel rims, reduced to metal shells. The twisted shapes merging into the molten river of tarmac could only be bodies.

As the wall of heat drove them back, the taller man reached out, straining for the push-bar, to drag the door shut again. Instead, he fell into it, and it began to swing out wide.

The air itself seemed to tear in two.

Instead of fire, there was water.

A wave slapped through the open doorway, and a gust of wind blew into the smoke-filled corridor, dragging a spiral of soot outwards and away. It curled into a blue sky studded with clouds shaped like torn sheets, and a bird – a seagull – darted by at head-height. It wheeled back for a second look, before flapping once and soaring towards a tall headland of jagged black rocks.

The bottom of the cliff was strewn with boulders that extended out in a line as far as the door, and the sea washed over them, hissing and foaming, then drawing down with a rattling gurgle.

The light was bright and clean.

Another wave spilled across the threshold, and the tall man – not wearing a bandage, but a turban – struggled back in from where he'd fallen, half in and half out the door. The lower half of his orange boilersuit was already soaked and dark.

Mary looked behind her. It was the same corridor, the same smell of heat and burning, the same taste of smoke and ash, the same sound of failing steel and masonry. The same people she'd cheated death with, filthy, dirty, wild-eyed and desperate.

Then she tried to take in what was beyond the door: the land, the sea, the sky.

'What the fuck have you done with London?'

She pulled the guy with the turban behind her, and hung out of the doorway, fingers clinging to the frame.

She felt the wind and the waves against her face. The spray was cold, a sudden shock after the heat, and she wiped her sleeve against her cheek. It came away wet.

Mary was afraid. The fire, the burning buildings, the cindered bodies: she'd been expecting that, had steeled herself to see it. But not this, this wide-open vista, nothing recognisable, no sign of brick or glass or plank or metal or dressed stone.

'Mama? Mama, can you see this?'

Mama roused herself enough to sit up. She'd fared badly. Her feet and hands were raw and, where not raw, blistered.

'Mary, girl. I see it. I see it.'

'What do we do?'

From below them, a boom sounded, rattling the walls, shaking the ceiling. Tiles and brickwork cracked and flew, tiny pieces of shrapnel that cut and stung.

The man with the shaven head and broad bouncer's shoulders stared out at the line of rocks that pointed towards the shore. His face was set, his body tensed.

Then he turned and spoke to them all: 'Nothing has changed. Either we die here, or we take our chances out there. I know which I choose.'

With that, he stepped over into the sea. The water closed around his ankles, lapped up his shins. He bent over to steady himself, one hand against the wet, barnacled boulder, and took another step. His foot slipped slightly, and he had to use both hands to stay upright. When he glanced back, he was smiling, his teeth white against his soot-streaked skin.

The roaring from inside the station was too loud to ignore now. It sounded like an oncoming train, but overwhelming and inexorable. Everything was shaking, and this, surely, was the end. The stray, the Chinese-looking woman who'd joined them in the tunnels, didn't hesitate. She jumped out and over, and didn't look back.

'Up, Mama, up!' Mary dipped down and dragged at Mama's arms. 'Everybody up.'

Mama responded slowly, uncertainly, and Mary rounded on the man in the turban. 'You. You've got to help.'

He did. He got behind Mama, pushed her towards the open door. Behind him, the red glow started to build.

'Hurry. Out. Out.' He reached out for the other two women and they climbed up him, almost pulling him over in the process.

Mama was still in the doorway, blocking it, feet against the jamb, hands braced against the uprights. Mary wasn't gentle. She put her hand in Mama's back and heaved her into the sea, letting the others jump past her and pick her up.

Then it was her and the turbaned man – boy, he was just a kid, like her – facing each other across the width of the open door.

'This. This is fucking nuts, right?'

'Where are we?' His brown eyes were wide and wild, struggling to take any of the impossible view in.

'We're in London.' She looked over her shoulder. The narrow door that led from the staircase to the corridor creaked, and jets of flame bored through the gaps. She watched Mama struggle and wail as a wave caught her full on, and heard the others shriek at the cold. She put one foot into the sea, felt the water rise up, fill her boot. The rest of her was burning. There was no choice, really. 'And now we're not.'

She pulled on the door, ready to swing it back shut, and the boy, already wet to his waist, jumped in again to help her wrestle it home. Neither of them gave any thought as to what the door might be attached to.

There was an order to it. The bar inside had to be raised again and the metal latch caught before it would close. They got it wrong the first time, and the second time too until the boy held the door to reach up and set the mechanism up right.

The corridor was on fire. Mary heaved as hard as she could, and felt the bolts catch. She staggered back, and caught her first sight of the façade of a glazed red-brick tube station entrance embedded in a lone stack of rock, the endless ocean behind it.

She fell on her backside. The sea rushed in quickly, so that it didn't matter how nimble she was at standing again. The moving water dragged at her, and she had to hold on to the black boulder, studded with sharp white shells, to stop herself from being swept away.

She looked up again at the lintel, where the weathered letters were picked out in cream: Down Street. Above that was the hint of an arch, where it seemed to merge into the natural rock. The door was still there, surrounded by bricks. Painted grey, with a blue sign fixed to it.

Even as she read the writing on it, it faded and grew more indistinct. Now she couldn't tell if there had been a door or not, whether the bricks were simply jointing in the rock, whether the letters over the door were just a trick of the light.

Then it was gone. No more than a slab of wet rock, imprinted with a vague impression of a door. If the light changed, or she looked away, even that would be lost.

A string of orange boilersuited figures stretched from the lone stack in the sea, along the half-covered blocks, to the rocky foreshore.

The boy's turban was deep blue, dirty and scorched in places, wet with spray. He had a sort-of beard, one she'd mistaken for soot stains. He was staring back at the place the door had been, and he, like her, couldn't quite believe anything anymore.

'Are we dead?' he asked her, even as the water washed up his back and made him shiver. 'We should be dead, right?'

A wave caught her, making her body rise and she lost her grip. As she scrabbled at the rough rock for another handhold, she grazed her palm on a jagged edge, and her skin split. Blood bloomed in red beads along the cut, and when she was able to get her feet down again and brace herself against the pull of the sea, she inspected the damage.

It wasn't deep, but the salt water stung. She turned her hand palm out as evidence.

'You might be dead. I'm not.'

The first of them, the man the boy had arrived with, had reached the shore, and was climbing out of the surf. The others straggled behind him. Mary wiped her hand on her thigh and started after them, clambering over the rocks when the waves went down, stopping and holding on when they came up again and tried to wash her off.

She'd gone only a little way when she looked back. The turbaned kid hadn't moved, still fixated on the blank slab they'd all emerged from. He reached out and put his hand against it, pushing at it and seeing if it was real.

'Leave it,' she called. 'Leave it, okay?'

'Where are we?' he shouted back at her, repeating his earlier question. 'Where?'

'We're not being burnt to death in some disused station corridor, that's where.' She turned her face to avoid a direct hit from a wave. 'Did you want to stay there?'

'No.' He didn't sound certain.

'Then get your fucking arse in gear and get moving. The water's getting higher and I'm not fucking drowning for you.' She couldn't swim. Float maybe, but not swim. If she got swept away, that'd be that, and it wouldn't matter that she'd escaped the heat of the Underground that had claimed almost everyone else. So she moved faster, took more risks, received more knocks and scrapes, got everything wet.

And she was certain that she was still alive, that she wasn't some hollowed-out twisted skeleton cooked so hard her bones had split open to the marrow. No, that wasn't her. She was up to her belly button in water so cold she was losing the sense of feeling in her toes, climbing towards the shore along a line of rocks sharp enough to cut her.

Like the kid, she had no idea where she was, but unlike him, she didn't much mind that she hadn't gone the way of all the others. She'd survived, because that was what she was good at. She moved on, hand over hand. She was right about the rising height of the water. The line of rocks was disappearing, the waves topping them more and more regularly, covering them for longer, leaving her less time to make progress.

She made it. She reached a point where a strong hand came down and helped her up the last part, and on to a rock that wasn't swamped with every wave. She climbed higher, well out of the wash, and finally got to sit with her back to the cliff. She was exhausted.

The kid struggled on. He'd almost left it too late, and the sea closed over his turban a couple of times. He re-emerged, spluttering and gasping, shaking the water from his eyes and resighting where he was heading.

Finally, he was up. The older man reached for him like he had her, and he all but fell as he was dragged over the lip of the last rock.

They exchanged a word or two, and the kid climbed further up away from the sea.

Behind them, the line of rocks submerged completely, white foam the only sign of where they'd been. The stack in the distance was now an island, the waves surging around it.

The sun came out from behind one of the quickly moving clouds, bright and strong, and the gull swooped down from the headland in a flash of grey, heading out towards the horizon.

A sinuous shape broke that same horizon, thick loops of shining green scales reflecting the light like mirrors. A streamlined head full of teeth twisted this way and that, scenting the air, before plunging back into the water. The loops grew smaller, and at last a finned tail flicked up into the sky before disappearing.

Mary was on her feet. They all were, reflexively backing away from the open sea and towards the base of the cliff, climbing up the blocky boulders.

'What the fuck was that?' Her wavering finger pointed at the bare horizon for a moment longer, then she dropped her arm by her side again. Perhaps it hadn't been as she thought, she'd got hair in her face, or something else. A trick of the light. Just a wave. It had happened quickly, and far away.

But who was she kidding? They'd all seen it, or at least they'd all seen the shape of it and none of them remained unaffected. And there they were, all dressed in orange, reflective strips sewn into their clothing, standing out against the dark rock like brilliantly coloured flies on dog shit.

The bullet-headed man stood on the rock above her, staring out to sea just like her. His eyes were narrow, his lips a thin, grim line.

'We should get off the beach,' he said, without looking down.

'I'm good with that.' She was surprised at her own voice, how tight and high it was. It didn't sound like her at all. She coughed it away, and added, 'After you.'

4

Getting off the beach meant taking the long route along the shoreline into the next bay, where the unclimbable rock cliff gave way to a shallower slope, and the boulder-jumping to clattering over a series of stepped pebble banks.

The sea monster didn't put in another appearance, despite Dalip's constant attention.

His boots were mostly ruined, the already inflexible soles robbed of any cushioning by being melted flat. The outer covering had gone at both toes and heels, with the curved steel inserts showing through. He'd emptied them of water and wrung his thick socks out, but he'd had no choice but to put them on again, wet. It made it difficult to walk. They were already rubbing, and he'd have blisters soon.

Stanislav, despite having all the same problems and injuries, seemed to be immune to their effects. He strode out, greeting each new vista with undisguised glee, even though the landscape appeared devoid of any sign of human activity.

Dalip trudged up the loose bank at the back of the bay, stones rattling under his feet and sliding down the slope behind him. Stanislav was already at the top, hand shielding his eyes from the glare of the bright sky, scanning inland.

'Can you see anything?'

'Lots of things.'

He was right. There was a great deal to see: to their left, there was a high ridge that ended as the sea-cliff, and started in a tall mountain in the far blue-hazed distance. Ahead was a broad valley, a river cutting and recutting its way across the flat land in a series of braided channels. To their right, hills, backed again by more than one mountain peak.

There were short scrubby bushes up the slope to the headland, mixed in with one or two stunted trees. Inland, the trees grew taller and more numerous until they became a forest.

There were no houses, no walls nor fences nor fields, no roads nor tracks nor paths, no cows nor sheep nor pigs nor goats, no structures close by nor far away, no spires of smoke nor mechanical sounds. It was just them, and the wind, and the birds overhead.

And the sea monster behind them. Dalip looked over his shoulder, just to make sure.

'Where is everyone?'

Stanislav frowned. 'What do you see?'

'Nothing. There's nothing at all.'

'Then what do you think?'

'That there's no one here? That can't be true.'

'So you know where we are?'

'No.'

'Then how do you know that it cannot be true?'

Dalip pressed his hands together, felt the burns and scalds, felt the clarity of his pain. 'Do you know where we are?'

'All I know is that we are somewhere which has big snakes swimming in the sea. Have you heard of a place like that?' Stanislav watched for his reaction closely.

'There is nowhere like that. Not ...' Dalip gave up. He wasn't going to say it. He wasn't going to let the words come out of his mouth.

And yet the landscape was untouched, wild, untamed. There

35

were impossible creatures abroad. They'd arrived by stepping through a door, from the Underground and into the sea. A door that had more or less disappeared as soon as they closed it. He was right: there was nowhere like that.

'I must be dead. Or dreaming. Or I'm unconscious somewhere. In hospital, in a coma.'

'You think? Okay. Say it is so. What are you going to do now?'

Dalip was suddenly, painfully aware that he had an audience. 'What am I going to do?'

'Yes, you. So you are dead, or asleep, or whatever. You are still here.' Stanislav stamped his foot, releasing a shower of pebbles. 'I am here. She is here.' He pointed to the girl with the light brown skin who liked saying 'fuck' a lot.

'Yes, but ...'

'We are all here. While we wait to wake up, or for our souls to be collected, we must choose what to do next.'

It was him and Stanislav on the shingle bank, the others arrayed around them. Dalip felt the wind tug at the material of his boilersuit: yes, drying it out, but he was getting cold. And now that he'd stopped running, he was tired, and just a little hungry.

He shrugged. 'A cup of tea would be nice.'

Stanislav looked momentarily nonplussed. 'Tea. You expect to find somewhere that serves tea?'

'It's as likely as anything that's happened since it all started burning. So, yes. Tea. I'll have a biscuit too, while we're at it.'

'I cannot see a tea shop.'

'Then I suppose we'll have to make our own.' Dalip waved his hands in the direction of the river. 'There's water. If we can start a fire and build a shelter and find a tea bush ... I don't know what I'm saying anymore.'

'Shouldn't we,' said the brown-skinned girl, 'you know, be looking for help?'

'Where from?' Dalip beckoned to her. 'Come up here and tell me where help's coming from.'

She scowled, and marched up to the top of the bank, knocking his hand out of the way when he reached down to assist her. 'I can fucking manage, all right?'

Confronted with the same blank canvas of sky and land, her scowl deepened.

'Anyone got a phone?' she asked.

No one had, because they were back at either Leicester Square or Hyde Park.

'Fuck,' she said.

'Got yours?' Dalip asked.

'Fuck off.' She whirled around, looking for something, anything she recognised. Then she ripped off her grimy bandanna, threw it on the ground and stormed away, down the bank and away from the sea. Scrubby, heavy-headed grasses whipped at her legs, and she disturbed a nesting bird which flew up with a flutter and squeak. It made her jump, and she flailed at it to fend it off before realising it was just a bird and it wasn't going to hurt her. 'Fuck,' she bellowed, and kept on walking.

Dalip bent down to retrieve the strip of red cloth.

'How can you just accept this?' he asked of Stanislav.

'I am alive. I do not know how or what or where or why. But I am alive.' He turned to look at the sun. 'We have a few hours before it gets dark. We should find somewhere to spend the night now, and worry about what to do later.'

He set off, roughly in the same direction as the girl, leaving Dalip behind.

Dalip helped haul the big black woman called Mama up to the top then, out of courtesy, the three other women. They all stood together for a moment, watching the two orange-clad figures slowly recede into the distance.

'We can all see this, right? We're all seeing the same thing.'

Mama nodded, her hands on her hips. 'I reckon we are. What's your name, young man?'

'Dalip,' said Dalip. It was about the only thing he was certain of at that moment.

'My parents called me Noreen,' said Mama, 'but everyone calls me Mama.'

'Do you know what happened?'

'Well now,' she said. 'I can't explain any of it. Doesn't mean it didn't happen.'

He looked at his hands, opened and closed his fists, watched his fingers curl and straighten. Every scald and blister told him it did happen, and that he wasn't dreaming.

'Oh, come on.' Mama nudged his arm. 'Your friend's right. We should find somewhere to stay, and worry about where we are later.'

'He's not my friend. I'd never met him before tonight. Last night. Before the shift started. He's just someone who was told to look after me.'

'Then he's done a good job, yes? He looked after you just fine.'

'I suppose.'

'Well, then.' She looked around her, and co-opted the other women into the conversation. 'We should stay together, at least till we get to go home. We'd all better follow along now.'

To pre-empt any more of his angst, she set off after Stanislav, and there was nothing for it but to go with her. They walked as a knot of orange, none of them feeling brave enough to spread out across the plain.

He didn't know much about plants or birds, but there was nothing unusual about the ones he was seeing. The seagulls? They had seagulls in London, and the ones here looked like those. The small brown bird that the girl had disturbed? He hadn't got a good look at it, but it wouldn't have been out of place in a nature documentary. The grasses were blue-green, the leaves on the stunted bushes similar, and he thought he could remember a geography field trip where they'd been shown salt-adapted vegetation that resembled what he was seeing.

Perhaps they were just somewhere they ought not be, and they'd got there by some weird physics. Everything seemed disconcertingly normal. Apart from the sea-monster. What was he thinking? There was an actual sea-monster. He hadn't imagined it. This wasn't any place that had ever been covered by the Natural History Unit of the BBC.

A thought struck him, morbidly funny: it'd be a privilege to end his time there being chased across a primeval landscape by a pack of allosaurs.

'What? Why are you laughing?'

Dalip coloured up, and stared firmly at the rough ground. He didn't have much experience talking to women. His mother and grandmother, yes, though his Punjabi was frankly shocking. Teachers, yes, but there was no question of any sort of social relationship. Doing an engineering degree was not-quite-but-almost an all-male affair.

The one who'd spoken to him was just smaller than him, with a wave of black hair with reddish highlights that may or may not have been cosmetic, and the beginning of crow's feet at the corners of her eyes. She wasn't Anglo – he didn't have the skills to tell from where. Her ... friend? Sister? She looked similar, though she wore her hair so that it shielded her face from view when she turned.

'Why am I laughing? Because I was wondering when the dinosaurs were going to turn up and eat us.'

She was looking at him, trying to work out whether he was serious or not. He still wouldn't make eye contact.

'Why dinosaurs?'

'Because it's as likely as anything else that's happened.' There didn't seem to be any giant footprints or egg-shells the size of saucepans, but who knew? He risked a glance at her, and quickly turned away again. He couldn't age her. Twenties, thirties, maybe. Wiry and strong. Confident. 'Are you scared by all this?'

'Scared?' She wondered for a moment. 'I do not know. I was

scared, very scared in the tunnels. I thought I was going to die. And now? We might be safe, so I am less scared.'

'But we don't know where we are.'

'Does it matter?'

'Yes,' he said, 'yes it does.'

'When you thought you were going to be burnt alive, did you think being anywhere else would be better?'

'Yes, that's what I thought.'

The ground beneath them was becoming increasingly gritty and damp, and where they'd walked pooled with water. The river channel had split into wide, shallow streams, with thousands of sand banks and islets between them. As the tide came up, as it was presumably doing now, the rivers went into reverse.

He bent down and put his injured hand in the clear water. It was cool, and when he let a drop fall into his mouth, it was somewhere between salty and sweet.

'Then that is where we are,' she said. 'Perhaps because we wanted it badly enough, it happened.'

Dalip didn't live in a world where wishing for something really hard worked. Ever. The only thing that ever worked was diligence, perseverance, and a willingness to be humiliated over and over again until it came right.

'That's just ...' He glanced up, at the river, the forest, the mountains, the sky. None of it made any sense, and perhaps it didn't matter who was right. Stanislav had insisted that all that counted was what he was going to do now.

'Luiza,' said the woman. 'This is my cousin, Elena. Where are you from?'

'Dalip,' said Dalip. He wasn't used to introducing himself to people – that was his mother's job – but she wasn't there. 'I'm from Southall. You?'

'Romania.'

'Okay.' He didn't know much about the place, and where they

were born seemed a strange thing to discuss. None of them had been born here.

The sweary girl was down in amongst the river channels, every so often kicking a plume of water into the air where it broke and fell. She stopped, and shouted, and pointed.

Stanislav was up by the tree line, exploring the edge of the forest, and Mama and the other woman were a little way behind, in easy conversation.

The girl didn't seem to be running away from anything, and her shouts were more indicative of something interesting than something terrible: Dalip, Luiza and Elena were closest, so they arrived first.

She was pointing down, at the water. 'Look,' she said, 'look.'

It took a moment to see past the rippling surface with its bright reflections, and not so far as the granular, speckled river bed.

Fish. There were fish, and not just one or two, but dozens of silvery, speckly fish that almost merged in with their surroundings. They were big, too, the length of Dalip's forearm and lazily swimming upstream with the seawater current at their tails.

Once he'd got his eye in, he could see there were hundreds, in every river channel. But where the girl saw novelty, he saw food. He had no net – no one had a net, or a line – but the fish were thick enough to walk on. And he'd seen that documentary, the one where the brown bears in Alaska waited for the sock-eyes to swim back to their spawning grounds. When they did, the bears could simply reach in and take what they wanted, flicking them up and on to the bank.

He could do that. It shouldn't be that hard.

He sat down and wrestled his boots off, the thought that he might not be able to get them back on briefly crossing his mind.

'What're you doing?' said the girl. 'Getting yourself one of those fish pedicures?'

'No. I'm getting us something to eat.' He scrunched his toes in the soft grit and waded out mid-stream. The water rose up to mid-calf, and predictably, the fish scattered at the intrusion.

'You've scared them all off,' said the girl. She seemed to be happy at his failure.

'Just wait,' he said. His feet were cold, and he didn't have a coat of shaggy hair like those brown bears. He'd lose feeling in them soon enough.

'I hope they're not those flesh-eating fish you get,' she said helpfully.

Dalip knew his salmon from his piranhas, and they looked salmony to him. Slowly, the fish gathered downstream, then moved forward again, slipping between his legs quite unconcerned as to his presence.

He crouched down slowly, like he was in the slips, poised for a catch. He slid his hands into the shallow water, and rested his knuckles on the river bed. Bits of grit, carried by the current and disturbed by the passing fish landed on his open palms.

'Well, go on then,' urged the girl, but Dalip was content to be patient and ignored her. He knew how it ought to be done, he'd just never done it himself before. He'd probably get it wrong, too, several times, until he got it right.

'I'd move back a bit,' he said, and just then a particularly indolent fish swam across his hands, so slow as to be almost moving backwards. He was never going to get a better chance.

His right hand moved towards his left, briefly trapping the fat, wriggling body between them, but the object wasn't to hold on to it – it was to move it, quickly and cleanly, out of its element and on to land. With momentum and surprise on his side, he threw the fish sideways towards the bank. It broke the surface, thrashing futilely, and flew up towards where the others were standing.

Straight into the sweary girl's face.

She shrieked and fell over. The fish jerked away, back towards the river, but Luiza pounced and scooped it up, flinging it into the scrub.

'What do you want me to do with it?'

'Break its neck, or something,' he called.

'You hit me!' said the brown girl. 'With a fucking fish!'

'I did say you should move.'

Luiza was still chasing through the grasses, so Elena went to help: not the prone girl, still wiping slime and scales from her face, but her cousin wrestling the fish.

In the stream, between his bare feet, the shoal had returned after the disturbance, seemingly unconcerned that one of their number was now gasping, open-gilled, on dry land. He was ready to go again.

The girl was lifted to her feet at last by Mama, furious with him, with everyone, while he was on the verge of smiling for the first time since they'd stepped through the Down Street door. He was doing something useful. He was doing something right. He looked at her, her balled fists and narrowed eyes, and perhaps he frowned at her, because she turned on her heel and stamped away.

He returned his attention to the fish, and he lowered his hands gently into the water, ready to catch another. If they could make a fire, then they could eat. Even if they couldn't, they could still eat, but fire was the next step, and then shelter.

Five minutes ago they had no food. Maybe they'd got lucky, but it was almost as if wherever-they-were was trying to feed them. Perhaps it would give them the other things they needed too. Maybe it wouldn't be so bad after all, making the most of their time before they got to go home.

Another fish lazed its way across his open fingers, and he tensed, the corners of his mouth turning ever so slightly upwards.

5

The East European man had a lighter, a big heavy slab of steel that looked like it had been through a war. It produced a tail of smoky orange flame whenever the flint was struck. He used it to catch alight a pile of dry leaves and twigs, and he'd clearly made fires before: he knew exactly what he was doing, and wasted no effort in telling the others what to do. Despite the exertions and the novelty of the day draining everyone, Stanislav was still working, still breaking fallen branches against his knee, still hauling wood back to the tree line where they'd set up a temporary camp.

Mary didn't help. She didn't know how to help. She was a city girl, who knew all sorts of tricks and scams, but none of them seemed useful here, where there were only trees and grass and water and rock and soil and sky.

She knew how to set a fire – pour the petrol, throw a match on it – but not how to build one out of raw materials, how to nurture it from tiny flame to crackling bonfire, how to feed it and with what. Neither did she know what to do with the fish: it had always come in either batter or breadcrumbs, never glistening and whole, and certainly never at her face.

And neither did the turbaned kid, which was almost gratifying, but Mama did, using a small knife that the kid had. It was blunt, and she'd said so, and he said it was never meant to be used, but she and the Chinese woman – Grace – went down by the river to 'clean' the fish, and by that she had to assume they meant cut them open and scrape their guts out.

That made her queasy, but she was also hungry.

Nothing was making sense to Mary, and the other six survivors seemed to be coping far better than her with what was going on. Even whatever-his-name-was, the kid with the turban, seemed to have shut up about being dead.

So she sat with her back to a tree, like she was in one of the local parks, and watched those around her. That was only good for a while, and she became bored. Little was happening: everyone seemed content just to stare into the fire and feel the warmth of it against their skin. It reminded her too much of the tunnels, and she got up to walk away.

'Hey. Where are you going?'

Stanislav had the top half of his boilersuit tied around his waist, baring a grey-looking vest spilling muscle and tufts of grey chest hair. To her, it looked grotesque. Old men were supposed to keep everything covered up.

'You don't get to tell me what to do,' she said.

The turbaned kid looked up. 'I'll go with her.' He was still barefoot, but he reached for his socks.

'Oh, fuck off.'

Stanislav, his stubbly head glistening from work, put the end of the branch he carried on the floor, then pressed his foot against it a third of the way up. It bent, and snapped with a sharp crack. 'We do not know what is out there. We have seen one monster already, there may be more.'

'That was in the sea. And I was just going for a walk.'

'No one will go and look for you when you do not return.'

'I wouldn't want them to.'

Stanislav shrugged, reduced the branch further, and threw

all three pieces on to the growing pile where they landed in a hollow clatter.

'As you say, I do not tell you what to do. In return, you cannot expect us to do what you want.'

'Whatever. Later.' She walked between the trees, waving her hand over her shoulder.

She'd barely got any distance before she heard footsteps hurrying after her. She didn't turn around, just kept walking.

'Haven't you learned anything from films?'

'Fuck. Off.'

'Seriously. We don't know where we are, we don't know what's out there. You can't just wander off like this.'

There was very little undergrowth: mostly small, thin plants and long looping briars. The leaf litter made every footfall release a deep, earthy scent. The overlapping branches above formed an almost complete canopy, throwing deep shade over everything below. Where a tree had fallen, there was a clearing, bright with sunlight and hazy with insects. They were like islands in a sea of gloom.

She stopped and looked around. She could see tiny flashes of orange boilersuit coming from the tree line, but if she went only a little further, she'd be lost, unable to find her way back.

It wasn't like a local park at all, with paths and play areas, and a lake with scruffy-looking ducks. This was the wild wood, stretching beyond this point for as far as it pleased. There were no tower blocks on the borders, and the realisation struck her with all the force of a punch to the side of the head.

The turbaned kid had a stout branch in his hands, his fingers digging into the rough bark. It was the best weapon and, unless his little blunt knife counted, the only weapon that they could muster.

She didn't want to lose face. Neither did she want to carry on any further. She could have gone down towards the river, but hadn't. Instead, she was in the middle of a forest with a stick-wielding kid in a blue turban and a ridiculous beard.

'Fuck.'

'Look. Stanislav's right: you can do what you want, but it'd be stupid to just wander off after all we've been through.'

'What if there's someone just over the hill who can help us, and we'll never know unless we go there.'

'And there might be someone – or something – just over the hill that might eat us. We don't know that either. So being together is always going to be better, right?'

Who was she going to be? Was she going to be the one who came through the fire and survived, or was she the one who was too fucking arsey to be with and eventually abandoned? Because that wasn't a pattern that had repeated itself throughout her entire life, was it?

Into the forest? Back to the river?

She looked one way, then the other.

'Fuck it.'

She turned on her heel and stamped back to the tree line, and the turbaned kid trailed after her, still carrying his stick.

'I'm Dalip,' he said.

'Congratulations.'

'Your—'

'I'm what? You don't get to say what I am.' She whipped around, and he was proffering her discarded bandanna.

'Bandanna,' and he held it out to her. 'You dropped it earlier.'

She could take it, she could snatch it. She stopped and thought about what to do. Then she reached out and held out her hand, palm up. He dropped the cloth, and she caught it.

'Thanks. Dalip.'

'That's okay …'

'Mary.'

She carried on walking ahead of him, and through the place at the edge of the forest where the fire was. It wasn't like anything had happened in the last few minutes to make her stay there, so she kept on, out into the sunlight. She went down by the river, to wash her bandanna, and her face.

The river had reversed its flow, and the fish had gone. The water was fresh, and she self-consciously filled her hands with it and tried to pour some into her mouth. She couldn't remember if she'd ever done that before; judging by the amount that disappeared cold and clear down her neck, she was, at the very least, out of practice.

The sun was going down, sinking behind the ridge of rock that had formed the backdrop to their arrival. The sky was now a deep blue, still with the white, ragged clouds blowing in from the sea, and the seagulls wheeled and cried.

Their cries were answered by a long, high-pitched wail that echoed across the open landscape. She'd never heard anything like it before, but she reacted instantly; she stood bolt upright and scanned the tree line, the river, the grasses, for movement of any kind. Mama and the Chinese woman did the same, a little way off.

Time stretched out, and her beating heart slowed enough to allow her to breathe again. As the sound faded into the wind and the memory, Mama shook her head and knelt at the water's edge again.

Mary wasn't so ready to let her guard down. The initial sounds of disaster had been nothing more than distant thunder above ground, a booming growl under it. Yet they'd all ended up running for their lives, and most of them had lost the race. She waited and watched.

And it came again. It sounded like it could have come from a musical instrument, a trumpet or a horn. Except it didn't quite, and the hairs on the back of her neck prickled as they rose. There was no way of telling which direction the sound was coming from: out to sea, from the forest, from the hills, or further away towards the mountains. It just seemed to be.

She tied her damp bandanna around her hair, and went to

see Mama, who was gathering up the gutted fish by hooking her fingers through the open gills. Grace did the same, and still there were fish left over.

'Mary, pick up the rest.'

Mary screwed her face up. 'They're dead.'

'They're dinner, girl. 'Less you want to go hungry.'

She didn't, but neither did she want to touch the cold, slimy things with dark, unblinking eyes. She changed the subject. 'What was that noise just now?'

'Some kind of animal? I don't know.' She looked down at the remaining fish at the river's edge. 'I do know that those aren't going to carry themselves.'

'But what sort of animal? I mean: there was that big snake in the sea. What if there are more on land?'

'Dinosaurs,' said Grace. 'The boy with the turban was worried about dinosaurs.'

'So what does a dinosaur sound like?'

'No one knows. They've been dead for millions of years.' She too stared pointedly at the fish. 'We don't need to worry about dinosaurs. Just those.'

Defeated, Mary forced her painted nails one by one into the gills, until she had three heavy fish hanging from each hand. She held them away from her body, as far as she could, disgusted by the touch and the weight.

The animal sound cut through the air again. Mary's stomach tightened, and she could feel her legs get ready to run. She forced herself to walk, all the way up to the tree line.

'Seriously,' she said, as she laid the fish out on the ground and wondered where she was supposed to wipe her fingers. 'What the fuck is that noise?'

'Wolves,' said Stanislav and Dalip at the same time. They shrugged at each other, and Stanislav continued. 'A wolf. There will be more.'

'There aren't any wolves in England,' she said.

'Then we are no longer in England,' Stanislav said. 'There are wolves in Europe. Perhaps we are there instead.'

'There are plenty in North America too,' said Dalip. 'Though I don't suppose that's helpful.'

Mary drew her lips in, and on cue, the wolf – if that was what it was – howled. It was the scariest thing she'd ever heard, and she'd run in riots with the roar of voices, the barking of fighting dogs and the wail of sirens.

'Are they dangerous? I mean, they're wild, right?'

'They sometimes attack people. The small, the weak, the injured.' Stanislav crouched down and picked up a long springy twig from a pile he'd made. He poked it through both gills of a fish, and held it up. 'We need a frame to hold these above the fire.'

Dalip nodded, and started to sort through the wood pile for suitable lumber.

'Can we keep on talking about the wolves?'

'Yes, of course.'

'Well, what are we going to do about them?'

'It depends,' he said, 'on what they want to do about us. They will stay away from us, and our fire, or they will not. Those are their choices. If they attack us, we will defend ourselves as a group, or they will pick us off one by one. Those are our choices. If we climbed trees, the wolves would still be there when we came down. But it is unlikely that we will have to fight. They are, as you say, wild, and they will either be afraid of us, or they will not see us as food. These fish, however, will bring them to us, and are better off inside us than not.'

He carried on threading them, one after another, on to sticks, while Dalip began to construct a short tripod next to the fire. Stanislav glanced over to check his design, then carried on with his own task.

Mary didn't know what else to say. There were wolves in the forest, and no one seemed to care.

'Do not go for a walk,' he said, without looking up. 'Night is falling, and we do not know how long it will last.'

She didn't like being told what to do, but she only went as far as just beyond the tree line, and stood with her hands in her pockets, balling her fists. The sky was darkening, and the sun was now below the ridge behind her, casting a long, dark shadow across the river valley. In the far distance, the light still caught the tops of the mountain range and they glowed like rosy lights in the sky.

It wasn't a sight she was used to. What she knew was the regular shapes of roofs and walls, spires and masts, reflections from windows and the steady sodium orange of the street lights. And the sounds: the city hummed, a deep bass rumble of traffic and machinery that infested even skin and bone. The only sounds here were the drone from the clouds of insects that misted the air over the river, the hiss of wind in the leaves and the grasses, and the occasional arse-clenching wolf call.

Natural. She wasn't used to it. Fortunately, she didn't need to get used to it either. They'd find a way back soon, and everything would return to normal. Of course, she might not have a job anymore, depending on how much damage the Underground had sustained. She might not have a room at the hostel anymore, either. That was for someone else to sort out – her probation officer, her social worker – not her.

She became aware of a sudden silence, and a white glow just over the horizon. Slowly, slowly, an edge of a circle appeared, pocked like the moon with blue craters and bone-coloured lines. Like the moon but most definitely not, because as she watched, it grew and swelled, inflating like a balloon until it seemed to take up half the sky. It was impossibly massive, full and fat, a huge ball of stone just … floating.

It was just her, and this thing. She knew then. She knew that everything was different and nothing was the same.

'Fuck.' She turned, and called out. 'You have to see this. You have to come.'

They walked towards her, and saw that she was silhouetted against the glow from the moon. She spread her arms out wide, and even then, her reach wasn't quite wide enough to encompass it all.

It was a terrifying sight, something that big rising above them. It would rise higher, and at some point in the night, be hanging over them. Their moon was so distant, so small, that it could be covered by a thumb at full stretch. This one, this world's version, wherever they were, couldn't be blocked out by both hands together.

'That's incredible,' said Dalip, eventually. 'That's,' and words failed him.

The rest of the sky was turning black as the mountain-tops lost their reflected shine. The last rays of the sun against the high cloud faded, descending through pinks into reds. Only the pearly moonglow remained.

'Where,' said Stanislav, 'are the stars?'

Dalip stepped out further, turned his back on the moon and stared upwards, his head tilted back and his mouth falling open. Mary hadn't noticed the lack of stars, and would never notice them. Her sky was an orange haze, growing thicker or thinner depending on the weather.

The dome of the night was – apart from the bright moon, which had now crested the mountains completely – utterly dark.

'There should be stars,' said Dalip, shivering. 'There should be thousands of stars.'

And perhaps for the first time, Mary looked up properly.

She knew something about stars – the stars formed pictures in the sky, some of which became star signs, and she was a Virgo. There was nothing. She turned her head to face the sea, then to face the mountains, and there was still nothing.

'Are you sure?' she asked.

'The sky should be on fire. No light pollution, no street lights or houses or cars or factories: you should be able to see everything. Stars, planets, nebulae, the Milky Way. Everything.'

'Maybe they don't have them here,' she said. 'Maybe this is all there is.'

'That's impossible. Even if it takes millions of years for light to cross space, it gets to us eventually.' He sounded close to panic, and no matter which section of the sky they checked, it always appeared blank. 'And that, that is not our moon. It's got none of the right craters, seas, anything. Where are we?'

'We've come further than we thought, that's all. It'll be okay.' She didn't mean to try and sound reassuring. It just came out, as if it was the right thing to say at that moment.

Dalip stared wide-eyed at her, and she could hear his breathing, fast and shallow at first, slowly subside into something more normal.

Then he nodded, and looked at the ground so he didn't have to look up. 'It's what we do now that counts.'

'I guess so.' She took one last look at the moon and started back to their camp under the trees. A wolf called again, and this time she didn't mind it so much. It was probably the least strange thing, including her own presence, about where she'd ended up.

Dinner, suspended over the fire, was ready, and she was ravenous.

6

Dalip woke up with a hand over his mouth. He started to shout around the fingers, to simultaneously rise and push himself away, when he realised it was Stanislav.

The canopy above was outlined in silver moonshine, and enough leaked down to cast shadows. The fire had burned low: the red glow from the embers shifted slightly and a trail of sparks twisted upwards. Arranged around the circumference like the hours of a clock, were six fitful sleepers – five now.

Stanislav raised his fingers to his lips in an exaggerated gesture, and Dalip realised that there was something in the woods behind him. He didn't need to turn around and look, he could feel it at his back, watching him, hot and hairy and hungry.

The only weapons they had were sticks, and his kirpan, which was more ornamental than not: blunt, as Mama had called it. He was supposed to use it to defend himself and others – that's what the Guru said – but he'd never needed to do either, until now.

His hand rested on the hilt, and he drew it, trying not to make a sound. It was a tiny thing compared with his grandfather's foot-long sword, but it was all he had and he felt better for holding it.

Stanislav rose from his crouch. He was holding a stout branch, with a heavy knot of wood at one end. The way he moved it easily from hand to hand showed he was no stranger to improvised clubs. He was testing its weight, how it would move and how hard he'd have to grip it to stop it slipping when he used it.

No one else was awake. That struck Dalip as a mistake, for surely they'd need everyone to defend each other. The Romanian woman, Elena, was closest, and he got down on all fours, ready to crawl towards her.

He glanced up. Wolves. And not only wolves.

There was a man. At least, he was guessing it was a man. He was tall and broad, with a hood that may have been made out of the actual head of another wolf. The detail of his face was lost, though his breath came in heavy clouds of mist that rolled out and down. In each hand, he had a wolf on a chain that was tight with anticipation.

He knew where they were, so there seemed little point in trying to be quiet and hoping he'd pass by.

'Elena. Elena, wake up.'

She rolled away from him with a moan, then rolled back, eyes white and open.

'Visitor,' he said, and nodded in the direction of the wolves and their handler, who he assumed for the sake of sanity was human. That they might not be caused his gut to tighten and his bladder loosen. 'Wake the others.'

One by one, they were stirred, and they instinctively retreated to the fire. Dalip reached into his pocket for his stubby torch, clicked the switch, and nothing happened.

He banged it against his leg, and tried again. When he lifted it up and shook it, drops of salty seawater leaked out. That, he presumed, was the end of the torch, and he dropped it by his feet.

In amongst the trees, a wolf shook its head, and its chain rattled: an odd, light sound. The man didn't move at all, and the time they spent staring at each other stretched past breaking point.

'What,' called out Dalip, 'what do you want?'

He wished his voice hadn't broken halfway through, because it made him sound as scared as he was.

When the man didn't answer, Dalip didn't know why. It was stupid to assume he'd speak English, but trying Punjabi probably wouldn't work either. Was he deaf? Did he want to fight? Were he and the others trespassing?

'Oi. He asked you a question.'

'Mary, that's not helpful.'

'Well.' She was shoulder to shoulder with Dalip. 'Maybe not, but he's given me the fucking fear.'

'We don't mean to be here,' he called. 'We just are, and we don't know why. We, we've not got any food left, but you can share our fire if you want.'

'What are you doing?' whispered Mary.

'Offering hospitality.' It might work. It might diffuse the stand-off and even be to their advantage. Dalip was pretty certain they'd collectively lose a straight fight with two wolves, let alone the man, or whatever he was. And this person was a native. He was going to know how this world worked. He might be persuaded to help.

It was his duty as a good Sikh, too, a thought that shamefully occurred to him after all the other, more pragmatic reasons.

A man, even one with two wolves, coming across seven orange-suited strangers when he didn't expect them, was entitled to be wary. It didn't automatically follow that they had to be enemies, did it?

The figure pulled on the wolf-chains, and both animals sat on their haunches. They suddenly appeared more like big dogs than they did wild beasts, turning their heads up to take their lead from their master. Dalip was sure that wolves couldn't be domesticated like that, even from pups, but the evidence confounded him.

'Where do you come from?' His voice was deep and resonant, curious and serious.

'There … There was a door,' Dalip looked at Stanislav for support, but the older man was still braced for an attack, and resolutely staring at the man and his wolves. 'We ended up here, down by the coast.'

'Where were you before that?'

'London. London Underground.' He had no idea if that made any sense to the man.

But it did.

'I'll share your fire,' he said, and made a ticking sound with his tongue. The wolves stood up and they all walked into the camp. Everyone moved out of their way, wary of the wolves, not so much the man, which struck Dalip as the wrong way around. Now he was close, he could both see him and smell him. The wolf pelt on his back was old and scraggy, the muzzle and ears certainly had seen better days: but as a statement of intent it was unequivocal. Here was a man who had fought fierce creatures and won.

He watched their separate reactions with amusement – at least, the small grunt he made as he sat cross-legged by the fire sounded like a laugh – and waited for them all to return. Stanislav warily lowered his club, and poked the fire with the heavy end, stirring the embers into life. He put more wood on, which instantly started to steam and smoke.

'What happened to your head?' the man asked, and it took a moment for Dalip to realise he was being addressed.

'My head? That's my turban.'

'Turban? Like the Mohammedans wear?'

It took a moment for Dalip to work out what a Mohammedan might be. 'No. I'm a Sikh. From India.'

'So you're from India?'

'No. I'm from London. My grandparents were from India. Rawalpindi. Except that's now in Pakistan. They left during the Partition.' He stopped and started again. 'I'm from a Sikh family now living in London. All the men wear turbans.'

The man pushed his wolf's-head hood back to reveal a head of black hair, thinning at the temples. 'Does that make you a man, then?'

Dalip thought of all kinds of answers, some of them entirely unsuitable to give to a man with two wolves crouching by his side. His grandfather had been in the Indian Army at sixteen – though Grandfather's age was a matter of family legend, so he could have been either younger or older. But if sixteen was old enough to carry a rifle and fight the Japanese, Dalip being nineteen was old enough to qualify as a man.

'So they say,' he finally managed.

'Good answer. The reputation you give yourself is worthless. Let others name you.'

The fresh wood caught with a pop, and flames jetted out, bright and lively. The man lifted his hands instinctively, palms out, to feel the heat, even though it wasn't cold.

Despite the presence of a wolf on either side of the man, Dalip sat next to him, cross-legged as if he were in the gurdwara. The closest wolf raised its head, shook its dense brown fur at him and leaned over to sniff at his leg. It spent a disconcertingly long time doing so, and the man pulled on its chain slightly, just to tell it that Dalip had had enough.

'Aren't you afraid?' The man jerked his head down to his side.

'Yes,' said Dalip. 'You seem to have them under control, though.'

'For now,' said the man, and grunted the same little laugh. 'When did you get here?'

'Today. Can I ask you something?'

'You can ask. Can't promise to answer.'

Everyone was looking at him, at them, and Dalip stared uncomfortably into the heart of the fire.

'Where are we?'

'Here,' he said, and shrugged. When he did that, Dalip could see past the front legs of his wolfskin coat to the thick-bladed knife he had, strapped down by the side of his broad chest. It put Dalip's little kirpan to shame, the kirpan he was still clutching in one hand.

He held it down by his leg to hide it. 'It's just that here is different to where we were. If we don't know where we are, how do we know how to get home?'

'You don't.'

His words caused a ripple of consternation and anger around the group, which he managed to silence with a mere look.

'I was born here. My ma was born here. My da – he arrived, like you did, but far to the north. He'd sometimes tell me of this place he was from, a city where there was nothing but streets and people, where you could walk all day and not go from one side to the other, and he called it London just like you do.' The man shrugged again. 'He started off trying to go back. Didn't do him any good. In the end, he stopped looking. Made the most of it here.'

'There's no way back?' said Mary. 'There has to be a way back.'

'Why? No reason why there should.'

'But there has to be!'

He tilted his head on one side as he looked up at her. 'Wishing it doesn't make it happen. Did you wish to get here?'

'No.'

'There's your answer then.' He gazed back into the embers. 'How did you get here?'

'There, there was a fire. And we ran.'

'Is that right?'

'It was more than a fire,' said Dalip. 'It seemed like the whole of London was burning. We thought we'd got out from the Tube, but the street outside was on fire too. Everything, everything was burning.'

'And were you in danger?'

Dalip turned to Stanislav. 'How many were in there in our shift?'

'Thirty or so.' He threw another log on the fire, and the sparks flew up into the leaves overhead.

'Two of us survived. Mary?'

'Twenty. Five of us got out.' She turned to look at Grace, who stared back. 'Something like that, anyway.'

'I'm told that's how it happens,' said the man. 'You think you're going to die, and you open a door, and this place is behind it. You can choose to stay, or you can choose to step through. I don't know how many people stay. Maybe most of them, maybe none of them, I can't say one way or the other. All I do know is that those who come here, stay here.'

Dalip sighed. 'But that still doesn't tell us where we are.'

'This is my home. This is where I was born, and where I'll most likely die. I've never been to your London. I suppose it must be a real place to you, but it's just a story to me. I've never seen a signpost or a map with it on, and I've never known anyone go there from here. You, any of you: ever heard of anyone who's come here and gone back? No? Then this is where you are now.'

'Forever?'

'Forever's a long time. Who's to say what might happen?'

Mary started to speak – several times, and each time the words got caught in her throat. She eventually gave up, her shoulders slumping.

Mama had no such problems. 'So what are we supposed to do, wolfman? Where do we go? Where do we stay?'

He regarded her with his pale eyes, as blue as the wolves'. If she was intimidated, she didn't show it. She put her hands on her hips and waited.

'Well?'

'What do you want to do?'

'Go home to my babies,' she said. With force.

'Apart from that.' He shifted diffidently.

'There has to be someone who can help us.' Mama tried again. 'Someone has to be in charge.'

'It might be like that in your London. It's not here.'

'What is it like here?'

'You can do whatever you want,' he said. 'There's no one to tell you what to do, no one who can make you do something you don't want to do.' He reached out his hands and laid them on the animals' heads, and they stretched their necks slightly to butt into his touch. 'You can be whatever you want to be.'

Dalip frowned at the idea. Almost his every waking moment had been planned, since he'd been old enough to remember. This school, that club, a friend's house, the gurdwara, plays and concerts and recitals, and family, so much family: brothers and sisters and cousins and second cousins and uncles and aunts. The thought that he might be free of all that was ... intoxicating. Even if it was for just a while, before someone was able to show him the way home.

It must have shown on his face, because he became aware that Stanislav was nudging him with his toe and shaking his head slightly. Was there any reason to believe the first person they'd met since arriving? No.

He swallowed. But what if it was true? 'We're not exactly set up for just, you know, starting. Where do the other people live?'

'Wherever they want,' came the infuriating reply. Then the wolfman relented. 'You mean a village.'

'Yes. A village, or a town. Do you have towns here?'

'If there are, I don't know of any. There are villages, here and there. Sometimes they're empty. You just have to find one.'

'And you know of somewhere?'

'You got a walk ahead of you. Or you could try the geomancer. She's close enough.'

The way he said it, it just tripped out like he was saying they could ask in the local pub.

'A geomancer?' Dalip sort of knew what that meant, because geomancy scored a lot of points in Scrabble. 'Would he know more about where we are?'

'She,' the wolfman corrected. 'Yes, if she'll wear all your questions. She'll want to trade, your knowledge for hers, so you'd better be prepared to answer, too.'

'Where does she live?'

'Up the river.' The man pointed. 'There's a gorge, steep, and best you went around it. There's a lake beyond it, and a castle by the shores of the lake, and that's where you'll find her.'

'How far?' asked Stanislav, and Dalip watched as the men eyed each other suspiciously. Stanislav still hadn't let go of his club.

'For you? Two days. If you don't stop to smell the flowers.'

'I will be certain to stay away from them.'

The exchange was apparently over. The wolfman sprang to his feet with a grace that belied his size, and the wolves were suddenly up, too, and straining to be back in the forest.

'Do we tell the geomancer who sent us?' asked Dalip.

'If you like. Oh, you mean names? A description will do,' he said. The wolves were dragging him away, and he was letting them. 'Names have power, little darkie. Best you remember that.'

He was running, chains in his fists, a wolf either side of him, away from the fire and between the trees, leaving only his words and his scent.

'Darkie,' said Dalip. 'He called me darkie.'

Stanislav finally dropped his club at his feet. 'I do not trust him.'

'Not after he called me darkie, no.'

'That is not why. I have met men like that before. Count yourself lucky you have not.'

'Dalip, what's a geo-thingy?' Mary stepped between them.

'Geomancer. A sort of priest. They tell the future using stones. You heard him call me darkie, right?'

'Better than Paki, I suppose.'

'I—'

'Enough,' said Stanislav. 'It does not matter to him what colour your skin is, only that you bleed red. He was trying to provoke you, and look, he succeeded.'

Dalip's fingers curled and uncurled around his kirpan. 'At least we learned something.'

'Did we? Perhaps we did. Perhaps we only know what he wanted to tell us.' Stanislav's gaze followed the path the man had taken back into the forest. 'This geomancer, if she exists: what is she going to want from us, other than our answers?'

7

For a brief moment between waking and sleeping, the dreams of being burnt alive faded – Nicholls' clip-board bursting into flame and the sheets of paper curling as they were consumed – and she thought she was back in her hostel.

Music, loud and fast, coming through the wall at her, sounds of an argument through her well-locked door, the grinding of changing gears from the road outside ... That was only a dream, too. Her reality was a vast open vista and the people she'd arrived with. That was it. That was all she had now. Literally, the clothes she stood up in, and nothing else.

There was nothing to eat. There was only river water to drink: it tasted odd, and no matter how often she cupped her hands, she always ended up with silt or something floating in it. Water came out of a tap and into a cup, not flowing past her face in a hundred different streams separated by sand banks. She had no real choice, and in the end she just shut her eyes and drank anyway.

She wasn't used to this. She was used to a bed, and coffee first thing, and if not a bed, someone's sofa. She was tired, with gritty eyes and a mouth that still tasted of last night's fish. Her neck ached, so that when she tried to stretch, things went crack.

The early morning light slanted over the far-distant mountains, bright and sharp, and the huge moon had thankfully disappeared over the opposite horizon. The sky was brilliant blue, with cotton-wool clouds piled up to the heavens.

If she'd stepped out of her door, draped in her favourite dressing gown, mug of coffee the same colour as her skin in hand, and been greeted with the same sight, she'd have been amazed. Her first reaction would have been to grab her phone and take some pictures. Here, it was different.

The wolfman who'd visited them in the night had told them to follow the river as far as the gorge. She squinted upstream, the direction they had to go if they wanted to find this priest, this geomancer. The horizon was hazy. Perhaps she could make out a notch in the mountain, cut by the river, or perhaps she was fooling herself. But priests were supposed to help people in need, even if the ones she'd encountered were long on advice and short on providing the everyday necessities like weed, fags, booze and burgers, phone credits and bus fares.

The wolfman had said the geomancer wanted their stories in exchange for her assistance. Mary could do that. She was good at telling stories, ones that tugged at the heartstrings and opened the wallet.

Dalip knelt by the river a little way off. He was washing, a great loop of jet black hair falling from his head into his hands, shining with water and sunlight. Face bowed to the stream, he was oblivious to her stares, so she carried on watching.

He massaged the water through his hair, twisting and squeezing it out then rewetting it several times. Then he twisted it for the last time, wrapping it tightly like a rope and coiling it around his head. A black bandanna held it close to his head, which he tied into place with deft, practised moves.

It was then that he looked up, and she looked away, too slowly. She could feel her cheeks burn for no reason whatsoever. It wasn't like he'd been hiding, and it wasn't like she'd been witnessing something private. A kid washing his hair and tying it up, that was all. She should probably do the same, except she wasn't going to without hot water, separate bottles of shampoo and conditioner, a towel and a hairdryer.

She daren't turn back, so she dried her mouth on her sleeve and walked back to the camp. Stanislav was using a long branch to open up the fire and pile on the last of the wood, while the others milled about and grumbled at their stiffness and hunger.

'Morning, Mama.'

Mama looked dishevelled, like she was laundry and she hadn't been ironed.

'I'm going back,' she said, and pointed with a fat finger. 'Back to the beach. Back to the door. I'm not spending another minute here longer than I have to.'

'The door's gone, Mama. Didn't you see? It closed behind us.'

'There's no door that ever existed that can just vanish. We opened it to get here. We can open it to get back.'

'But the tunnels, the fire—'

'Fire's don't burn forever, girl. They get put out. I'm going back, back to my babies. They need me.'

'Mama …'

Mary got the look.

'There's no way I'm walking for two days in the wrong direction, no roads, no tracks, no transport, just to talk to some crazy witch with a crazy name. The way out is back the way we came in, am I right, ladies?'

The three other women were close enough to overhear, not that Mama was trying to be quiet.

'We should go and see,' said Luiza. 'We need to be there in case the door only opens at low tide, or at the same time every day.'

'Perhaps it will not open again for a hundred years,' said Stanislav as he passed by. Mama drew herself up, ready for an argument, but the man didn't wait and went off towards the river.

'What if he's right?' asked Mary, watching him go. 'The rules are different here.'

'We don't belong! There's nothing here for us, girl, and the sooner we get away, the better.' Mama's hands were on her hips. She wasn't going to back down.

But Mary was struck by a thought: what if Mama was wrong, and the wolfman right? What did that mean for her? There was nothing waiting for her in London, save her probation officer. Here, she could be whatever she wanted to be. For a moment, she felt giddy with unfettered possibilities.

'Mary?'

She was aware she'd taken a step back, away from the others.

'I don't know,' she said. 'What if the door won't open? What do we do then? We can't just stay here, can we?'

She knew that Mama was used to getting her own way, but it was different this time. Bending Nicholls to her will had been easy. Trying to force a, a what? A whole world to do her bidding? Could she do that?

'I'm not spending a second here that I don't have to,' said Mama, 'and you're coming with me, girl, to keep you out of trouble.'

'I'm not in trouble.' Mary took another step back. 'I'm not in trouble here.'

'Every moment you stay, you get into trouble with the folks back home. You've got meetings of all sorts you've got to attend, and don't pretend you haven't. Oh, you know what I'm talking about. They're going to throw your sorry backside in prison if we don't find a way to leave right now.'

She felt the rush, the flow of blood and passion from her heart to her head. Everything she'd been taught about controlling the Red Queen was forgotten.

'Fuck you. Fuck all of you. You don't get to tell me what to do. You don't tell me to do anything. So fuck you. You'd be dead if it wasn't for me. Dead in the tunnels and I'd be glad because

I wouldn't have to put up with your fucking nagging. You don't get it, do you? We're stuck here. This is it, all right? We are never going home. Fuck.'

She screamed her last word, and if Mama had been any closer, Mary would have been hitting her with her closed fists, anywhere she could but mainly the face because that hurt the most.

The women had drawn together behind Mama, eyes wide, mouths open.

And behind them, just in the open ground, were Stanislav and Dalip. The older man had his arm stretched out across the Sikh boy's chest, barring his way, holding him back. They weren't going to interfere. They were going to make their own choices, but what was more, they were free to make their own choices. No one was telling them what they had or hadn't to do.

'I'm not one of your fucking babies, so stop talking to me like I was. Fuck off, then, if that's what you want to do. There's no door, and you'll drown looking for it. If you do, at least it'll be quieter. Go on. Go.'

She was done. Spent. Her throat was raw, and she was shaking with the effort. She turned away, and stumbled into the woods. She couldn't go far, because her legs wouldn't take her. She found a tree, slumped with her back to it, and slid down the trunk. She'd deafened herself, and she could hear nothing of what was happening behind her.

She knew though. Everyone else would be shaking their head and saying how disgraceful her behaviour was, how no one could help her. How it'd better for them to simply abandon her, because she was just too difficult. She couldn't be tamed. She was self-destructive, and better that she destroyed herself, rather than take anyone else down with her.

She sat there, staring at nothing between the brown trunks and the green leaves, while they came to the inevitable conclusion. She waited for what she thought was long enough – it may have been minutes, but it felt like hours – before getting to her feet again.

What would she do? She supposed that she'd start walking, see if she could find this geomancer by herself. It wasn't like she had anything better to occupy her time.

The moment she came out from behind the tree, she could see Dalip, working away at collecting firewood over to her left. There was no one else around.

If he was collecting wood, then it looked like the decision to stay in the clearing for another night had been made. Or at least, he'd made the decision to stay there another night, while the others went back to London. Or tried to go back to London. Or, as she'd cruelly predicted, drown in the sea.

And what did that matter? She could do whatever she wanted: she could go in whichever direction she chose. The kid wasn't going to stop her, not after what she'd said and done. No one was.

He slowed briefly when he saw her and then, by the way he carried on dragging the thick, dead branch over towards the fire, decided to ignore her. He passed in front of her, glancing briefly at her feet.

'Where is everyone?' she asked.

He kept on going, and if she was going to hear his answer, she had to follow him.

'They've gone back to the door. Well, Stanislav hasn't. He doesn't think they'll get it to open, but in case they do, he's going to watch them from the shore.'

'Your mate doesn't say much, does he?'

'No. Perhaps he doesn't think he has to.'

Which was more than a little pointed, and she could feel herself rise to it. Then it was gone, like a fast car in the street.

'What happens when they all come back?'

'Those who want to, will go and see this geomancer. It just seemed stupid to split up now, especially after last night. We know we're not alone here.'

'The wolfman seemed friendly enough,' she said.

Dalip dropped the wood, rubbed his hands free of bark and moss, and immediately started back to where he'd been foraging, again forcing her to go after him.

'There were seven of us. You don't know how friendly he would have been if he'd found any of us alone.'

'That's not you talking, is it?'

'Stanislav's right, though. We don't know. Even if everything the wolfman told us was true, we still need to check with someone else to make sure.'

He spotted another fallen branch, and diverted towards it.

'Do you think we can get back home?' she asked.

'I don't know. There's stuff happening that just shouldn't happen. You know ...' He wasn't going to say it, so he bent down and started stripping the branch of its smaller twigs.

She said it instead. 'Magic.'

'We've seen a sea monster, but we already have giant squids and whales and we've had plesiosaurs and ichthyosaurs. The moon's huge, but it could be bigger, or closer, or both. No stars could mean we're in a dust cloud or something like that. But I saw the door disappear, right in front of me, just go from a door in a wall to rock face with nothing to show where we'd come through, in less than a minute. I've been thinking about that. And other things. A lot.' He picked up the narrow end of the branch and pulled it around, ready to drag. She had to step back to accommodate his arc.

'You're smart, right?' she said, and he shrugged in response. 'So where do you think we are?'

'We're not on Earth. Or if we are, we're so far in the past or in the future that we may as well not be. I'd still expect the rules to be the same, though, and I don't think they are. If we got here by,' and he shrugged again, 'a wormhole that just happened to open at the right time, then okay, but we're obviously not the first to have made the journey. Other people have crossed over at different times and different places, but no one can ever get back. Either we're dead, and this is the afterlife, or we're not, and I have no idea. Do you feel dead?'

She checked herself, actually patted herself down and made certain.

'No.'

'Then get the other end of this log and help me carry it back. Then when we've done that a few more times, we need to search for food.'

Her automatic response was to put her hands behind her back. 'Fuck off.'

Then he looked at her – actually looked at her, right in the eyes and wouldn't break off no matter how belligerent her expression grew.

'There's no one else to do it,' he said. 'No one else is going to bring us anything. This isn't paradise, where we can just pick fruit off the trees and it's no effort. We're going to have to work at this.'

'Doesn't mean I have to do it, does it?'

'No,' he said. 'But,' he added, then stopped.

'But what?'

'I'm not going to get shouted at like you did at Mama.' He started dragging the branch back towards the fire, on his own. 'I think you're smart, too. I also think you're right: we're no one's babies and we get to make our own decisions now. That's something different, at least.'

He left her standing in the wood, feeling – she couldn't tell what she was feeling. Everything was churning around. Yesterday, she'd known how everything worked. She'd always been at the edges of society, looking in at it through a double-glazed window, banging on it, demanding attention. She'd eventually got that attention, and while it wasn't the good sort, at least it was something. In London, she'd had professional people chasing around her, finding her somewhere to live, getting her a job, keeping her out of prison.

None of that applied today. It might never apply again.

If Dalip was struggling with the idea of a world where nothing quite worked the way it ought, she was struggling with the idea that it was going to work exactly the way she'd always wanted it to. There were no rules. No one to tell her what to do. No one to make her do anything.

What she was feeling was fear.

She put her hands over her mouth, pressing down hard as she realised that she was free, bottling up what would either be a yell of triumph or a cry of defeat. In the end, after a long while, she did neither.

She started to laugh. If she couldn't be queen of the old world, she could at least be the queen of her own life. She didn't need to go home. She didn't need to miss home. There was nothing and no one she was waiting for there.

She hoped that the others would fail – not that they would drown, because they didn't deserve that – and they would set off together to see the geomancer. And not because she might show them how to get home, but because she'd lived here longer, and could tell them everything she knew.

Mary checked herself again. Definitely not dead. She was still afraid, but accompanying that was a thrill of anticipation, like the moment between receiving a present and opening it. She wasn't going to be disappointed when the wrapper came off. Not this time. Not ever again. This would be the gift that she'd never tire of, that would never break, that would be new every morning and not old by evening.

'Wait,' she called, and even her voice had changed. 'Wait.'

He was almost at the fire, but she still picked up the end that had been dragged through the leaf mould.

'Go on, then,' she said, and gave the end of the branch a shove.

He stood there for a moment, uncertain as to what to do, before readjusting his grip and carrying the wood the short distance to the growing pile of broken timber.

'This will do,' he said, and they dropped it more or less at the same time.

'Do we need more?' She didn't know. Last night, she hadn't paid any attention to what was going on the fire and how fast it was consumed.

'About half as much again.' Still bemused, he added: 'There's two of us: it won't take long.'

'Where've you already looked?'

'Over there,' he said, pointing in a rough direction.

'Then let's try the other side.'

This time, she led the way.

8

By the time he'd wasted half the morning trying and failing to fix his hopelessly corroded torch, he'd almost missed the turning tide. The fish had run again, though not as many as the day before – Dalip guessed it was some sort of migration, and that it wouldn't last. There were also geese-like things nesting on the flat plain of the estuary, on the sandbanks and in amongst the grasses. While the birds flew away when he approached, they couldn't carry their fist-sized eggs with them.

The first nest he came across filled him with uncertainty. In the centre of the woven reed basket, reinforced with dried mud, were four white eggs still warm from brooding. Everything he'd learnt told him he shouldn't even be touching them. Collecting eggs was illegal. Wild birds were protected by law. Just standing there, looking, seemed incredibly transgressive and he already felt guilty, because he knew what he was going to do.

He picked up two eggs out of the four, and walked back across the channels to where Mary was trying to emulate his fish-catching exploits. She was impatient, and therefore less success-ful. By waiting longer, she'd catch more. He knew that she knew, and he didn't remind her. He put the eggs down next to the beached fish. In his family, the women worked in the kitchen, and men were excluded. He wasn't going to let on that he had no idea what he was supposed to do with the eggs. If Mary didn't know, someone would, he was sure.

Her face was fixed with so much concentration that she barely acknowledged him. She was strange, and he didn't understand the first thing about her. As far as he knew, she was a cleaner, and gleaning what he could from her earlier shouting match with Mama, she'd been in trouble with the police more than once. That made her highly unsuitable in his mother's eyes and someone he shouldn't be spending any time with.

His mother wasn't there though, and he didn't have much choice as to his companions at the moment – and neither did they. He probably wasn't the kind of person Mary would hang out with, either. They'd simply have to make the best of it, no matter what.

She wanted to help forage. That was good. It was a change from earlier too, but he'd rather have it that way than the shouting or sullenness.

He straightened his back, and watched the distant others for a moment, returning in a long, stretched-out line of orange figures. By the set of their shoulders, they'd been less than successful and less than satisfied with the state of affairs. They looked beaten, in fact: all except Stanislav. He seemed to still be walking with purpose.

'This'd be easier with a net,' Mary said, not taking her eyes off the river between her feet.

She was right. They didn't have one, though. Could he could make one?

He was used to wires and circuits, motors and controls. A net wouldn't need more than a forked piece of wood, and a bit of thin cloth. Still cross with himself over his earlier failure with the torch, he thought about construction without suitable tools as he went back out on to the estuary to look for more nests, and more eggs.

He had supposed there was going to be a main channel to the river, but he blundered into it to above his knees before he realised. The wide stretch of water was rippling as the tide ran up against the downstream flow.

The fish, which on the edges of the estuary wafted their tails lazily, had to swim hard against the current. Their sail-like fins and gleaming backs flashed as they broke the surface, scattering light and water.

There was a sudden roar, and an eruption of white foam. Dalip fell back into the reeds, and a black shape with scales the size of shields leapt up and lunged forward. The wave hit him hard, and the backwash dragged at his boilersuit. The creature shook its head, spray flying from its closing mouth, pin sharp teeth ivory white against its skin.

It ducked back down. The water slapped closed over it, and the waves subsided.

He scrambled further back, using his feet to push him away. It took him a moment to realise that he was whole, and another to realise that the first rush of water had been more fish than river. They flapped and wriggled, eventually squirming into the nearest channel and darting away.

The sea serpent was so much bigger than he'd expected. He sat up in time to see the tip of its tail churn the water with a v-shaped wake. A moment later, upstream and swimming hard, it burst out again, mouth wide and full of prey.

Mary was running towards him. What she thought she could do escaped him, and he quickly waved her back, while setting off at a jog towards her across the braided streams and sandbanks. He was soaked, and must have looked more like a drowned rat than anything else, breathing hard, heart hammering in his chest.

He finally turned and tried to see how far the serpent had gone upstream. From where he stood, both it and the deep channel were invisible.

'Are you all right?' Mary called.

'I'm fine.' He bent over, his hands on his knees, puffing. 'Did you see that?'

'I saw it.'

'Good. Because I don't think I'd believe me.'

'Did it go for you?'

'No. I don't even think it knew I was there. It was after the fish.' When he reached her, he sat down and wrestled with his boots, unlacing them and emptying them of water.

While he was sorting out the second, Mary picked one up to inspect it.

'You made a fucking mess of these.'

'We had to run through molten tarmac. They're,' and he made a face, 'uncomfortable. There's no give in them at all.'

'What're you going to do when we have to set off up the river?'

'I'm just going to have to cope.' He took his boot back off her and peeled off his socks to wring them out. 'It's not like I'm going to find another pair soon. If ever.'

'The wolfman had boots. They must make them here, somewhere.'

'Cobblers,' he said.

She snorted. 'Well, fuck you.'

'No, they're people who make shoes. Cobblers.'

'Fuck you anyway,' she said, and smiled. 'Your feet aren't that big. One of the others is probably the same size as you.'

'Won't they need them?'

'Not if they're dead.'

'I am not killing someone for their shoes! I'm not killing anyone.'

'I'm not saying you have to. Just if something happens, you can take them.'

'I can't do that either.'

She counted the number of fish she already had. 'All I'm saying is that you won't get far in those. Have you sorted out that net for me yet?'

77

'I … Yes. Give me a bit of time, and I'll try something out.'

'Get on with it, then. The others are coming back.'

Dalip walked barefoot for a little way, before putting his thick socks back on. She was right; the soles of his boots were barely hanging together. There was already a crack that traversed the width of the left one, which when he flexed it, showed the construction deep inside.

At some point soon, he'd need to replace them. The bottoms of his feet were soft and coddled, vulnerable to pea-sized stones that felt like bricks. The forest floor wasn't harsh to walk on, though, and he quickly hunted out a clearing where a mature tree lay rotting on its side, and saplings competed with each other to climb towards the circle of light.

Getting one of those saplings to break at the base was another thing entirely. They were supple and strong, and they fought back. He used his kirpan to dig a ragged notch in the bark, then further into the wood beneath, and eventually he managed to get enough leverage. The trunk snapped unevenly, and not all the way through. He still had more twisting and bending to do before it came away from the ground.

Hand-sore and tired, he sat down with the y-shaped tree, and undid his turban.

He suspected that his parents would tell him he was committing a terrible sin, ruining his pagh and breaking his vows simultaneously. They were strict, and above all, proper. Outward behaviour was a discipline. It trained the mind and the body to obey until rightness and decency became an ingrained habit, difficult to break and impossible to forget. That still mattered to him. But he knew there was more to being a Sikh than just following the traditions: justice, mercy, compassion and, yes, feeding everyone.

The cotton cloth of the pagh was a long strip, folded, folded, folded and folded again. He wouldn't need much, and his subtraction wouldn't even show. He used his kirpan to start him off, forcing the blunt point hard through the material, then tearing it along its length. When he judged he'd gone far enough, he made another cut, and tore from the side.

He'd been a Scout, and could even remember some of his knots. Nicks in the cloth allowed the forked tines of the sapling to interweave it, and he tied it off using the spare material. There: possibly not as deep as he'd wanted, but perfectly serviceable as a scoop. If his kirpan had more of an edge, he'd have been able to fashion a fish spear, like the Inuit, or the South Sea island-ers used. Not that he knew how to use one, but form followed function. He knew how it ought to be used. After that, it was all practice.

He stopped, and leaned forward and hugged his knees. What was he doing? Making nets and thinking about spears? There was a monster in the river, and he'd just avoided being eaten by it. Just for a moment, he'd had nothing to worry about, and he'd let his mind wander. Despite him saying that this place wasn't paradise, he'd believed it was safe. Even the wolfman's wolves, chained and controlled, had seemed benign in the end.

He remembered the wall of scales, the surging wave, the needle-like teeth. Whether or not its preferred prey was fish, it would make short work of him; a couple of bites then swallowed. They didn't have giant sea snakes in Southall. Perhaps he should think harder about trying to get home, rather than toying with the notion that he might have finished his formal education, moved out of his parents' house and become independent in one giant, irrevocable step.

He forced his legs to work, getting them under him, standing him up. He retrieved his pagh and rolled it back on neatly, tuck-ing the frayed end in. He resheathed his kirpan, and picked up the net.

By the time he got back to the fire, the first of the others had arrived: Elena, and her cousin, Luiza. They looked defeated as well as exhausted.

'I guess it didn't work.'

Luiza sat down hard and stared into the heart of the fire. Elena shook her head in warning and mouthed something at him he didn't catch. The meaning of it was clear enough, though. Their stay here would be longer than a single day.

He didn't know what he should feel about that. He didn't dare ask himself, in case the answers weren't what he anticipated. They were all going to have different responses to an open door back to London: what he should do – what they should all do – was obvious. And yet no one here was going to scold him to do what was expected of him.

He knew Mama wanted to go. He didn't know what the Romanian women wanted, so he made some suitable noise of consolation and threw some more broken branches on to the fire.

Stanislav was the next to appear. He jerked his head for Dalip to follow him, and they walked together down to where Mary was still fishing. As they went, the older man took the makeshift net from him, examined it with an approving nod, and handed it back.

'They tried,' he said. 'They tried all kinds of incredible things. The door would not appear to them. It was just rock.'

That was, apparently, all that could be said about it. They tried, they failed, they came back.

'The sea serpent came up the deep part of the river,' said Dalip. 'It was chasing the fish on the tide. I ... got quite close to it. Closer than I'd like.'

'You survived.'

'Yes. It's probably something we don't want to meet on a dark night, though.'

'Agreed. Was it big?'

'Oh yes.'

'Was it impressive?'

Dalip caught the inflexion in his voice, and then the twinkle in his eye. 'Yes. That too. I never imagined such a thing could even exist. Yet, if I hadn't been trying very hard to get out of its way, I could've reached out and touched it.'

'You are both drawn to and repelled by this place. It seems wild, and—' He spent a moment searching for the word. 'Untamed. This is outside of your experience.'

'Lots of things are. My parents keep me on a pretty tight rein. Kept. I don't know. This is all very new.'

'This is very new to all of us. None of us know what we might find here. Just keep in mind this freedom means you are also free to fail. Badly.'

'I understand. At least, I'm beginning to understand.'

They looked at what Mary had caught. There were another two fish on the bank.

'Shall we worry about varying our diet tomorrow?' asked Dalip.

Stanislav bent down and held one of the eggs in his hand. 'Fruits, vegetables, grains: all change with the seasons. We do not know about seasons here, though it appears to be spring or early summer. 'Are there more eggs?'

'I think so. The geese – if that's what they are – nest on the ground. I took two out of four, and I was going back to look for others, when the sea serpent happened.'

'You should have heard him,' said Mary. She took the net from Dalip, and poked at it, testing its robustness. 'Did you know you screamed like a girl?'

'I was surprised, that's all.'

'Course you were.' She lowered the net into the river, and tried to chase a fish with it. It swam away with a flick of its tail. 'This isn't any easier.'

Stanislav looked over his shoulder. Mama was walking in, a solitary and dejected figure in the distance. He frowned, and turned to where the thin stream of white smoke was rising through the tree canopy from their fire.

'Where,' he asked, 'is Grace?'

'She went with you.' Dalip turned a slow full circle, looking for a tell-tale flash of orange, even as a fleck of ice lodged in his stomach.

'She stayed only a short while. Long enough to see for herself that the door had disappeared. Then she said she would return to you.'

'We never saw her, and we were in and out of the camp all day.' He swallowed. 'Mary?'

She carried on trying the net out, but she shook her head.

'Not seen her since this morning.' Then she realised the importance of the discussion and splashed out of the riverlet. 'So where is she?'

Dalip did what he thought was sensible. He drew in a deep breath and cupped his hands around his mouth. Stanislav closed his fist over them and dragged them inexorably down.

'No,' he said.

'But if she's wandered off—'

'This is not an accident. If she has been taken, we can shout for her until our throats bleed: she will be unable to answer. And if, as I suspect, she has left us to find the geomancer on her own, she will not want to answer.' He made his lips into a mean, thin line.

'Shit,' said Mary. 'The ungrateful bitch.'

'We can't just assume that,' said Dalip. His heart was starting to race. Even faster than when he'd been surprised by the sea serpent. 'We have to try and find her.'

'Do we?' Stanislav's whole face was now set and sour. 'How?'

Dalip spun around again, knowing what he'd see: the ocean, the estuary, the forest, the distant mountains. They could search from now until … whenever, and not scratch so much as a tiny fraction of this vast wild space.

'But,' he objected. 'We can't abandon her.'

'It is decent and noble of you to want to try to find her.' Stanislav's voice rumbled deep in his chest. 'If she had come to harm between the headland and the camp, one of us would have seen or heard something. If she had made it as far as the fire, then she would have met either you or Mary. No. She has abandoned us. Deliberately. You worked with her, Mary.'

'No, it wasn't like that. She wasn't part of our crew. She just tagged on to us after it all went tits up.' She leaned on the net's pole. 'Fuck. What does this mean?'

'It means we three should talk.' Despite there being no eaves-droppers, Stanislav beckoned them, and Dalip and Mary moved closer. 'We are thrown together by an accident of chance, yes? We will have different views and different goals, and there is no reason why we should agree on everything.'

Dalip was still looking around him, wondering what might have happened to Grace, even though he hardly knew her – and it turned out that no one did. Now, she was gone.

'Concentrate,' said Stanislav. He pressed his thumb and fore-finger together and gestured in Dalip's face like he was jabbing his point home. 'We cannot help her, or hinder her. We must consider our own safety.'

'You want us to form a gang, right?' said Mary.

Stanislav equivocated. 'A gang?' he said. 'An alliance, perhaps. A formal agreement between ourselves that we will stay together, at least as far as this geomancer. None of us know what we are doing here. We do not know this world, or our place in it. We cannot tell whether Grace has stolen an advantage over us and put us all in danger, or whether she has made a terrible mistake in going on alone. There is so much we do not understand, but staying in this one place will not help us. We cannot get through the door, and we are unequipped to live here: the food will become scarce, we lack shelter, and if there are tame wolves, there will also be wild ones. We need to go and seek wisdom. All of us. That would be best, I think.'

'Best for us, or best for everyone?' asked Dalip.

'It is the same thing. If Grace believes she gains something by getting to the geomancer first, we must seek an advantage of our own. We must stay together and act together. If we three all argue that we should leave here in the morning, we should persuade at least one of the others to join us. If we do that, it is likely that they will all come.'

'But that's going to happen anyway,' said Dalip. 'The door back to London won't open. We haven't any other choices.'

'Well, that's not true is it?' Mary kicked the bottom of the net pole. 'If Grace fucked off on her own, she's going to be halfway to the geomancer already. And Mama, she's going to want to go back to the door tomorrow, and the next day, for as long as it takes her to see it's not going to open.'

'Dalip. Listen to Mary.'

'Someone had to make those wolf chains, right?' Mary hefted the net again, and looked to the river. 'That must mean there's somewhere else we need to be.'

'She is right. What do you say, Dalip?'

He gave in. Searching for Grace was going to be futile, especially if she didn't want to be found. 'Yes, yes okay. Let's try that.'

'No,' said Stanislav, 'we must be more determined than that. We must move on, we must go together and we must not let anyone else leave us. Talk to them. They will listen to you.'

'Me?' He raised his eyebrows. 'They'll listen to Mama.'

'Then do not speak to her, but to Luiza and Elena. Use Grace's absence to scare them into agreement if necessary. Mama will not remain here while the rest of us go upriver. Here,' he said, and reached into his pocket for a wide, flat stone. 'You will need this.'

Dalip took the sea-worn rock and hefted it in his hand. 'What's this for?'

'For sharpening your knife. You must grind an edge on it for it to be useful.'

The rock was smooth, fine-grained, black and heavy. 'I'm sorry,' said Dalip. 'I don't know how.'

'Then I will show you. Now: tell me where the eggs are to be found. If we are to walk far, we must be fed.'

9

The moon rose later and less full than the previous night, but it still resembled a huge skull of cratered bone hanging over their heads, casting its light through the canopy. Beneath its ponderous orbit, they spoke, argued, shouted and finally decided. There were tears and red faces, and eventually capitulation and sleep.

In the morning, Mary went down by the river to wash, scrubbing at her skin and scalp with her fingers. The water was cold when she wanted hot. She had sand when she wanted soap. She told herself that there was no point in wishing for things that none of them had, but it didn't stop her wishing anyway.

Stanislav had emphasised that none of them should ever be on their own, just in case. So Dalip was nearby, and she wasn't watching him as such. Not closely. He was downriver from her, secluded but not private, going through the ritual of washing his hair, combing it straight, tying it up and imprisoning it under his turban. Every so often, that plain steel bracelet he wore high up on his forearm slipped down, and he'd reposition it again before carrying on.

And when it was time to go, they just left. There was nothing to carry, except the net, nothing to pack, except Dalip's sharpening stone. Stanislav raked out the fire with the end of a branch and gazed at the embers as they grew dull. With everything unspoken, he threw the stick he'd used on the ashes aside, and simply started. One by one, they followed, leaving the coast, and the door, behind.

She remembered that stupid kid's joke – she couldn't remember where from or who told it to her first – about 'when is a door not a door?' Who knew there was another answer, one which involved the door merging with a sheer cliff?

They kept to the tree line for a while, but as the estuary narrowed, so did the distance between the bank and the forest, until it became necessary to walk amongst the trees and keep an eye on where the river was.

The sun slewed around behind them, but they were shaded. It was cool under the canopy. Insects turned slow loops in the shadows, and skittered over the face of the running water. Sometimes a fish rose for one with a soft approach and a powerful escape. Birds called unseen from the upper branches.

Back when social services were still trying, they'd tried to make Mary do one of those adventure holidays – they said it'd be character building. The pictures they'd shown her to encourage her, the ones of stark rock ridges and barren, boggy moors where the wind and rain spotted the camera's lens, had the opposite effect. She wasn't doing that. Why should she? What possible purpose would it achieve? She'd started with a hearty 'fuck off', and it escalated from there.

She hadn't gone.

Perhaps the mistake they'd made was making it too safe for her. Where was the challenge in climbing a hill thousands had already climbed that year, and getting roped up to abseil a few metres down a rock?

Now, with no one to plead with her, cajole her or compel her, she was walking and camping out, foraging for food and eating with her fingers, all the things she swore she'd never do, because she wasn't a fucking animal.

She didn't even want a cigarette. She couldn't normally make it five minutes after waking without one.

With slow inevitability, they became strung out. Spotting each other was easy enough, though; there was nothing that particular shade of orange in the forest. Stanislav was always out in front, Dalip not far behind as if he had something to prove – which perhaps he did, if only to himself – and her third. Elena and Luiza walked close together, with Mama in the rear.

Mama really didn't like the idea of the journey, let alone the journey itself. Every step was further away from her babies, as she called her seemingly endless collection of children, grand-children, nieces and nephews.

She could remember all their names, and their birthdays. For someone like Mary, that seemed astonishing enough, but Mama knew every part of their lives, too. Mary would have found it all too claustrophobic and oppressive, but apparently the kids were all fine with it, voluntarily surrendering every intimate detail without the threat of sanctions hanging over them.

Mary was happy being on her own, happy that no one was questioning her, happy that her life which had swung between chaotic to strictly ordered had found a third path she'd never actually known existed.

Stanislav stopped. Dalip caught him up, and the older man pointed at something ahead of them. They looked behind them and saw her approaching, and together they waited for her too.

She saw it before she had to have it explained to her. It was a house. Or at least, it was a corner of one, deep green with moss, the same colour as the forest. She moved her head this way and that. What had been a complete structure, four walls and a roof, was little more than sagging timber uprights being inexorably reclaimed by nature.

'I don't think anyone lives there,' she said.

'No. Not for many years. Twenty at least.' Stanislav stared at the ruin as if it had been his own once.

'How can you tell that?'

'The trees,' he said, circling his finger. 'They are all younger here. This land was cleared, farmed, and then abandoned.'

'Do you want to take a look?' asked Dalip.

His fleeting expression told her that no, he didn't. Really didn't. But he looked away, then back, and he wore a different face. 'Yes.'

The three of them converged on the house from different angles. It wasn't big, but big enough for a few people who really didn't mind seeing each other every waking moment. The roof had collapsed completely, and a single sapling poked out above the tottering walls.

The rude wooden door was still in place, but only for as long as it took Dalip to rest his hand on it. It fell, neatly and cleanly, backwards to join the ferns and fungi that were growing out of the scattered shingles and beams.

The walls were rough timber, overlapping split logs on a frame with the bark facing outwards. For all that, it was carefully and skilfully made, and it would have been dry inside.

'I wonder what happened?' said Mary. She ducked under Dalip's arm and stood on the fallen door. There wasn't any evidence of furniture, or anything on the walls.

'The wolfman said—' started Dalip, but Stanislav interrupted.

'We know what the wolfman said. It is very convenient that he told us about the possibility of empty houses before we found any. As he knew we would, because he also told us the direction to go to find this geomancer.'

Mary walked in further, and began kicking through the debris with the toe of her boot. 'You think he's lying?'

'I think it is convenient, that is all. If we accept his explanation, all we think when we see these falling-down walls is that the people who lived there have moved somewhere else.' He looked up at the sky, at the trees reaching out over the ruin. 'There are other reasons for houses to be abandoned, not all of them good.'

'You're very suspicious,' said Dalip. 'Sometimes an abandoned house is just an abandoned house. We see them all the time on London streets: you know, with those steel shutters over the doors and windows.'

'How often were the occupants forced to leave?'

'I don't know. I suppose that happens sometimes.'

'It happens a lot,' said Mary. She'd made a hole in debris, and had dug as far as a layer of thick bark sheets. 'In squats, or you can't pay your rent. Bailiffs come round and give you the evils, throw your stuff out on to the street, and it's fuck you very much.'

Dalip conceded the point with a shrug. 'Okay. But it's not like anyone owns this bit of the forest, do they?'

'So you believe,' said Stanislav. 'What if they do?'

'I don't know. We can't go back, because we've nowhere back to go to. We can go in a different direction, but then we're more lost than we are already, which would be saying something. At least we have a destination at the moment.'

'Which the wolfman gave us.'

Mary bent down and pulled at the bark tiles: the original floor, like the walls, was made of split logs, but these were flat side up. As she exposed more, she started to find things that had been protected from the elements. A wooden platter, with rounded chisel marks across it. What looked like a broken stool, a sawn piece of trunk and three stout legs splayed around it.

She passed them back for the others to examine.

'If the people who lived here had moved of their own accord,' said Stanislav, 'they would have taken their plates, if not their chairs.'

Dalip turned the platter in his hands. 'We don't know that. For all we know, the farmer was old, out working alone in his fields, had an accident or just died, and everything just fell apart with no one to keep it up.'

Mary stood up and wiped her hands. 'If this was a farm —'

'Twenty years ago.'

'Then is there still going to be food here? I don't know how these things work. Are we going to find chickens and things like that running around? Or potatoes. They grow in the ground, right?'

'We don't even know if they have potatoes here,' said Dalip, but Stanislav nodded in agreement.

'It might be food we do not have to work for, which is always worth collecting.' He checked the position of the sun and pronounced it midday. 'We need to rest for a while anyway. Here is as good a place as any.'

'You realise I don't know what I'm looking for. Veg comes out of packets.'

'Then,' he said, 'do you know what a chicken looks like?'

She thought about it. Probably. It wasn't going to arrive in breadcrumbs, but yes, she'd seen one before. 'Sure.'

'Then we are all agreed. If there is any sign of Grace, or if she has been here, tell me immediately.' Stanislav stepped back out of the doorway and walked off to catch the others as they arrived.

'Your mate's a bit weird,' said Mary.

'Weird? In what way?' asked Dalip, and added, 'And he's not my mate.'

'He's closer to being your mate than anyone else here. And weird in a serial killer sort of way. Paranoid.' She went to the other corner of the room, picking her way between the leafy ferns. 'No one's tried to kill us yet, unless you count your sea serpent. So why's he got the fear?'

'Fear? I wouldn't say that.'

'I would. It's like he's seen all this before. Where did you say he was from?' She bent down again, and started pulling up plants. They came away easily, and she threw them to one side, creating a shower of soil that made Dalip step back.

'I didn't say he was from anywhere, and I don't know. Eastern Europe somewhere, I suppose.' He shook the dirt from the uppers of his boots. 'What if he's right? What if we're trespassing on someone else's land?'

'We've walked for half a day and we've seen no one. We've been here two days and there's only been the wolfman. There's no one here. This place is empty.' In London, everywhere was someone's; the council's, developers, some rich Russian bloke, it didn't really matter – there were rules wherever she went, even in places that seemed to have fallen down the cracks of the city. Here? No.

She uncovered a few more pieces of detritus. Shards of a small stone bottle. A wooden handle, worn smooth with use, but no clue as to what it was attached to. Something that may have been once string, but fell apart on being picked up.

There was nothing to indicate one way or the other whether the farmer had simply upped and left for pastures new, or been forced out by some crooked landlord.

By the time the rest of the group arrived, Mary was already out in the forest. She could see, now that it had been pointed out to her, where the former fields had been: thinner trees this side of the line, fat trees, the other. In places, she could even see the remains of a fence, now only a series of rotten posts in the ground.

She couldn't see any chickens, or pigs, or cows, or sheep. That exhausted her knowledge of nursery rhyme animals, but there didn't seem to be anything moving except the occasional flash of orange boilersuit on the ground, and glossy feathers in the air.

She followed the old fence around. It wasn't far, enough to encompass the land that someone could reasonably work and live off. It went in a strip from the river to beyond the house, roughly square. And as she walked the boundary, she saw another structure in the distance, between the straight trunks and slanting branches of the trees.

Looking around, Mama was closest to her, but she didn't say anything. It wasn't like it was important. She stepped over the fence line and through the mature wood until she came to it. The house was also a ruin, roof gone, walls sagging, but there was no evidence of fields around it. Instead, there were jumbled piles of logs, slowly returning to the soil.

She poked her head inside the rectangle of wood. There was nothing remarkable to see, just a chaotic mix of rotting debris and new life. But outside, she found an axe embedded in one of the logs: an actual hand axe, haft as long as her forearm, brown blade the size of her fist.

She worked it free. The head wobbled slightly on the handle, and it was badly rusted. It was, however, an axe. She made a few experimental swipes with it, then let it hang by her side as she slowly turned.

There was another house even further away.

It looked to her like the whole village had just packed up and gone, leaving things behind that shouldn't really have been left. Perhaps Stanislav was right after all. She walked halfway over to the third ruin, growing increasingly uneasy for no reason at all. Everything around her was green and brown, with even the man-made structures being eaten by nature.

Perhaps that was what had happened. The plants themselves had risen up at the order imposed on the land and dragged the people down, into the ground, burying them with roots and vines. Flowers grew on their graves and rot consumed their houses. All that remained were ghosts.

She stopped. She could feel her legs start to tremble. Concrete was what she knew, concrete and glass and tarmac and noise. Not this. Not the forest.

She turned around, and hurried back to where she'd found the axe. She was breathing fast and shallow, and leaned against a tree to recover. Orange in the distance meant that she was safe, back in sight of the others.

A crash, a shout, and she raised the axe instinctively.

Dalip stumbled back from the house, which he'd accidentally

partially demolished. Then he heard her, or sensed her, because he spun around, hands up, ready to defend himself. For a moment, they didn't recognise each other, seeing only a threat. His gaze went from the axe, to her, and his shoulders sagged with relief. She looked up at her hand, and lowered it.

'Sorry,' he said.

'You, you … What the fuck do you think you're doing?'

'Just looking. Just … looking, that's all.' He held his hands up again, but this time palms out. 'I didn't mean to frighten you.'

'Well, you did.' She wasn't angry, but startled and scared instead. 'I, I found this. And there's another house further on. There used to be people here, loads of them, and now there aren't.'

Dalip didn't seem to want to get close to the axe, not when she was still waving it in front of her.

'Everyone's going to keep looking for a bit longer. I came over here because I hadn't seen you for a while.'

'I don't need looking after,' she said automatically. 'I'm fine.'

He didn't believe her, but at least he pretended he did. 'Okay. I'll leave you alone.' He pointed towards the river and slightly upstream. 'I'll be over there. Call if you find anything.'

He left her, moving off between the trees, every so often slowing and examining the ground by his feet. She leant back against the tree again, the back of her head resting against the bark. She started to realise that freedom for her meant freedom for everyone and everything. She was at their mercy, and they were at hers.

It wasn't that no one could tell her what to do anymore. It was that she couldn't tell anyone what to do anymore; that all she could rely on now was either trust and friendship, or fear and coercion.

She weighed the axe in her hand, and wondered what to do.

10

Whatever the reason for the village's abandonment, they found so very little of use. No crops growing wild in the undergrowth, no feral chickens scratching their way through the dirt. They did find what Stanislav thought might be an old orchard, but the fruits were barely swellings behind the hairy remains of the blossom.

Dalip realised that the presence of a farm meant that they couldn't just rely on foraging for food, or if they did, that their existence would that of a nomad, chasing calories around, always in that delicate balance of food burned against food earned. Plenty and famine were precarious states to sit between.

Perhaps the geomancer could help after all. If the name suggested anything, it was a close connection with nature: they'd be someone who watched the way the seasons turned and how the land reacted. He was keenly hungry – he was certain they all were – but he wasn't going to complain, because what would be the point?

When he was younger, he'd always tried to wheedle something from the kitchen, no matter what time of day it was. But food was always there, and his mother was the gatekeeper. Occasionally she would relent. Most times she would not. Here, there was no food, no morsel being kept back. Only finding or catching something would change that.

They started upriver again, heading for the notch between the two peaks ahead. There were no more houses, at least that they could see. It felt like they were walking through forests so ancient that no one had ever walked that way before, and though Grace must have passed that way only the day before, there was no sign of her passing.

All the woods he'd ever been to – with the Scouts, with the school, or on holiday with his parents – had had paths worn into them by the persistent feet of people, even if planned routes, marked and laid out with posts and signs, hadn't been present. The closest he'd ever come to this was the one time he'd gone – his father had called it 'going back home', to a place alien to Dalip – to the Punjab. They'd gone as a party up to the high mountains, where the patchwork quilt of cultivation ended and the forest reigned. He'd stepped off the path, away from everyone, just for a moment. It hadn't been quiet, or still, but it was a world apart from the roar and dust of the cities.

That had been just a flavour, a mere hint, of what he was experiencing now. Once upon a time, the whole world had looked like this. Trees grew, seeded, died, and more trees grew to take their place. Some of the saplings were eaten, but the eaters were in turn eaten. There was no one to cut and burn and clear the forest, until the coming of man.

That thought had him hurrying to catch up with Stanislav, who once again had taken the lead.

He drew up behind him, and the man waited for a few seconds to let him catch up the rest of the way. They'd have to stop soon, anyway, to gather firewood and try harder to scavenge food.

'This place,' said Dalip. He was not so much out of breath as simply tired. 'This place, it's untouched.'

'This is true,' said Stanislav. 'But you mean more than that, yes?'

'When people – when we – stopped being hunter-gatherers and started being farmers, we lost all this. Even where we didn't cut the forests down, we lived in them, managed them. Here, that never happened. If we believe the wolfman—'

'If.'

'Even if he's lying to us, he might be telling the truth in parts. He said his father was a, a traveller, like us. What if everyone here is one, or their children? That there's no other people here at all, except those who find their way here by accident?'

'I see. That would mean that there are no real natives, that there is no deep knowledge to pass down, and that people we meet vary only in their levels of ignorance depending on how many generations back they go.' He lowered his chin, deep in thought. 'It might be that this geomancer is the pinnacle of lore here, but there will be limits even to her knowledge. This is important.'

'Also ...'

'Yes?'

Dalip's gaze followed Stanislav's, down to the ground. 'People, you know, have babies. Even by the end of the Neolithic, most of Britain had been worked over once. By the Middle Ages, everywhere was lived in, and that's with a tiny population, a couple of million.'

'You are very knowledgeable.'

'School, that's all. But everything we know about where people live: along rivers, on the coast, especially where rivers flow out into the sea. We should have already found a town, a couple of villages, and farms everywhere. There's nothing. Nothing at all.' Dalip spread his hands wide. 'There's no one here. This is a, I don't know what to call it, a blank slate, a new world.'

'Yet,' said Stanislav, 'when we do find what we could call a village, it has been deserted for many, many years. The number of people should be increasing, not decreasing. There is no lack of space for them to spread out into.'

He rumbled deep in his chest, a noise that made Dalip look askance.

'Have you seen this before?'

'Yes,' said Stanislav. 'Twice before. Once when I was young, and again when I was not so young.'

'And?'

'The cause was the same. War.'

'That's not good.'

'No.' Stanislav looked over his shoulder, either to see who might be listening, or to check that the others were still there. Dalip looking behind him, too. There was Mary, and further back, possibly Luiza.

'But you think this might have been twenty years ago.'

'Yes. There is another question, of course. How did the wolf-man find us so quickly, if this is an empty land?'

'I ... don't know.' Dalip didn't, either. 'Chance?'

'Perhaps. Have we met anyone else? By chance?'

'No. No, we haven't.'

'So he was waiting for us, yes?'

'But we didn't know we were coming,' said Dalip. 'How could he possibly do that?'

'When I mean waiting, I mean watching. He did not know when we might appear, but if he knew where we would appear? Then it is very possible. Then we must consider why he would keep watch over a door which, until we passed through it, we did not know existed.'

'Other people must have come through.'

'Yes. What do you think happened to them?'

'The same thing that happened to us.' Dalip stopped walking, right there in the forest within earshot of the slow flow of the river. 'They were told about the geomancer. They went to find her.'

'The wolfman did not explain any of this. He had the oppor-tunity to do so, and yet did not. He led us with his answers, so that we would choose to go in this direction, to choose to find the geomancer, choose to knock on her door and ask to see her.' He pursed his lips. 'I think we should reconsider.'

They stopped and waited for the others. Mary arrived first.

'Is this where we're stopping for the night?' She looked up and around. 'I suppose it doesn't make much difference, right?'

She started to head off towards the river, to see if it could offer them anything, when Dalip called after her. 'Don't go far.'

'Fuck off, all right?' she said, and kept going.

Stanislav jerked his head in her direction, and Dalip got up to follow her.

She was lying down, looking over the river bank at the slack water beneath, trying to see if there were any fish there, when Dalip came up behind her.

'We need to stay together,' said Dalip.

'Fuck off, Dalip. I'm fine.'

'No,' he said, and tried to explain, but the words got stuck. He sat down, back to a tree trunk. 'Stanislav thinks we're walking into a trap.'

Now he had her attention. She rolled over and leaned on one arm. 'We're what?'

He wanted to explain, and he tried, but Mary wasn't at all convinced.

'This geomancer is paying the wolfman to be her lookout, to send people up to her, whatever, church? What the fuck is she going to do to us when we get there? We can just walk out if she gets heavy on us.'

'I don't think it's that simple. I don't think the wolfman's on his own.'

'He's got a gang? So have we.'

'He's got wolves, Mary! I mean, look at us. We're dressed in bright orange clothes, we have a cigarette lighter, a small blunt knife and a rusty axe between us. We're not a gang. We're just a bunch of people thrown together by the fact that we didn't die.'

Then the final penny dropped. 'He's watching us now. We'll never spot him, but he's followed us this far, and he'll follow us until we get where we're supposed to go.'

She sat up and stared into the forest, checking random directions.

'You're scaring me.'

'I'm scaring myself. But it's too much of a coincidence that he's the first and only person we've met. We should've been more careful.'

'There's nothing wrong with what we did,' she said, and was suddenly distracted by something happening behind Dalip.

Shouting. Rushing. A scream.

'Get down.'

Dalip rolled to one side, pressing himself against the ground. After a moment, he started to raise himself, to see over the undergrowth. It was as if the forest itself was moving, brown and green shapes darting from cover to cover, and the few orange boilersuits he could see were running.

'We've been so stupid. Naive, trusting ... idiots.'

Mary crawled next to him. 'Who are these people? Why are they doing this?'

'I don't know, and we need to find out. But not from them.' He looked forward, then back at the river. 'We're going to have to go that way.'

'We can't just leave the others,' she said, and straight away doubted her words. 'Can we?'

'We have literally nothing. If we can cross the river without being seen, it might mean we can get away. Go. I'll be right behind you.'

There was another scream, and more shouting. Something that sounded like a laugh.

'I can't swim.'

'Bank to bank, it's not even the length of the local baths. Just do it.'

'I really can't swim.'

'You can probably walk halfway across.' He raised himself up again, and dropped down immediately. 'They're coming.'

They were several shapes he could barely make out, as tall as a man but blending with the background in a way he couldn't quite believe. They were close and closing.

'Come on!'

He sprang to his feet, grabbed Mary's wrist and pulled her toward the river. She wasn't even standing by the time he got her to the bank and he pushed her in.

There were noises right behind him. If she was to get away, he would have to stay. Even if she drowned because for some inexplicable reason she hadn't learnt to swim, and he wasn't there to hold her up.

He reached into his boilersuit and drew his kirpan, then turned to face them.

Perhaps they realised by the way his hand shook that he'd never used the blade in anger before. Perhaps it was because there were three of them, lean, toothy, skin tanned like leather, all used to casual violence and pain.

Could he keep them at bay for long enough for Mary to escape? They had knives in their hands: proper knives, almost swords, thick bladed and curve-edged. Never mind. It was his duty. It was his honour. It was the first time he'd had to act out his faith on his own accord, and it felt like something inside him had finally shifted into place.

Any fight would be quick and dirty, and it'd be him losing and losing badly. These men in brown and green were fighters, warriors. He was an engineering student with decent batting average and a fierce spin.

And still. He jabbed forward with his kirpan at the face of the man on the left, causing him to dodge back. The man on the right caught his arm, stepped close and punched him hard in the kidneys.

The pain was extraordinary. He felt his legs start to fold, and decided that he'd be better on his feet. He brought his arm back, elbow first. He made some sort of contact because the grip on his wrist loosened.

They'd had enough of his nonsense, clearly. The other two laid into him with no finesse. A fist to the gut, a blow to the side of his head, and he was reeling. He couldn't see straight. He lashed out, hit something, and his hand felt like he'd struck solid wood.

Then he was down, and the blows didn't stop falling. His back, his legs, his head. His turban saved him: that, and a clear command stopped the beating before he was crippled.

'Hello, little darkie. You must think you've very clever to have worked it all out. Better you hadn't shouted it out so all the world could hear, though.'

Dalip forced one eye open. Everything hurt so much, it didn't matter which bit of him was damaged.

'Hello, wolfman,' he said. His lip had split open. He may have lost a tooth, he couldn't tell.

The wolfman crouched down and plucked the kirpan from Dalip's fist. He waggled it like a finger. 'You weren't going to do much with this.'

'I had to try.'

'Of course you did. Now where's your little darkie friend?'

Dalip spat out blood on the ground.

'Cat got your tongue? She can't have gone far. Go,' he said to the other men, 'bring her back.'

Dalip couldn't breathe through his nose, so he lay there, curled up, mouth open, panting. The wolfman was missing something.

'Where,' he managed, 'where are your wolves?'

'My wolves?' He rubbed the end of his nose, and gave a sly smile. 'Is that what you're worried about?'

The wolfman dropped the kirpan and held his hands out in front of him, curling his fingers around imagined chains. He clenched his jaw, and his eyelid twitched.

His hands did hold chains. Those chains looped around the necks of wolves. The wolves sniffed at Dalip, smelling his blood and his defeat.

'These wolves, you mean? They're right here.'

11

Mary stayed very still, even though the water was cold and the current pulled at her boilersuit. The voices were right above her, above where she crouched amongst the roots and the weeds, with only a thin overhang of soil hiding her. Her chin was in the river, and she was prepared, no matter how much she'd hate it, to take a deep breath and submerge completely. Anything, just so long as she wasn't discovered.

She could hear the men beating Dalip, the steady grunts of effort as their fists rose and fell. She could hear the wolfman's taunts. Then she heard him call for her to be found.

She was almost numb with cold by the time they moved off, and she sat, balanced on her haunches, for a good while longer. It could have been a trap, another one, with someone sitting on the bank above her, waiting for her to emerge, and with her in no state to either fight or run.

She listened. The sounds she recognised – traffic, music, doors, shouting – were absent. The sounds she was now hearing – trees, birds, the slow churn of the river – were alien to her, but she'd rather hear those than anything else. She was alone. Truly alone now.

She still wanted to cross the river, and put broad water between her and her pursuers. It looked, at least from down at water level, a long way. Especially for a non-swimmer. No one was going to help her, no one was going to offer her a reward for just trying. She steadied herself and moved her waterlogged legs out towards the middle.

Her feet lost the bottom quickly. Her head ducked under, she splashed her way to the surface, gasping, and for a moment couldn't remember which side of the river she'd just left. One bank was a lot closer than the other, so that was decided for her quickly. The current was carrying her, and the one thing in her favour was the trapped air in her closely woven boilersuit.

She floundered, arms and legs moving in contradictory motion, her boots dragging her down, her sleeves holding her up. The current slackened, her foot struck something soft and she grunted, pulling it back fast. But it was only the river bed's soft mud, and she was able to stand a few metres from shore, sodden, freezing, dirty, scared.

She looked behind her, to where she'd come from. She could see no one, though she knew the wolfman and his gang were able to blend in to the forest in a way that was almost spooky. They could be watching her now, just like they probably had been, all the way from the sea to here. Watching her wade to the far bank and crawl out, lying on her belly like a worm, in the brown leaves and broken twigs and earthy decay.

Where was she going to go? What was she going to do? How was she supposed to do anything?

Something was sticking in her ribs. She rolled over, reached inside, and pulled out the axe. Dalip had been right. It was very rusty. She wasn't going to throw it away, though. It was all she had.

She wasn't going to be able to rescue the others, even if she could find them. She didn't owe them anything, really, even though the thought suddenly struck her as, if not wrong, certainly unworthy. She didn't know where such an idea came from.

Perhaps she could find someone to help her rescue them, or better still, who would do all the rescuing for her.

No. There would have to be a rescue at some point – she assumed that was a given – and she had to be involved in some way. She wouldn't be alone, though. The Red Queen needed soldiers.

The problem was, there was no one here. The woods were empty. She'd have to start walking until she found someone. Not upriver though. Away from it. If she'd started the day with the sun on her right and ended with it on her left, she'd have to travel towards where it rose and watch it circle around.

She was also fucking freezing, and if she didn't make a move soon, she'd never go anywhere at all.

She emptied her boots, wrung her socks out, and straight away put them back on, hurriedly brushing off the leaf litter and the tiny bugs that had crawled out of it to investigate her toes. Her fingers were stiff and shivery, and tying wet laces was hard. When she put one foot in front of the other, she was so uncomfortable, it was all she could do not to sit down and weep.

What drove her on was the certainty that the others would swap places with her in an instant. She was free. They were not.

She walked. The forest looked the same in every direction. She couldn't see the distant mountains; she could barely see the sky. The sun was behind her, but she couldn't tell how far it was from setting. She could be walking straight back the way she'd come, just on the other bank of the river.

And when it did set, she would be alone, in the dark.

She kept on going. She started to pick up on subtle changes in the land around her, though it was muted and dormant under the green canopy. The small streams she crossed, where she slaked her thirst with loamy brown water, ran downhill, diagonal to her path. The ground went from flat to gently undulating to a series of ridges and dips. The trees themselves started to be shorter and narrower, and maybe their leaves looked a little different too.

On one ridge, the rock broke through to the surface, black

and weathered. There were no trees there, and she climbed and climbed, hands slipping on the mossy covering, legs aching with effort, until she was finally in the sunlight and above the tops of the trees.

It was evening. The light slanted across the forest, turning it golden, except for a thin broken band where the big river ran. She looked at how far she'd travelled, and it seemed both a long way and not enough at the same time. If she could cover it, so could the wolfman. The notch between the two peaks they'd been heading for was obscured by the angle she was seeing it from, but as she turned, she saw more mountains beyond, blue with distance, rising like a line of filed teeth.

The forest was thinning in the direction she was going. The land rose and fell, and there were large patches where there were no trees at all. Neither was there anything else that she could see. A village might not be visible, but a town might, and a city certainly would. There wasn't a single building in sight, nor a spire of smoke to indicate a fire.

Empty. The world was empty but for her.

She knew that wasn't true. There were other people, and if there were those who would trick her, trap her, and – then what? What would they do to her once they'd caught her? She'd heard things, wild, wicked things, of women and men treated as slaves and subjected not just to endless hours of work, but every other kind of degradation too. If that could happen in London, where help was often no more than a shout away, it could happen here, where a girl could scream her lungs to bloody ruin and no one would either care or hear.

If there were those sorts of people, there had to be some of the other kind, the ones that would take her in, feed her, teach her, help her rescue Dalip, Stanislav, Mama and the others. Why? Because there did. It was a law of the universe, wasn't it? For every gold-plated bastard, there was going to be an angel. She just had to find them in this green wasteland.

Where should she start looking? She shaded her eyes against the brightness of the sky, and studied the view in front of her, carefully this time.

Assuming she didn't want to throw herself at the geomancer, she didn't want to go near the closest mountains. There was nothing at the coast for her. The hill country, then, where houses might hide in the folds of the ground, where they'd only light fires at night and put them out by morning, like those people who kept their curtains closed and their door unanswered against the debt collectors and the police.

Perhaps the hill country was just that: a different country. It didn't look it, but there weren't lines on the ground like there were lines on the map.

She felt hopeful, like she'd discovered something for herself that was useful.

Then the wolf began to call.

Her heart stopped for a second, before beginning to race. She'd stayed still far too long, gazing into the far distance and making plans, when she should have been walking. Now she might have to run. Something she could do, but not for very long. Enough to outrun a store detective or the drugged-up wildlife she grew up around. Not wolves, though. Not them.

Mary stretched her calves, rising up on her toes, like she might have known what she was doing, and started down the ridge to go back among the trees.

She lost sight of all her landmarks, and felt only the pressure on her back, pushing her on. She ran a little, walked a lot, and tried to keep a good pace overall. In keeping with the pattern of when the wolfman put in his first appearance, the gaps between howls were almost unbearably long.

He had wolves, so she guessed he was going to find her. That part was out of her control. What she was determined to do was find someone to protect her from him before then. As she kept on, it grew darker, and the tree trunks began to merge with the gaps between them.

The moon hadn't yet risen, though the threat of it was in the sky ahead, the highest clouds rimed in white. When it did, she'd be able to see again, but for now, her advance slowed to a crawl, banging between trees like the steel ball in that old pinball machine they'd had in the games room of the first home she'd been in.

The wolves called again. They sounded closer. No, they sounded close. She didn't know how that worked. Did they pick up scents like dogs, follow them with their noses to the ground, and drag their handlers behind them, like she'd seen in all those cop films? If so, she'd done the right thing in crossing the river to break her trail. Could she do that again?

But there were no more big rivers, just little ones, so she made as much use of those as she could, jumping in their shallow courses and splashing upstream for what she knew might not be long enough before she leapt out and resumed her course.

The moon finally rose, huge and pale and three-quarters full, turning the black forest into a silver miracle. She could see again, and it was enough. She was more tired than she'd ever been, but she knew there was no time to rest. Keep moving. Don't stop.

The stupid thing was, the old her would have given up by now, sat sullenly against a tree and waited for capture. It was inevitable, wasn't it? The wolfman had her number, and he was going to track her down with a tenacity beyond that of the most vindictive Met officer.

The new her, the Mary that was slowly emerging under the bright sun and pale moon of here, was made of different stuff. Maybe the old Mary was right, but there'd be no long-suffering social worker to dig her out this time. What she did now actually mattered. It was for keeps.

Up and down another ridge, the sparse woodland clinging to

its flanks providing little cover for either of them. She looked behind her, saw nothing, and pressed on.

Almost immediately, there was a howl that sounded like it was right behind her. It wasn't ridiculous. They'd come out of the woods at her and Dalip like they were ghosts before. So what should she do if they were just over the last rise? How was she going to slip to the side, so they'd miss her completely?

By doubling back on herself.

It felt so wrong, running towards the threat, not away. Any moment, the wolfman and his two pets would be standing in her path, blocking her way, forcing her to the ground with fists and feet and claws and teeth. She ran parallel to the ridge line, where the exposed rock rose from the thin soil like broken bones, and at a place where two huge boulders almost met, she climbed back up and squeezed herself through the gap to the other side.

'Do not move,' said the voice in her ear, close enough that she could feel his breath against her hair. 'Do not speak. They might not be able to see you, but they will be able to hear you.'

Mary froze. The shadow unwound around her, covering her, as if a black veil had dropped over her face. She could still make out the landscape bathed in bright moonlight, but she was one step removed, as if she was watching it rather than living it.

Stone scraped on stone, close by. A clatter of pebbles, a heavy footfall as they steadied themselves. Hard breathing, a soft groan. The patter and pad of an animal and the cackle of a chain looping and straightening.

The wolfman walked right by her, looking into the slit of space afforded by the boulders. The moon shone silver off his wolfskin hood, and his breath condensed in the air in a glowing, transitory cloud. The nearest wolf stretched towards her hiding place, nose in the air, drinking deeply of the night's scents.

She was in plain sight, and yet it was still searching for her. Nostrils twitching, teeth partly bared, muzzle turning in tiny angles; it knew, it knew she was there, precisely within a single leap of her, and it could do nothing. Confused, it let out a whimpering growl and put its head down in an acknowledgement of failure and submission.

The wolfman, oblivious to the subtle clues, was searching ahead with his own dark-adapted eyes, and pulled on the chain to hurry his pets along. He stepped out of view, but Mary knew well enough not to break cover. She stayed wedged, back and knees pressed against cold stone.

Eventually, a wolf howled, further away, mournful, unfulfilled by the hunt, and the veil about her lifted.

When she tried to move, she was so stiff she fell over, landing hard on her side and stinging her hands. One of the rocks above her moved, unwrapping itself to become the figure of a man.

'I heard the wolves hunting. I wondered who their prey was.'

'That trick you did; it looked straight at me, and it couldn't see me.' She turned herself over on to her back and bent first one leg in the air, then the other. 'How did you do that?'

'Study, hard and long. Practice, painful and repetitive. Will, strong enough to make your nose bleed.'

'Really?'

'No. If you have the knack, I could teach you in an hour. It is nothing more than a bit of simple hedge-magic.'

'Could you?' she blurted. Magic: actual magic. 'Will you? Teach me, I mean.'

'Teach you?' he said, unfolding himself further, and spidering down the rock towards her. 'I do not even know your name, girl.'

He wore darkness like a cloak, but it really was a cloak, black and ragged, voluminous and flowing. When he stood over her, he seemed impossibly tall and thin, like a lamppost draped with wind-blown plastic.

He held out his hand for her, and it was like the rest of him: hard, bony, spare. He had no problem hauling her to her feet, though. The top of her head came somewhere below his jutting chin.

'It is usual, when you save someone from their enemies, to be thanked,' he said.

'Are they? My enemies, I mean.' Mary didn't know. She'd run anyway. 'Yeah, okay: thanks,' she added.

'My pleasure,' said the man. 'And yes. At least, they are my enemies, and we still need to have our wits about us. Stay close.'

It was difficult, as he moved like a stain, visible when slipping from cover to cover, vanishing when stationary. And he moved so quickly, climbing and jumping and crouching, that she, already exhausted, could barely keep up.

When he finally stopped, she slumped to the ground and lay there. The burning in her legs was exquisite, the taste of blood in her throat less so.

'You have determination,' he said. She weakly acknowledged the compliment with a raised middle finger.

She became dimly aware of a floor that wasn't leaves, and walls that weren't wood. She coughed and choked on what came up, and coughed again, hollow and barking. The sound echoed away.

There was stone under her face, flat, worn and dirty, like a pavement. She got her hands down and raised her head. They were in some sort of building: behind her was a wide arched doorway that led directly into the forest, and the forest seemed to be creeping in through it, along with the moonglow that gave the only illumination. She could hear her own panting, the man's footsteps in the dark corners of the room, padding about, and above her, the soft mutterings of roosting birds.

He set a bowl in front of her that reflected moonlight off its trembling surface. She unceremoniously plunged her face into the bowl and started sucking. It wasn't water, but some sort of beer, and she didn't care. It was as far removed as possible from the cans of cheap lager she'd beg, buy or steal, but she picked up the bowl when she couldn't empty it any other way. Yeasty froth stuck to her upper lip.

'Finished dying?'

She coughed one last time. 'Where am I?'

'My castle,' he said.

'Does that make you a king?'

He laughed. 'The King of Crows, if anything.'

'You could do with a new front door.'

'I will tell my craftsmen to saw the timber first thing in the morning.'

Mary drew herself shakily to her feet, peering around her in the gloom. It was a ruin. If she looked up, she could see the sky through the ragged rafters and birds' wings. Dark doorways led further in. The man took the bowl from her, and disappeared into one of the rooms beyond.

'What do I call you?' she asked. He might have rescued her from one set of dangers, but that didn't mean he was safe.

'Your Majesty?' came his disembodied voice.

'Fuck off.'

'Crows, then. Call me Crows. You know about names, do you? What they mean?'

'I know that the wolfman wouldn't tell us his. He said others should give us our names.'

Crows returned holding the bowl. He'd pulled his hood back to reveal his face, a fine black face with a long oval head shaved close. 'So what should your name be? What are you famous for?'

'I'm ...' and she trailed off. She ended up shrugging. 'Nothing really.'

'That is a poor title,' said Crows. He handed her the bowl, and she drank deeply, almost greedily. 'What do you call yourself, when the lights go out and all is dark and quiet, in those moments between waking and sleeping when you dream and can still remember?'

'I can't tell you.' She stopped drinking, and looked at him over the rim of the bowl.

'Cannot or will not?'

'It sounds stupid.'

'Others should be the judge of that.'

She muttered it into the bowl, and he cupped his long fingers around his ear.

'Too soft. Louder, so all the crows can hear.'

'The Red Queen.' Her face burned.

'Oh, oh oh.' He laughed, and all she could see of him were his fine white teeth. 'The King of Crows and his Red Queen it shall be. But you're not a queen yet, are you? What shall we call you in the time before you claim your throne?'

'Mary,' said Mary. 'When do we start?'

12

When they dragged Dalip's hood off, he was sitting in a chair, wrists tied awkwardly behind his back by someone who enjoyed their work just a little too much. There was also a rope around his neck, a noose that would tighten when jerked.

That was all there was. Him, in his chair, and on the stone floor in front of him, a single candle. The light barely reached him, let alone the walls. He was inside, he could tell that much, and he'd passed through a corridor and another room to get where he was. Beyond that? He'd been force-marched, blind and bound, for a night and a day, along with the others.

Everything hurt. He was bruised and battered. They'd taken his kirpan, his kara and his kangha. They'd taken his turban and his patka, leaving his hair to tumble, sweaty and knotted, over his shoulders.

They'd all but stripped him of everything that made him who he was and set him apart, and the only thing that stopped him from slumping to the flags were the last vestiges of his pride. Whoever had hold of his hood now was walking away into the darkness, leaving him alone.

He tried to pull his hands apart. The cord used to tie them was stiff and strong, and all his struggling seemed to do was make the bindings dig deeper into his skin and threaten to cut off his circulation.

That he couldn't see the knots made it impossible to even try and undo them. If he could bring his arms down under his body, and slip his legs through – he'd seen it done once, but the escape artist had limbs seemingly made of rubber.

He forced his shoulders down and tried to straighten his arms, but his wrists had been held parallel and in opposition to each other before they were bound. There was no slack to take up, and he didn't think he could physically do it, even if he could stand the pain. He stopped and waited for his muscles to uncramp.

He had, as far as he knew, done nothing to deserve this. He had been the one to offer the wolfman hospitality, and he'd been repaid with violence and betrayal. The ember of anger burning inside ignited into righteous fury.

Dalip stood up, deliberately knocking the chair over on to its back.

'How dare you treat us like this! How dare you! Untie us at once and let us all go.'

His voice rang out, and came back to him distorted and hollow. A big room, then. If he had the patience, he could work out just how big merely by listening to his words return to him.

'Show yourselves. I know you're watching. Come out where I can see you, or do you just hide in the shadows? You can't be scared of me, not like this. Come on!'

He was panting with effort. He knew it was dangerous, trying to goad whoever had taken him into action, but he'd had enough. Dangerous and stupid: there were far worse indignities they could heap on him – rape, torture, slavery, execution – but he wanted to see his captors, look them in the eye and spit in their faces before they did any of that to him.

He circumnavigated the circle of light provided by the candle, stepping around the fallen chair, searching the darkness for a sign that he'd been heard.

The flame flickered with a sudden draught. A distant boom signalled a closing door. Slow, deliberate footsteps, accompanied by a metallic tapping, grew louder. Dalip stopped his pacing and straightened his spine.

The steps sounded outside of his vision. They circled him just as he'd circled the candle.

'Pick up the chair.'

'I'd rather stand, thank you.'

'It's not a request. It's an order.'

He considered it. 'Make me.'

'How tiresome.' The voice was male, cultured, urbane, and bored. So very bored.

'Pick it up yourself. You can untie me at the same time.' Dalip turned to face the shadow of the man. 'What did we ever do to you?'

'I don't think you appreciate the gravity of your situation, young man.'

'So why don't you tell me? Why don't you come where I can see you?'

'Knowledge is power, and I'd be a fool to give you anything. Since I'm not a fool, let me tell you the way this works: I ask you questions, and you answer them.'

This wasn't the geomancer. But the geomancer would be listening.

'What,' said Dalip, 'what if I refuse?'

'Then you will be beaten, starved, chained, and eventually – after a very long time – you will die. It doesn't have to be that way. All that is required is your cooperation, and we can avoid that. You do want to avoid that, don't you?'

'I'm not keen on pain.'

'There, that didn't take long, did it? Sit down, and we can begin.'

He almost did. His foot reached out for the seat, to pivot it upright.

He pulled his leg back. 'No. Do your worst.'

'How ... disappointing.'

'You've not given me a reason to want to please you.'

'Things will go badly for you. You should reconsider.'

'Badly? They're not exactly terrific at the moment.' Dalip watched the candle flicker again. Someone else had entered the room. So let them work for it, since they were going to thrash him and he was completely defenceless.

He spun around and kicked the candle away, out of its molten wax socket and into the dark. The flame stretched, tore, and was extinguished. He could just about remember where the chair was. He took a shuffling step towards it, and another. Something hard tapped his shin, and he crouched down, turning the chair legs so he could pick it up one-handed by its back.

He listened very carefully. Now he'd stopped moving, there was no sound. The darkness was total. Or was it? Every time he'd looked at the candle, he'd ruined his night sight. With that distraction gone, he could make out – dimly, but there all the same – an inconstant rectangle of light. The door.

The light occulted, right to left. Someone had walked in front of him.

He hefted the chair as he stood, and it scraped on the floor. He stepped right, and the air rushed past him. Now he could hear and smell his attacker. He swung around, let go of the chair, and as it connected with the hidden figure, there was an audible grunt of pain.

The chair clattered away, and he made for the door, not directly, but off to one side. His broken, melted boots crunched on the gritty floor, and running with both hands tied behind him made him step more heavily.

He felt, rather than saw, the wall ahead, the deadness of sound and the absence of space. He slowed, turned, bounced off it with his shoulder, and squatted down again.

'Enough,' said a woman's voice, high and imperious.

But it wasn't enough. The door was at the end of a short tunnel, and he rolled around the corner and headed, crab-like, for it.

Something heavy and fast-moving tapped his skull and he went down. His ankles were lifted and pulled, and he was dragged back into the centre of the room. A light came on, high above him, up on the wall. Then another. And another. All around him, the flames seem to leap from candle to candle until he was surrounded by a soft orange glow.

Someone took Dalip's shoulder and turned him on his back, none too gently, either. A man, heavy-set and smelling of piss, stood close by his feet, while another, a thin man with a thin, silver-topped cane was by his head.

The room was shaped like a drum, a perfect cylinder, except that high up were rings of open balconies, each ring illuminated by the candles. A gloved hand draped over the lowest balcony's rail.

'Enough,' she repeated.

Dalip was hauled to his feet and dropped on the chair. He squinted, one-eyed, up at the balcony, at the woman in the white and gold dress. She inspected him down the length of her nose.

'You're quite brave,' she said.

'And you're not,' he managed before the silver-tipped cane swung at his head again, a sharp tap to the back of his skull that left him with a bitten tongue and blood in his mouth. He spat on the floor and glared at the wielder. 'Why are you doing this to us?'

'You're going to be useful to me.'

'You could have asked us first. We could have, I don't know, come to some sort of deal that didn't involve having the crap kicked out of me.'

The man with the cane drew his arm back again, but the woman raised her hand. 'I said, enough.' She rested an elbow on the parapet and leaned forward. Her blonde hair was caught in a net that twinkled with jewels. 'You don't know what it is that I want yet.'

'Information. Knowledge, your man said. We want that too. For God's sake, we don't even know where we are, or why.'

'Is that so?' She cocked her head. 'Are you sure you don't have anything to tell me?'

'What do you mean? None of us have any idea of what this place is or how we got here.' He tried to get up, and was forced back down by the hand on his shoulder.

'Two of you have disappeared since you came through the portal.' She sat back. 'And no one escapes my very talented wolves. I'll have the truth from you, one way or another.'

Dalip tried to stand again, was forced down again. 'You've already got the truth. Torturing me won't change that.'

'Experience tells me otherwise. Take him away and make him uncomfortable, then bring in the next one. Perhaps they'll see more sense.'

The guard took a handful of Dalip's hair and pulled him up and swung around, launching him in the direction of the door. Without being able to use his hands, he landed heavily on his side, and once again, his head hit something hard.

He was reeling and half-blind, and that was before they put his hood back on. The world went dark and stuffy again. He was pulled and pushed, dragged and thrown. He tripped and fell, was kicked into walls and doors, and finally pitched head-first again to the ground.

He lay there, waiting to be coerced into moving again, but there was nothing. A door banged shut behind him. A bolt worked into place. Footsteps faded.

The only way to get the hood off was to drag his face along the floor, twisting his head left and right to work it free. Eventually he reached a point where he could shake it loose and cast it aside.

He was in a tiny room, barely longer than he was tall. A slit of a window – more like a crack in the stonework – let in light and air, but not much of either. The floor was bare, and his hands were still tied.

And he had no idea how he'd ended up there. What had the woman – the geomancer? – meant when she'd intimated that he might be lying? That he knew where he was? That was preposterous. The geomancer must be wrong, or mad, or both.

He'd done nothing wrong. He'd never done anything wrong. From earliest memory to the moment the supervisor had called Stanislav's name, and the two of them had appraised each other on the station platform: he'd always behaved, always acted honourably, always told the truth, always been kind. He'd been told that if he did those things, then he'd never know shame, that he'd never be the one in his father's study or the headmaster's office or the police interview room, staring at the door and thinking of what best to say to get out of trouble.

And now, he was a prisoner, in a prison cell, held captive by someone who wanted him to confess to who knew what? And there could be no appeal to a higher authority, because there was none. No black-suited solicitor would sweep in, demand his release with threats and promises, and drive him back to his parents.

It was up to him.

And he had nothing to bring to a situation like this. Nothing he'd ever done had prepared him remotely for action. All his learning, all his good manners, all his religious devotion: could it really have left him so grossly unprepared?

Yes. No. Perhaps.

He could shout and scream and kick at the door until his toes broke. Or he could work out why he was there, what the geomancer thought he knew, and how to escape. No doubt that kicking the door and making himself hoarse would feel better, but enough bits of him were broken already.

There was the door, there was his foot. He took a deep breath.

What he really wanted was his hands free. The walls were old and the stone coated with powdery grit. There were no protrusions or sharp edges to grind the bindings against, but there was the recess made by the door frame. In lieu of anything better to do, he pressed his back against the angle and started rubbing his wrists against the stone work.

It was long, boring, and repetitive. Like simultaneous equations, but with added muscle ache. He had to stop every once in a while, just to rest and let his arms hang in a more natural position. But when he'd rested, he went right back to it.

There were noises from outside, so far, twice. He heard Stanislav's resonant voice echo down the walls, then fade away into the distance. He was questioning the guard, but getting no answers. Sometime later, a woman's sobbing came and went. He couldn't tell who it was from the sound, and the door had no grating. The shadows under the door flickered as they passed, then it was quiet again.

He kept on rubbing. He couldn't see if it was doing any good, neither could he feel any extra give. Eventually, if he kept it up long enough, one of the cords around his wrists would wear thin, and then he could break it. Once broken, he should be able to work out the loose end and the whole knot should unravel.

This, he knew. He'd learnt this: a little bit of his schooling was useful after all. This was how materials behaved.

His legs started to cramp with the tiny up-down movements he was making. As he stretched his calves, his shoulders flexed, and something snapped.

A third person was led past. Voluble, outraged Romanian infiltrated his cell, and like before, faded away. It ended with a sharp bang – a door being closed, but nearby. If he pressed his ear against the wood, he could still hear the complaints.

He wriggled his wrists, easing them apart, slowly unravelling the cords, pulling and relaxing, twisting and turning. Then his hands were free.

They hurt, not just from their prolonged captivity, but from shielding himself from the kicking he'd received. He had a lump on the back of one hand that hurt exquisitely when he pressed it with his thumb, and now that normal circulation had been restored, it started to throb with every beat of his heart.

All his fingers seemed to work, however. That was something. He squeezed his wrists and felt the deeply indented grooves in his skin made by his bindings.

He looked around his cell again. He had a bag, and a long twisted leather thong, still tied at the loose ends but broken in the middle. He gathered up the thong and put it in the bag, which was rough hessian, like a potato sack.

Without his turban, his comb, his sword, his bracelet, he felt naked. Four of the five symbols of his faith had been stripped from him. Part of him, the zealous part that felt the affront most, wanted to get them back, as soon as possible and at whatever cost. Only then would he be ready and fit to deal with whatever came next.

But the other, more wary part, the whisper from a deeper teaching, was telling him that he should be patient, that he wasn't going to offend the gurus or go against their teachings if he waited and watched and yes, learned from his captors.

Another prisoner passed in front of his cell door. He listened carefully to see if he could tell who it was, but she was silent. She and her guard scuffed down the corridor outside. As they moved further away, there was banging and shouting – Romanian and English – but it was all in vain. A distant door opened, closed, and something heavy banged into place.

That made five. Because Mary had escaped – or at least, because Mary was still on the run, and there was a huge difference between the two – that was it. They'd be left to stew.

There was no bucket in with him, not even a hole in the floor that he could find. Given that he'd been casually beaten up, arbitrarily bound and blindfolded, force marched and imprisoned, he supposed that this was just the start. There was no reason why, above the simple expediency of keeping him alive long enough to answer questions, he wasn't going to end up living night and day with his own excrement, slowly starving to death and driven mad by his incarceration.

He wondered what would have happened, what would be happening now, if he'd literally and metaphorically thrown Mary to the wolves, and swum the river himself. He decided that he'd have found that choice impossible to live with, and that he was, if not exactly glad, content with the way things had gone. He was supposed to protect others, even at a cost to himself. That he'd never had to do it before might have made it easier: he had none of the messy practical experience to dilute his pure motive.

But being locked up to rot wasn't what he wanted, either. As the guard's footsteps tracked back down the corridor, he knocked crisply on the door and said: 'I want to see the geomancer.'

It wasn't quite a demand, and was far from grovelling for mercy. That might come later, of course, but he didn't know what that might look like and he really didn't want to.

The footsteps had stopped. Under the door, he could see the slowly shifting shadows cast by a lit candle.

'You saw her already.'

'I want to see her again.'

'Why's that?'

Dalip judged his words carefully. 'Because she wants to ask me some questions.'

Nothing about giving her the answers she might want, but yes, she did want to ask him questions. He'd misplayed the situation before. Perhaps he was doing so again, but it was perfectly clear that regular beatings eventually followed by death would be the result of his opening gambit.

'Wait there,' said the guard, then laughed at his own joke. He went away, his hiccoughing chuckles receding with the light he carried.

Dalip invested the time in trying to climb up to the window-slit. The wall wasn't smooth, and the rough stonework was pocked with gritty holes. That made it easy to get a little way up, and just as easy to slip down again. Because the wall was deep in shadow, he used his hands more than his eyes, reaching and feeling over his head. He was young and fit, and reasonably supple. Climbing the corner of the cell made it possible to brace himself, rather than rely on the strength in his fingers. His melted boots weren't helping, so he took them off. He had his thick socks on underneath, and they were growing increasingly crisp with wear.

The outer wall was broad, as deep as his arm was long. The gap was far too narrow for him to pass through, even his head, let alone his shoulders, but if he could see outside and look down at the ground, he might have some idea of what lay beyond.

He was almost there, raised up off the floor, feet stuck in adjacent walls, and about to traverse towards the window, when there were three bangs at his cell door.

He scrambled down and dusted himself off, quickly kicking the sack into a dark corner. He stood away from the door: he genuinely wanted to do the question and answer thing, not fight. Not this time, at least.

Something slid aside, and the door opened outwards into the corridor. The guard was holding a lantern, a crude black iron cage, pierced with holes to let the light out. There was no point in trying to trick him by pretending he was still tied up; Dalip showed him his hands, and the guard reached for his knife.

'I'll come quietly,' he said. That was what all the criminals in the TV shows said, and they were treated reasonably. He didn't know if it would work here, but it was worth a shot. 'You have my word.'

And that, strangely, seemed to have the desired effect.

'A knife in the back if you break that. Out, then.'

It was the first time he'd seen the corridor. It was mean and narrow, just wide enough for one. There were doors all the way down, both left and right, but there was no way of being able to tell what was behind any of them.

At the far end was a T-junction. The finger in his back told him he was going left, though he was able to steal a glance the other way. A bigger door, better made. That way, then, was out.

The way he was facing was a short blank-walled corridor, with just one small door at the end to go through. There were bolts, and a bar, but they were pulled back.

'Through here?'

'Through there. Whatever you're asked, you answer, right? Whatever you're asked to do, you do it.'

'I've got the idea. Now I have, anyway.'

'Don't you forget it. In.'

Dalip lifted the latch, pushed, and the door swung open. It was as light inside as when he'd left it, with all the candles ringing the various balconies in the drum-shaped room.

No chair, though. Not this time.

The door closed behind him, and he looked up to see the woman in white and gold, seated behind the balustrade, and standing next to her, the man with the silver-tipped cane.

'I never give second chances,' she said. 'Tell me why I should make an exception for you.'

'I'm more likely to tell you the truth now, than later, when I'll tell you whatever I think you want to hear, just so you might stop hurting me.'

She frowned, a shadow on her pale forehead. 'A good answer. But I have all the answers I need for now, and I'm disappointed that it was you who prevented me from taking the coloured girl. So now you have to make amends.'

She nodded, and the man with the cane threw something at his feet. It bounced and clattered, making Dalip jump back. When it had stopped moving, he could see it was a knife, with a long blade and a short crossguard. Not a kitchen knife, but a combat knife.

He looked down at it, but didn't pick it up.

'What am I supposed to do with that?'

'You're not a child, are you?' said the man. 'Do we need a wet-nurse to flop her teat out and suckle you?'

Dalip had done Shakespeare. He knew what those terms meant, but he wondered why the man would use them as insults.

'I'm not here to fight.'

'Then why are you here?'

Dalip thought that a very good question.

The door opened again. No one stepped through, but Dalip turned and saw something crouching there, two eyes reflecting the golden light back at him. A dog. Not a good dog for certain, he could tell by the way its hackles were up and its teeth were slowly becoming bared.

The geomancer gave an open-handed gesture towards the knife. 'Take the knife. Show me how brave you really are. Or,' she seemed amused by the idea, 'fail and have your throat ripped out.'

Dalip slowly bent down and his hand felt for the knife's handle. The dog started growling, deep in the back of its throat. He pulled his hand back, and it stopped. He reached forward again; it began snarling again, and took one step forward. This time, when he eased his hand away, the animal took another step. Closer, always closer.

Dalip curled his fingers into a fist, feeling the weight of the blade for the first time. This was his new reality and he needed to embrace it fully.

13

If Crows had slept at all, she didn't know where or when. The tumbledown ruin – perhaps a victim of the same wars that had claimed the riverside village – still had a couple of rooms that were mostly weatherproof. The blankets she'd found smelled of cold air and flowers, and despite the terrors of the night and the uncertain quality of her saviour, she'd not woken once.

She found him on his doorstep-without-a-door, hunched over, staring over the woodland beyond. The castle had been set on a rock outcrop, on the highest point of a ridge, and the trees swept away like a carpet before them.

'Does the wolfman know we're here?' she asked. She leaned against the stonework, watching the sun cut away the early-morning mist.

'He knows nothing of this place, so both you and I are safe here. He knows I come and go into his mistress' domain, but he cannot catch me.' His words were accented but precise, his voice pitched higher than hers. 'I have places to hide, and ways to hide those places. Sit, Mary. Drink in the view, for there are few sights finer.'

She sat beside him. 'So what am I looking at?'

'Down,' he said. 'Whoever first named it, named it right.

Down is where we are: it is both a destination and a direction, it is how we fall and where we land.'

'And how did I get here?'

'Like everyone else. You needed it to be there. I take it you had reason enough?'

She remembered the heat and the noise. 'I thought I was going to die.'

'Down is a gift of grace, a last-minute mercy, unlooked for and unheralded. You do not find it: it finds you, when you least expect it but want it the most.'

'I don't get it, though. Why us? Why me? Almost everyone else I was with that night died.' She remembered, and shuddered.

'You are asking if you have been especially chosen. Hmm.' Crows steepled his long fingers in front of his face. 'I have thought long and hard over this. Is there a thread of meaning, linking all those who have come to Down, marking us out like gold amongst the dross?'

She huffed. 'Is there a reason why, then? Why us and not others? Why it didn't appear sooner and save more of us?'

'If there is an answer to those questions,' he shrugged, 'I cannot find them. Why you, why me? You may as well ask the moon, Mary. What makes us special is that we are here, Mary, not the why or the where or the when of it. We were granted an unexpected second chance, but it is a blank sheet, a tabula rasa as the Romans say.'

Crows paused, as if to contemplate his own words, and Mary grew restless again.

'Crows …'

'Can you write, Mary?' he asked, pre-empting any more questions.

Not often, not well. 'Sure.'

'Have you ever written your own destiny?'

'I don't even know what that means.'

'What were you, on the other side of the door? Did you give

orders, or take them?' Crows turned his head resting his cheek on his hands, staring at her intently with his wide eyes.

She had to look away. 'You can probably guess.'

'I was a sailor,' he said. 'Far away from home. London was the centre of the world, but that did not mean its streets were paved with gold. I took some dark turns, for certain, and I was not much older than you then. And here I am, now, the King of Crows in his own castle. What about you?'

'I ...' She may as well say it. It wasn't like Crows could do anything with the information. 'I was in care.'

'Care?'

'You know. In a home.' She watched his eyebrows knit together. 'For kids. A kids' home.'

'Ah. An orphanage.'

'No one calls them that any more. How old are you?' To her eyes, he couldn't be more than thirty.

Crows smiled and looked out over his kingdom of trees. 'Who knows? If you do not count the days, keeping count of the years is impossible. The answer to a different question is nineteen thirty-eight.'

She looked him up and down. Eventually she said, 'Fuck off.'

'It is true,' said Crows. 'I take it you are from later.'

'Fuck off! There's no way you can be from the nineteen thirties. You should be an old man. And there weren't any black people in London in the thirties; that was, I don't know, after the war.'

'War?'

'Fuck off! World War Two, Crows. Bloody Battle of Britain and stuff. Churchill and Hitler. It's history.'

He blinked at her. 'Your history. Not mine.' He waved his hand. 'Actually, I've heard of the Second World War. I think a lot of people come from then. London was bad, yes?'

'The Blitz. I can't believe you don't know about that. Bad? Bombs and everything. Fires and buildings falling down.' Just like her London. She took several deep breaths. 'You're a fucking time traveller.'

'No more than you. Down is joined to London, at different places and at different times. There are people here who are from different whens to both you and me. I think,' he said, tapping his lips, 'there will be a great deal of interest in you.'

'Fuck.' She sat back, bracing herself on her arms. 'The geomancer.'

'The one you call the wolfman works for her. He makes sure that those who pass through the portal get to her. One way or another. Were there others with you?'

She shook her head. 'Seven of us.'

'That many? I've never heard of such a thing happening before. Tell me, Mary. What do you do? What special knowledge do you have?'

Mary snorted. 'I know nothing, Crows. School was a bit, you know, difficult. When you say "special knowledge", what you mean?'

'Scientists. Engineers. People who can recreate the machines of their world in this one.'

'Is that sort of thing important?' she asked. Dalip was just a kid like her; how much did he actually know?

'It is one reason why you were being hunted by the wolfman.'

'I ... not me. There's this one boy, he's a university student. Something sciencey, I think.'

'Did the wolfman take him?'

'Dalip stopped them from getting me. So yes. Not before they beat the crap out of him though.' She chewed at a fingernail. 'What are they going to do with him?'

'It is difficult to tell,' said Crows. 'This ... boy. He must be very intelligent, yes?'

'I guess so. A lot more kids go to university now than, than in your day. But, he'll be one of the smart ones.'

'This portal you came through, what year was it?'

'Twenty twelve.' She tutted. 'I'll miss the fucking Olympics. I love all that running and shit. Watching it, at least.'

Crows sucked air through the gap in his front teeth. 'That is late. Very late.'

'Does that make it worse?'

'It might do. Who else?'

'We were cleaners on the Underground. You know what the Underground is, right?'

'Yes, we had that,' said Crows.

'So I don't know. I guess if you're a cleaner, it's because you can't get a better job elsewhere. There's Stan – Stanislav – he was with Dalip, but he's just a workman, I think, laying train track.'

'Navvy, they used to be called.' Crows unfolded himself and stepped out into the sunshine, shrugging off his cloak and standing there, warming his spare frame. 'The question is, will she know what she has in your boy?'

Mary stretched her legs out in front of her, and compared his clothes to hers. Obviously, he hadn't come through from the nineteen thirties, wearing trousers that ended mid-calf and a plain linen smock.

'So what happens to people who come here? Where do they live? Where is everyone?'

Crows turned slowly, baking first his front, then his back. 'Down is big. Very big. The portals are spread wide across the land. And the people are few. You can, if you want, find places where no one else has ever been, and just live there, perfectly alone, and not see another soul until one morning, you are too old to get up. For most people, well … there are the castles. There is one place, far away, which you would call a town. I saw it once, many years ago.' He held his arms out, let them drop back down. 'Do you see? You are used to London, yes? Millions of people. Here in Down, people are rare. Few come through the portals, and of those some die of injuries they gained while on the other side.

Once here, they are vulnerable. Many become victims. Some get new injuries, and they die, or they get sick because they are unused to finding their own food. Some get into fights.'

'You mean like the others who came through with me?'

'They have been taken, but she is unlikely to kill them. They will have to answer her questions, and they'll work for her in whatever role she sees fit.'

'What? As slaves?'

'Yes. They may become accustomed to their slavery, and become trusted. But they are still slaves, even though they wear no chains.'

'Can we do anything about that?' asked Mary.

'She is a geomancer. Her power increases, while mine?' Crows snorted. He lifted his hands to embrace his tumbledown battlements and open-air halls. 'I have an army of birds and nothing more.'

'There must be something we can do.'

'Why must there be anything? Why can it not be hopeless and useless and all the other lesses? There is no law, that those that think of themselves as good must triumph over those they believe are evil: sometimes the best we can hope for is to get out of the way. We have the whole of Down to explore, so why fight over this little piece?'

She didn't know why, but then a thought entered her head and lodged there.

'You fought, didn't you?'

'Ah. And I barely escaped with my life.'

'So why are you still here, Crows?' She stared into the far distance, beyond the broad, dark lake that started where the lines of hills stopped, to where she thought she could make out the coast. 'Why not take your own advice and find somewhere else?'

Crows looked sour for a moment, his lips pursed as if he was sucking on a vinegary chip. 'Something keeps me here. I do not know what.'

She did. 'You don't like losing, Crows. No one likes losing. What happened?'

He flopped back down next to her. 'Before she came, there was peace here. People mostly got on, grew food, kept animals, cut wood, drew water, brewed beer, baked bread, hunted and fished, and there were enough of us to scare away the beasts.'

'Beasts?'

'Perhaps there is something in the way that this world is made, that if there is magic, there have to be beasts, too. Beasts are mostly just animals, but they don't come from where we live. They come from our imaginations.'

'Like the sea monster, you mean? It nearly ate Dalip.'

Crows nodded. 'Yes, like that. So then she came, she and her men. She had discovered a new portal, and her devices told her that people would pass through it soon. She wanted the farmers and the trappers and the woodcutters out of the way, so that those who came through came to her, not them.'

'But why didn't she just camp out on the beach, rather than setting up shop miles away?'

'When I say she had discovered a new portal, no one had yet come through it. She knew it was between her and the sea, but no idea where. The land was almost empty; it became so when she took the people and made them work for her. They cannot leave, because they believe there is nowhere to leave for.' He smiled sadly, and hugged his knees. 'They try. Even if they manage to get out of the castle, they are hunted down and brought back by the wolfman.'

'That's why you stick around. And you thought I was one of them. That's why you helped me.'

'I would have helped you anyway, Mary. Slavery is not our natural state. We were born free, and we are no one's when we die. Why should we live in bondage between times?' He shrugged shoulders that were like bony wings. 'This is not your fight. You should go – no, I should take you to the edge of this land and see you safely away – and look for somewhere where you can settle, and prosper.'

He was right, she should. She didn't owe Mama, or any of the others, anything at all. They were accidental acquaintances, people who'd washed up on the same beach as her. She had no ties of family or friendship to them.

So why did she feel the need to rush in and save them from the geomancer and her wolfman? It wasn't like she'd ever felt that way about anyone at all ever. Where she lived, it was every man, woman and child for themselves. Everyone knew that.

'You said you'd show me how to do that magic trick,' she said. She saw that he was watching her, and she didn't look away.

'If you have the knack. Only some do.' He flexed his fingers and dragged them through the air in front of her face. They trailed darkness, which he wiped away as he moved his hand back. 'And I never said I would show you: I said I could teach you.'

'Crows,' she said. 'Will you teach me?'

She was never very good at lessons, but this: this was different.

'Let us say I teach you everything I know: what then? What will you use it for? Will you go out and conquer yourself a kingdom, and rule it as the Red Queen? Or will you be Mary and help protect the weak from the strong?'

'Can't I be both?'

'I don't know,' said Crows. 'Can you?'

He jumped up and walked into the ruined hall behind them.

'But an empty belly has no ears. You cannot learn if you are hungry.'

She followed him in, avoiding the bird droppings by skirting around the edges of the room. She looked up: the crows had gone, and presumably they'd be back at nightfall. Sky showed through the broken beams above her head, and it didn't seem safe.

Crows lit a candle – no matches, he just clicked his fingers at the wick until it caught – and rummaged through the meagre stores he had. His back was to her, curved in the act of searching, and she bent down to look at the candle flame.

It was warm against her face, and when she held her hand over it, she could feel the heat build until it was almost, but not quite, burning. It began to hurt, but she didn't snatch her hand away. There was another way to stop the pain.

The candle flickered. She didn't know if that was her breath or not. It flickered again, blown ragged, and she knew for certain it wasn't.

Then the flame went out, the last gasp of the wick a tiny red coal in the darkness before it too winked out.

'I ...' She sat back and fell over something. 'Fuck. I did it.'

Crows snapped his fingers again and his serious face loomed. 'Eat first.'

'But magic,' she said, scrambling to her feet. 'I can do fucking magic.'

'A child can blow out a candle, Mary.'

'But you don't understand. I've never been able to do anything. No one ever wanted me. Everything I touched turned to shit. My life was one big fuck-up, and whatever I did, I was always going to fuck it up further. I was trying, all right? I was trying to be better. I was trying so fucking hard, and there were always people like Nicholls with his fucking clipboard, ready to knock me back.'

She was crying. She didn't know why. Just that everything she had inside was emptying out, spilling on to the floor, draining away. Bile, bitterness, guilt, shame, rage, fear, hate. She was sobbing and shaking, and Crows was content to let her. He placed one of his hands on her shoulder, just to let her know he was still there, and he was waiting.

'Sorry,' she said eventually. 'I must sound fucking nuts.'

'When I came here, I was a sailor, a stoker, working below decks, a man who fed the boilers and oiled the machines.

I sweated while the Chief got drunk and got paid a hundred times what I did. I was chased here, to Down, by a gang of knife-wielding men who wanted to carve their names on my belly, to see if I bled black.'

He reached down and lifted her up. Easily. She would remember that moment, of being picked up and set on her feet.

'I have scars, like you,' said Crows. 'But that was from then. You are here now, and Down welcomes everyone equally. The magic is not in what you do, it is in what you become. Down changes everyone according to their nature: the good become saints. The wise become sages. The compassionate become healers. The strong become heroes. But it also turns the greedy rapacious, the liars into traitors and the genuinely wicked, oh, you must watch out for them ...'

14

Down. She'd called it Down. That was all she gave away. Dalip had given more in exchange, much more.

The guard who'd shown him in had dragged the dog out by its hind legs, leaving a trail of shining blood from the wounds that Dalip had made. The biggest thing he'd killed up to that point had been a fish, and that had been the day before yesterday. And fish were different: cold blooded, scaly, slippery and a source of food. He was used to seeing it on his plate in a variety of guises. Dogs were different. His next-door neighbours in Southall had two pugs, ugly but endearing little things. While people had fish as pets, the quality of the relationship they had with dogs made knife-fighting with one, even one as dementedly angry as his opponent, a different prospect entirely.

He'd first kept it at bay, turning and keeping the blade-point at its muzzle as it circled him, looking for an opening. Then as it lunged at him one more time, he caught it on the nose. What had happened after that hadn't been pretty, but at least it had been relatively quick.

Its claws couldn't get to him through the tough material of his boilersuit, but its teeth had been a different matter. Dalip knew that if it had bitten him on his face or his hands or his feet, he'd need antibiotics that probably didn't exist, and he'd also be bleeding heavily with a dog chewing on part of him.

He'd bunched the material on his arm, and offered that instead. It had clamped on, vice-like jaws closing hard, and he'd stabbed it. In the back, in the sides, and when it wouldn't let go, the back of its neck.

The actual fight, from first nick to final, fatal blow had taken mere seconds. He'd left the knife in the dog, assuming he was still a prisoner, and wasn't going to be allowed to keep a weapon.

She'd applauded him politely. Told him that Down was his true home. Then she'd left, taking the man with the silver cane with her.

That was all. Dalip had sat down in the centre of the circular floor and started to shake, the dog still and bleeding next to him. Then the guard had re-entered through the small door and taken the dog away. He'd left the door open, though. The invitation was obvious, one Dalip wasn't quite ready to accept.

He pulled his sleeve back slowly, uncertain as to what he was going to see. Standing at the crease while some six-foot-tall fast bowler, only twenty-two yards away, launched a small hard ball at ninety miles an hour? Sometimes there were injuries: big, fat circular bruises, and once, a broken rib.

The skin on his forearm was torn, but only in a couple of places, and more shallow grazes than deep cuts. He could move his fingers and turn his wrist. The dark mottled arcs, top and bottom, showed where the teeth had dug in. It wasn't that bad, but he might not be able to move it come the morning. And he'd had to kill the stupid dog, too.

He wondered where he'd got the courage to do it, to do something so alien to him as to stab another living creature to death. It might have been instinct, he supposed, but it was certainly nothing he'd learnt.

He looked up. The balcony was out of reach: he knew he'd never jump high enough to even get his fingertips on it. He looked at the pool of blood, and the smears leading from it, away and out the door. It was that way or no way.

Realising that he didn't have an option, he dragged himself up. Beyond the door, he could go back to his cell, or keep following the blood, which trailed straight ahead, through the other door he'd noticed on the way in. That door was open too, and there was no one stopping him from going through.

There were high narrow windows, a fire, a rough table and some stools. Another door opened, and the guard came back through, blocking out the view outside – a courtyard, a wall, a fire issuing black, greasy smoke – before closing the door behind him.

'Get yourself cleaned up,' he said, jerking his head at a barrel.

'Why am I here?' said Dalip, not moving.

'To fight.' The man went to the barrel himself, and plunged his arms up to his elbows into the water. 'What else?'

'I didn't come here to fight.'

'Then why are you here?'

The circular argument infuriated Dalip. The guard scrubbed at his hands with a brush, then cast it aside.

'I'm here by accident.'

'No, you're not.' The guard took a towel, if the scrap of filthy material could be called such, and rubbed himself dry with it. 'No one comes here by accident. You were going to die, right?'

The fire, the heat. 'Yes.'

'That's when you made your choice. Die there or live here.'

'But killing dogs? That's not living.'

'It is if that's what you have to do to keep living.' The guard threw the towel at Dalip who instinctively reached up and caught it before it slapped him wetly in the face. 'Wash. Sit.'

Dalip did as he was told. The water wasn't clean, but it was cleaner than he was. He carefully avoided washing the wound on his arm, though. But he did gather up his hair and thrust his head into the barrel, emerging with a gasp.

On the table was a wooden plate, with some crude bread and a wrinkled apple. Now he realised just how hungry he was. Opposite was the guard, again indicating with a jerk of his head that this was Dalip's.

He sat warily. 'Is this my reward, then?'

'You've had your reward already. This is just food. Eat it or don't, I don't care.'

The cup next to his plate had water in it, hopefully not from the same barrel he'd just washed in. He was going to get sick if he didn't drink it, just as he might if he did. If there was no alternative, like everything else he was having to endure, he'd have to cope.

His teeth still felt loose from the beating he'd had when he'd been captured, so he chewed slowly, watched all the time by the guard.

'What's your name?' asked the man as Dalip moved on to his apple.

Perhaps he shouldn't tell him, mindful as he was of the wolf-man's words. 'Singh,' he said.

'Singh. What does that mean?'

'Lion.'

It may have been funny, but it shouldn't have been funny enough to make a man fall off his chair. When his gaoler had recovered, wiping his eyes and his mouth, and righting his stool, Dalip had reduced the apple to a thin woody core. The pips were lined up on the edge of his plate.

'So, little lion man. Why are you here?'

'I'm not here to fight.'

'Then why are you here?'

'We've done all that.' The urge to wipe the table clean of plate, cup and the guard's grin was strong. 'None of us have done anything to anyone. Yet we've been lied to, taken against our will, locked up, and now, you're making me kill dogs for some mad woman's entertainment. Why?'

'Because.'

Dalip howled in frustration. 'That's not an answer. We don't deserve to be treated this way.'

'How else do you think you should be treated?' The smile slipped. 'Listen. Until you do something that earns you better treatment, you're lower than maggots, you're lower than that, even. Just dirt. You came with nothing, you are nothing: you can stay nothing, I don't care. No one's going to be kind to you – you can forget all that. You work, and maybe she'll pay attention to you.'

'I will not live like that.'

'Then,' he said, 'you'll die like that.' He took Dalip's plate away, and tipped the pips and crumbs on to the floor. 'It's not that bad. You'll get used to it.'

'That's what they said about people calling me nappy-head in the street. I didn't get used to it.' Dalip clenched his jaw. 'I want my patka back.'

'Your what, now?'

'Patka. My head covering. The black one.'

'They were taken away for a reason.' The man reached out for Dalip's cup, but Dalip snatched it away and drained it.

'What's the reason?'

'Because she wanted me to.'

Dalip passed the cup across the table. 'It's important to me. That and my turban, and the steel bracelet, and the comb, and the little sword. They're what marks me out as a Sikh.'

'So earn them.'

'How?'

The man got up from the table, banged the plate against the top and simply put it back on the pile with the others. The cup went unwashed on to a shelf. Dalip looked up and around him, at the soot-stained wooden roof-beams, the cobwebbed corners, the rough, unfinished, unloved nature of everything.

'Everyone's different. For you? You know what you need to do.'

'Fight? I won't do that.'

The guard put his hand on the knife at his belt. 'You'll do it when you're told to.'

'No. I'm not going to be some sort of, whatever it is. Performing seal.'

'Then the next time you go into the pit, you'll die.'

'I'm not going in there again. I'm just not.'

The knife, drawn in a flash, lunged across the table at Dalip, and he stepped back. 'You'll fight or you'll die. Doesn't bother me where you do it.'

Had Dalip imagined a hint of desperation? 'She won't be happy if I die in my cell, will she?'

'I'll drag you out by your mane, little lion man.' The guard passed the knife hand to hand and began circling the table. Dalip began to side-step, keeping the man opposite.

'The moment you touch my hair is the moment you'd better be ready to finish it one way or the other. Just because I won't fight in your pit doesn't mean I won't fight in my cell.'

'We'll come in mob-handed and take you down. Fists and feet, just like they did in the forest.'

'And once you've beaten me up and thrown me in front of her, what then? I'm not stupid. I know that that dog was just the beginning. Next time it'll something bigger, with more teeth, and sooner or later I'll slip or fall, or drop the knife, or just get beaten. So you can either stop this nonsense, or kill me now. I'm not dying because someone thinks it's fun to watch.'

He'd moved around the table far enough that the door leading to the outside was at his back, and his guard was between the table and the wall. There was an opportunity, if he was willing to take it.

He slapped his palms on the table's edge, then quickly turned them so that his fingers were underneath. Then he heaved.

The guard didn't realise what was happening at first. The table top reared up at him, and caught him squarely in the chest. As it started to fall it kept on turning.

Dalip didn't wait to see where it landed. He bolted for the door, wrestled with its unfamiliar latch for a second before dragging the wood aside and running through, heedless of where he might end up.

Sun and sky. Momentarily dazzled, he tried in an instant to spot a way out, or somewhere that might lead to a way out. Whichever way he looked, there was a wall: tall, wide enough to walk on. Between him and it were, to his left, a short stone building, surrounded by crude wooden ones, and to his right, a patchwork of vegetable plots.

Dead centre, a gate, which he'd missed the first time.

He started to run.

The gate was open. There was no one even near it. The two bent backs over the rows of cabbages were turned against him. He was closing on them fast, head down like he was heading for the boundary, then past them without either of them looking up.

He glanced behind him, to see what lead he had. The guard, knife in hand, face screwed up in rage, was just emerging from the door.

Plenty. He'd make it with time to spare. He'd worry what lay beyond the wall when he was outside it. It couldn't be worse than what he was running from.

No shouts. No alarm bells. He didn't care why not. The view through the gate was widening: a lake, a mountainside, and open sky.

A shadow flickered over him. By the time he looked up, it was ahead, over the wall, turning back, a roar of wind under leathery, translucent wings. Dalip was almost at the gate when the scene beyond vanished, and the gap was taken up with a lunging, grinning reptilian head and a lithe, coiling serpentine body. Wings unfurled, it blocked his way, even if he was going to chance the razor-sharp teeth and two powerful sets of claws. The black scales only served to highlight the red of the open jaws.

It flapped its wings. The gale it created almost blew him over. He skidded to a halt. It hissed, and snapped at him, prevented from closing on him by its sheer size.

This was his gaoler, not the men. How could he possibly escape if this monster was loose?

Something heavy met the back of his skull. He was almost too surprised to fall. An arm came around his neck and a knife blade was pressed to his ear.

'That was stupid, lion man. Very, very stupid.'

'It's a dragon. It's really a dragon.' Dalip didn't struggle. There was now no point to struggling, or escaping, or any act of defiance. The geomancer had a dragon.

'Wyvern, she calls it. I've seen it eat a man in two bites.'

It hissed at him again, its forked tongue rippling. Dalip could feel its hot, moist breath, smell its last meal rank on the wind.

'I didn't know. I didn't understand.'

'If I cut you, if I slice through your ear so that you bleed, I don't think even she could hold it back. The scent, you see, it drives it wild. You'd be dead meat before you'd run another yard.' The guard tightened his grip and the keen edge of the knife kissed Dalip's skin.

Dalip swallowed against the man's arm. The wyvern pulled its head back through the gate and stretched its wings. In two beats, it was perched on the wall, peering down at them, head cocked to one side to see them better.

'What's it going to be, lion man? In the belly of the beast, or back inside with me?'

The wyvern's claws scrabbled for purchase, and it flapped to keep its balance. To Dalip, it looked like its wings were blotting out the sky.

'Back inside. Take me back.'

'On your feet then, and I'll stick you if there's any nonsense. Come on, little lion man, back to the pit where you belong.'

Dalip managed to get upright, and started the long walk back to his cell. Despite the knife at his back, he did his best to look around him. The central tall tower, with its conical roof. The more substantial gatehouse to the right. The two mountains, one behind him and one ahead, looming over the circular wall. An arched bridge leading from the main tower's first floor to the shorter nearby cluster of buildings where he'd fled from, and was being led back to.

It was all a little ramshackle, like everything had been new once, a couple of hundred years ago, and now it was fading, slowly being returned to the ground from which it had been raised. But it was still formidable. And guarded by a dragon.

They'd reached the door. With an extra push between his shoulder blades to send him sprawling, it was slammed shut behind him, and bolted top and bottom.

'Pick the table up.' A toe jabbed his ribs. 'Be quick about it.'

He did it, and he set the stools around it, and waited for the next instruction.

'Why are you here?' asked the guard.

Dalip remained mute.

'That's better. Next choice is whether you want to live for a short time or a long time.' The guard sheathed his knife, and squinted at Dalip. 'I'm guessing a long time, right? You don't look like a kid who wants to die any time soon.'

'I still don't understand why you're doing this to me.'

'Because she's seen it in the stones, in the leaves and the feathers, lion man. She's seen you. And she's right, isn't she? There's plenty of fight in you.'

'I've never fought anyone, ever.'

'Then you've wasted your time. You were born for this.'

'I don't know what I'm doing. I don't know how to fight.'

'You need a teacher. I'll find you someone.'

'No,' said Dalip without thinking. He didn't want this stinking, pig-faced lackey or anyone connected with him.

'Suit yourself.'

'Stanislav. The other man you took. I want him.'

They stared at each other, and eventually the guard broke first. 'All right. He doesn't seem the sort, but why not?'

15

They were walking through the forest below Crows' tumbling tower.

'Can you find your way back?' he asked her, and she turned around to see the way they'd come.

'I reckon.' The ground sloped up, either side of them, and if she gained a ridge-top, she thought she'd be able to see the ragged battlements easily.

'Then we haven't gone far enough.'

'You're not trying to get rid of me, are you?'

'You're very suspicious, Mary. Not everybody is trying to hurt you.' He held his hands up above his head and embraced the sky. 'This is not even magic. You find your way around with street signs and familiar buildings, yes?'

'And?'

'Where are your street signs? Where are your parks, your big shops, your busy junctions? They are nowhere, and even though we have barely gone any distance at all, you are already lost.'

'All the trees look the same,' she complained. 'That's not really fair.'

'Being able to hide from the wolfman will not help you if you do not know where you are, or where you are going. So I will show you a few simple tricks.'

'Magic tricks?'

'That depends on whether you think the sun rising in the morning is magic, or the folds of the land are magic, or the way the wind blows is magic.' He raised his eyebrows at her.

Mary looked up at him. 'I'm guessing they are.'

'Then you would be half-right. They are not magic, but they may bring magic with them.'

He said nothing else until they suddenly stepped out of the forest and on to the shore of the lake she'd seen from the castle. Close to, it was more of an inland sea, and even though they had been walking for what seemed like ages, judging both time and distance without a watch or familiar landmarks was hard.

Crows walked down to the shingle beach, where little waves lapped the stones. 'Can you find your way back now?' He held up his finger as her mouth opened. 'Do not tell me yes or no. Tell me how, and take your time. Think.'

She took a deep breath and turned around. Now the tower had vanished completely, along with everything else she'd walked by on the way. Trees; nothing but trees, taller than she was, blocking the view. Yet this morning, she'd looked out from Crows' front door over the whole vista.

She joined him on the shoreline and tried to remember. There'd been the chain of mountains that both the sun and the moon rose over, and there they were again, blue with haze, off to her left. She remembered those from when she'd been catching fish in the estuary. Straight forward was the lake, and beyond that the bay, where the river they'd followed washed out to sea. Then to her far right was the sharp line of rock that eventually made the headland where they'd arrived.

Then she imagined herself there on the beach, looking towards the twin mountains where the geomancer was supposed to be waiting for them, where the river cut through and they were supposed to go around the steep gorge. When she'd run, she'd crossed the river and through the forest until the trees had started to thin and the lines of ridges began.

'I think I've got this,' she said, and tentatively pointed. 'The river's over there. The geomancer lives beyond the gorge, which is there.' She turned. 'The sun rises over those mountains, and between there and here are hills, which means your castle is at the edge of those in …'

She turned again, and decided that if she was going to be wrong, she was going to be definitely wrong. She jabbed her finger.

'That direction. On the tallest ridge.'

Crows bowed low, his scarecrow body bent double. 'You were paying attention after all. Could you draw a map?'

'I don't know,' said Mary. 'I was never any good at drawing anything. I could give it a go, if that's what you wanted.'

'Here in Down, maps are power. They mark out the portals and the spaces in between. You can trade maps, barter them for whatever you want. Just make sure you hold them in your head, so that no one can take them from you. So, with that lesson over, are you ready for another?'

She nodded and he held up his hand to her.

'What do you see?'

'Your hand,' she said.

'Yes. What else?'

His palm was a little pinker than the jet black of his knuckles. The creases on his skin at the joints and across the width of his span were like hers and yet unique to him.

'Am I supposed to be doing some sort of fortune telling?'

'No,' said Crows. 'Look carefully.'

She did. She looked for patterns in the lines, scars or calluses. He had those, but they didn't mean anything except a past and a present of hard work.

'Have you looked?' he asked.

'I don't know what I'm looking for.'

He turned his hand around to show her the back of it. 'You are looking for the same thing as you were before.'

Crows had no hair there. His nails were pale and chipped, ridged like the land where he lived. His fingers were almost impossibly long, and she wondered how hard it had been for him to heave shovel after shovel of coal into the furnace, in the heat and the smoke of the engine room.

He turned his hand again, palm forward. 'Do not look at the hand. Look at what the hand becomes.'

She wasn't seeing it. A hand was a hand was a hand, however it was held. She held up her own, but she was facing into the sun, so she moved it to block it out. The light peeked through the spaces between her shorter, fatter fingers.

'Shadow,' she said. 'I can see a shadow.'

'Good. Now, this is the trick. When you move your hand, the shadow it casts follows it. Always. Unless you can persuade it not to.'

He stood next to her, held out his hand again, and wiped a line of darkness across the clear lake air.

'Do I have to believe it'll work before it does?'

'It helps. There are three reasons to do something, anything. The most obvious is that you know that it will work. You have done it before, and the outcome every time is the same. Then there is a belief that it will work. You have seen it done, you have been shown how to do it, though you have never done it yourself. And then there is the third way.'

She waited. And waited. 'Crows?'

'Hope,' he said. 'You hope it will work. You have no idea how it might be accomplished, but you need it to work so very badly.'

'So all I have to do is hope?'

'It is all you ever have to do.'

'A world can't run on wishes. It can't.'

'Surprise yourself,' he said. 'Do you want it to be true?'

'I do. Fuck, yes.' A talent, once latent and now woken, was

poised on the tip of her tongue and the tips of her fingers, ready for her to speak and shape it into being.

He laughed. 'Then make it true.'

She looked at the black smear in front of Crows, the way it slowly crisped and crumbled at the edges, falling like soot but melting before it reached the ground. It was his shadow, dissolving in the sunshine.

Mary took a deep breath, stuck her tongue between her teeth and wiped her hand as if she was clearing condensation from a window pane. The image was so strong that she was on the top deck of a bus, night outside, and using her sleeve to scrub the sheen of water away so she could see out.

She pulled down mist, not darkness.

It swirled about her hand, tiny tornadoes of cold steam that floated off on the shore-side breeze.

'Interesting,' said Crows. 'But ill-disciplined. Try again.'

She wreathed herself with fog, and whichever way she turned she just produced more of it. She ran along the shingle beach like she was laying down a smoke screen, then ran back through the fog bank she'd created, dragging it with her. She sprinted past Crows, dancing around him, then on up the beach to weave through the trees.

When she finally stopped, the air was thick. Tendrils of vapour curled and twisted, and the wind only slowly unpicked her impromptu, unexpected manifestation.

'Crows?'

The fog was bright, a luminous cloud with no beginning or end. Without the sky, she didn't know which way to go, but she could still listen for the movement of the waves on the shore. Perhaps that way. She took an uncertain step forward and called Crows' name again.

He answered, distant and indistinct, and she sighed with relief. The mist, even though she'd created it out of nothing, was acquiring a solidity that unnerved her. She started to head towards where she thought Crows was, when she stumbled. She looked down, and a white rope of smoke was coiling around her ankle.

She jerked her foot through it. It unwound and reached forward again, its indistinct tip questing and probing. In her enthusiasm, she'd done something else other than summon fog.

'Crows!' She broke into a run again, and it was like a thousand little hands pulling her back. She twisted to shake them off, but they were insubstantial and momentary, forming and dissipating at will.

There was something building behind her. She could feel it growing and forming a shape, and she wasn't going to outrun it. She'd made it. She'd have to confront it. No more running.

Mary stopped, clenched her fists, and closed her eyes. Then turned and opened them again. It was like staring up at a wall of albino squids, tentacles writhing without purpose or rhythm, moving ceaselessly and never resting.

She'd done this. She'd brought it into being from her own mind. It was her, though, her life manifested as a monster, in-choate and unreasoning. From birth, through life, nothing but thrashing and never anything solid to grip on to.

Until now, paradoxically when she had only the clothes she stood up in.

She held up her open palms. 'I'm not you anymore.'

The tentacles continued to churn. They reached for her, recoiled from her, an endless dance.

'You can go if you want. I'm different now.'

They faded, grew back, faded. The fog and her fear gave them permission to exist. And actually, she didn't mind that much. Perhaps there'd always be a part of her that'd be wild and chaotic, formless and searching.

'Okay. Stay, then. But you don't rule me. The Red Queen is going to be fierce and brave, and never run away from anything ever again. She's going to be beautiful and strong and happy, and she and Crows are going to rescue her friends. If you're coming along, you do what I say from now on, not the other way around.'

She stood her ground, and the monster folded itself back into the mist, slowly, until there was a moment when she thought it had gone, but it hadn't. Then the whiteness faded, stretched out and grew ragged. She could see the trees, and through the trees, the lake, and by the lake, Crows.

He raised a sceptical eyebrow as she approached, breathless.

'You know that, like most things, magic is not safe.' His shadow-drawing hung in tatters behind him.

'Now you tell me.' Her own mist was a few streamers still curled in the hollows of trees. She straightened her back. 'It didn't hurt me.'

'It could have done. You are unteachable, and we should stop this at once before you come to harm.'

'But it didn't hurt me, Crows. It was nothing in the end. I'm fine.'

'You did not do what I told you to.' He was adamant. 'How else will you learn if you do not pay attention to your lessons?'

She took a step back and held her hand up to the sun, so that one side was in the light, the other in the shadow. She brought her hand down, painting the sky with a thick black stripe.

'I always paid attention when the teacher told me something useful. It's just that they didn't do that very often.'

She added legs and arms to make a black stick figure, and finished it off with a coal-black head.

'Look,' she said. 'It's you.'

For a moment, she thought she'd misjudged the situation, that he'd take offence and storm off. She needed him, and he didn't need her. She should apologise.

'I ... Crows. I was so bored in school. I learnt next to nothing. And that was when I could be bothered to turn up. This – this is different. I'm actually excited by something. I'll try and do my best from now on.'

'You are very good, Mary, a natural. But while magic is not

something you do by rote, you have to learn the techniques before you can create works of great beauty and power. It is an art, and all artists start by learning how to hold a brush.' He grinned at her, his white teeth bright in the sunlight. 'No more mist monsters. For now, anyway. You were lucky to survive that encounter, so let us not tempt fate by doing it again.'

The grin wasn't happy. Crows was nervous, edgy.

'How much trouble was I in?'

'There are stories. Some of those who have such encounters swear never to use magic again. There are those who never recover. They are broken by seeing themselves as they truly are. So said the man who taught me. And you conjure your demons on the first attempt. What you did was very dangerous.'

'But I know what I am. It's just that I don't like it. I want to be something different.'

'The Red Queen.' He was calmer now. He picked at her stick figure creation, like it was peeling paint, or an old black bin-liner left out in the sun and the rain for too long. 'You are unusual. Most people imagine themselves to be better than they are. Not you. You are better than you believe yourself to be. That saved you, but please, do not do it again.'

'What did you see, Crows?'

He turned away, and muttered.

'What?'

He couldn't look at her, so he addressed the clouds.

'I saw nothing. Nothing at all.'

'Nothing? But that's …' Then she understood. Not nothing as in nothing at all, but everything, and Crows' place within it. 'Oh. You're not, though.'

'I am a child from a place that no longer exists, I am a man invisible to other men. As the King of Crows, I was unable to protect the people I thought I could protect. I am drawn in darkness and to darkness I will return. I have seen it, and even though I fight against it every day, I will fall eventually.'

'You can be whatever you want to be, Crows,' said Mary.

'Despite my best efforts, it is what I want to be. I know about new beginnings and becoming your heart's desire, but we must realise that some people's dreams are darker than others.' He scrubbed his fingers against his face and looked haunted for a moment. 'Can you swim?'

'Me? No.' She was unsettled by Crows' gloom, and was glad for the change of subject.

'Are you scared of water, then? It was said that it was unlucky for a sailor to learn to swim: by who, I do not know, because they were idiots. Swimming is important. Bridges are rare on Down, and lakes and rivers are not.' He took off his shirt in one fluid motion, and threw it to the ground behind him. She caught the barest glimpse of a series of ridged scars on his otherwise smooth belly, before he turned. He started wading out into the lake, the water enveloping his legs.

'I haven't got anything to wear,' she said.

'My intentions are wholly honourable, Mary. It does not matter what you do or do not wear, only that you learn.'

She thought about it. She hadn't washed properly in days – apart from the river crossing, and that didn't count as being washed.

'There aren't any monsters in the lake, are there?'

'If I said yes, would you learn to swim quicker?'

'No.'

'Then no, there are no monsters in the lake.' Crows was up to his waist. He ducked down and disappeared. After what felt like forever, he reappeared, far off to one side. 'No monsters but us,' he called.

He was lying, obviously, but seemed totally unconcerned about being eaten by sea serpents or giant sharks or whatever. She had a vest top on under her boilersuit which, yes, would turn transparent, but it wasn't like she'd be spending much time with even her head above water.

She sat down and kicked off her boots, dumped her socks in the tops, and pulled at the heavy zip on the boilersuit, listening to the way it growled as she dragged it down. Crows was busy diving down under the surface, emerging elsewhere, spitting water in a tall fountain, then jackknifing under again, all away from her.

Did she dare do this? Crows was sad and alone, but she got the impression that her presence wouldn't change that, that he didn't want her to change that, that he simply wasn't interested in her in that way. He'd never looked her up and down with predatory intent, and she – no: he was too different, too otherworldly and out of time. But they could be friends, and if they were friends, what else mattered?

She shucked the boilersuit and left it on the shore next to her boots, and ran the short distance across the sharp grit into the water.

It was cold like a knife was cold.

'Fuck. Fuckfuckfuck.'

She was up to her calves, her knees, mid-thighs, wading forward, ice water splashing on her pale brown skin like glitter, goosebumps making her skin puckered.

She tripped, and fell. Her arms came forward to stop her, and she plunged headfirst into the stirred-up silt. The water closed over her, and the shock of it, the way it thieved the heat from her, almost made her gasp. Her lungs strained for breath, and her arms and legs flailed as she tried to find her feet. It didn't occur to her to close her eyes, and she caught a fleeting glimpse of another kingdom, of weeds and fishes and green sunlight.

Then she came up with a shout, hair coiled like oiled springs behind her and over her shoulders, the sun warm against the chill of the lake. Crows flipped himself under, reappearing wide-eyed and closer, and Mary used her hands to manoeuvre herself towards him, feeling the embrace of the water against every inch of her body.

16

Dalip sat on the stone of the pit, back against the curved wall, facing the door. He'd been told by the guard to wait: he had no reason to give the man a nice name, so he hadn't, and started thinking of him as Pigface.

He was more Cowface, broad and bovine, but Pigface seemed to sum up his raisin-like eyes and sticky pink complexion. He was casually, almost indifferently, brutal, as if that was the only way to behave and he'd known no other. Perhaps that was true: perhaps he came from a long line of Pigfaces, slave keepers who were little more than slaves themselves.

Then Stanislav appeared, entering the pit cautiously, looking up at the surrounding balconies and the rings of lit candles. Behind him, Pigface was watching.

'Why are we here?' asked Stanislav.

'That's the question I keep on asking. The answer, for me at least, is to fight.'

Satisfied, Pigface turned away to the guard room, leaving both doors open, and Stanislav toured the circumference of the pit.

'And you have agreed to such madness?'

'I didn't really have much of a choice.'

'No. You cannot fight. I will go and tell them this instant.'

He clenched his fists and started back up the corridor to find Pigface.

'Stop. Stop. You don't understand.'

'I understand that you are just a boy, a child. If they want someone to fight, they can pick me.' Stanislav seemed more than ready to start there and then.

'They have a dragon.'

That stopped him. He put his hand on the door and leant against it. 'They have a what?'

'A dragon. They call it a wyvern – snake's body, bat's wings, two legs like a bird. We're stuck halfway up a mountain and it'll eat anything that goes beyond the wall. I managed to get out, tried to make a run for it. There's literally nowhere to run to.'

'We walked here. We can walk out again.'

'Not with that thing flying around.'

Stanislav came back again. 'You saw this wyvern, this draco?'

Dalip nodded sourly. 'We're in some sort of castle. Buildings surrounded by an outer wall, where there are two gates, at least. They don't even bother to close or guard the gates, but I guess they don't need to.'

'You still do not have to fight. That is barbaric.'

'I don't think they care. They're going to drag me here and give me a weapon, then set … things on me, whether I want them to or not. Either I fight back or I die.' Dalip looked up at Stanislav. 'I don't want to die.'

'Have they told you how many opponents you will face? What kind? Men? Beasts?'

'They used a dog for the first time. A fighting dog of some sort. I have to assume it gets harder.'

Stanislav sat down next to him, and rested the back of his head against the same wall as Dalip.

'This is how you win your freedom?' he asked.

'I don't think it works like that.'

'To the death?'

'I'm here to fight. Apparently.'

'This is, this is …' Stanislav raised his hands, then let them drop uselessly in his lap. 'Evil.'

'I didn't know what to do. I thought this might buy me some time.' Dalip shrugged. 'Something might come up. An opportunity, a rescue. I know I can't keep going forever, but it's better than being dead now.'

'Is it? There are worse things than dying.'

'I don't know how to fight. Pigface said one of the guards would train me. I didn't want that. So I asked for you.'

'And you think I do?' Stanislav pressed his chin into his chest. 'You should not have picked me. Anyone else but me.'

'I'm sorry. I wanted someone on my side, someone who'll care enough to give me a chance.'

'You will die in this ring of cold stone. You have no chance, none at all. By saying yes to them, you have given them control over you. Only by saying no do you keep your honour and your dignity intact.' He ground his jaw. 'You have made a mistake, Dalip. If you will not let me go and tell them you will not fight, go yourself, and let them do their worst.'

'Their worst will be to let some other wild thing in here, and it'll kill me.'

'If you want understanding, understand this: you will not hurt them by fighting their animals. You will only hurt them by fighting them. The only way you have of hurting them is by not playing their cruel games.'

'Stanislav: they'll kill me. One way or another, they'll kill me.'

'This is true. But they will gain pleasure out of seeing you fight, not seeing you win. It is the fighting they want. Deny them that.'

'I shouldn't have brought you into this,' said Dalip. 'Okay, I do have a choice. Die now, die later. And everything you said is true. I just don't want to die now. I want to live.'

He got up and dusted himself down and started to prowl.

'What will you do,' said Stanislav, 'when they bring in another man? Or a woman? Or a child? Will you kill them to stay alive?'

'No. No, I won't.'

'You are sure of that? Once you begin to kill, it will become almost impossible not to kill. What if they push this Pigface into the ring with you? He is a prisoner of the geomancer as much as we are.'

Dalip said nothing. He hadn't thought that far ahead, and he was ashamed that he hadn't. If it was Pigface facing him, knife in hand, sweat streaming down his forehead and stinging his eyes? The guard would stick a blade in him without a moment's hesitation. Did that give him the right to do the same?

Killing him could be seen as protecting the others.

'No,' he said.

'So you would be prepared to let Pigface kill you?'

He imagined the knife going in, into his belly, being dragged out sideways, his guts spilling out over the floor. 'No.'

'It must be one or the other. Those are the rules of their game. Two go in, one comes out.'

'I know, I know.'

'So you must decide whether you will be prepared to end another man's life for the purposes of entertaining our masters, or whether you will not. What if,' said Stanislav, 'it was me?'

'No.'

'Why not? We are together through circumstance alone. Neither of us chose the other. If I am just another man you must kill in order to survive that day, then why not?'

'You've not done anything to hurt me. Stanislav, please. I just want to live a little longer.'

'And you call this living?' He shook his head. 'I do not blame you. I would have agreed with you once. You are young, you have experienced mostly kindness and generosity so far. You cannot quite believe what is happening to you, so you choose to

161

put all that to one side and cling on to the idea that everything will be all right in the end.'

Dalip pressed his hands to his face and blinked back the tears. 'It will be.'

'I have seen it with my own eyes. I have seen men, and boys not much younger than you, believe until the very last second that everything will be all right in the end. They died with a look of astonishment on their faces, that the world had somehow tricked them into thinking that people were good and kind and fair, only to reveal that underneath, we are all brutes, savages and murderers.' Stanislav pulled up his legs and hugged his knees. 'We are prisoners, not of any state that has rules that mean we must be fed and clothed and well-treated, but of people who own us like property, to do with as they wish. Do we cooperate with such people? Only if we want to lose our souls as well as our lives.'

'But useful slaves—'

'Are still slaves! Pigface is still a slave. The wolfman is still a slave. Perhaps they want to be slaves, good slaves. I do not, and you should not either. It is not a condition that anyone should become comfortable with.' He got up, and stood in front of Dalip. 'What is it that you want? Do you want to fight? Is that it? To show you are a man? To kill and kill again because that is what men do?'

'No, I don't want to fight. But they're going to make me fight anyway, so I may as well not die at the first attempt.'

'You know of the Christian martyrs, yes? The ones that the emperors put into the arena with the wild animals? They did not fight, but prayed as they died.'

'I'm not a Christian.'

Stanislav took a step closer, and pressed his extended forefinger into Dalip's chest. 'What is it that you want? What do you really want?'

'I want them to let me go. I want to make them let me go. I

want to make them give me back my turban, my kangha, my kara, my kirpan. I want to make them glad to see the back of me. I can't do any of that if I'm dead.'

'That is true,' he conceded. 'Will you fight to make them let you go?'

'Yes.' Dalip looked away, then back. 'I think so.'

'You have to more than think. You have to know. And you have to fight them, every second of every day until you are either free or dead. Can you do that?'

'Yes. Yes I can.'

'If this is ultimately futile, and the geomancer and her men are too powerful for us, then we might only make them pay in some small way for what they have done. Would you be content with that?'

Dalip stared at his hands and wondered if he could do it. He was a student, a son, a brother. Not a fighter. Why was he here? He was here because he was being held against his will by people who wanted to feed him to dogs. That was why. That was the answer: not 'fight'. So they were wrong, and he'd show them they were wrong, one way or another. If that meant pretending to become what they wanted, then he'd do that, only for as long as it took to work out a way of escaping.

'Yes.'

It was Stanislav's turn to come to a decision. His gaze wandered up to the first balcony, where the geomancer had sat. He pursed his lips and looked pensive.

'Yes, then. I will attempt to train you. I know the basics. If nothing else, you will leave a better-looking corpse.' He checked that Pigface wasn't in sight. 'Strip,' he said.

'Sorry, what?'

'Strip. Let me see what I have to work with.'

Dalip kept his kachera on. Otherwise, he was naked, and felt utterly uncomfortable as Stanislav circled him, sizing him up as if he was a joint of meat. The air chilled his skin, and what hair he had rose up.

'I have seen worse. You do a lot of sport?'

'Cricket, mainly.' Dalip looked straight ahead.

'Cricket. How very … English. Can you run, throw, catch?'

'I'm not bad, I suppose.'

'The ball is small and hard. Are you scared of it?'

'I know it's going to hurt sometimes, and more if I get it wrong. But no, not really.'

'This mark here.' Stanislav pointed to Dalip's arm. 'This is where the dog bit you?'

'That's where I let the dog bite me. Then I stabbed it in the back and neck.'

'We want to avoid that. A bigger creature will break your arm, even if they do not break your skin. A dog has blunt claws, made for running. A cat – a big cat – is sharp at every corner and will slice you like one of your Sunday roasts.' Stanislav sized up the floor space. 'This is small. Speed will only count for so much. Once you have made contact, ending it quickly will be your only option. Do you know any judo, or karate, or wrestling or boxing?'

'No. I never really got into fights at all.'

'Not even with racists or neo-Nazis?'

'I got thumped a couple of times, but I was always able to run away.' He shifted awkwardly. 'Can I put the boilersuit back on? I'm cold and …'

'Embarrassed? You will not die of embarrassment.' Stanislav kicked Dalip's boilersuit further away. 'No. You cannot run away in here. Against animals, predators who will be used to killing for food and for dominance, there can be no running. You must dodge, close and strike, use your mind as a weapon as much as a knife. The longer a fight goes on, the more likely you are to lose. When you are tired, you will make mistakes. Out there, you have the chance to do it again. In here, it will kill you.'

Despite the cold, Dalip found his hands damp with sweat. Of course he was nervous. He'd be a fool not to be.

'So how do we start?'

Stanislav weighed up the options. 'You know what this is?'

He dropped to the ground and balanced his straight body on his fingers and toes. His elbows bent, his body dipped, then he straightened them again.

'A press up,' said Dalip.

'You need more strength in your back and shoulders. Your arms are like sticks. One hundred. Start now, and I will find some weapons to practise with.'

Dalip assumed the position. He was quite light, and the first twenty weren't too difficult. He could hear voices off, away down the corridor. He raised his head enough to see Stanislav and Pigface engage in, at first, an animated conversation with a lot of gesturing, and then it escalated to a full-throated shouting match. Pigface turned to walk away: a brief struggle ensued, ending up with the guard's head squashed against the stone wall by Stanislav's meaty hand, while the other relieved him of his knife. It had happened so quickly, almost effortlessly, that Dalip had no idea of the order of events.

Pigface slid down the wall when released, and Stanislav re-entered the pit. He stooped to put the knife on the floor and acted as if nothing had happened.

'How many have you done?'

'Twenty-six.'

Pigface was picking himself up off the ground, pressing his palm to the side of his head, staring narrow-eyed at Stanislav.

'More, then,' said Stanislav. 'And faster. This is not meant to be easy. While you are doing that, tell me what you saw outside: tell me about the buildings, how far away they are, how many soldiers you saw.'

He gave the details as best he could, and then talked about what he presumed was the geomancer's stronghold.

'There's a tower attached to this one, by a bridge that links the first floors. If that's where she lives, then she can just walk from there to here without going down to the ground. But the only way out of here for us is through the guard room.'

'How high is that balcony? Three and a half metres? Four? If one of us could climb that, then there is another way out.'

Dalip's arms were beginning to burn. 'It's smooth stone. I don't think anyone could climb that.'

'No? I will show you how it can be done. Not today, though. Let them get used to us being here, then they will take less notice of us. How many now?'

'Forty-seven. Forty-eight.'

The strain was showing in his voice.

'Keep going. Do not stop. You are not weak. You are strong.' Stanislav glanced up again. 'If the geomancer was there, we could catch her by surprise. She does not look like a fighter herself. Incapacitate her guards, and you have her.'

The pain was building, and all Dalip could do was grunt.

'Once you have taken her hostage, we can free the others, and whoever else wishes to leave. Her dragon cannot attack us without attacking her. When we are safe, we can decide what to do with her. Remember what she is and what she has done. There may be no justice other than what we give, and if we let her go, she and her men may hunt us down, or simply go back to slaving.'

Dalip's arms were trembling with effort. He locked his elbows to rest, but Stanislav wasn't letting him slack off.

'In this ring you fight until you finish. You cannot stop before then.'

The fire. He couldn't feel his arms any more, but he kept on going for another one, another two, then he collapsed face-first on to the cold, hard ground.

'Your legs are not tired. Get up. Run from the door to the

door, then reverse. We may have just one chance at this, and you must be ready. Up. Up!'

Dalip dragged his bones upright, his arms dangling uselessly at his sides. He started to run.

17

She had to step over a wall that hadn't been there before. It was just about knee-high, wide enough to have to stand on on the way across it, made of rough stones that were more-or-less fitted together.

Having crossed it and jumped down the other side, she looked back at it. Crows was already heading up the hill, carrying the fish he'd caught – she still wasn't quite sure how – while she was paddling up and down in the shallows.

The wall extended left and right. Soil and shrubs were piled up against the inside of the wall, and when she checked, the outside too.

Like it had pushed its way out of the ground.

She looked up the hill. Crows had disappeared into the ruined tower, so she took the opportunity to follow the line. It ran all the way around the tower, following the same contour, and she arrived back where she'd started a few minutes later, breathless and not a little confused.

She climbed after Crows, to find that the wall wasn't the only addition. There was a new pavement in front of the doorway, and somehow the tower seemed taller and more substantial. If that had been all, she'd have just put it down to her faulty memory, but the circular wall was something else. She hadn't forgotten it, and neither could she dismiss it.

And inside, the roof, or at least, the floor above, had been repaired. But not in a new wood way. The boards now over her head looked old and tired, the beams supporting them rough and soot-stained.

'Crows? What the fuck is happening to your castle?'

'You've noticed,' he called from the back room where he kept his stores.

'I'm not blind. Or stupid.' The ceiling was too far away for her to jump up and touch, but it obviously wasn't at the top of the tower. There were going to be stairs somewhere, and she started searching for them.

She found a dark alcove that, when she looked up into it, she could see faintly. Uneven stone steps led upwards, and with a quick glance behind her, she started up them, hands feeling the way against the walls of the narrow staircase. It grew brighter as she climbed: the stairs ahead of her grew more ragged, until there were whole sections of tread missing, but there was a doorway to her right just before it became unusable. She stepped through, and found she was standing on the boards she'd been looking up at before.

They seemed solid enough when she pressed them with the toe of her boot, and she walked out on to them, listening to them creak softly.

Above her, the crows had moved up a level. There was another threadbare set of rafters hanging from the sockets in the walls, and the birds returning to roost seemed perfectly at home. She paced the square sides of the tower, and ended back at the door.

She wasn't imagining it, and Crows wasn't denying it.

'Dinner is cooking,' he said, appearing behind her.

'How is this even possible?' she asked him, throwing her hands up in disbelief.

He shrugged. 'I cannot tell you why, but I can tell you how.

There are lines of energy that flow under the surface of the land. Where those lines cross, the energy pools as in a well. Miracles happen there.'

'So, what? The castles just appear?'

'Yes.' Crows shrugged again. 'What can I say? Down was like that before I got here. I did not make the rules.'

'What about the villages?'

'Yes, those too. If you stay long enough in one place, a house forms for you. Those are along the lines. Where two or more meet, you get castles.'

'Fucking hell. That's crazy. Why isn't everybody running around trying to find their own castle, then?'

'As you can imagine, it is not as simple as that.'

'And this one's repairing itself because?'

'Because you are here, Mary. The land responds according to our natures. Some people are weak in magic. Others are strong, like you. You can drink deeply from the well beneath us. The castle was never very big, and I lost heart, so it fell into ruin. Now, it is responding to your presence, and grows once again.'

'Me? What did I do?'

'You do not have to do anything. You just have to be.' Crows tapped his foot on the boards, and they sounded hollowly back.

Mary looked around her with wonder. 'This grew, out of nothing?'

'Again, not out of nothing. Out of the ground. It rises and falls with the power of the men or women under its roof.'

She pressed her hand against the wall, where the individual stones fitted with each other in blocks and courses, like a gigantic jigsaw. 'That is still fucking nuts. So how do you find these lines of energy?'

'You search for them. Tease them out. Remember how I told you that maps were powerful things? This is why: if you have a map, you can start to find the lines. Once you have drawn the lines, you can find where they cross. Where they cross is where castles rise. And sometimes, you can, if you are clever and you have more complete maps than anyone else, you can find a place that no one else knows of.'

'Do you?' she asked.

'Do I what?'

'Have maps?'

Crows pursed his lips. 'I might.'

'Can I see them?'

'Mary,' he said. 'They are fragile, and very precious. They are not objects to be idly toyed with. But perhaps … yes. You must start a map of your own, and mark everything you know of so far on to it. Come, and eat, and then while it is still light, we can make a start.'

Crows wasn't much of a cook, Mary decided, not that she could do better with the ingredients to hand. There was steamed fish – bony and tasting oddly of weeds – and boiled grain that was a step firmer than porridge. He thought it was fine: he extracted every last morsel of grey flesh from the skeleton, scooping out the difficult to reach bits near the head with one of his long fingers, and sucking the juices from the tail, all the while using the same fingers to cup small balls of grain and feed them past his white teeth.

If she didn't eat, she'd be too weak to walk to all the places that Crows thought it necessary to take her to, and too weak to weave fog from the air she breathed and darkness from the shadows she cast.

She could do magic. If that wasn't astounding enough, the very land itself was magical, with castles springing up from the ground at her unspoken command. Eating some mediocre meals was a small price to pay for such wonders, and she'd do it without complaint.

Then when they'd finished, and she'd washed her face and hands and bowls in what had been that morning, a stream, and was now a stone arch sluicing water down a trough before it turned into a stream, she sat on the still-open doorstep while Crows fetched a sheet of paper and some ink.

She wasn't sure where he'd get paper from, or pens. They spoke of being manufactured, while everything about Down was crafted – handmade, bespoke, using only raw materials.

The ink was made from soot and oils, the pens from stripped-down feathers, and the paper, she was both fascinated and disgusted to learn, was actually a scraped-clean square of animal skin, the size of a school exercise book.

She'd always been an inveterate doodler, tagging everything with the art she saw on the street. This was different. Even the ink was rare and precious, delicate and worryingly permanent. No hesitation, no erasing.

'How do I do this?' she asked.

'You mark down everything you've seen, as accurately as possible. Mark where you have walked, the mountains you saw in the distance, the curve of the rivers, the lines of the hills. Guess the distances if you cannot measure them. Start where you started, finish where you are.'

'And what do I do with it when I'm done?'

'You keep it,' said Crows. 'This is the beginning of your wealth here in Down.'

'Oh,' she said, looking at the blank parchment. 'Okay.'

She looked out over the land from the doorstep and the newly restored pavement, and the sun that was sliding around to her right. The long ridge that made the headland was a dark smudge.

'Everything?'

'It is most important that you put in every last detail, while you still remember it.'

She'd never used a quill pen before: she dipped the nib in the little pot of ink tentatively, before making an equally uncertain mark on the parchment at the top and right of the page. That was to mark the door they'd come through. Then another, bottom left, to indicate Crow's castle. What she knew of Down would fit somewhere in between.

She scratched out the lines to represent the bay and the estuary, the river and the lake they'd completely missed because they were on the wrong bank. She added dots for where they camped and the village they'd found.

She was concentrating so hard on getting it as right as she could make it, it was only when she looked up did she see Crows staring intently at the picture she'd drawn.

'How does it look?' she asked him.

'Carefully done. When it is dry, we will put it some place safe.' He bent low to blow softly on it. 'The portal is on the beach itself?'

'It's in the sea, facing the beach, set in a big rock that stands on its own. I could show you if you want.'

'No need. I know where you mean. There used to be an arch there, but it collapsed in a storm.'

'Crows, will I ever get back home?'

He sat back on his haunches. 'Why do you ask?'

'The wolfman told us that going home was impossible. Was he lying?'

'He was telling the truth, as far as he knows it.'

'But does that mean he's wrong?' She held her map up to the reddening sun, watching how the light played through the thin sheet and emboldened the black lines she'd made.

'That is a geomancer's great dream, the grand project, to discover whether or not those in Down can pass through the portals to London.'

'No one has, then.' She didn't know how to feel about that. She was trapped, but the prison was far bigger than the freedom she'd previously taken for granted.

'Yet,' said Crows. 'Geomancers fight for control over land, over castles, over portals. Your friends have been taken in case they know something about how the portals work: even the smallest clue might help open the way.'

'What's going to happen to them?'

'If I know her, she will never let them go: what they know will be useful to others and part of being a good geomancer is to deny knowledge to other geomancers. She will force them to work for her, like she did the villagers under my protection.'

'Slave labour.'

'Yes.' Crows sagged at the thought. 'I wish I could do more.'

'Has she got a castle?'

'Hers is large, with high walls and a commanding view over the land. She has soldiers at her beck and call, and workers in her fields. She does not have to worry about finding food, or keeping warm. She spends her whole day in study. I was no match for her, and I barely escaped her myself.' He curled in on himself further, and worried at his thumb with his teeth. 'She shamed me.'

'We can get them back.'

'We are not enough,' said Crows. 'We would need an army to take her castle, and we are not going to find one. This part of Down is empty.'

'Maybe we should just go somewhere where there are more people and, I don't know, hire an army. Can we do that?'

'The only city I know of is hundreds of miles away. There are people here and there in the hills to the east, but they enjoy their peace, and it is not their quarrel. We cannot make them fight for us, and we will not be able to persuade them either.'

Mary looked again at her map, at the tiny amount of land it actually covered. There was so much more to explore, but she still felt the urge to at least try and rescue the others.

'Can we go and look at her castle? Just to see what it's like?'

Crows looked up. It was clear he didn't want to.

'You know where it is, right?' she asked.

'Yes, yes. I know it, but it is too dangerous. If she catches us, then she will kill me and enslave you.'

'Crows, my friends need me to help them.' She felt the first stirrings of irritation. 'And I need you. You can't say no.'

'It is too dangerous,' he repeated. 'There is nothing to gain by going, and everything to lose.'

'You're scared.'

'Yes, and you should be too. Her power is terrible. She is far stronger than me, and that is that. I have run from her once, and I am not so great a fool as to confront her again. I will do what I can around the margins, saving those who escape from her, but if they are within her walls, I can do nothing.'

'I can't do anything, either.' She let the map drift to the floor. 'I've only just got here, I don't know how anything works. I thought,' she said, 'you were going to help me.'

'I am helping you. And I am helping you by telling you that we cannot stand against her. We would be throwing our lives away, and in doing so make her stronger still.' Crows shied away from her, rising on his thin legs and going out on to the pavement. 'There is a time to fight and a time to hide. Perhaps when her fortunes are reversed, we can help your friends. Until then, they will come to no real harm – they are too valuable alive.'

'They're fucking slaves, Crows! It's not the fucking Ritz they're staying in. If it was the other way around, and they'd got me instead of Dalip, I bet he'd be thinking up some sort of way to get us out of there, no matter how long it took.' She looked up at the man, how his black skin glowed with the orange of sunset, and remembered the fire of the tunnels. Yes, she'd been terrified, but that had been no reason to abandon everyone else. They'd saved each other once before, the best they could. 'We have to try.'

'We do not "have to try". No one is forcing you to do anything. No one will think better of you for failing. Those few people who know you will soon forget. Nothing you have done will be written down. Even if you succeed, who will thank you? There is no reward to gain, no medals to win, no one will make you queen.' He waved his hand at the darkening land. 'If you want to be queen, then be one here. This is your country. Rule it how you see fit.'

Her fingers and toes were tingling. The end of her nose. Her ears. This was what she was like just before she blew. The rage growled like a trapped animal, desperate to escape. The only way it could go was out of her throat.

Crows was right, and yet he was so very wrong. If Down meant she could walk away and begin again where no one had ever heard of her, it also had to mean that she could stay and work out a way to save those she came here with. No one was forcing her: she wanted to do it. Win, lose, medals, empty hands. It didn't matter. She was going to save them all, with or without Crows, because that was the task she'd set herself.

Her anger slid through her like fog through her fingers. And she felt calm and strong.

'I'll find her myself,' she said. 'You can come if you want, but I'll go alone if I have to.'

He had all manner of objections, but they seemed to die on his tongue.

'I rescue you and yet you are determined to go back and throw yourself into her shackles. So be it.' He threw up his hands at the futility of it all. 'I will take you only close enough for you to see her castle. After that, you may do as you wish. A waste, I tell you. A waste.'

He stalked off, leaving her and her map on the ground. But at the edge of the pavement, he turned around.

'You should sleep,' he said. 'It is a full day's walk, and we will be up early.'

Mary looked at her map, at the discarded ink and quills, and began to gather everything up. She'd roll the map up and keep it in her room, and return the rest to the store room. She'd light the candle there with a flick of her fingers, just like Crows, and she'd extinguish it with sheer force of will.

18

Pigface came for Dalip sooner than he'd thought. Three days of merciless physical training had left him aching in places he didn't know he could ache. He felt all but boneless, loose and unconnected. He'd had extra food – for all he knew it was Pigface's own rations, and Stanislav had bullied them out of him – but nowhere near enough time for anything to make a difference.

The older man's demeanour had changed in captivity: he was now all sharp edges and abrupt actions, as if he knew exactly what would put their gaolers on the back foot. And Dalip was afraid to ask where he'd got that knowledge.

'On your feet, little lion man. She wants you.'

Dalip raised himself from the stone floor. He'd been stretching, feet out in front of him and bending from the hips, trying to get his head as close to his knees as he could. He was, as Stanislav had told him, stiff like an old man, and he needed to be supple in order to fight.

Despite the hours of knife-work, of slow, deliberate blocks, slices and stabs, he was certain that he didn't know enough to defend himself yet.

'No. I'm not ready.' He stood at the back of his cell, so that

Pigface would have to come all the way in and drag him out.

'She doesn't care, and I don't care. To the pit with you.'

'Where's Stanislav? I want Stanislav.'

'The Slav's not been called for. You have.' Pigface had armed himself with a club, as well as his knife.

'I need to talk to him before I fight.'

'No. Get to the pit. She's waiting, and you don't keep her waiting.'

'Then go and get Stanislav, and you won't keep her waiting.' Dalip put his hands behind his back and planted his feet, and they stared at each other, both in shadow, one silhouetted by the door, the other limned with light from the window.

Pigface took a step towards Dalip, but it was hesitant and betrayed his weakness. It would come down to whether he wanted a fight with Dalip, risking the fight he was supposed to be putting on for the geomancer, or whether he thought he'd be able to get his work done quicker by letting the prisoners dictate the terms of their imprisonment.

He muttered something under his breath, and left, heading up the corridor to Stanislav's cell, leaving Dalip's door open. He wasn't a very good gaoler at all: either that, or he was a coward and a bully, and didn't know how to take being challenged.

He heard voices. He hadn't been allowed to mix with the others at all, only Stanislav. He knew from him that Mama was diagonally opposite. Elena and Luiza were further on. The women had been put to work in the kitchen gardens he'd seen on his abortive bid for freedom. As far as Stanislav could tell, they were being treated tolerably.

Grace? No one knew where she was. She didn't appear to be a prisoner with them, though she could have been somewhere else in the castle. Perhaps she never made it this far: taken by some creature with sharp teeth, or fallen by accident and he'd passed her by within shouting distance.

Perhaps she was dead. It was impossible to know. Pigface

seemed to not only know nothing, but also lack the curiosity to find out.

The cell doors were barred with a plank of wood that fitted into hasps on the far side, preventing them from opening. Dalip took the bar from where Pigface had laid it against the wall and took it back into his cell. It was too wide to be useful as a weapon, difficult to grip and swing.

He lifted it up and offered it to the window slit. It would just about fit through, and if there was a time when he'd need to conveniently lose the bar – and free the other prisoners – then he could just slide them all outside.

He returned it, just before Pigface came back around the corner, walking behind Stanislav and tapping his cosh into the palm of his hand.

'You are to fight?'

'Apparently.'

'What?'

'He hasn't said.'

Stanislav idly turned around, and in one fluid move, pinned Pigface's throat and club hand to the wall. When the guard tried for his knife with his off-hand, Stanislav pushed his forearm harder against the man's Adam's apple.

'We need to know before he goes in the pit.'

Pigface couldn't turn his head, couldn't swallow, couldn't speak. He just made a little gasping noise from somewhere inside.

'What animal does the boy have to fight?'

Pigface's lips moved, but they were starting to turn blue.

'If you kill him,' said Dalip, 'Actually I don't know what'll happen if you kill him.'

'We might get someone with some balls. That would make things more difficult for us.' Stanislav released his hold and Pigface staggered away, wheezing and cupping his neck with his hand.

'You're crazy,' he gasped. 'You're mad.'

'Yes, all of us,' said Dalip. 'We're more trouble than we're worth.'

Pigface coughed and leant against the wall. 'She's waiting. You're late.'

'What does the boy have to fight?' said Stanislav again. 'Are you going to tell me, or do I beat it out of you?'

Pigface held up his hand to ward him off. 'Boar. There's a boar.'

'A ... what?' Dalip looked askance.

'Pig. Wild pig. Strong. Dangerous.'

'I know what it is. But I'm fighting a pig?'

'No, a boar.' Stanislav ignored Pigface and walked slowly back to Dalip. 'They are difficult opponents. Their vital organs are deep in their bodies, under many layers of fat and muscle. A knife will not be enough to kill it.'

'But a pig?'

'It will open your belly and root around in your guts if you let it. It has teeth like razors and is angry, always angry. It is your opponent and you must treat it with respect.'

Dalip conceded the point. 'Okay. But if a knife's too short, what do I use?'

'In old times, a spear. Big one, broad. With something to stop the boar pushing down the shaft and attacking you, even as it dies.' Stanislav raised his eyebrows. 'You see?'

'Right.' It wasn't a pig, then, all pink and squealy.

'A knife is all you get, lion man,' said Pigface, pushing past.

He ended up pressed against the wall again.

'Find him something longer,' said Stanislav.

'I'm not allowed,' he grunted. 'She said so.'

'What else did she say?' Stanislav tightened his grip. He had no hesitation in inflicting pain on the man. 'Tell us.'

The confusion that washed through Pigface's little button eyes almost provoked sympathy from Dalip. It wasn't supposed to be this way, with prisoners assaulting their guards with impunity.

'The knife is all he gets. Ever. She wants him to be afraid. Terrified. That's what she wants.'

'Why?'

'I don't know why. "Make him afraid," she told me. "Make him think he's going to die," she said. She's not going to tell me her plans, is she?'

Stanislav let go, and deliberately wiped his hands on his boilersuit.

'The man that is with her. The one with the silver cane. Who is he?'

'He's ...' Then Pigface checked himself. 'I don't answer to you.'

All it took was for Stanislav to take step closer, and the guard brought up his club to defend himself.

'Who is he?'

'He does everything for her.'

'Does he have a name?'

'He's the steward. We just call him "sir".'

Stanislav sighed. 'I expect you do, you worthless pig-faced coward. Go. Go and do what you have to do.'

Pigface shuffled away, and they watched him go to the end of the corridor, turn right towards the guard room.

'Why does she want you scared?' asked Stanislav.

'Because I stood up to her. Now she wants to break me.' Dalip squared his shoulders. 'I ...'

'All men break, eventually. There is no shame in that. All men: there is no one who ever lived who could not be taken beyond what they could endure. Now, this boar. It will try to knock you down and gore you. Stay on your feet and away from its head. The front end is very dangerous. When you get the chance you must stab it in the arse.'

Dalip blinked. 'I have to do what?'

'Stab it in the arse. It will bleed to death quickly. It may even take just one blow.' He shrugged. 'It is what wolves do. Attack from behind, rip out its arse.'

'You have got to be joking.'

'No,' said Stanislav. 'This is no joke. Wild boar can kill people. If you do not wish to be one of them, then you must—'

'Stab it in the arse. I get it.'

'Do not hesitate.' He put a hand on Dalip's back and began to guide him down towards the pit. 'Show no fear. Now we know that is what she wants, the less she gets of it, the more you will hurt her.'

'Right.' Dalip's mouth had gone dry, and his palms sweaty. He waved them down by his sides to dry them. He could hear a commotion from the guard room: raised voices, something banging against heavy wood, and a most awful, high-pitched shrieking that cut straight through his resolve and left it in tatters.

'Remember: it is nothing but a brute animal. It will act on instinct, while you can out-think it.'

Dalip wasn't so sure. The dog had been one thing, sprung on him almost before he'd had time to work out what he was going to do. This was different – this was deliberate, planned, and he was a willing participant, no matter how much his situation had forced him into it. He was growing almost light-headed.

'Breathe, boy. Breathe slow and deep.'

That was it. He was hyperventilating. He caught himself and put his hand to his chest so he could count the space between inhaling and exhaling.

He was in the drum-shaped pit, and the geomancer and her steward were looking keenly at him, trying to gauge just how close he was to begging. He wasn't going to do that. Not today. He breathed in, counted to five, breathed out. Stanislav was with him, staring belligerently up through narrowed eyes at the woman.

She leaned over to confer with the steward, their voices too quiet to hear. He nodded and scratched at his chin thoughtfully. Dalip wondered what was more important than his fight, and possible death.

Pigface came into the pit and threw his knife down on the

ground at Dalip's feet. He was sweating as much as Dalip was.

'This one's a bit lively, if you take my meaning. We'll be having pork one way or another tonight.' He was more confident now, with others behind him, backing him up.

Dalip scooped up the knife, even though he could barely hold on to the haft. He clenched his fist over and over.

'If the boy kills it,' said Stanislav, 'it should be his to give to whoever he wants. His risk, his reward.'

'His reward is that he lives, Slav.'

'And what is your reward, Pigface? The chance to be a bully?' Stanislav spat at him, the gobbet of saliva arcing through the air and landing squarely on Pigface's boots.

'I should—'

'Make me lick it off? Yes. You should. But you are powerless.' He jerked his head at the geomancer. 'She is the only reason we are still here.'

'Stanislav?' said Dalip.

He ended his confrontation with the guard with a dismissive gesture, and turned to Dalip.

'You will be fine.' He slapped his big hands on Dalip's shoulders, nearly causing him to drop the knife. 'Remember to move, to strike, to finish it quickly. It will charge you: when it is past, then it is vulnerable.'

'I can't do this.'

'You can and you will.' Stanislav grabbed him by the back of the neck and pulled him close so that their foreheads were touching. 'This will be over in less than a minute. Then we can continue to plan our escape.'

Dalip nodded, and watched the man's broad back disappear through the door. Pigface was directing two other men, shoving a rickety crate towards the pit. The crate was shuddering and jerking side to side with each lunge of the dark shape within: the shrieks of the boar and the taunts and slaps of the men combined to create an unholy cacophony.

The crate was pushed through the door. One of the men took a crowbar to the planks, while his mate stood outside the door, hand poised on the latch.

Dalip took one last opportunity to wipe his hands, and resumed his grip on the knife. He bent his knees slightly, readying himself for the onslaught.

The geomancer raised her hand, glanced at the door, and it slammed shut, just as the crate began to disintegrate. A black snout jammed through the slats, forcing them apart. When it pulled back, the wood cracked and splintered.

The guard turned for the door, and if he hadn't realised it was now barred to him before, he did in that moment. He threw himself at it, scrabbling for purchase that just wasn't there and wailing to be let out.

The geomancer leaned forward, as if it was the most interesting thing she'd seen all day, and the boar, with a frenzied energy, reduced the rest of the crate to shards. It stood there for a second, quivering with rage, while it took in its new surroundings, and charged the nearest enemy.

Which wasn't Dalip.

He shouted a warning, but the man wasn't even looking in his direction. The crowbar, the only weapon the man might have feasibly used, lay forgotten on the ground, while the man banged uselessly against the thick door. He was trapped in a short tunnel with a beast that filled it widthways.

It took him down by slashing its tusks through his calves, then just kept on going, shaking its head left and right, cutting and cutting him into bloody ruin.

Dalip ran forward, over the broken remains of the crate, and just like he'd been told, rammed the knife blade up to the hilt under the boar's squirming tail. Just like he'd been told, he twisted the blade, and just like he'd been told, dragged it out sideways with as much force as he could muster.

From rooting around in the still-screaming guard's body, to

turning on Dalip, was almost instantaneous. Its sheer bulk belied a speed and agility of an animal half its size. Its head went down and it rushed him. Dalip jumped clear, springing back and sideways. It was dripping blood from its snout, but it was pumping it from the other end.

They were in the pit proper now, Dalip balanced on the balls of his feet, hand and knifeblade shining wetly red, the boar, bristles caked in gore, its deep-set eyes murderous. But nothing could disguise the thick trail of spatters and splashes that marked the stone floor.

It came at him again, slower, misstepping, uneven, and Dalip spun away again, leaping aside and letting the beast ram the wall with its thick skull.

He could have stabbed it again, in the time it took it to recover, but he backed away, carefully avoiding the sticky ribbons of blood on the ground.

The boar limped around, breathing heavily, trembling with effort now, not with anger. It staggered, its forelegs slipping underneath it. It rose and made a drunkard's walk towards Dalip, who circled away, forcing it to follow.

Halfway around, it sagged to the floor, shivered all over, and didn't move again, save for the slight rise and fall of its ribs. Once. Twice. Then nothing.

Dalip kept a wary distance, and closed on it from the rear. There wasn't much blood left to pool, but what there was shone thickly around its hindquarters. He prodded it with the outstretched knife, pushing the point into its hairy back, through the skin and into the fat below.

The boar didn't move, and he thought it safe to assume it was dead.

The guard, on the other hand, was weeping as he tried to hold his wounds together. In the shadow of the tunnel, Dalip found it impossible to tell where clothing finished and flesh started. Both were bloodied rags.

'Why? Why?' the guard sobbed.

Dalip didn't know, beyond naked barbarism and utter contempt for life. The man couldn't be moved – he screamed in agony when Dalip tried – and perhaps with modern medicine and a team of doctors, he might have survived. Scarred inside and out for certain, but alive nevertheless.

He died too, slowly, sadly, knowing he was going, sliding inexorably into darkness and terrified of it. He died clutching at Dalip's forearm, and only let go when he slid to one side, awkwardly trapping his head in the angle between the wall and the door. Not that he cared any more about comfort.

Dalip walked back out into the pit and stood centre stage. He threw the knife down and looked up at the geomancer, dressed in her finery.

'Are we done here now?' he shouted at her. 'Are we?'

'Yes,' she said, and stood, adjusting her skirts, readying herself to leave. The steward tapped his silver-tipped cane against the balcony, in annoyance or impatience or just out of habit, and scowled at Dalip.

Who bent down and caught up as much blood as he could off the floor, before flinging it up at his captors.

Most of it either fell back or flecked the high walls of the pit. But one or two drops reached their targets. The steward stiffened as something touched his cheek, and the geomancer saw it without knowing her back had its own darkly shining jewel clinging to the fine fabric.

'There. That's your share of this butchery.'

He stared up, his bloody hands raised to them, while they stared down. Whatever they were expecting, they got defiance, not supplication. They got his red palms and drying scabs instead of his fear.

They still left, and he had to drop his arms by his side at some point. He hung his head, and went to pull the body out of the way of the blocked door.

19

Mary made the top of the last rise. Even at a distance, the gorge that divided the two peaks was discernible. The base of each mountain was forested, like most of Down that she'd seen so far, but higher up where the slopes grew steeper, bare grey rock dominated. The peaks, facing each other over the chasm, were high but rounded, scraped clean by the wind and the rain.

She still couldn't see the geomancer's castle which, Crows assured her, was behind the rightmost peak, tucked in a hollow with a lake.

Crows puffed up behind her. 'We should turn back before it is too late.'

'Shut it, Crows,' she said. Between them and the gorge was uninterrupted forest, and this was the last chance she had to get her bearings and see if there was a different route. But the best choice seemed to be the simplest: meet the river that bisected the mountains, then climb up past the gorge to the very top, where they could look down on the castle unseen. It looked like hard going, with a lot of scrambling over loose rock especially just below the summit, but far from impossible. By going for the more difficult ascent, she hoped to avoid anyone guarding the way from the valley up the lea side of the slope.

The sun was creeping lower to the horizon, and the moon would only rise halfway through the night: enough to hide her once she was in position, and enough to let her climb down while it was still dark.

She took one final look and pointed her toes in the direction they needed to go, angling down the ridge and heading for the start of the gorge. The forest covered her, and she tried to keep to the right path, even though she'd lost all her landmarks.

She seemed to be doing this all by herself. Crows was dragging his feet, and she was fed up of waiting for him. She'd given him the option of not coming, and he'd said he'd take her to where she'd be able to see the castle. She understood he didn't want to get closer, but he should at least keep his promise, and without complaining every step of the way.

And then, almost on cue, she heard a wolf howl. She stopped and rolled her eyes.

'Just what we needed.' She didn't know if it was the wolfman, or a regular wild wolf, but actually, she did know. She didn't even have to bet herself which it was.

Crows drew level with her, and licked his lips nervously.

'We can avoid him, right?' she asked. 'Like we did before?'

'Perhaps someone else has come through the portal. If so, he's far away, and not looking for us. If not, he could still be looking for you. He doesn't hunt on his own, Mary. Ever.'

'He did that first night. It was just him.'

Crows shook his head. 'No. The forest would have been full of them. When you moved off, they followed you. When you started questioning the wisdom of where you were going, they attacked you. The wolfman is never on his own: he is scared of Down, scared of its spaces and its silences, scared of being alone and scared of not being owned. He joined with the geomancer to stop himself going mad, and he lives in fear of her sending him away.'

'Oh. Okay. Let's hope he's after some other poor bastard then, and not us. At least for now.'

She checked the direction of the sun through the canopy of leaves, and set off in what she guessed was the right direction, which was downhill. They reached the river, and walked upstream alongside it – there was no need to go all the way down to it, just keep it on their left. Then uphill towards the clear, bare rock beyond the forest.

The ground bent upwards, and the trees began to sprout from between weathered boulders and moss-covered outcrops of stone. Soon the river was below them, rumbling away between the walls of the deepening gorge. The wolf howled again, plaintive and symbolic in a land devoid of human habitation, a wilderness made more wild by desolation.

The vegetation stopped abruptly at a steep ledge. Above it, there was no cover, nothing to mask her from view. She was, of course, still wearing orange.

Down's gifts only seemed to run to buildings, not clothing. She almost turned back then, realising what a stupid thing she was doing, and that any half-blind idiot would be able to spot her, the only splash of colour pinned to a mountainside. Then again, if she could draw down darkness and make fog, could she camouflage herself with what she had around her?

There was only one way to find out. She stooped down and collected a double-handful of dry, brittle leaves, all browns and dark reds. She knew what she wanted, and she could see it in her mind.

A cloak like Crows', not black and ragged, but the colours of nature, muted and ending beyond the edges of the cloth so that it looked like a storm of leaves, continually moving and changing.

She threw the leaves she held up in the air, and let them fall around her. She scooped up more and cast them backwards over her.

And when she straightened, it was done. She was wearing a shifting mirage of browns and greens and reds which trailed out behind her and flowed over her arms. She brought her hands together, and the folds of the cloak closed over her orange boiler-suit, concealing it beneath the fluttering, rustling cloth.

It wasn't her, and was still part of her. Like the hem which had no definite beginning or end, neither did she now. No longer isolated and self-contained, she was growing into the landscape as it was growing into her. Let the wolfman and his gang find her now.

'You should go more slowly,' said Crows, puffing up behind her.

'We're not going to get there if we don't get a move on.' She gazed up at the steep slope, and tried to work out her route.

'That is not what I meant.' He too tilted his head back, scanning the sky. 'You know how dangerous magic is. If you do not control it, it will control you. I have seen the results and they are not good.'

'I can handle it, okay?'

'Being lucky once does not make you invulnerable.'

'I know that. Crows, you're not my social worker, all right?'

'Am I correct in thinking you did not listen to them either?'

She gave him the look, and he turned away, holding his hands up in mock surrender.

'You are free to destroy yourself in any way you see fit. Just that it would be a waste, that is all.'

The wolf howled again. It seemed closer, but that could have been her imagination.

'It's almost like you care,' she said. 'What about those people who you were supposed to be protecting?'

'Mary, they are not here. You are.'

'They don't stop existing. They're still there, locked away in her castle. They're people like you and me, who were running from something terrifying: they ended up here and tried to make the best of it. They don't deserve this any more than my lot do.'

'The strong do as they want, and the weak suffer what they must. I cannot protect them: I built myself up for a role I could not fulfil. Now, we all suffer, they in their prison and me in my ruin.'

'Fucking hell, you sound like me, and I sound like someone else. Things change, Crows, and there's no reason why we can't make them change.'

'Strong words. Perhaps once you have seen her castle, once you have seen her, you will realise how pointless all this is.' He swirled his own cloak about him, gathering the darkness and blotting himself out for a moment before reappearing as the cloth settled again.

'Maybe I will. There's no harm in looking, is there?'

'Yes, there is. We are deep in her territory, almost up to her door. If you think there is no risk in this, then why are we hearing the wolf's howl?'

Mary pushed her hair away from her face. It felt tangled and greasy, and her scalp itched. Perhaps Crows did have a point, but she was certain she did too. She wasn't doing this blind, but naively? She shrugged.

'Is there any way of working out whether the wolfman's hunting us?'

'Only by finding him before he finds us. Which is not very wise.'

'So let's get on with it.' She clambered up, and turned to look at the last rays of the sun touch the crowns of the trees. She had no idea where this sudden courage had come from. First sign of danger and she'd always run. And sometimes not fast enough.

Crows was still below her. 'You may go if you wish,' he said. 'I have done my duty, and I will go no further.'

'Shit, Crows, what is wrong with you?'

'Whatever follows, you cannot say that you were not warned.' He flapped his cloak a second time and was gone.

'Well, fuck you too.' She set her jaw hard, and turned back to the ascent.

The summit was above her, and close up it was now clear that gaining it wouldn't be straightforward. The direct route took in at least two bands of loose scree and a vertical cliff just below the top, where the rock had broken away and tumbled down into the forest beneath. To her left was a steep incline that merged with the sheer side of the gorge, and only to the right did the mountain become easier to navigate.

She didn't want to climb in the pitch black, so she started off again, zigzagging up rather than confronting the whole edifice at once.

She worked her way around to the shoulder of rock that sloped down from the summit, scaling the last ridge in the last of the light. She was almost there, a few more steps and she'd be on the very top. It didn't seem at all likely, the girl from the tower blocks, on a mountain, exhausted, exhilarated.

The view opened up to take in what looked like the whole world. At her back were seas without end, at her front, a mountain range so tall that the snow didn't carry all the way to the top. Left and right were bays and islands, and everywhere between was cut with rivers and leavened with lesser peaks and hills. Up on the darkening mountain, her leaf cape was now redundant. She discarded it, and unlike Crows', hers caught the gusty wind and came apart, leaves separating and spiralling away, chasing each other across the bare rock like children.

The last sliver of reflected sunlight died in the sky, and it was night. With no stars to appear, she was left entirely unsighted, at least until moonrise. She couldn't tell where the mountain ended or began. She realised that if she took a step anywhere, she might end up broken at the bottom of the gorge, or bouncing down the way she'd come in an avalanche of loose rock.

She crouched, felt around her, and sat down. She wouldn't have that long to wait for the moonglow to begin glimmering on the underside of the clouds far away on the horizon. A couple of hours before the massive moon ground into view and thundered across the heavens.

While she sat, aware of the unseen vastness around her, she began to see things. Flashes of light where there were none, trails of luminescence in the sky, bright sparks dancing around her: none of it was real, and yet it didn't matter. She'd never experienced anything like it before, and it was her reward.

The land turned silver, and the lights were gone. The moon hung low, a huge half-circle of white bone carving its way into the night sky. The illumination it gave was nothing compared to the majesty of the full moon, but it was not just sufficient, it was generous.

She picked herself up now that she could see. The crystals embedded in the rock made it twinkle like frost, and she could skip over the puddles of shadow towards the far side of the mountain. As she jumped from high point to high point, she could see an edge forming ahead of her. She slowed, and stepped cautiously. She could see into the valley below, but not the slope that led there.

Eventually, she was crawling on her stomach. It was a cliff, high and long. It swept down the mountainside to form a huge bowl of land that was itself perched halfway between summit and river. At the bottom of the bowl was a lake, and next to the lake, the geomancer's castle.

Like Crows', it had a ring wall, but it was no mere collection of stones thrust out from the ground. This wall was tall and broad, set with gates and towers. Inside were various squat buildings, and two towers, one broad and short, the other tall and thin, with a roof that pointed upwards like a wooden rocket.

Fires lit the yard, and plumes of silver-lit smoke drifted away in spirals. She was close enough to see the shadows of the men around the largest fire, black shapes against the orange of the fire glow, but too far away to catch any of the sound they made.

The castle was large and impressive. It was guarded both by walls and by people. The central tower had commanding views over both within and without, down the mountain and beyond.

The ground immediately outside the castle was bare, and unless she learnt to fly – unless she learnt that she could fly – the geomancer would get plenty of warning of anyone approaching.

She looked harder. The gates were pointing at the lake and toward the valley, which left a lot of the wall nothing but blank stone all the way to the battlements. There didn't seem to be anyone patrolling them, either. She'd known warehouses like that, where security had a warm cabin and control of the CCTV, which they sometimes even watched when they weren't reading a paper or napping in their chair.

If no one was watching, it made getting in and out easier: only the physical barriers would cause a problem. But once she was in, what could she do? Even if she managed to sneak in, find Dalip, Mama and the others, where would they go? Back to Crows' castle if they could. If the wolfman and his crew came looking for them there, they'd just have to have moved on first.

It wasn't a great plan. It was barely a plan at all. And it'd be far easier with Crows' help than his recurring lament that he'd already fought his battle and lost.

The wind on top of the mountain was starting to batter her and make her cold. She decided that she'd go away and think about things again. She had one last look, and the more she looked, the less likely it seemed that she'd be able to get anyone out at all. Maybe one or two, if they were quick and quiet, hidden beneath shadow-cloaks woven from her own fingers.

That wasn't going to be good enough, though. She wanted everybody: her lot, and anyone else who would come, free of the person who'd enslaved them.

She glanced behind before she backed up.

And saw a dragon, perched on a rock near the summit, staring at her with its hard, black-marble eyes.

There was nowhere to run to, and nowhere to hide. The only way down the mountain not barred by a giant winged lizard was straight over the cliff.

'Fuck. Me.'

Crows hadn't warned her about this possibility, and he really should have. Or perhaps he had, and she hadn't been listening. Though casually mentioning that there might be dragons ought to have got her undivided attention. It flexed its wings and blotted out the half-moon. The gust of wind it caused raised a hail of grit, and she had to blink it out of her eyes.

Its scales glinted in the silver light as it loosely folded its wings against its sinuous body. Its two clawed feet rasped against the joints of the stones, and its snake-like head danced on its neck, tasting the air with its tongue.

She placed her hands firmly on the rock and shuffled around on her knees to face the beast. She had no idea what to do. The East End had many dangers. Massive fuck-off dragons wasn't one of them.

Perhaps it would just fly away. Perhaps it didn't see her as food, and if she wove a shadow-cloak around herself and crawled away, it'd leave her alone. Perhaps it was a tame dragon, and she could coo to it until it let her scratch it behind its ears. She couldn't see any ears, though. Its head was smooth and dart-shaped.

In the absence of anything else to try, she swallowed hard against the brick in her throat.

'Good dragon?' She knelt up, very slowly, holding her palms out in what she hoped was a calming, non-threatening way. She was a fair way away from it, and if it got lairy, she could stop and back up again.

The dragon opened its mouth very wide and lunged at her. Its teeth were like rows of knives, except for the incisors, which were swords. It covered the distance between them in a single leap, and its jaws snapped shut, just where her hands would have been if she hadn't snatched them back and dropped to the ground.

Not a friendly dragon, then.

Its head wound back in, coiled for another strike, and she still had nowhere to go. Her hand closed on a frost-edged shard of stone that cut into her fingers as she instinctively picked it up. The dragon's mouth gaped wide and she threw the rock, as hard as she could. She didn't think she could miss from that range, but she did. It sailed out of sight, over the creature's head, and again she had to press herself to the mountain to avoid being swallowed whole.

It seemed surprised that it hadn't got her, impaled on its teeth. Not as surprised as Mary was. The next time for sure.

It flapped its great wings again, rising into the air and battering her with a gale that almost hurled her over the edge. She grabbed another saucer-sized chunk of rock from the ground and half rose from her crouch.

And just when the dragon was settling again, claws closing against the loose surface, head rearing back and wings cupping the air, there was a clatter of falling stones from behind that distracted it.

It twisted sharply around, fearing an attack and, in that moment, Mary stretched her legs like a sprinter from the blocks. The moonlight wasn't sufficient for what she was going to do, but she didn't have a choice. No matter that she was on top of a mountain, she was going to die if she stayed there a second longer. She ducked under the outstretched wing and ran.

It was downhill all the way. She could feel the wind in her face, the wind at her back, and the roaring in her ears was either the speed she was moving at or the dragon's displeasure. Whichever, she was going too fast to stop, the ground bending away from her feet and forcing her to take larger and larger strides.

She realised her descent was out of control at the same time she knew she couldn't choose to avoid the drop-off formed by a ledge of rock. She'd climbed up it on the way. She knew how high it was. She could only guess how much it was going to hurt on the way down.

She sort-of-jumped, arms and legs wheeling. She landed in the scree beneath it, feet first but overbalancing. Then she was over. The mountain rose up and smashed her in the face.

It hurt, but more disorientating was seeing the land and sky becoming interchangeable. Moon and mountain passed each other. With each rotation, the dragon hanging above her grew closer, a silver outline against a black sky.

She stopped, eventually, abruptly, catching herself around a boulder like a ragdoll, all the air in her lungs forced out by the impact. The shadow deepened around her in a rush, and her back opened up to cold air and hot blood.

The most remarkable thing was that she was still alive enough to register the pain. She reached up a ragged hand and pushed herself away from her anchoring rock, rolling over and staring at the darkness of the sky and vastness of the moon.

Apart from her own heart, she could hear the steady pulse of beating wings. The dragon was coming around again. This was it. Could she stand? Could she work out how? Nothing seemed to be responding properly. She had one arm, one hand, and the rest seemed useless.

Not like this. She turned over again, on to her front, and somehow managed to wedge a knee under her. Here it came, all night and teeth, and she was determined she would face it. As she half-rose, because that was as much as she was able to manage, the stones of the mountain rose with her.

The dragon, full of pomp and arrogance, checked its advance, uncertain as to the threat. Mary didn't dare look away, in case the slowly turning rocks fell. If this was her doing, then breaking her concentration as well as her bones would be the end of her.

Whatever instinct or intelligence drove the dragon on told it that it would come to no harm. It bent its head low and clawed at the ground, then rushed her.

She willed the rocks to stop its charge, and they flew at it, a solid storm of stone, battering its scales and membranous wings. The dragon stumbled and fell, and still the stones kept coming. It turned, lashed its tail, and ran.

The rattle of falling stones like rain marked the end of her resistance. She was alone in a world that was not hers, more than half-dead, halfway up a mountain she'd just fallen down.

'Enough,' she said. 'Enough.'

20

Something had changed, possibly because the guards now realised that they were no more valuable, and no more protected, than the prisoners they were keeping. The man who'd died – Dalip heard him referred to as 'Charlie' or 'Old Charlie' – had been, if not well liked, not so unpopular that his singling out by the geomancer made any sense. His fate could have been theirs: they knew it, and resented it.

The harsh regime the prisoners had been kept under relaxed by degrees. Inside the cell block, the individual cells were only barred at night. They could talk to each other freely outside those times, as long as it didn't interfere with their chores. The women were made to work in the vegetable plots inside the walls, fetching and carrying water, doing laundry in vats of boiling water, from sunrise to sunset. It was back-breaking, exhausting labour that would have been hard if it had been done for themselves or with the promise of pay.

Neither Stanislav nor Dalip were compelled to join in. The pit was deemed sufficient for them, but, led by the older man, they turned up every morning to do their share. Hoots of derision had joined the slaps and kicks which had been common enough to begin with. They tailed off as the prisoners got used to their roles. And now, a week later, casual violence was mostly redundant. Of course, the guards weren't going to boil washing or weed between rows of cabbages. Then again, they'd thought they weren't going to die in the pit either. That they might made them realise the geomancer didn't care about them one way or the other: prisoners, guards, they were all the same in her mind.

The threat and the promise was that the regime grew to be normal, when it was anything but. Their lives consisted of mean meals, hard physical labour, beatings and captivity.

Dalip was with Stanislav in the pit, training with short wooden sticks instead of knives.

'We must rebel. While the memory of Charlie's death remains fresh,' said Stanislav.

'Before my next fight?'

'Your next fight will be against something that you cannot hope to defeat. Remember that you are supposed to be scared. You are not. You are simply too angry at her to be scared. That is why she shut Charlie in with the boar. He was scared when you were not.'

'But I was scared,' Dalip protested.

'She does not want ordinary frightened. She wants you to experience such terror that you piss yourself and run screaming for the door. You will not give her that, whatever they put in here with you.'

'Don't be so sure.'

'And if it is the dragon?'

Dalip thought about that. They had all seen it early on: almost as if it had made a show of itself. Then it had been conspicuous by its absence. The sky above the castle was strangely blank without it. But the gates had remained open, and the guard not reinforced. It was still around, that was certain.

'Well, maybe,' he conceded. He ought to be terrified of it, but he was already thinking of ways of cutting it, if only he could get close enough.

Stanislav lowered his stick, not in a feint or a ruse, but in a way that meant they were no longer sparring. 'Undress,' he said, and when Dalip hesitated, he grunted: 'Just do it.'

Dalip dropped his stick at his feet and wrestled the heavy zip down to his navel, then shucked the top half of his boilersuit. He pushed it down to his knees, and straightened up.

'Look,' said Stanislav. He walked around Dalip. 'Look at yourself.'

Reluctantly, he did so. It was him. It was still him. Yes, he had visible muscles now, even at rest. He had broadened, and he stood taller even if he hadn't actually grown.

'This. This should not have happened. Not this quickly. Training, yes, over weeks and months, to make you strong and fast, will bring about such changes. Not days.' He stood in front of Dalip, his hands on his hips, appraising him. 'There is something else at work here.'

'I just thought ...'

'You thought wrong. It is this place, with its wolves and its dragons and whatever else.' He looked pensive for a moment, disturbed even. 'I thought this was a new start. For all of us. Perhaps it would be better if we just went home, yes?'

He jerked his head, and Dalip pulled the boilersuit back on. They were still alone, and Stanislav took up a place under the geomancer's balcony.

'Let us make use of this gift you have been given,' he said, and crouched down, feet planted wide, forearms on his thighs and hands cupped. 'Go and stand by the wall opposite.'

When he was ready, he nodded.

Dalip understood what was required of him. He pushed himself off the wall and started his run-up. Speed was good: he needed forward momentum, but what he wanted was height. Timing was everything.

He lightly jumped off one bare foot and pressed the other firmly into Stanislav's already rising hands. He straightened his leg and swept his arms up. He was flying. He clawed his fingers, caught the edge of the balcony, and the rest of his body smacked hard against the stone. The impact tore him loose, and he bent his knees before he broke his legs.

Stanislav grunted his irritation. 'You must hold on.'

'I can't. I don't think anyone could. I haven't got a grip of anything at all, and when I hit the wall, my hands just slide off.'

'Is there nothing you can hold?'

'The top of the wall's too wide. If,' he said, staring at his target, 'I went straight up, I could hang there, but then I'd have to pull myself the rest of the way.'

'You can do that.'

'Yes, and the steward would be hitting me with his cane all the time. And she: we have no idea what she can do.'

Stanislav scratched at his chin, where a white beard was showing through.

'Can you go higher?'

'Can you throw me harder? And move a bit away from the wall. Ideally, I'd want to hit the top when I wasn't rising or falling. If I can get my elbows on it, I can push myself up and over, before they can react.'

They took up their new positions. Dalip would have to run faster now, and timing was critical. The first time, he was too tentative, and missed the wall completely. The second time, he left it too late.

When they'd both picked themselves off the ground and thought about blaming each other for their bruises, they tried again.

'Concentrate,' said Stanislav.

Dalip bit back what he was thinking, that this was all too much like school except there, if he'd failed a chemistry test no one would have had him killed.

'Just, just do your bit.' He bared his teeth in a grimace and launched himself at the tiny sweet spot contained within Stanislav's hands.

His heel connected and he pushed off hard. At the same time, he was propelled upwards. If he missed this, it was going to hurt.

He reached up, always closing on the wall. Then his head could see over. He bent his elbows, spread his fingers wide like nets, and slammed them on top of the parapet. He was still moving forward. He was almost bent double over the wall before his legs hit it. He started to go backwards, and no matter how much he scrabbled, his weight was always off balance, always dragging him down.

He slipped down the face of the wall with a gasp of disgust and landed in a heap at the bottom.

'You had it,' said Stanislav, standing over him.

'I know I had it! You don't need to tell me I got it wrong. I know I got it wrong.' He angrily waved away an attempt to pull him upright, and got to his own two feet. 'Again.'

'Tomorrow.'

'No. Now. We practise until I can do it.'

'But can you do it?'

'Yes.' Dalip was breathing heavily, and his humility regained momentary control. 'Eventually.'

Stanislav chewed at his already bleeding lip. 'Okay. Again.'

He didn't manage it the next time either. The same thing happened. Almost, then he lost his grip on the smooth stone and the sharp edges. He couldn't judge how many attempts he had left in him. He was tired. His legs hurt. He felt like he'd banged his ribs one too many times. And Stanislav couldn't keep this up all day.

One more, then stop. Two more, then he'd slink back to his cell and lick his wounds.

He pressed his back to the wall on the far side of the pit, one foot against the stone work. Stanislav readied himself, gave him the nod, and tensed.

Dalip ran: step, step, step, then jump. He connected clean. He was in the air, and rather than trying to stay upright, he brought a knee up, turning his whole body sideways. His feet cleared the top of the wall, and he reached out with his hands, slapping the stonework as it passed underneath him.

He hit it hard, and rolled.

This time he didn't fall far, just at the feet of the geomancer's empty throne. He lay there for a moment, quiet and still, checking that he'd actually done it, and that he was alone.

The circular balcony wasn't that deep, enough room for him to fit between the parapet and the chair, and the same space behind it. He could see a door, set into the wall in front of him. He pulled himself up and looked down at Stanislav. He glanced up, circled his finger and thumb for an okay, and purposefully stared in the direction of the pit door, which was merely ajar.

He wouldn't have long. He circumnavigated the narrow balcony with its low ceiling, found no surprises, and ended up back at the only door. It was closed with a latch, which he lifted very slowly. He pushed, inching the door away from the jamb, listening at the crack he'd made for any sounds from the other side. The hinges groaned, and he ceased all movement. Nothing. No sudden clatter or shout of alarm.

He dared himself to push a little more, when he heard Stanislav's extravagant throat-clearing. They hadn't agreed on a warning, but it couldn't be anything but. No one must know that he could escape the pit, until the moment he did so. Dalip pulled the door shut and sprinted for the edge. He lay on the top of the parapet, and swung himself over. His nervous fingers slid, and he fell the rest of the distance to the floor, which was where Pigface found him.

He turned his gaze between Dalip and Stanislav with an expression of disdain. Nothing was out of the ordinary. Dalip looked like he was resting, propped up against the wall. Stanislav had his stick in his hand, as if berating the boy for being weak. He snorted, and turned his back on them.

'You've had enough for one day,' he said.

'We decide that,' said Stanislav. He threw his stick at the door, where it clattered near to Pigface's head.

'Push it too far, Slav, and I swear I'll do you.'

Stanislav shrugged, flexing his shoulders. 'Come, then. It will end up as before, with my hand on your throat and you gasping for air.'

Pigface half-turned, and hesitated.

Dalip picked himself off the floor. 'We shouldn't be fighting each other. We know who the enemy is.'

'And who's that, little lion man?'

'Your mate Charlie worked it out, didn't he?' He dusted himself down. 'I'm just sorry I wasn't quick enough to save him.'

Nor quick enough to save himself from waking up in the night, cold but sweating, as a phantom boar tore through his own guts.

Pigface took the apology with a shrug. 'Stupid bastard got himself stuck the wrong side of the door, didn't he?'

'You know that's not what happened,' said Dalip. 'She trapped him in here, held the door shut, then watched him die. Maybe you should ask her why she did that.'

Genuine fear washed over Pigface. He shuddered and shook his head.

'I'm not stupid.'

Stanislav grunted. 'No? Stupid enough not to realise that you are a slave like us. Can you leave the castle for somewhere else? No? Then you just have a better class of prison.'

Again, Pigface turned to leave, and couldn't quite bring himself to go.

'What is it? You want more?' demanded Stanislav, but Dalip waved him quiet.

'When's the next fight?' he asked.

'No one knows. She's been in her rooms, last few days. She'll tell us when it's time.'

'What about the steward, the man with the cane?'

'He's around. More than usual.'

Dalip beckoned Pigface closer. After a moment's reluctance, he crossed the pit floor, but still remembered to stand out of lunging range.

'Is this the life you want for yourself? When you ran from whatever was trying to kill you in London, and you had your new start, is this what you imagined?'

Pigface worried at the ball of his thumb with his crooked teeth and listened very carefully.

'Because this isn't what I want. I want to go back home, but if that's not possible, I won't live like this. I didn't run from the fire to become a pit-fighting slave in some witch's dungeon. Do you understand?'

The guard nodded slowly.

'You can get in the way, you can ignore us, or you can help us. Up to you. Just remember what happened to Charlie before you run off to the geomancer.' Dalip bent down and retrieved his stick. 'You're as expendable as we are.'

Pigface left the room this time, shoulders slumped, back bent.

'It will not work,' said Stanislav. 'I have met men like that before. They are broken. They prefer living in their own shit than the trouble of cleaning themselves off.'

'If we don't have to fight them too, it'll be easier. Easier still if they're with us.'

'You cannot count on Pigface, or any of the others. Our plan will not include them because they will let us down.' Stanislav punctuated his speech with finger-jabs into Dalip's chest.

He knocked the man's hand away. 'I don't know where you get this from, but not everybody is a ...'

'Bastard? There are two kinds of men. Corruptible bastards and incorruptible bastards. That is all.'

'What are we, then?'

'We make common cause. Pigface has already shown his true self, so we do not trust him.'

'Why should I trust you, then? I mean, I don't really know

you. We just happened to be in the same shift. That, and we survived together.'

Stanislav walked away, ostensibly to retrieve his stick. He scooped it up, and idly scraped the thin end against the wall.

Dalip persisted. 'Like where did you learn to fight with a knife? Some of the things you say, they're ... hard. Like nails hard.'

'My history is the other side of the door, and that is where it will stay. The wolfman was right when he told us all that matters is what we do now. You ask me to help you train, yes? How and why I can do that, is something you do not need to ask.'

Dalip wanted to know. He wanted to know how a railway engineer with an Eastern European accent and a better command of English than most English people knew which end of a pig to stick with a knife. He also didn't want to know, because none of the scenarios that he was constructing were ones in which Stanislav had been a good, decent man. By not knowing the truth, he didn't have to make a decision.

And, he discovered, he was content with that.

'I'm sorry,' he said. 'It's none of my business.'

'That is not true. However, it is not relevant for now. When we have killed the geomancer, her dragon and her steward, freed the slaves and escaped from the castle, then perhaps we can talk more.' Stanislav raised his stick. 'One more bout.'

'I'm tired.'

'You think that matters to your enemies? You think they will wait while you have a little sleep, a meal? When you can fight exhausted better than they can fresh – then we can stop.'

Dalip ached. He was tired and hungry and dirty. His hair, normally washed and combed every morning, was a bound rope thick with oils. His boilersuit was becoming stiff with sweat and dirt. His kachera ... he was ashamed of them. He should be clean. It was one of his sacred duties.

And this man, this gadfly, wouldn't let him rest. Dalip wasn't lazy. He worked hard, at everything, as was right and proper. A moment's respite was all he wanted.

'First strike?'

'Then make sure it counts. None of your dabbing at me.'

Dalip assumed his stance, and so did Stanislav, and they began to circle each other. Now, the older man seemed tireless: relentless would be a better word. Driven. Determined never to lose. He was the same last thing at night as he was first thing in the morning, pushing himself, and pushing Dalip. He saw any slackening of the regime as intolerable weakness.

Dabbing indeed. He'd show him dabbing.

They feinted, lunged, dodged, retreated. Dalip remembered what Stanislav had said about getting tired, and making mistakes. He was already tired, so he ought to just close and attack, but the older man was still a stronger and faster and moreover, a filthier fighter. There was nothing pure about his style – whatever worked.

Then he was aware of being watched; a slight change in the air, a presence behind and above him that Stanislav in his singular focus hadn't spotted.

In that moment, he was distracted, and his opponent struck, trying to tangle his feet and push him back against the wall. Dalip fell, but rolled out of the way before the stick poked his stomach, or his neck, or his groin, or his kidneys, or sideways into his ribs. So many ways that he was vulnerable, so many ways to be killed.

'She's here,' he said, and Stanislav, thinking it might be a trick, ignored him and tried to rush him again. In his haste, he left himself open. Dalip dropped, thrust his arm up and delivered a palpable blow that would, had it not been a blunt piece of wood, gone up under the sternum and into the heart.

It was one of the few times he'd won: it left Stanislav winded, and him with sore fingers.

'She's here,' he repeated, holding out his hand for Stanislav to grasp.

And she was.

Even by the candlelight, it looked as if she'd been beaten. Her face was battered, two black eyes, one she could barely see out of, a ragged purple cut on her pale forehead, her jaw swollen and seemingly misaligned. Her hair, normally straight and golden, was dishevelled and patchy, as if clumps of it had been cut or torn out. What could be seen of her shoulders and chest were mottled in colours from black to yellow.

She was staring down at the two men, just as they were staring up. Then she turned and left, slowly, painfully. The door up on the balcony opened, then closed again.

'Soon,' said Stanislav. 'As soon as we can. We may not get a better chance.'

21

She dragged herself back to the castle. At times, it was literally that: when her legs were too tired, too painful to use, she'd pulled herself from one tree to the next. Her back – why did it have to be her back where she couldn't see – felt strange. Numb one minute, burning the next. If she knew anything about dragons, which she didn't because how could she, she guessed that whatever wounds she had were infected, and that she was going to die soon.

Which was, she considered, a fucking stupid way to go. Not that she wanted to go at all. She was eighteen and everything that life had so far thrown at her, and everything she'd thrown at life, had taught her that she was immortal. Stupid, irresponsible, impulsive, angry, alone: but immortal all the same. No matter what she did, no matter how much trouble she got herself into, nothing was actually going to kill her.

Not even the fire that drove her to Down. She'd watched other people die in flames, but it hadn't claimed her.

And now she was going to get blood poisoning, like some skanky needle-marked junkie. Unless Crows showed up and helped her.

She'd shouted for him. Softly, because she didn't want her

voice to carry as far as a wolf's cry, but he never came.

Eventually, after stumbling and falling and crawling and rising, she recognised where she was, and spotted the unfinished crown of Crows' tower through the forest. She hoped he'd be there. She was still hoping when she passed under the gateway that hadn't been there when she'd left. She still hoped when she banged her little fist against the dark stained wood of the door, which also hadn't been there before.

But the door opened slightly with her knocking, and she knew he wasn't there.

It didn't stop her from shouting for him.

'Crows, you bastard. Why didn't you tell me about the fucking dragon? Crows? Crows!'

He didn't come, and she slumped against the door frame, immediately falling forward because she knocked the cuts on her back. The waves of pain left her on her hands and knees, gasping and nauseous.

She could feel fresh blood leaking down her sides, soaking into what remained of her boilersuit. She needed water. She wouldn't feel so dizzy, so exhausted, if she drank more than the few scooped handfuls she'd managed from tiny, earthy-tasting rivulets. And she needed food, whatever she could find. Most of all she needed the pain to subside so that she could move again.

When she woke up, she was face down on the cold, hard stone and the shaft of sunlight through the open door had moved around. Her lips were dry, her mouth parched, her tongue stuck. She almost choked as she gasped, and her coughing was enough to make her whole body ache.

The rest, enforced and reluctant, had helped. She could now creep on all fours back out of the door – with difficulty as she seemed to blunder and sway into either the wall or the door as she tried to pass through – and across the pavement towards the spring.

It had, like the gate and the door, improved itself. From

the trough that had contained the run of water before, it had become a circular pool. The water poured out of a stone spout at one side, and out again at the other, into a gutter that carried it through the now-impressive wall.

Even though she knew she shouldn't, once she'd drunk her fill of cold, clear spring water so that it sat heavy and potent in her belly, she levered herself up and slid into the pool, pushing herself up and over the rim.

She held her face just over the surface of the water, while it soaked up her arms and legs. It wasn't deep. It barely came to her elbows. But it was enough. She pressed her head down and turned it side to side, wetting her hair and scalp, watching the water tint pink in front of her wide-open eyes.

Then she rolled on to her back, spreading her arms wide and letting her body float. The water around her, constantly refreshed, gradually grew clearer as she lay there, her clothes once again becoming loose about her, rather than stuck to her skin. With her arms up, only the oval of her face – eyes, nose, mouth and chin – was above the rippling surface. She reached under for the boilersuit's zip and dragged it down, easing her arms out one at a time, and pulled it down to her waist.

It wouldn't come. It was stuck against something on her back. And yet when she tugged, it didn't hurt. It just didn't move.

The material was too tough for her to tear. She didn't have a knife, though Crows might have left something in the castle. She couldn't see her back anyway.

She gave up and tried to sit. Even that simple task seemed almost beyond her. She felt so weak, it took an age to manage upright. Something broke the water behind her, distinctly, long after she did.

She didn't dare turn around. As the coldness of the water faded and the warmth of the late afternoon air touched her, she realised that there was something clinging to her back, hanging between her shoulder blades, heavy and wet. She sat very still, screwing her eyes up so that she wasn't even tempted.

She shifted slightly, and the weight shifted with her, slow and large.

She couldn't sit there all day. She couldn't avoid whatever it was. She had no weapons, but she did have magic. What good that might be against something that held her so close without her noticing until now was only ever going to be a guess.

She opened her eyes and turned her head slightly, her gaze falling on the frayed strap of her top, her bruised brown skin, the slope of her shoulder, and the tawny ridge of feathers behind.

No hesitation now. Her head snapped around to the other shoulder, and there was another mass of mottled plumage. It didn't matter over which side she looked, the view was identical and reversed.

She had wings.

Actual wings. Sodden, bedraggled, dripping water, but they were incontrovertibly wings. They hung off her back, still and lifeless, on her and part of her, and she couldn't move them because she had no way of knowing how to move them. Which muscles should she flex, which part of her brain should she spark to trigger that? She knew how to move her fingers, her toes: she just thought about it, and it happened. But wings?

How did she even get wings? Where did they come from, and what did they mean? Was it what Crows said, about doing too much, too soon? Had she become so infested with magic that it was breaking out, changing her without asking, taking her over.

She didn't know if she should be scared or not. She'd grown wings because ... she'd wished for them. Trapped on the mountain with only an angry dragon for company, with a sheer drop behind her, she remembered what she'd thought, what would have helped at that moment. If she could have flown.

And now she had wings. She didn't know if that meant she could fly. Perhaps it did, if she could work out how to use them. On the other hand, if she did, then she knew nothing about how to fly. If she'd been given a car, she wouldn't know how to drive it any more than being given wings gave her the knowledge of how to swoop and dive and soar.

Still sitting in the pond, she forced her legs out the boiler suit, then worked it backwards over the wings until she was free of it. She felt awkward, that standing would make her overbalance. But she couldn't just stay there. Afternoon was stretching into evening, and soon it would be night.

As well as awkward, she felt restless. She hadn't eaten for a day, two days, maybe longer – however long it had taken for her to get back to the castle. She was battered and bruised and bewinged, but she was also hollow.

Gripping the side of the pool, she got herself to crouching. Then slowly, slowly, she stood, more water pouring from her, giving her goosebumps as it evaporated away. She felt the wind catch the feathers behind her, and she shivered.

Her wings flexed, and tugged against her. She splashed her feet, scrabbling for stability, and after five or six steps, was able to stand mostly upright again. Gingerly, she lifted a leg over the edge of the pool, then the other, and she was on the pavement, leaving damp footprints trailing up to the door.

She was getting used to it, to them. There was nothing to it, really, just a difference in her gait, a change in her posture, a slight delay in her turn. She'd have to open the door wider. That was fine, too.

Wings. She had wings. Her breath caught in her throat, coming out like the first sob. She'd wanted this – not this exactly – but this: to bend the world to her will. It had always been coldly inflexible before, uncaring, unresponsive to her wants and wishes. Now Down was giving her her dreams in a piecemeal, overgenerous way that didn't make any sense and wasn't controllable.

She could snap her fingers and light fires. She could drag light and dark out of thin air. She could weave the natural world around her for camouflage and for weapons. A castle was grow-ing out of the ground to her unbidden command.

No one had said Down was safe. It was the ways in which it was unsafe that confounded her. Friends that turned out to be enemies, she could understand. Growing wings was incompre-hensible.

She could ignore that for the moment, despite the ever-present weight on her back. The first thing she did was check the little room she'd slept in for the map she'd drawn. It had gone, taken by Crows.

Of course it had. Maps were power and wealth. Why did people tell her the truth and then betray her with those same truths? Because they could. Draw a map, said Crows, put everything down that you remember. How stupid could she be? He'd told her exactly what he was going to do, and she hadn't even noticed, in the same way that the wolfman had: in Down, there was no one to stop you doing whatever you wanted. She hadn't asked, what if you wanted to be very wicked?

So the map had gone. She could make another one, with the right materials, which inevitably had gone too, with the rest of Crows' supposed hoard of knowledge. It became more of a question of what he'd left than what he'd taken.

The candle was still on the table, and she lit it almost casually, even though the act itself was extraordinary. There was grain, which she could boil, but there was also a cake of something dark and heavy and sticky. She licked her fingers and tasted the dense flavours of sweet, rich fruit, dried and compressed into a single solid block.

Which she tore into, pulling and clawing, and when that wasn't fast enough, picking up and worrying chunks out of it with her small white teeth.

What was she doing? She put the pressed fruit down on the table and backed away like it was something live and dangerous. She spat out what was already in her mouth and not yet down her throat or her front. She liked sweet stuff, but not that much, not that intensely. Yet she could see her fingers glistening and had the overwhelming urge to suck the syrup off them.

She made a conscious effort to stop herself. Boiling the grain up, making a porridge, it would take time. She could do that: she didn't have anything else do. Crows wasn't around, and judging from what was missing, he wouldn't be coming back. This was her castle now, and it certainly seemed to be responding to her presence by becoming more complete. She filled a metal pot with grain, listening to the way they bounced against sides, and carried it outside to fill it with water.

The sun was setting, and the sky was turning purple with dusk. The crows were coming back to roost, their black shapes wheeling above her and around the incomplete tower. They called to her, and she watched the way their wings snapped and flapped as they turned.

She felt a longing, a terrifying ache, that told her she should be up there, with them, and not concerning herself with such mundane things as cooking. Birds didn't do that; they lived off the wild bounty of the world.

She clenched her fists and closed her eyes, and the feeling passed.

Crows had piled up firewood and set the pot over it. She tried to copy what he'd done, but inevitably she was unpractised, and she hadn't been paying that much attention. The wood, she could find, stacked away in another room, but it came with no instructions on how much to use or how to lay it out. She guessed, and caught it alight by willpower alone. When the first flames had died down, she dropped a scorched, sooty flat stone into the middle of the fire, and carefully placed the pot on top of it.

The heat reached her, and made her shy away, her feathers trembling. The pot settled on the stone at an angle, but it didn't spill. She'd need to remember to pad her hand when she retrieved it later. When she looked up, the crows were still circling and calling. It would take a while for the grain to cook down. Time enough to climb the tower.

She tried to resist. She tried so very hard. But wrestling with her compulsions was harder, and she was exhausted and confused, and in no state to feel strong. She gave in. She almost ran. Back inside, up the steps, past the room she'd entered previously because that too was now enclosed by timbers stretching overhead and boarded out. The steps, where they'd petered out into space now carried on, and so did she.

The tower now had a top, a parapet of stone that was waist-high, and the rafters that would make the roof had already grown out. All that was missing was the floor beneath, and the shingles above. The crows swirled around her, cawing and cackling, but those already roosting merely hopped out of her way as she stepped on the exposed beams on her way to the edge.

She planted her feet, held on to one of the angled uprights, and stared out over Down. From the height she was at, she could see more, even the distant mountain with the twin peaks, which the geomancer ruled and where she'd fought a dragon and at least not lost.

When she leaned out and looked down at the cooking fire, she didn't feel a visceral turn in her stomach. Rather, she felt the opposite. Elation. Her wings fluttered against the gusting wind, rising of their own accord.

A crow hopped on to the parapet beside her, its head turning to inspect her with one dark eye. The same wind that she felt riffled the purple-black plumage on its back, and it flapped its wings with sudden violence, making the wing-tips snap like whips. It settled, and its pale beak announced a caw.

'Caw,' she said back. 'Caw.' Her own wings, brown, speckled with white and black, remained mute.

The crow stretched its wings out again, and flapped them hard. It rose into the air, and glided back into place. It looked at her again, its bright eye shining. She could see her reflection, strange and inhuman.

For a third time, the crow flapped and rose, fell and folded.

It was trying to teach her how to fly, and she still didn't have the muscles or the motive. All she had was wings, that were surely insufficient to carry her aloft.

She stepped up on to the stonework, and spread her arms wide.

She wanted to do it. She wanted to leap out into the sky and not hit the ground. She knew she mustn't. That it was a dangerous, lethal delusion, brought about by Down's magic. It was going to kill her if she jumped, because there was no way she'd survive the impact with the unforgiving pavement below.

The crow looked at her, daring her. They were both birds. With a flap of her wings, she'd be away, rising over the darkening land, wheeling and calling with all the others. How simple and straightforward that would be.

She wavered between flying and falling, caught between what she knew to be true and what her dreams told her to believe. The wind whirled around her bare legs, her exposed midriff, her outstretched arms. Her hair, still damp in its depths, quivered with anticipation.

How could she contemplate this? This was craziness, drug-fuelled, bad trip psychosis. She wasn't going anywhere but back, on to the wooden beams and down the stairs and collect her meal that was steaming merrily away over its bed of brightly glowing coals.

But despite everything, she knew that if she missed this opportunity, that she'd wake in the morning and the gift would be gone. Down gave, and Down would take away. There was no guarantee that she'd ever find this road again.

Tricked by the wolfman, abandoned by Crows, alone in two worlds, and only Down had stepped in to save her when death had seemed certain, each and every time, hiding her in the folds of its land and rising up to drive off the dragon.

She steadied herself, gripped harder with her toes, and shouted out over the tops of the trees to the lake and sea beyond.

'You seem to be helping me. I don't know why. I can live small, and regret it for however long I've got, or I can risk everything now to live large. And I'm tired of living small.'

She leaned forward, over the parapet, over the pavement, and stretched her whole body out towards the sky.

22

There was no fight. Not that day, and not the next.

Stanislav was the one who became like a caged beast, prowling and snapping, being forced to wait and finding that waiting impossible to endure. Dalip was calmer than he thought he'd be: he had the prospect of a fight to the death, yet he'd come to some measure of acceptance that the older man had not. He'd accepted the plan they'd devised, and it was now Stanislav who wanted to change it, strike pre-emptively while the geomancer was incapacitated.

The guards bore the brunt of his bad temper, and it was a constant surprise to Dalip that they wore it as well as they did. They were the guards, they were in charge, and they should have had no qualms about putting him back in his place. But they understood. Perhaps they were waiting for something too.

The day's work had ended, and the slaves were being herded chaotically back to their cells. They were, briefly, all together. Mama, as usual, waited to be pushed across the threshold.

Then Stanislav turned around and said he had had enough.

Pigface pushed past the other guard. 'We don't want any trouble, Slav. Just do as your told.'

'No. Now is as good a time as we will get. Dalip? Take his knife.'

Dalip stepped around Stanislav. He reached out, got his hand slapped away, but in that narrow corridor, it was easy enough for him to immediately bring his other hand across and pull the knife free of its scabbard. He held it high, and Stanislav reached up to take it from him.

'Hey. Give that back.' Pigface tried to find the space to wrestle with Stanislav, but there was none.

'You want it back?' Stanislav slipped his arm under Dalip's and stabbed Pigface. Not once, but repeatedly, the blade going in and out into the man's stomach like a sewing-machine needle. Both the other guard and Dalip watched the sudden series of impacts with shock, as if it was happening to someone else, somewhere else.

Then Pigface folded, leaning against Dalip before sliding wetly to the floor.

The remaining guard stared and stared, then tried to run for it.

'Stop him.'

Dalip, used to obeying that voice, and that tone of voice, leapt after him, brought him down and tangled his fingers in his hair. Then he jabbed his wrist forward, and the man's forehead connected with the stone flags. His captive went limp.

'Did you have to?' Dalip said, getting to his feet.

Stanislav rolled Pigface flat to search him for anything else useful. Pigface wasn't dead yet, but would be very soon, and as he was turned, he made a sort of wet, gurgling noise that elicited quiet moans of dismay from the others.

'He is the enemy. He is complicit in our slavery. You want to show him mercy?' He slid the bloody blade over to Dalip. 'Then do so. It will be more than he would have done for any of us.'

Dalip wasn't going to stab a dying man. And neither was he going to have the other guard stabbed either. He dragged him into his own cell, pulled the door closed and started to lower the bar across it.

'You have not finished him.'

'No. I'm not going to either.'

Stanislav scooped up the knife with an exasperated sigh. 'This is weakness. This will get us all killed.'

'We can just leave him there.'

'When he begins to scream and shout, others will come and free him. Then we will have to kill them to escape.' Stanislav jabbed his finger hard against Dalip's temple. 'You are not thinking.'

'We cannot kill an unconscious man.'

'You want to wait until he wakes up?'

'We can't.' Then: 'I won't let you. You might not have any scruples, but I do.'

Stanislav made to lift the bar, and Dalip slammed his hand on top of it, holding it in place.

'We don't have time for an argument,' he said.

Pigface coughed, his whole frame shaking, and Stanislav broke the stand-off. 'The pit, then. Mama, go to the guard room and bar the outside door. Elena, Luiza, bring the table there through into the pit, and a chair.'

The women stood the other side of the dying man, the other side of the thick lake of blood that was welling up and out of him, across the floor, up to the walls.

'Sweet Jesus,' said Mama, 'Sweet merciful Jesus. Look what you did, Stanislav. Look what you did to this man.'

Elena shrank back behind her, using her bulk to shield the ruination from sight, but Luiza grabbed hold of her cousin, and started barking at her in Romanian. Stanislav was already down the corridor, at the junction. His face was set hard, and he shouted one word: 'Hurry!'

Dalip took a deep breath. 'Mama, we don't have a choice now. We can't go back. But we can get out of here: just come with me.'

Reluctantly, Mama took hold of Dalip's proffered hand and she jumped over Pigface's body. The man was no longer moving, breath no longer rasping, fingers no longer twitching.

'Go. The door. Do what Stanislav told you.' Dalip eased her past him and away.

Luiza all but threw Elena at him, and leapt the obstruction herself. Dalip muttered his apologies as they squeezed by, but Luiza merely tutted her frustration and shoved Elena hard in the back to speed her up.

They diverged at the end of the corridor. The women went into the guard room, Dalip into the pit. It was completely dark, something that neither he nor Stanislav had bargained for.

'We need a light,' the older man growled, and hurried out, coming back with a lantern from the guard room.

The glow it gave was feeble, and Dalip could barely see the edge of the parapet. Even though he'd jumped up to it several times now, groping around in the dark wasn't going to make it any easier.

Stanislav put the lantern on the floor and judged his position. Dalip trotted over to the far wall and braced his back against it.

'Ready?' he called.

'Yes.' The shadow was so deep that it was almost impossible to tell. They'd just have to trust that they'd trained enough.

'Okay. Three, two, one.'

Dalip ran, half-blind, hoping that Stanislav could see him better than he could see Stanislav. He raised his foot and stamped it down at the undifferentiated mass of darkness, and then he was flying. He remembered in time to raise his leg, turn his body, reach out in case he hadn't risen quite far enough.

The landing was brutal. He'd overcompensated and so had Stanislav. He slammed, sight unseen, on to the balcony, having cleared the parapet completely, crashing into the throne and shoving it across the floor until it wedged against the wall. Parts of him were tangled with the legs of the chair, and not for the first time, he could taste blood in his mouth.

He'd also made enough noise to wake the dead. If there was

anyone within earshot, they'd be busy raising the alarm and arming themselves. A slave uprising always had to be a possibility for a slaver: even though there were only five of them, and calling it an uprising was nothing more than a bad joke.

He staggered to his feet, spitting, and leaned back out over the pit.

'The knife. Throw me the knife.'

The lantern was there, but Stanislav wasn't. The confusion at the door was Luiza shouting at Elena, trying to get the table through the gap. They tried repeatedly, and only succeeded in blocking it for Mama.

Dalip spat on the ground again, wiped his mouth, and realised that if anyone came through the door behind him, he'd have to deal with them himself. His only weapon was the throne, too solid to break up, too heavy to wield. He could still drag the chair against the door until they were ready, so he did, and went back to the parapet.

They'd finally negotiated the doorway and were carrying the table in.

'Here, just here,' he called. They looked up, changed their path, and placed the table against the wall below him. Mama stacked the chair on top of it, and Luiza climbed up straight away.

When she stretched up her hand, Dalip could reach down and clasp her wrist.

'Okay?' he asked, and he could make out her nodding.

He thought that it'd be a strain, an effort, something he'd struggle with. It turned out that either she was very light, or he was now very strong. When he could, he used both hands, and was even able to ease her over the top, rather than dump her like a sack of rice on the floor.

'Still okay?'

'Yes ... yes.'

'Go and stand by that door. Listen out for anyone coming.' He pointed, and she nodded again, brushing her hair back from her ear in readiness.

Elena was next, and again, despite all her weight being on one arm, he could lift her and hold her until she was able to swing herself over the edge of the parapet.

Mama was next. A more substantial challenge, and there was still no Stanislav.

'Mama, get on the table, then on to the chair.'

She was surprisingly limber despite her rolling curves.

'Oh, that poor man. That shouldn't have happened,' she said as she clambered up on to the tabletop.

'Yes, Mama. I know. I ... it's wrong, but what else are we supposed to do? Ask them nicely to let us go?'

'Oh, he was a bad man for sure, but kill him?' She put both hands on the chair back and looked up. 'Can't you, I don't know, keep Stanislav under control?'

'You're joking, right?' He lowered his hand over the side. 'Come on. Whatever happens next, we need to stay together.'

'I don't think I can climb, Dalip.'

'Let me worry about that.' He waved his fingers. 'We have to hurry.'

She got her knees on to the chair, then one foot, then the other. Slowly, shakily, she stood, her arms out wide trying to hug the wall.

'Reach up. Right up.'

She was shorter than both Luiza and Elena. They both stretched, and could just about touch.

'Elena, hold my legs. Stop me going over.'

He leant right out, over the parapet with both hands, and with Elena gripping his knees, he was able to take hold of Mama's wrists.

'You ready?'

'No,' she whispered.

'We're not leaving without you,' he said. He started to

straighten up, taking all her weight through his arms and into his back. Her feet left the chair, knocking it over in the process.

It clattered to the pit floor, and she looked down at the sudden height. She started to wriggle in his grasp.

'Don't do that,' he said.

'It's too far.'

He kept on pulling, and she was rising despite herself.

'You want to get back home? You want to get back to your kids and grandkids?' It hurt, from his elbows, through his shoulders to the small of his back. He was speaking through clenched teeth. 'This is the only way.'

Luiza left her post at the door, leant herself over and took a handful of boilersuit at Mama's side. She pulled as Dalip leant back, and that was enough to drag Mama up as far as the parapet, getting her on the wide stone wall and over the right side.

They lay together, in a heap.

'You're strong, Dalip,' said Mama. 'You're a strong man now.'

'Maybe.' He didn't feel strong at that moment: he was breathing hard, and everything felt over-stretched. But it seemed Stanislav had been right. He couldn't have managed to pull any of them up, not even himself, before he came to Down. He heaved himself up and looked over the edge. The pit was empty, save for a table, tipped chair, and weakly burning lantern.

'Where is he?' asked Luiza, extricating herself from under Mama. 'What better thing does he have to do than be here?'

'I don't know.' He stared at the pit door, as if it'd make the man appear. 'Stanislav? Stanislav!'

It was more a stage whisper than a shout, and even that seemed too loud.

'What do we do, if he does not come?'

'He'll come. Go and listen at the door again.'

He didn't know what to do. It seemed like an age before Stanislav trotted back into the pit, though it was probably no longer than a minute. He was holding a hessian sack heavy with loot in one hand, and Pigface's knife in the other.

'Where the hell have you been?' hissed Dalip.

'Taking care of business. Catch.' He threw the bag up, and Dalip caught it neatly, setting down beside him. 'Now the knife.'

That, he threw slightly to Dalip's right, so that it landed ringing on the floor. Then he reset the chair on the table, put the lantern next to it and climbed deftly up. He held up the lantern for collection, then both hands.

'Pull.'

Dalip didn't. 'When you said … You've killed him, haven't you? The other guard.'

'You are so squeamish. Have you never seen Spartacus?'

'What's that got to do with it?'

'When the slaves revolt, they kill their overseers. They have to. They are owned. This is the only way. Now pull me up.'

Dalip looked at Mama, at Elena. He didn't want to be a slave, and he didn't want them to be slaves, either. He warred with himself, balking at killing, railing against what he'd already been forced to do. Of course Stanislav was right. He was squeamish. He'd never thought of himself as someone who'd kill even in a just cause. Southall wasn't like that.

Clearly, wherever Stanislav had lived had been exactly like that. He was uncomfortably comfortable with violence. And they needed that. They all needed that. Without it, they were as good as back in their cells.

No matter what the others thought, then. He reached down and Stanislav clamped both his hands on Dalip's wrist. He pulled him up, more difficult than Elena, easier than Mama. Once he could reach the parapet himself, Stanislav could haul himself over.

While he did that, Dalip collected the knife, and hung on to it. The bag contained Pigface's club, and smaller knives from the kitchen, which he distributed. They were all armed now. Just how dangerous they collectively were was doubtful, despite the two corpses they were leaving behind.

'Any sounds?' Dalip asked Luiza.

'No, nothing.'

'Then we have to go. Find the bridge to the geomancer's tower. Cross it without being seen. Then we find her, and—'

'Take her hostage. Knock her out, tie her up. We need her to get past the dragon.' Stanislav heaved the throne out of the way and raised Pigface's – his, now – club. 'If she tries to use magic on us, we might have to kill her anyway. Any one of us who has the chance.'

He lifted the latch on the door, and to forestall any further qualms or questions, swung it wide. 'Bring the lantern, Mama. Hold it high.'

They were in uncharted territory now, outside what any of them had seen. The light showed mainly shadows, and the glimpse of stonework, a wall, stairs up – and another door. It rattled on its own, making them jump and step back, but it was just the mountain wind, whipping cold around the ill-fitting frame.

'This must be outside, yes?' Luiza felt the door for the latch, found an iron ring, and twisted it. The door resisted opening, then eased ajar. More of the cold air swirled in.

Stanislav crouched and peered through. 'No moonlight. We need the lantern, but we must keep it low so that it is not seen. Remember, we must be quick and certain. If someone sees us, they have to be silenced before they can raise the alarm. Afterwards is too late. Once we have crossed the bridge, we search every room in the tower for her. And we take no prisoners but her.'

'What about her steward?' asked Dalip.

'What about him? He is part of this, so you know what to do.' He took charge of the door from Luiza. 'I will go first, Dalip will go last. Watch for the dragon.'

Stanislav heaved the door wide and took a moment to check the bridge and the sky above it.

The bridge itself was clear – it ran straight and flat across from the pit to the geomancer's tower, where there was another door. The waist-high parapet either side was going to give them some cover, but the tower loomed tall, and there were narrow windows that overlooked the bridge: anyone so much as glancing down would see them.

The top of the tower, with its conical slate roof, was almost invisible against the sky. There could have been a dragon wound around it, and none of them would have been any the wiser. The side of the tower to the right flickered with firelight, so they'd have to keep down, but Dalip wasn't so worried about that as he was by the prospect of that far door being barred shut from the inside. If he was in charge, leaving doors to the slave quarters open seemed not just averagely stupid, but lethally so. It was the whole reason why they'd been going to strike just after one of the fights.

'Look,' he said, 'we don't even know if we can get into the tower. Why don't I go across first and check?'

It made sense, and Stanislav could tell by the shifting body-language that the others weren't now going to cross until they knew the way was clear.

'Mama, give him the lantern so he can signal. Go, then, and quickly.'

Dalip found himself at the front, the wind dragging at the candle flame inside the lantern. He squeezed the knife handle and took one last look. That he couldn't see a dragon was no promise that there wasn't one. The lights at the windows in the door stayed constant, and there was no better time – or at least, it would get worse the longer he left it – to run.

He held the lantern low, so that it almost scraped along the walkway, and crouched down. It wasn't far. He covered the distance quickly and quietly, and nestled the lantern in the corner of the door recess.

He listened and, on hearing nothing, reached up and turned

the iron ring. The latch lifted on the other side of the door, he could hear that, but when he pushed, the door moved only a fraction before pressing against something immovable.

Dalip's stomach tightened even further. He tried again, to make absolutely certain, but he'd been right the first time. The door was barred or bolted, and they weren't going to be able to shift it.

He took a step back and looked up. There was a window slit right over the door, the same height again above it. He might, if he could get up there, squeeze through it, then open the door from the inside.

It seemed their only option, and they were running out of time. Sooner or later, someone was going to check where Pigface and the other guard had got to. Then there'd be no hope of escape, and certainly no going back to captivity.

He left the lantern where it was, and raced back to the others.

23

She could see everything. Every last leaf, rock, blade of grass. Every fold of the ground, every lake, the course of the rivers and the line of the ridges. Everything, like it was the map she'd painstakingly drawn and then had stolen from her.

The crows had kept up with her as they'd taught her how to flap and turn and glide and land – how difficult that had been, when she would fill her vast wings with air and snap them almost in front of her to try and brake herself. She ended up pinwheeling into the ground, and then going backwards, and then almost hovering in flight as she tentatively dabbed at the ground with her coal-black talons, unwilling to commit.

As she circled higher and higher, she left the smaller birds behind, and as she spiralled upwards, Down became a sheet of beaten copper, lit by the dying sun. She watched the shadows lengthen, deep pools of darkness stretch out and cover the land like ink, then the last threads of light hung on the western horizon while the forests and mountains settled into slumbering dusk.

And she could still see, her preternatural vision catching movement far below: animals emerging from cover, the wind-waves on the crowns of the trees, the rising spire of smoke from a fire.

Her fire. She remembered. She'd set it, and lit it, and now there was a thin column of sooty smoke marking its place. She wheeled away. She didn't want boiled grain any more, if she ever wanted it in the first place. Meat. Raw meat, running with blood, hot and vital. Only that would satisfy her. But she was huge. The crows she had flown with were like flies to her. She could crush them by the handful and still not be satisfied, and they were her crows, not to be slashed out of the air and broken on the ground.

She needed bigger prey.

She turned and spread her feathers wide, gliding like she had been born a bird, and started searching in the growing gloom for something to catch and kill.

Even though she spotted, and swooped low over, cattle the size of cars, they didn't excite her or give her the same thrill that the discarded thought of catching crows had given her. Not some beast tied to the ground for her. Her quarry should be airborne, like her, so that she could dive on it from above, wings swept back and feet clenched like fists to break its wing and send it tumbling to the ground.

Where was she going to find such creatures, something worthy of the effort? She could almost taste them, the breast feathers torn out with her hooked beak, the puckered flesh beneath, the first burst of flavour.

She turned east to look across the hill country, and north towards the high plateau, south over the ocean and east to view the islands set in the darkling sea, but there was nothing. The sky was void and empty, and it would be hours before the moon rose. She turned for home, to the tiny red glow of the fire on the pavement in front of the castle.

She landed in a flurry of feathers, as disappointed as an unfired gun. Folding her wings, she strutted forward to inspect the remains of the cooking pot that was now a foul-smelling cinder on top of a whited-ash heap.

Her head turned sideways to look at it, her talons gripping the cracks in the pavement, and she was distracted by a flash of colour off to one side. She couldn't walk – the motion was unnatural – so she hopped over, and found a circular pool. She pecked at the thing floating in the rippling water, a shed orange skin with a rent and stained back, and dragged it out to get a better look at it.

She knew it should mean something more to her than it did, because it was her skin, the one she'd worn before she'd spread her wings, and what? Jumped from the top of the tower, that tower above her, its edges ragged and unfinished, full of roosting crows.

There'd been a man, too, with skin as black as a crow's coat. He'd helped her, or had pretended to do so, and then he'd stolen from her that which he considered most precious.

The door. The fire. The stepping into the surging sea. The cold saltwater washing around hot burns.

Mary. Her name was Mary.

This was Down's doing, then. The wish first, followed by the act. That was the art of magic, and the danger of it too, because it could so easily destroy her: the transformation of her from human to avian almost had her lost in the now of flight, of hunting, of seeking. That was what Crows had warned her of, too much, too soon.

Where would Crows be now? He'd be making his way downriver, towards the place he called a portal. With that, the unbidden urge to stretch her wings again launched her into the air, flapping quickly to gain height, climbing over the growing wall and heading south.

The land was in darkness, and still she could see. There was the lake she'd swum in, half a day's walk she could now make in a fraction of the time, there was the river, flowing out to sea, the broad, braided delta with its shallows and bars, there was the bay, curving like horns, where the waves tore in and broke themselves on the sloping shingle beach.

And there, there was the long ridge, looking like the spine of the world, except that when it reached the coast, its back was broken and beyond the cliff was a line of broken rubble extending as far out as a stack of rock, surrounded by the ever-moving sea.

She flew towards it, and a thin sickle of a moon had started to rise when she had proper sight of it, still miles away in the distance. Below her, the forest stretched out, and the river shone silver. There was movement there, and her sharp eyes picked out dark figures moving through the scrub and reeds.

Yes, there were wolves, but they were not all wolves. Two wolves, six men, in a ragged line, from the main, broad channel of the river to the edge of the forest. If any of them had looked up, they would have seen nothing. She was far above them, and travelling silently.

She circled them as they made their sweep towards the sea. They were looking for someone, someones, but didn't have a scent yet. Perhaps there were more survivors coming through the portal, and the wolfman had been sent to collect them in the same way he'd come for her group.

Or perhaps they were looking for Crows. She thought she'd find him first, and depending on what he had to say, she might tell him he was being hunted.

The seas around the stack boomed and shook, the swell heaving against the broken rock around its base. She flew once around the pillar of rock, twice, three times, getting lower with each pass. She instinctively avoided the spray, but in amongst the flashes off the rock faces, she could detect something moving at the wave-washed base, clambering over the boulders.

It was no more than a pool of darkness, gliding from shadow to shadow, but she knew what that meant and who hid beneath it.

She swung back up to the top of the stack, contending with cross-winds and updraughts, and landed on the weather-struck rock. The wind continued to ruffle her feathers, and when she looked out over the ocean, she could see the lowest quarter of the moon blocked off by a band of black cloud.

The stack was larger than she'd thought: any bigger and she would have called it an island. To seaward, it sloped down to a rocky beach, but it rose from that low point to form cliffs on the other sides. She couldn't climb, and she couldn't talk. All that came out was a screech. Having found Crows, she couldn't get close enough to him. Not as a bird, and even as she crouched low over the ground to stop the wind buffeting her, she wondered what she could do.

She hadn't always been that way, even though it felt as natural as breathing. She remembered walking upright, swinging arms as she did so. She'd had hands that gripped, a strange flat face with a curious button nose and lips that could pout, and hair that fell from the crown of her head in black coils. She had a tongue, sharp and quick.

She was cold. She stumbled, and she steadied herself with a five-fingered thing that it took her a moment to recognise. She was still bruised and cut, and now she was also in her vest and pants, exposed to the strengthening salt gale.

The muscle in her mouth lengthened and thickened. She could taste copper and bile.

'F... Fu ...' she mouthed. She had teeth, and tried not to bite herself as she formed the word. 'Fuck.'

For a moment, she wrapped herself in the strange-angled limbs she had instead of wings and lay in a rough rock-bowl, rocking against the sudden pain and shock, trying to cushion her mind from the sense of howling loss.

She could no longer fly. She'd put it down and she didn't know whether she could ever take it up again.

Slowly, she unwound, and had to relearn how to stand on feet, and how to use knees, and how to swing hips. Awkwardly, stutteringly, she started down the slope to the shoreline.

It came back to her. She could fumble her way around the base of the cliffs. Sometimes she had to cling on to the rocks as the waves rushed up and tried to suck her down. From cold, she went to freezing numb, but she carried on.

'Crows? Crows, you bastard. Come out.' She'd lost her falcon's sight when she'd lost her falconhood.

A wave drew down strongly behind her, and returned twice as hard. She gasped as the wall of green water hit her, and gasped again as her fingers started to tear free.

A hand came down and lifted her easily out of the surf.

'Climb higher,' said Crows. 'There is a ledge.'

He half-carried her up, and set her down before shrugging off his sea-drenched cloak and wrapping her in it.

'How did you find me? Where are your clothes?'

'You stole my map,' she said, drawing the edges of the cloak around her as tight as she could.

'And you lied about the portal.' The whites of his eyes and the white of his teeth as he hissed out his words were all she could see.

'I did not. It was here.'

'It is not here now, Mary, and portals do not vanish. They exist in both worlds: that is what gives them power.'

'This one disappeared. It just went.'

Crows took her by the shoulders and shook her. 'They do not vanish,' he repeated. 'Where is it, really?'

'It's here. Here.' She shook herself free and looked around. There was the headland, and the line of broken rock leading to the stack. 'There. We stepped out into the sea right there.'

He left her and went to where she pointed, and she followed, still trying to hold his black cloak around her.

'There is nothing here,' he shouted over the boom of the waves.

'It disappeared. It looked like the entrance to an Underground station, and then it disappeared, even as I was looking at it. What does it mean, Crows? Why did it go?'

Crows slapped at the rock with his hands and gave a grunt of frustration. The cliff was blank: no door, no brickwork, no faded sign. The sea swallowed up their feet, regurgitated them again.

'The portal I came through is still there, though it is closed to me. I have seen other portals too. I have never heard of one just vanishing before.'

'But it was here. Just ... here.' She scrubbed the spray from her face. 'I thought they all did that, after you pass through. Fade away until they're opened again.'

'No. And the power that comes from them connects with other portals. With this one dead, the lines will have shifted.' He hit the rock again, just to make sure. 'Are you telling me the truth, Mary? Was the portal really here?'

'Yes. It was right here. Now it's not.' She turned away and started to pick her way back to the seaward slope.

He was following her, but only when she was out of the surf and up on dry land did she face him again. 'Why did you do it?'

'Why? Because I had to. Such knowledge is precious, and we each guard our own carefully. I told you as much.' He reached out for his cloak, his long fingers snagging the hem and pulling it towards him. She resisted.

'You could have copied my map, and I wouldn't have minded.'

The thought seemed to confuse him.

'You watched me do it. All you had to do was ask. I even owed you: you saved me from the wolfman, you took me to your castle, you fed me and taught me about magic.' She was cold to the bone, and still she shivered at the realisation. 'You did all that just to get me to tell you where the portal was, didn't you?'

'No. Not all. My motives were ... confused.'

'The fuck they were, Crows. I thought we were, I don't know, friends.'

He looked away. 'People like us do not have friends. We are kings and queens, Mary, and we are naturally rivals. We raise castles, we must rule alone: it is for others to obey us willingly or otherwise.'

'Fuck you, Crows. Fuck you.'

'You want it,' he said. 'You want to be your Red Queen. It is always what you want to be.'

'Not like that.'

'However else? There is only one way: seize power and keep tight hold of it. I have let mine slip away, so now I must take my leave and try my luck elsewhere: this portal has gone, and without it the castle will fall.'

'I'm sorry. It wasn't my fault.'

'Sorry?' He blinked. 'Sorry? Do not be sorry. This is momentous. This will shake Down to the roots of its mountains. I can sell this knowledge, and it will make me rich. Do not be sorry, Mary.' He pulled harder at his cloak, and gathered a handful in his fist. 'Now, I have to go.'

'You can't,' she said. She wasn't going to tell him, but it just came out. 'The wolfman is on the shore, looking for you.'

'Is he? You managed to slip past him, didn't you?'

'I didn't ... It wasn't like that.'

'The wolfman can howl at the moon until his throat is raw. He will not catch me. I doubt he will even see me.' His expression softened slightly. 'A geomancer – like her, like me, like you – does not suffer rivals. Stay away from the wolfman, yes?'

He walked towards the shore, and the cloak inexorably slipped from her shoulders. She was cold again.

'Crows?'

'Do you remember how you got here?'

'I, I flew.'

He looked sad and shook his head. 'I know. I know what you are, I know what you are becoming. I have done what I can to help you, but this has come upon you too soon, Mary. Far too soon. It will master you and leave you nothing but a beast, with a beast's mind, and no memory of what you were. Even now you are struggling to remember.'

He kept on walking, down the rocky shore and into the sea.

She wondered what he was doing, what he thought he was doing. The waves lashed him, breaking over his head, and still he kept on.

When he was past his waist, he turned, opened his arms wide and fell backwards into the foam-flecked water. The sea took him.

'You're wrong! I do remember,' she shouted after his wake. 'I remember everything.'

The sea boiled and seethed, and a sinuous coil of scales burst out and up. It roiled and rolled, then submerged with a smack and a clap. A head, serpentine, sleek and glistening, emerged in its place, blinking a pale membrane across its dark eyes. It kept on rising until it towered over Mary, then it looked down at her, indifferent to her fate, peering at her as if she was nothing more than a rock or a flower: a specimen, interesting for a moment, but ultimately forgettable.

The head turned, plunged down into the deep, the body following in an arc of writhing water. The tail, fringed with spiny fins, flicked up for a moment – and then it was gone, and she was left freezing to death on an island in an unknown sea, the wind and the waves tearing at her.

She knew there was only one way off, the way she'd arrived. She'd never swim to shore, and if she tried, the wolfman would only find her drowned, limp body washed up on the strand line.

By the time she reached the edge of the cliff overlooking the headland, she could barely feel her skin. She was disembodied. And as if in a dream, a dream in which she could fly, she staggered – just like Crows had walked into the water – stiff-legged to the precipice and tumbled over the edge.

24

'I can get through the window, if I can get up there.'

Stanislav thought hard, chin on chest. Then he raised his head. 'If you fall, you will alert the guards. But it is our best option. Otherwise, we will have to face them anyway, and the geomancer will know we are coming.'

Dalip had never climbed anything more complicated than gym equipment. There was a parapet he could stand on, and then a rough stone wall to ascend. He'd have to traverse to the window. He had no idea if he could actually accomplish what he'd just said he'd do.

'I'll do my best,' he said. He looked up at the tower, at its shadows and shapes, and he felt sweat prickle his fingertips.

'Go, if you are going,' said Stanislav, pushing him back out the door.

'Good luck,' whispered Mama, and Dalip caught her nervous smile. He nodded, then did the crouching run back across the bridge. In the darkness of the recess, he peered over the parapet at the fire in the courtyard below.

It was bright, bright enough to rob anyone near it of their night sight. A couple of benches had been dragged out of the squat building near it, and there were three, no four, men sitting, drinking and talking. If he was careful and quiet, he'd not be seen. How was he going to carry the knife so that it wouldn't drop out? He thought about the waistband of his kachera, and a pocket in his boilersuit. Neither of those was certain. He looked at the blade, and lifted it to his mouth. He closed his teeth on it, and now the taste on his tongue wasn't his own blood.

He climbed up on the parapet on the far side from the fire. It was wide enough that he could get both feet side-by-side on the top. The drop to his left was precipitous, though, and perhaps he shouldn't think about that.

His hands, resting on the wall, explored its surface. The blocks were big, but there were gaps between them. With boots on, he'd have no chance, but because he was barefooted, he could squeeze his toes into the holds.

There was nothing else for it. He'd run out of reasons to delay, and he reached above his head to feel for a crack. Once he was as confident as he was going to be that he could maintain his grip, he slid the inside of his foot up the cold face of the wall and turned his big toe into a piton.

He straightened his leg at the same time as pulling with his arm. He was up, clinging to the wall like a spider. He took his time to find the next foothold and handhold, and when he'd pulled himself up on those, his initial arm was sore with effort. He was trying too hard: he needed to be more instinctive, climb it like he would a ladder.

Smoothly then, foot and fingers, up, drawing level with the bottom of the window. Again, and now he was halfway up. The wind pulled at him. The loose grit in the gaps needed brushing out in case it caused him to slip. He didn't need to look down, so he didn't.

Part of him was aware that what he was doing was dangerous, outrageous, ridiculous. The other part told him he was doing something good and brave, and his grandfather would have argued against Dalip's parents for him to be allowed to do it.

That this was his duty, his honour, his right, to risk everything to help his friends.

He was at the same height as the window. He stretched out with his foot, found his next foothold, and slid across the wall, turning his head to the direction of travel. Below him, across the courtyard, the men were still drinking. If they'd looked up and away from the fire, they'd have spotted him, an orange figure spreadeagled against the side of the tower. But they concentrated on the dancing flames and their conversation, and Dalip carried on.

Another move closer. If he reached out now, he could stand on the window ledge. It'd also make him visible to anyone in the room beyond. He listened for voices, and decided that he'd just have to risk it. He eased himself across and got a good handhold on the other side.

There was a curtain over the window, hanging down inside from a rod on the lintel, obscuring him from view – a stroke of luck. He listened again, and when he heard nothing, he quickly slipped through, still behind the curtain, turning sideways and searching for the floor with his foot. He found it. The effort of the last few minutes burned in his muscles, but he'd done it. He made sure he had firm hold of the knife before unclenching his jaw.

He peeked around the side of the heavy curtain. It seemed to be a dimly lit room, and after a moment's hesitation, he stepped out, knife ready.

There was no one there. He quickly crossed the bare floor to listen at the only door, and only then took notice of what else was there. He was in some sort of store room, with floor-to-ceiling shelves on the walls holding jars and boxes of all sizes and shapes. A table was covered with clutter, things that looked like the results of a primary-school nature ramble: stones rough and smooth, mottled leaves and snapped twigs, the bleached white bones of small animals long-since passed.

He wasn't there to poke around, though. He lifted the latch on the store-room door and opened it a sliver. The curtain behind him rustled and lifted in the draught, and the wind moaned through, carrying with it the unmistakable tap-tap of someone on the staircase beyond. He eased the door shut and waited for them to pass.

The tapping got louder, and against his expectations he recognised it as the sound of the steward's silver-topped cane on the stone floor. Dalip held his breath. The tapping stopped with a scratch, and the latch clacked up on its own.

He had nowhere to hide but behind the opening door. He squeezed himself in the angle and stayed utterly silent as the steward, dressed in his customary black, entered and went straight to the table with its collection of dead things.

The steward had a tray with him. He pushed it on the table and began to arrange some of the items on it. His gloved hand hovered over some, rejecting them, and plucking others up as worthy.

Dalip realised that he was going to be spotted the instant the man turned. He wondered if he could sneak out while the steward was busy, but he was scared even to move. The heavy boilersuit wasn't the stealthiest of clothing, and he was certain to be heard.

There was only one possible course of action. He raised the knife and took the two short steps up behind the bent black back. He snaked an arm around the man's neck and pressed the knife hard into his side.

'Don't,' said Dalip. 'Whatever it is you think you can do, I can kill you quicker.'

The steward stiffened. The hand that was resting in the top of his cane flexed, and Dalip tightened his grip.

'Put it on the table. Slowly.'

He lifted the cane and gently slid it in amongst the discards, next to the tray.

'You're not the Slav. The little Sikh boy, then.'

Dalip didn't respond. The cane safely out of the man's hand, he dragged him back a couple of steps so that it was out of reach too.

'If you're hoping to escape, it's not going to work.'

Dalip thought they seemed to be doing all right so far, but kept it to himself.

'We're going down the stairs.' He thought of all the hackneyed phrases he'd seen in films during situations just like this, and decided that his captive was intelligent enough to know what was required of him.

He steered him out of the door. The staircase was a spiral, stone steps that were wedges around a central column. It was going to be difficult to keep in close contact down them, but his prisoner's comfort wasn't his concern. There were noises off: the creak of wood from above, a more metallic clatter from below. He couldn't hope to deal with everyone – what was important was letting the others in so they'd have a chance at getting to the geomancer.

Dalip and the steward descended awkwardly, the knife an ever-present inducement to good behaviour, Dalip's bare feet gripping the narrow steps better than the steward's booted ones, which slipped on occasions, stretching his neck in the crook of Dalip's bent elbow. There were other doors off the staircase, but they hadn't descended quite enough.

'That one. Open it slowly.'

The steward reached out and twisted the ring, pushed at the door. It swung open. Two women in drab dress looked up from the collection of stone bottles they were refilling and froze in place. Dalip quickly scanned the room, spotted the door he needed to undo on the far side, then looked back at the women.

Were they slaves, too? Could he enlist them or at least get them not to give the game away?

'If you make a sound, he dies. If you don't, you get to do

whatever it is you want. You can join us, or not, as you choose.'

They glanced at each other, at the steward, at Dalip, but mainly at the floor, their hands, the bottles on the table. Dalip eased the steward into the room and knocked the door closed with his heel. It didn't look like he was going to get either co-operation or defiance from them.

'The door over there, the one that leads to the bridge. Can one of you open it?'

Again, they looked everywhere but at each other. Then, the older one's head came up, and she brushed a strand of grey hair away that had fallen loose from her tightly tied knot. Despite the hesitant restraining hand of her companion, she walked deliberately around the barrels and racked bottles, and lifted the first of two heavy bars blocking the door.

'Don't,' managed the steward before Dalip cut him off with a tightening of his arm.

She put the bar to one side, then heaved the other from its hasps.

'Open it, and step away. I don't want you to get hurt.'

She rested the other bar next to the first, and put her shoulders to dragging the door open. The outside blustered in, and she walked back to Dalip.

She spat in the steward's face, then she walked out.

Dalip felt the steward stiffen, smelt their sour smells of sweat mingle.

'You can go too, if you want,' he told the other woman. 'But don't do anything that'll stop us.'

She nodded. She looked young and scared, not just of the steward, but of him. He'd always thought of himself, on the rare occasions that he did, as a quiet boy, a good boy, dutiful and diligent. Certainly not someone to be frightened of, yet there he was, ready to drive a knife into someone's side if they so much as spoke out of turn.

Luiza poked her head around the opened door, and waved

the others on. They crept in, doubled over, then stretched out. Stanislav was last in and pushed the door firmly shut.

'Where is she?' asked Stanislav.

'Up, I think,' and he had the presence of mind to ask. 'The geomancer's at the top of the tower, right?'

The serving girl was watching them all with amazement, her hands clutched over her mouth. Then she nodded.

'Why is he still alive?' said Stanislav. He barred the door behind him, pushing the thick wooden bars back into place.

'Because he's useful.'

'His use is at an end. Finish him.'

'He can get us close to the geomancer.' Still, despite everything, Dalip was reluctant to be ruthless, even though he knew it was costly and he wasn't the only one paying.

'He will get us all killed.' Stanislav held his club low and squared up to the steward. 'I have met his kind before: the ones that are more vicious, more cruel than the generals they serve. They are not driven by any ideology, only by the desire to do evil and the permission to do so.' He leaned forward into the man's face. 'Am I not right?'

If he was, the steward didn't offer an opinion.

'Gag him, tie his hands. Elena, keep a watch on the stairs. Mama, check the room for anything we can use.'

Dalip forced the steward to his knees. Luiza grabbed a scrap of cloth from the bottling table, wodging it into a damp ball and presenting it to the steward's mouth. He resisted, and Dalip had to make him open his mouth by twisting the knife-point through his close-woven clothing and into his skin. When he gasped at the pain, Luiza jammed the cloth in. His breathing became noisily nasal, and he tried to cough it out. She slapped him hard, once, twice. He glared at her, and she raised her hand for a third time. He flinched, and her lips twisted into a smile.

She tied the gag into place with length of cord, and since she seemed to know what she was doing, Dalip forced him to the floor and made him offer his hands for her to bind behind his back. It looked to Dalip that she was cutting his circulation off, the bonds digging deep into his wrists as she twisted and wound. But she was taking some degree of pleasure in doing so, and the steward was in no condition to complain.

The man was going to die soon, and it didn't really matter how tightly he was tied: Dalip still couldn't accept that, though, and tried to imagine a scenario where he didn't have to kill everyone in order to make them leave him alone.

Mama had found nothing much useful, but she'd dragged a crate of stoneware bottles containing a sharp, clear spirit into the open space. She unstoppered one of the bottles and held it up for Stanislav, who sniffed at the open neck. 'That will burn. Bring some of them.'

Dalip dragged the steward upright. Since being bound, he had become more compliant.

'Is there anything we should know before going up the stairs?' Dalip asked the serving girl. 'Anything that'll make it difficult for us?'

'Are you going to kill her?'

'That depends,' he said. Stanislav narrowed his eyes at him, but said nothing. 'We need to know how to get past the dragon, so we're guessing we need her alive for that.'

The serving girl blinked.

'We must go,' said Stanislav. 'Strike now, while we still can.'

'No, wait.' Dalip held the steward's coat by his collar. 'What are we missing?'

The serving girl was shaking with confusion. 'The mistress and the wyvern.'

'Yes?'

'She is ... she is the wyvern.'

'I don't understand,' said Dalip.

'She changes between woman and beast.'

'You have got to be joking.'

'No.'

No wonder the steward had been so confident, so arrogant. They burst into the geomancer's room at the top of the castle, and within seconds they're facing a massive, angry dragon. And not some animal, either, but human intelligence and guile.

'What the hell do we do?'

After a few moments, Stanislav said: 'Nothing has changed, and now that we know, we can use it to our advantage. If we can get the geomancer before she changes, then we kill both her and the dragon at the same time. We go in hard, all of us. Bring her down. Stop her any way we can.'

'What if she changes first? What if she's already changed?' Dalip looked at his knife. It didn't seem very big now.

'Then we have to kill a dragon instead.'

Stanislav had only seen the creature in the distance: he didn't understand quite how fierce it was, nor how large it was. Some of them were going to die in the fight, and the thought made Dalip hesitate.

'What does she value most? If we got hold of that, would she negotiate with us?' He shook the steward. 'What about him? Does he mean anything to her?'

The serving girl looked as if she was about to faint. 'I don't know. I don't know. She keeps all of her treasure with her.'

'This discussion is over,' said Stanislav. 'We must attack, kill her, escape. It is all we need to understand.'

'I'm trying to do the right thing here!' Dalip's voice started to rise, and he clamped back down on it. 'There has to be another way.'

'There is no other way. That much is clear.'

'Give me some time with her. Ten minutes. Quarter of an hour. I can talk our way out of this, and no one has to fight.'

'This is foolishness. She will kill you, and she will be warned.' Stanislav shrugged off Luiza's hand. 'I did not think you a coward.'

'I'm not ... Look, she's not going to kill me if she thinks you're going to burn her tower down with all her treasure in it. Even if she turns into a dragon and flies away, she can't carry it with her.'

'Once she has turned into a dragon, then killing her becomes so much more difficult. She can keep us trapped here until we starve. Or make another mistake such as this one.'

'I'm not making a mistake. If we rush her, we might win, but we might all get eaten and we're smarter than that. None of us wants to face a dragon, not if we can help it.' Dalip pushed the steward in Luiza's direction. 'We were told, right at the start, that we could be whatever we wanted to be. We still can. Let me talk to her, tell her we've taken her steward and the tower. She's not stupid.'

'Evil and intelligent is worse.'

'Killing her is not our only option.'

'For God's sake, Stanislav,' hissed Elena, 'let him try.'

Mama nodded. 'We can fight, but if we didn't have to ...'

'Make it good,' said Luiza, and Stanislav could only growl in frustration.

'This is not the plan.'

'The plan went out the window when you decided we'd not wait for the next fight. So don't complain.' Dalip wrapped his fingers around the knife handle and stepped to the door. 'I'll, well. Do my best.'

25

She flew along the silver length of the river, with the storm chasing her all the way. The wind blustered at her back, and the black line of cloud came at a gallop, pulled in from the wild ocean by white horses.

She didn't know what she'd do when she got there. There was a dragon, and she would fight it in the sky, while the rain lashed down and the thunder cracked. She would throw it down and feel her beak close on its neck, her head shaking with its death-throes. And then she would ... what? What could she do after that? Find her friends and perhaps find a way home.

She thought about that. There was, according to both the wolfman and Crows, no way back to London: but neither of them were the most trustworthy of witnesses, and she'd have to make that judgement for herself, later. The geomancer would have maps of her own they could look at, and once the dragon had gone, she wasn't going to be able to stop them going through all her things and asking as many questions as they wanted.

She flew low over the trees, the rush of silvery crowns a blur beneath her, the mountain rising ahead of her, split in two by the river gorge. She flew lower, the walls of rock rising up either side in blank-faced slabs and drawing together, until she was forced to twist and turn in the gap, threading her way like a needle through the weft of the landscape.

Then she was out, back into the clear air, with the rising wind under her wings. She banked left, spiralling up, keeping an eye on the castle on the flank of the mountain opposite. Once she'd gained height, she overflew the courtyard. The guards had left the security of their fire, and were all at the door of one of the low buildings, rhythmically hammering a long log into the wood, shouting incoherently at each other.

She dipped her wing and made a tight turn around the main tower, spotting for the first time the balcony cantilevered off the top floor, just below the conical roof. She made another pass and saw that the balcony was not only wide enough to land on, but that a perch – a monstrous perch – had been erected on it.

Twisting in flight, doing a roll so that she could take in all of the darkening sky, she searched in vain for the dragon. But that perch, scratched and worn by long claws, spoke of its existence. It was here, somewhere.

The guards had gained access to the building they'd been trying to break into, stumbling in their haste to push through the doorway and into the room beyond. She watched them disappear, and watched them again as they spilled back out, still shouting. After a moment's argument, they set off at a lumbering run either towards the tall tower, or to the closest set of gates in the outer wall.

Of course this castle had grown from the ground, just like Crows' had: it followed that it sat on one of the confluences of energy from the portals, and that the size of it depended on the power of the geomancer and the number of people she could command. Not caring whether the inhabitants were slave or free, Down did the rest.

But she judged that something was seriously wrong below: guards didn't normally have to force their way into what they guarded, and the tall tower was at the centre of the noise. The gates leading to the mountain lake were closing, and the ones overlooking the valley would be next. She'd not been able to spot an enemy, either single or several, crossing the bare ground before the castle walls. They were under attack, but from within, not without.

As she glided over their heads, two of the men went back to collect their impromptu battering ram. The tower, too, was sealed to them.

Not her, though. She could land and enter: there was still no sign of the dragon, so she decided that it was safe to do so.

It was as she slowed to grasp the perch that one of the guards spotted her and pointed with a shout. Her wings fluttered against the air as she braked, hovering for a moment before closing her claws on the scored wooden bar. There was nothing that they could do to her from down there: if they'd had a gun, or even a bow and arrow, it'd be a different story. Those with the battering ram renewed their efforts. The others, after gawping up at her, pressed their backs close to the tower's wall in case she swooped at them.

The doors in front of her needed hands to open properly. She leant forward to peck at them, her sharp beak rattling the bolts. That didn't work, but there were other ways to get in. She started a more concerted jabbing and scratching as she tried to break her way through. Every time she pushed, the crack between the doors widened, and she could see flickers of what was inside: a splash of red, a line of silver, something deep green. She kept on, battering at the doors, using her size and her lightning-fast kicks to weaken the fastenings.

And all of a sudden, they gave, and the doors swung open, banging against their jambs. Her keen eyes noted all the places inside the room within – bed, table, wall-hangings, boxes, wood, brass, bone, cloth, light, shadow – and finally rested on the woman standing in the centre, leaning heavily on a stick.

She was dressed in white and gold, her skirts down to the

floor, her sleeves as far as her hands. Almost weddingy, but her expression – her whole purple-bruised and black-blooded cut face – held no celebration.

'Have you come for me?' asked the woman.

Mary's gaze skittered behind her to the intricate metal machines set up on benches around the circumference of the room, and didn't answer. She turned her head in short, sharp jerks to take it all in.

'What are you waiting for?' The woman's voice was sharp, used to being obeyed. Mary knew the type. Her neck feathers prickled.

She could just about squeeze in. She'd be at a sudden, and huge, disadvantage. No room to stretch her wings, her head forced against the ceiling, difficult to raise her talons in front of her. Difficult to leave in a hurry, too. The boom-boom-boom echoing up the tower told her that the guards hadn't broken in yet, but also that it was only a matter of time until they did.

She had cunning, both as a hawk, and as a veteran of the care system. So no, she wasn't going to do what the woman wanted. She'd stay outside and keep watch for the dragon. She had almost turned away, when unexpected movement caught her attention. There was a hole in the floor, surrounded by what she'd thought was an odd metal cage, but now she could see was a curving banister.

A dark mass of long black wavy hair, the hint of an orange collar. He was facing away, then slowly, slowly, his head came around to reveal his face.

It took her a moment to recognise him. It was a longer moment than it took for him to gasp, and longer still than him spotting a massive bird of prey peering intently at him from the broken balcony doors. That the geomancer stood between them, her back to him, was mostly lost as mere detail.

The geomancer turned as quickly as her injuries would allow, and Dalip stayed where he was on the staircase, his empty hands raised.

'You.'

'Yes,' he said. His gaze left Mary, alighted on the geomancer, then was back on the bird. Which had gone, and only the coffee-coloured girl remained.

'And me,' she said.

The geomancer was confronted front and back.

'Mary?' said Dalip.

'It'll take too long to explain. Is everyone else all right?'

'They're downstairs. If the guards get in, then ... I don't know.'

'Then she has to call them off.'

'She's only going to do that if we threaten to hurt her.'

The geomancer banged her stick against the floor. 'Stop discussing me like I wasn't here. You – you are my slave, and you – I should have killed you on the mountain-top while I had the chance.'

'I refuse to be your slave.'

'And ...' Mary frowned. 'You weren't on the mountain-top.'

'You silly little girl. Are you really that stupid?'

'Fuck you,' was her automatic response. 'And fuck your wolf-man, too. You're shits, the pair of you.'

The geomancer lurched towards Mary, raising her stick to strike that foul mouth. She staggered as she swung, and she fell against a bench, upsetting the delicate brass instrument on it. It teetered for a moment, and she scrabbled to save it, all thought of violence lost.

The effort left her sprawled on the ground at Mary's feet. Mary looked down at her trying to rise, and she realised what the pattern of cuts and bruises meant.

'You're the —'

'Dragon,' said Dalip. 'One of the servants told us. But you, you're a ...' He flapped his arms uselessly. 'You're a bird.'

'Yes, I am, when I want to be.'

'You're also not very dressed.' He shook his head to clear his mind. 'How do we prevent her from turning?'

254

'I don't know. I don't think we can. Perhaps I hurt her badly enough to stop her, for a bit.' Mary snatched the geomancer's stick away. It didn't seem like it was a magic wand, or wizard's staff, like she'd seen in films, but there was no point in risking it. It might just be a smoothed length of wood, but it might be as lethal as a loaded gun.

'You did this to her? How?'

'I came to find you, see if I could sneak into the castle and get you all out. She came at me as the dragon, tried to kill me.' Thinking about it, even though she'd been utterly desperate and out of her depth, she'd been brave and resourceful, and in the end, despite her injuries, she'd won. Her chin came up. 'I still beat her.'

The geomancer hung on to the edge of the table and pulled herself up. The brass thing rattled and rolled.

'You were lucky.'

'I beat your arse good and proper. Now, call off the heavies.'

'That would be very stupid of me. And I'm not stupid.'

'Dalip,' said Mary. 'You should leave.'

Everything close by that was loose, started to hum, chatter or buzz.

'Mary, what are you doing?'

'Finishing what I started.'

'We can't fight everyone.'

'We don't have to. We just need to fight her, and the whole place falls apart. Isn't that right, your ladyship? This castle wasn't built by you. Down gave it to you, and it can take it away just as easily.'

'Mary, what are you talking about?'

'She knows. She knows exactly what I'm talking about.'

'Oh, I know far more than you do, girl. You caught me off guard before: not now. I know how to deal with you this time.'

'You threw everything you had at me and you fucked up.' Mary was still holding the stick, and she swung it at the geomancer's head.

The blow was blocked by the sudden interposition of the same brass apparatus that the geomancer had gone to all the trouble of saving minutes before. Rather than a skull being cracked, it was metal that bent and twisted.

It fell, broken, between them.

Then it was the geomancer's turn. After the first flung object came from behind Dalip and nearly took his head off on its way to bludgeon Mary, he ducked back down into the stairwell.

Mary squared up for the fight. She dodged the jar easily – its arrival had been telegraphed for longer than a drunken punch outside a kebab shop – and heaved the now-empty table up to be her shield.

The wood shuddered and groaned, and the legs scraped towards her. The impacts came regularly, a continual barrage of heavy concussions that was going to leave nothing in the room intact. She knew that this was treasure the geomancer was wasting, destroying it all in an attempt to destroy her, but also to deny it to her when Mary inevitably triumphed.

She let her pound the table for a few moments longer, crouching behind it as debris exploded in cogs and dust, then retreated a little way. She took a step to the side, then another, and blindly, everything was still directed at the table, taking the brunt of the geomancer's fury.

Quickly, quietly, she skipped across the room. She hadn't done so much physical activity as this since she'd faced the dragon: the cuts on her back and the bruises in her flesh dragged and ached as she ran and jumped up on the big bed, leaping down on the other side. Something sailed past her ear, fast and bright, but it was only passing.

She thought she should have a weapon of some sort, but even then, it wasn't very street. She'd settle this like a true Londoner, with fists and feet and nails and teeth. As the geomancer orchestrated her destructive volleys like a demented conductor, Mary came up behind her and threw herself at her back, pulling at the wild blonde hair with one hand, and clawing at her face with the other.

Mary's knees punched down, and the geomancer went over. Her face smacked the floor, and there was a spray of blood, thick and red, across the stone flags. Oh, Mary knew how to do this, savage and relentless and utterly without mercy, yanking handfuls of hair and battering her face, half-letting her up only to shove her back down and keep going. There was no one to intervene: no police or social workers or care home staff to drag her away, trailing scraps of skin and cloth, to be forced into some Home Office-approved restraining position until she'd calmed down; not even other kids who'd cheer her on for the first few minutes and end up pulling at her arms because she was taking it just too far.

She could keep on until she'd reduced her opponent to bloody ruin and beyond.

'Mary. Mary.'

She slowed, and then stopped. Something heavy – one of the wall coverings, thick and rich – draped over her shoulders, and she was gently guided aside. She sat with her back against one of the bed posts, while Dalip peered uncertainly at the geomancer.

'You've,' he said, dry-mouthed. 'I mean, she's really ...'

'I know,' said Mary, and pulled the covering tighter. 'What were you going to do?'

'I don't know. I talked Stanislav out of just killing her. I wanted to see if I could,' he shrugged, and his hands fluttered, 'reason with her.'

The geomancer covered her ruined face with her ragged hands, and wept. Dalip clearly had no idea what to do and, if she was honest, neither did Mary.

This was the woman who, a couple of nights ago, tried to cut her into strips with her sharp teeth and sharper claws. This was the woman who had turned her friends into slaves, and she didn't know how that had gone: Dalip had clearly been changed by his experiences, because the shy, uncertain engineering student was nowhere to be seen. This was the woman who had forced Crows' villagers out of their homes and staked out this part of Down as her personal kingdom, making a claim on everyone and everything in it.

The geomancer was, despite the tears, or even because of them, not a good person. She was a boss, nails-hard, ruthless in the pursuit of power. She had her crew, too. There was noise coming from below – shouts and cries and the sound of breaking things.

'Go and get them to stop. Just tell them we have her, and it's up to us to decide what happens to her.'

Dalip nodded and went to the top of the stairs, stopping to pick up one of the damaged brass instruments. 'Are you going to be okay with her?'

She raised her weary gaze. 'What do you think?'

He shrugged and hurried away, his bare feet padding on the stone steps, and she was alone with the geomancer. The situation was now very different from last time. She could take her to the broken balcony doors and pitch her over the edge. If she could change before she hit the ground, she'd live. If not, then the castle and everything in it would be Mary's. She might not even give her that chance, and simply finish her with something sharp, or heavy. The geomancer would, if left alone, heal and grow stronger until one day, Mary would be forced to do something.

In her experience, that was the way it had to be.

'Just … stop crying, okay? It's over.'

It didn't help. If anything, it made it worse.

'Look, I know what I'm supposed to do now. I'm supposed to take out the competition, move on to their manor and pick up where they left off. It's what you did to Crows, and it's what you expect of me.'

At the mention of Crows' name, the geomancer stiffened.

'Oh, Crows. He might be a bullshitter, but he taught me a few tricks. The rest, I seem to be learning by myself. He's gone now, though, with my map. And that hurt. I trusted him, like how we all trusted your wolfman: how come no one in this fucking place seems to be able to open their mouths without a lie coming out?'

The geomancer slowly lifted herself from prone to sitting, wedging herself against the wall. The white and gold dress was tattered and torn: one sleeve was down by her wrist, and the other's stitching had all but unravelled. Her front, bare chest and sculpted bodice, was stained scarlet from the copious nose bleed Mary had given her. She lifted a hand and scraped her hair away from her face enough to reveal one baleful red eye.

She wiped her puffy lips with the back of her hand. Her teeth were white against the red.

'Why are you letting me live?'

'Because I don't feel like killing you, right? You want to die? There's the window.' Mary glared at her. 'This should have been different. You could have been nice to us. We would have answered all your questions. We'd have probably stayed here while we found our feet. Instead, you treat us like shit, then wonder why we don't do as we're told. You can fuck right off with that. You're going to have to answer our questions now, and you'd better tell us the truth.'

26

Dalip found a stand-off at the bottom of the tower. The guards had forced the door, but those inside had barricaded the stairwell making it impossible for them to pass further.

'Let me through,' he said to Mama, and even though it was a squeeze to get by her on the stairs, they were both past the point of embarrassment. Elena was next, and it was no more nor less awkward. The front line consisted of Luiza and Stanislav, and Dalip peered between them over the jumble of furniture at the thwarted guards. He threw the geomancer's broken toy into the midst of the snarling men.

'What was that?' asked Stanislav. He'd been cut on the forehead by some flying object, a raised lump with a gash at its centre had streamed blood down the side of his face and neck.

'I've no idea what it was, but it should mean we can stop fighting for a bit.'

'You've taken her, then,' came the shouted response.

'It's over. She's still alive, but she's our prisoner now.'

'You should have finished her,' hissed Stanislav. 'She is dangerous.'

'Look, just ...' Dalip screwed his face up in concentration. 'Shut up about that. We know what we're doing.' He returned his attention to the guards. 'Leave the tower. Leave the castle if that's what you want, we can't stop you and we wouldn't want to. Everything's changed here – we're not slaves anymore.'

He could see the guards individually weighing up the balance of power: one by one, they left the downstairs room. There was no door to pull shut behind them – it was lying flat on the floor – but once the last of them had gone, the only thing stealing back through was the night.

Mama huffed. 'Well, that's that. We're free to go, right?'

Dalip put his shoulder to the barricade, just to see how firm it was. 'It's a bit more complicated than that, and I really don't have the words to explain it. It'd all be better if you just took a look for yourself.'

Luiza offered him the long knife. He thought about declining, but he took it. It was a kirpan by any other name, and he hoped that he'd be able to get the geomancer to tell him what she'd done with his kangha and kara. And his pagh.

The two serving women came with them, up the narrow winding steps all the way to the top. Mary had heard them coming, and was sitting on the bed, still wrapped in the tapestry.

'Hey,' she said.

'Everything okay?'

'We need to clean her up. Find her some new clothes.'

'Are you sure about that?'

'We can't just leave her like that.' She gestured at the raggedy woman, who sat with her legs drawn up and knees hard against her chest. 'Just because we won doesn't mean we have to behave like shits.'

'She tried to kill both of us.' He stepped off the staircase and in to the room. Mama followed, cautiously, eyes wide.

'So we'll be careful. Good to see you, Mama.'

Mama slowly turned, taking in the whole room, and eventually her gaze caught the slight figure of Mary.

'Good Lord and Sweet Jesus,' she shrieked. 'Where've you been, girl?'

'Out and about. I'm fine.' She smiled. 'I'm better than fine.'

'What happened to your clothes?'

Dalip had to stand back lest he got trampled by Mama.

'They got wrecked. By her. When she was a dragon.'

The others emerged. Mary nodded her welcome, taking a kiss on the cheek from Luiza and Elena. Mama drew back the wall hanging to inspect Mary's back, causing her to wail and invoke God again.

Stanislav stared for a moment at Mary, then fixed on the geomancer. He marched straight to her and grabbed her by one thin wrist, pulling her upright and leaving her legs struggling to find purchase.

He pressed her against the wall, his hand around her throat, and slapped her, forehand, backhand, her head snapping one way, then the other. His fingers tightened, and she started to scrabble at her own neck, trying to prise him off.

'Stanislav. Stop.' Dalip started towards him, but Luiza was already moving.

Stanislav's hand fastened on the front of dress, hooking the cloth away from her already-bruised and blood-smeared skin and ripping it apart. Luiza jumped up on him, her momentum knocking him sideways and forcing him to let go. They landed together, all three of them: the geomancer was desperate to get away, Stanislav just as desperate to attack her, and Luiza clinging to the Slav like a burr.

Mama interposed her bulk, shielding the geomancer and shoving hard at Stanislav. Now separated from his target, he half-rose and shook Luiza clear with a shrug of his broad shoulders. She landed with a squeal and tried to scramble back into contact, but Dalip got within range and brought Stanislav down.

The man raged and frothed and bellowed, and Dalip could

barely hold him, let alone control him. It was like riding a tiger, and not even his fabled grandfather had done that.

Luiza threw her club next to him. She was right: it was either that or the knife. He snatched it up, got his arm around Stanislav's neck and smashed the club against the crown of his head. The first strike seemed to have little effect. The second knocked him back flat against the floor. The third was ill-timed and weakly done, and only the fourth, where he was able to get a better swing and connect with the wound already on Stanislav's temple, stunned him.

'Get him out of here,' demanded Mama. 'Just get him out before he does that again. And when he comes to his senses, tell him we do not do that – to anyone! That man is becoming too much of a liability to have around.'

Dalip threw the club aside and dragged Stanislav by his collar to the stairs, then bundled him down them and into the room he'd first entered via the window. He slammed the door shut and put his back against it, bracing himself upright. He swung wildly between shock and fury.

'What was that? What did you think you were doing?'

Stanislav, sprawling half under the table that still held the specimen tray, groggily put his hand to his head where Dalip had coshed him.

'Answer me!' He thought of all the words that the other boys at school used, openly, between themselves. 'You were … you were …'

'You don't understand,' slurred Stanislav.

'That, at least, is right. Mary – Mary can do magic now. The geomancer wasn't a threat any more. She was beaten. She was our prisoner.'

'She is still dangerous—'

'No. She isn't. It's you who's too dangerous. You've already killed two people tonight. One of them in cold blood. And then you want to kill the steward, and the geomancer, and then you,

you were tearing her clothes off. That's just not …' All the long words had failed him. 'That's just not right.'

'She is dangerous,' roared Stanislav. 'She needs to be, needs to be – subdued. Conquered. Looted. Like a city. Her walls must come down, yes? It is not enough to force her to her knees, she needs to remember why she is there.'

'That's—'

'She was using you to fight animals to the death. Have you forgotten that?'

'No, I haven't, but—'

'She deserves to be trampled into the dust. We were slaves! We were owned! She is beaten, but she is not humiliated like we were. Make her cower. Make her flinch when we raise our hand to her. That is all she understands, that the strong do what they want, and the weak have to suffer what they will.' Stanislav sat up, back to the table. 'She will try to kill us if we do not do these things. Break her will, and we will be safe.'

'I can't go along with that.'

'Then you are one of the weak, and you will always be a slave.'

Dalip stared at the man, who'd he'd spent hours with. He knew Stanislav was hard, driven, and unsympathetic, but as long as he'd worked hard and not spared his effort, his teacher had seemed not just satisfied, but actually pleased. Yes, he'd had moments where he'd disliked the man, but they were fleeting, because he could see the point to his training – staying alive long enough to escape.

It had turned out that Stanislav wasn't putting on an act, and that he was actually like that.

'Mary had it all under control, and look, I'm not the only one who thinks you went too far.'

'Not far enough, I say.'

'You were trying to rape her in front of everyone! What the hell did you expect us to do? Watch?'

'That is how humiliation works.'

Now Dalip slipped into despair. 'Where did you learn this stuff, Stanislav? Normal people don't think like this. They don't. They just don't.'

'This is war, you stupid boy. This is anarchy. This is all the places you read about in the newspapers and see on the television and are glad that you do not live there. Do you think normal, civilised, nice people live in such places? No, only two sorts of creatures: wolves and sheep. No shepherds. The wolves eat the sheep whenever and wherever they like.' He snorted. 'And now the sheep have the chance to kill one of the wolves and still they bleat.'

'So which are you?'

'I had to become a wolf because I did not want to be a sheep. You, you were becoming a wolf too, but no. The sheep have dragged you back into their fold.' Stanislav screwed his face up in disgust. 'Baaaaa.'

Dalip slid down the door, still barring the man opposite from leaving.

'Where were you?'

Stanislav equivocated for a moment, pressing at the various lumps on his head.

'Bosnia.'

Dalip had heard about it, briefly and in passing, but it had started before he was born, and ended when he was still a baby. That some of those responsible had gone on trial later was the only reason he knew there'd even been a war. His parents had been uncomfortable enough about what had gone on that they'd talk over the reporting, exchanging family gossip until the report had finished.

The images, however, remained: mass graves, shattered buildings, haunted people in the backs of cars and trucks piled high with their belongings.

Stanislav had been there. More than been there: had fought there, and it didn't really matter for who, or why. What was important was that he'd brought that war with him to Down; in the same way, Dalip supposed, that everyone who came to Down brought only what they were with them. Their hopes and dreams, their fears and nightmares, the past they'd lived and the future they were destined to live.

'You have to leave that behind,' said Dalip. 'It's destroying you, and us.'

'Do you know what it is like, to be weak?' asked Stanislav.

'Not until recently. I only got through that because of you.'

'Do you want to be that weak ever again?'

'No, of course not—'

'Can you not see that if we fail to act now, then we are condemning ourselves to always being that weak?'

After everything that had gone on that night, Dalip was abruptly exhausted. He'd done everything asked of him, and more. His head sagged, and he gathered up his loose hair and dragged it over one shoulder.

'We cannot do a deal with our former owners,' said Stanislav. 'They are not people we can trust. They will seek to own us again, and they must be stopped.'

'We have stopped them.'

'For now. When they regroup, they will try again.'

'Then we'll fight them again. Stanislav, it doesn't have to be like this.'

'Tell them that and see if they agree with you. They did not have to take us as slaves, but they did. They did not have to make you fight in the pit, but they did. They will do it again unless we – you and me – finish it now. There is no one else: even if we walk out of here, they will take others. Do you want that? Do you want to say to yourself, "We let the slavers go", knowing that you have condemned others to the same state as you were?'

'I know we have to do something.'

'You know what you have to do. You know!'

Dalip scrubbed his face with his fingers. 'We don't have to do that. We don't. We just don't.'

'You know the right thing to do. You refuse to do it.' Stanislav pulled himself up by the table-top. 'I will have to do it myself. To protect the sheep.'

'You're staying here. The others don't trust you for the moment.' He got to his feet too, and they were both as uncertain of vertical as each other. 'Give it time, and we'll work something out.'

He left him there, and closed the door. Stanislav wasn't a prisoner, and there was nothing but words keeping him in the store room. Dalip hoped all the same that he'd stay there.

Truth be told, the man had a point. They'd been tricked and trapped and enslaved, and they had a moral duty to make sure that it didn't happen to anyone else. There was no justice in Down, no higher authority to appeal to. It was the strong against the weak, or the strong for the weak: what other way was there?

Dalip climbed up the steps to the top floor. Mama was seeing to the geomancer's wounds, while Luiza and Elena were carefully checking the contents of each box, each drawer. Mary had moved on to the bed, and lay there against the headboard, still wrapped up in the tapestry.

'What are they looking for?' he asked her.

'Maps,' she said. 'She should have lots of maps, but there don't seem to be many at all.'

'And why maps?'

'Because,' she said, 'maps are power and wealth. It's what geomancers need to … Look, this is fucking complicated and I can barely get my head round it myself, let alone explain it. She should have a fuck-ton of maps somewhere in this tower, and they're like gold, so I'm guessing that they're somewhere here, in this room.'

'Have you asked her where they are?'

'She's not exactly in an answering mood: between me and your mate, we've terrified her into silence.' She shifted uncomfortably on the bed, and sat up, revealing her scars as she slid her hands down to her shins.

'Who, what happened?' The wounds were new, barely healing, wide and glistening.

'She did. She happened. A few days ago now. She would have killed me if she could.'

Dalip sat on the edge of the bed, his back to her. He watched while the two Romanian women systematically went through everything, lifting things up, moving them around, checking behind them.

'What are we going to do with her?'

'I don't know. I thought I was coming here to kill her. It turned out I didn't need to.'

'I thought we were going to have to kill her too. But I didn't have the stomach for it. I wanted to see if I could reason with her instead.' He looked at her over his shoulder, her coiled-spring hair, her skin opened up in broad red trenches. 'Was that a mistake? Stanislav seems to think so. He says if we leave her alive, then either us or someone else will become her victims. We have to remember what sort of person she is.'

'She's no saint. Neither am I. You might be, I guess. What do you think we should do?' She drew up her legs and hugged her knees.

'That the only way to stop her may be to kill her. And that I'm not going to be the one to do it.' He shrugged. 'I don't know if that makes me a coward or not.'

'A lot depends on her. If she even looks at me funny, I'll have her.' Mary pointed down behind her neck. 'The last time I turned my back on her, I got these.'

'I'm supposed to protect the weak – that's what the gurus say. I don't know who the weak are any more.' Dalip reached into his pocket for Pigface's knife, and considered his distorted, dim reflection in the blade. 'This isn't over yet, is it?'

'No way. But at least we can do what we came here for – ask some questions of her, and work out if we can go home or not.'

Dalip caught her gaze, and held it. 'Do you think we can?'

'I'm told if we do, we'd be the first.' She blinked her big brown eyes. 'We might have to stay.'

He didn't know what he thought about that, and looked away.

27

They couldn't find any maps, just some half-complete outlines of the coast to the south, with scratches marking a few prominent features. Mary knew that this wasn't right, that the geomancer had to have maps, because that was the whole point. How could someone hope to divide Down with criss-crossing lines of energy without detailed maps?

The wind had picked up, and the broken doors on to the balcony were beginning to heave and yaw. Dalip went to wedge them shut, while Mary went to sit opposite the geomancer, who looked up through closing eyes at the woman who'd beaten her. Her split lips reopened as she pressed them together.

'What do we call you?' asked Mary.

'Whatever you want.'

'Pick a name. Yours would be good, but any name will do.'

Mama frowned at Mary and went to wipe away some of the freshly blooming blood with a damp cloth dipped in what might be wine. The geomancer pushed her hand firmly away.

'I'm not a cripple.'

'You seemed grateful enough for my help before,' said Mama. 'What's changed?'

'It's me,' said Mary. 'She can fool you as to what she's really like. She can't fool me.'

'She's just a—'

'She tried to kill me, Mama.' Mary shrugged off the tapestry. 'She did that. She did everything that's happened to you and the others. All this is her fault, and she can fucking tell me her fucking name right now, or we'll go another six rounds.'

The geomancer looked sour. 'Bell. I'm Bell.'

'Like the Disney princess?'

'The thing that rings.'

'Okay. Bell: where are your maps?'

'I don't have any.'

'That's just bollocks. I know you have maps. Where are they?'

A flash of defiance burned in Bell's face. 'They were stolen.'

'Convenient. By who?'

The fire flickered, and was extinguished. 'It doesn't matter.'

'It matters to me. We want to know where the fuck we are and what the fuck is going on, and whether we can get the fuck home again. So, you're going to tell me where your maps are, or I'll beat it out of you right now.' Mary balled her fists, and the muscles in her bare arms flexed.

'A man called Crows stole them when he left me.' Bell put her hands to her face to cover her shame.

'Left you? Like he was your boyfriend? Oh, you have got to be fucking kidding me.'

'You know this Crows man?' Mama looked askance. 'You get around, girl.'

'Yes, I know him. He stole my fucking map too.'

'Mercy! Will someone please, in heaven's name, explain what is going on?'

'Right.' Mary glanced up to see she had an audience. The longer she left it, the more interested they became, and the more embarrassed she turned. 'No. I'm going to let Bell do it.' She pushed her with the flat of her foot, and the geomancer tried to slap it away. Too slow.

With the focus of attention off Mary, she moved back and waited with the others.

'Down,' said Bell, with a shuddering sigh, 'Down isn't just a direction.'

'It's a destination,' said Mary. 'Get to the good bits.'

'Down is a world separate to where we came from, but connected to it in lots of different places and times. These places we call portals, and they're doors where people can enter Down, but not, apparently, leave. Someone, a long time ago, discovered that if you draw a line between two portals, there's nearly always another portal on that line. You can get villages on those lines, too. Where those lines cross, you get castles. That's why maps are important. And Crows stole mine.'

'She's missing some stuff out,' said Mary, 'but that's pretty much what I got from Crows.'

'So what did I miss out?' asked Bell. She pushed her hair back from her face, to better show off her black eyes, torn skin, and dew-drop of blood clinging to the end of her nose.

'That the villages and the castles grow, depending on how many people live there.' Mary watched the others' consternation rise. 'Those houses we found in the forest? They grew there, and were just sinking back into the ground. The same with castles. She needs people to live here in order to keep the walls and the towers intact.'

'Is that why she took us?' Elena was as bemused as she was angry. 'Is that all?'

'No, that can't be all,' said Dalip. 'Why did you make me fight in the pit?'

'Fight? Pit?' asked Mary.

'Like a, a gladiator. She wanted me to be afraid. Isn't that right?'

Bell shifted awkwardly, painfully. 'I ... I was carrying out an experiment. When we came to Down, we were all running from something, someone. I thought that by making someone scared enough, I could open a portal back to London. Didn't work though, did it? You were too bloody honourable.'

She said it with grudging admiration, but hadn't counted on Dalip not taking it as a compliment. Luiza just about stopped him from dragging the geomancer up by the hair and throwing her through the closed balcony doors.

'It wouldn't have worked if I'd told you why you were being trained to fight,' said Bell. 'It wasn't about you being scared. It was about those other plebs being scared of you.'

Luiza pushed Dalip away and stood in front of him. Dalip's chest heaved, and he seemed to only control himself with the utmost effort. 'It didn't work at all.'

'You can't blame me for trying,' Bell offered.

Luiza's hand pressed hard against Dalip's sternum.

'I do blame you for trying.'

'To be honest,' said Mary, 'it sounds like a really shitty thing to do, over and above all the other shitty things you did. And though Crows might be shady as fuck, at least he never tried to kill me, or any of my mates. He saved me from the wolfman. He taught me how to use magic. Why don't I guess why he left you?'

Bell stayed defiantly silent.

'If I said he left you because he thought your idea was fucking nuts, would I be wrong?'

'Yes. You don't understand anything.'

'So make me understand.'

The two women stared at each other. Mary was acutely aware of the cold wind rattling through the tower, brushing against her wounds in a way that didn't happen when she was a bird, but also that Bell was sitting opposite her in a fine white dress turned to scarlet rags. The gravity of the damage they'd done to each other should have been worthy of comment, but neither of them were ever going to be called to account for that.

'Crows was my lover,' said Bell. 'We planned everything together.'

'Hang on,' said Mary. 'Where's Grace?'

'She's not here.' Mama shrugged. 'She's not here and we don't know what that means.'

'Okay. We'll have to look for her after this. Go on, Bell: you were making plans.'

'We knew there was a portal around here, but didn't know where. We found this crossing point using ...' Her voice trailed off as she contemplated her collection of broken brass instruments. 'A device. We searched – him by water, me by air.'

The others frowned at this.

Mary sniffed. 'Remember the huge sea snake we saw after we got to the shore? That was Crows. He knew at that point that the portal was probably somewhere on the island. When he couldn't find it, he got me to tell him exactly where. They're not supposed to disappear.'

Bell suddenly showed more than passing interest. 'The portal vanished?'

'There's nothing but rock there now. It's gone, and Crows didn't know what that meant. Do you?'

Bell shook her head. 'Portals are attached to London. They don't go anywhere. They're fixed points.'

'What if,' said Dalip. 'What if London ceased to exist?'

That caused disquiet, but he persisted.

'I don't mean to ... I've got as much to lose as everyone. But that fire wasn't normal. We ran and ran, and it wasn't enough. Even a plane crash wouldn't have been that bad. And if – I don't know – a nuclear bomb, maybe, with a firestorm afterwards. Would that be enough to break the connection?'

'When are you from?' asked Bell.

They were all too surprised at the question to answer, except Mary.

'Twenty twelve. You?'

'Nineteen sixty-eight.' Bell looked at them again, each one, checking for differences between them and her. 'How did it go, those forty years?'

'Good for some. Not so good for others,' said Mary. 'This is well off the point, though. Crows said that whoever controls the portals, controls Down.'

'And London,' said Dalip. 'They'd control London too.'

'That. But no one's ever managed to open a door going the other way, right?'

'No. But there has to be a way to do it.'

'Why?' asked Mary. 'Why does there? Why can't this just be it?'

'Because it doesn't make sense otherwise. If things can pass from London to here, then it stands to reason they can pass back.'

'You mean like you can turn into a dragon and fucking castles grow out of the ground?'

Bell faltered. 'This place just has different rules, that's all.'

'One of which might be, you can't go back,' interrupted Dalip. 'Do you have any evidence at all that anything has ever gone back to London, over and above simply wishing it was true?'

'No,' she whispered. 'No.'

'Great.' He turned away, then abruptly towards her again. 'You were going to have me fight people to the death because you hoped something might just happen that had never happened before. That's just ...'

'Fucking nuts?' offered Mary.

'Pretty much covers it. If you were going to experiment on someone, at the very least you should have started with yourself.' The wind rattled the balcony doors open, and Dalip went to close them with something more substantial.

'These maps,' said Mama. 'Are they that important?'

Mary nodded. 'Without them, we don't have a fucking clue where we are or where to go next. Geomancers like her spend years making them, finding them, hiding them away. Get it right, and you get a massive fuck-off castle like this, people to follow you, and maybe, if you're the first to work out how everything works, you get to run the show.'

'Then we should concentrate on getting the maps back,' said Mama, arms folded.

'Problem is, Crows is long gone, turned into a sea snake and away.'

'He can't carry the maps like that,' said Bell, shifting awkwardly. 'He can't get them wet, and he needs hands to carry them.'

Mary looked at the ceiling. 'He lied to me. Again.'

'He does that,' said Bell.

'I'm not feeling sorry for you, if that's what you want. If I was him, I'd have lied to you too.' She tutted. 'He'd have to have them stashed somewhere, somewhere close. Not at his castle—'

'He had a castle?'

'It was a bit shit, but yes. Full of crows, which is why I thought he was called Crows.'

'Those weren't crows,' said Bell.

'Then what the fuck were they?'

'The crows were Crows. You've met Daniel and his wolves.'

'The wolfman?'

'Him. The wolves were Daniel. Projections from him, controlled by him. He can see through them, like a witch's familiar. Crows does the same, but through a flock of crows.'

Mary wiped her face with her hands. 'Oh fucking hell. I thought Crows had vanished, and he was there all the time. He played me. Fuck. He even taught me how to fly.'

'So where are the maps?' asked Mama. 'Does this Crows have them?'

'He wouldn't have left the area without them. They were in the castle, so he probably stashed them nearby, where I wouldn't find them. And if he can only carry them when he's a man, then … somewhere near the river. We know he swam up it, don't we, Dalip?'

'I thought he was going to eat me,' said Dalip. The increasing wind rattled at the shutters again, threatening to tear them loose. What might have been thunder rumbled distantly.

'The wolfman was down by the portal,' said Mary. 'I thought he was looking for Crows. Or me. But what if he was looking for the maps?' She thought about it. 'Where would he go with them? If he wanted to sell them, or just start again? Or maybe the other thing, trade the fact that portals can disappear.'

'There's really only one place. The White City. But it'll take him weeks to get there. There's still time to find him.' Bell murmured an offer: 'I can help you, if you want.'

'You are not going to turn into a dragon again. No. You with the maps is more dangerous than Crows with the maps, we've already found that out for ourselves. If anyone's going to find him, it's me.'

'She can turn into a bird,' said Dalip. 'A big one. A hawk.'

The others exchanged more glances, and Mary shrugged, pulling on her wounds.

'I'll go in the morning, just before it gets light. Where is this city?'

'In the far west. If I had my maps ...'

'You're a regular joker, aren't you? I'm tired of having to drag everything out of you, one bit at a time. I'm just tired. I feel like I could sleep for a week.'

'It's the transformations,' said Bell. 'They're exhausting.'

'Crows said there's a chance of getting stuck. Is that right?'

She looked equivocal. 'It's been known.'

Mary wondered what it would be like, to forget everything, to give it all up and live each day, free of consequence from yesterday and free of thought of tomorrow, her whole world just flight and wind and feathers. That wouldn't be too bad, would it? Except she had responsibilities now, to protect this ragged band of survivors. Her crew: her gang, in other words.

Not that she'd done a good job so far, but she was going to change that, and their fortunes.

'Okay. In the morning, I'll go out and look for Crows. In fact, what I'll do is look for crows. If I find some, he might be nearby. What we need to do is make sure that dragon-lady here doesn't try anything before then. Any suggestions?'

No one, apparently, wanted to kill her. At least, they weren't saying it out loud.

'Tie her up and lock her in a room?' said Luiza. 'A small room so if she changes, she hurts herself and not us.'

'Is she that dangerous,' asked Mama, 'that we have to tie her up?'

'I don't want her coming for me in the night,' said Mary. 'And it's going to be me, isn't it? I'm the threat to her, no matter how brave Dalip is or how mad Stanislav is.'

'We should watch her,' said Dalip. 'Take turns. But that means one of us is alone with her. Two of us?'

'I've never done anything like this before.'

'Stanislav will have,' said Elena.

'We're not going to ask him for advice,' said Dalip. 'Why don't I check the rooms and see if there's anything without a window? Or ask someone who knows, which'll probably be quicker.'

He wasn't gone for long, when he came running back.

'Stanislav's gone.' He paused. 'He's also killed the steward.' He paused again. 'It's ... not good.'

Mary caught his meaning better than the others. She looked at Bell's reaction. She'd just lost her ... what? Servant? Slave? Friend? Lover? And there was nothing except barely contained glee that their plans were going awry.

She knew people like that, back in London. They were the ones to avoid, the strange, dangerous ones who ended up getting locked away for the rest of their lives.

'Then we'd better go and find him.'

28

The steward was over by the door to the bridge. And under the table. And halfway up the wall where something, some part of him, had been thrown with great force and stuck.

'It looks like a fucking abattoir,' said Mary, and retreated quickly, intercepting Luiza with a muttered, 'You don't want to go in there.'

Dalip had been to an abattoir, where they killed animals to eat according to Sikh rules. Quick, clean, one cut. The room – the killing floor, because that's what it was called – had been almost spotless. The store room was far from that.

He stepped across the threshold and looked around. Stanislav could now be anywhere, either in the castle or even outside it. But he could still be here, hiding behind the barrels and the shelves, and he needed to check. The far door was still barred, but he peered into the shadows made barely lighter by the meagre lantern.

The steward had been decapitated, his head torn off with a force that was beyond human capacity. Hopefully, he'd been dead before that, because the thing that was glued to the wall was the sticky remains of his burst heart.

Dalip walked the room as if he was in a dream, the knife not even in his hand. What could he possibly do in the face of such primal forces except succumb? But Stanislav wasn't there, and he stepped outside and back on to the staircase to report.

'If he didn't come up, he had to go down.' He tugged at the hair on his chin. 'We need to stay together. I think … I think he's having some kind of psychotic episode. He was in a war where he came from, and he's pretty much reliving it now. The very worst parts of it.'

'Was that the guy's head?'

Dalip nodded. 'I don't think Stanislav used anything but his hands to do that.'

Mary grimaced. 'Seriously, he should be easy to find. He'll be covered in blood, everything. Just, where the fuck are his footprints? Hand-prints? I've seen places where some kid got stabbed, and it's everywhere: floors, walls, ceiling, and there's always footprints and smears and marks on the walls where you brush against them. I mean, just look.'

Dalip did. His bare feet were leaving almost perfect dark impressions on the stonework, like a child's printing set.

They searched the stairs, inspected the stonework, went down to the kitchen at the bottom of the tower, where their barricade was still mostly intact.

'He can't have come this way,' said Dalip, rattling a big chair hard enough to make the table resting on it fall to one side. Once it had all finished moving, he added: 'See?'

'You climbed in the window,' said Luiza. 'He must have climbed out.'

'I don't know if he could. He doesn't seem the climbing sort.'

'He doesn't seem the kind of bloke who'd rip someone's head off, either,' said Mary. 'But here we are.'

Dalip leaned back against the wall. Stanislav had saved his life, more than once. And now this. He'd been brought up to be loyal, and deferential to his elders. This … this was difficult for him.

'Luiza. The two women we found in the room above. Where did they go?'

She blinked. 'They came upstairs with us.'

'But they're not there now.'

'No.' She tutted. 'I suppose we must look for them too.'

'This is getting stupid, right?' Mary stared into the darkness up the stairs, and Dalip couldn't help but see how her scars shifted.

'We should go back to the top floor,' said Luiza, 'and wait until morning. We cannot see what we are doing.'

'At this rate, there may be no one left by morning.' Dalip pulled out the knife. 'We brought him here. We have to deal with this. One way or another.'

'Well, he's your mate,' said Mary.

'In which case, I might get a chance where no one else will. I'm not saying we have to do anything, you know, permanent, but who else is going to stop him? There's no one but us.'

'Every room, then. Every door. If he's not in the tower, then that's something.'

When they got back to the store room, Dalip made to go in again. Mary was about to stop him, and tell him they'd already looked there. Then she caught his expression and said nothing.

He opened the door, pushing it with his foot. It was exactly as he'd left it, except that the bars that should have been sealing the way to the bridge were lying on the floor, and the door chattering and rattling in the rising wind. The draught stole around his ankles on its way through the tower.

Luiza, in charge of the lantern, held it high over Dalip's head. 'He was in there all the time,' she said.

Dalip moved back on to the stairs and pulled the door firmly closed behind him.

'Mary, when you turn into a bird, how do you do it?'

'How? I just … I don't know. I just can. I want to be it, and there I am. Some big-arse bird.'

'And the first time, what happened?'

'I grew wings. Bell's dragon cut me open, and when I got the boilersuit off, I had wings. I really don't know how this works.' She stopped, and asked: 'Why?'

'So you can turn into a hawk, she can turn into a dragon, this man Crows turns into a sea serpent. I think Stanislav can turn into something, too. Something not good. Very strong.' He struggled with the whole idea, even though he himself may have been changed, and was in the process of changing. 'Do you get a choice?'

'Of what you change into?' Mary shrugged. 'Maybe, but I think you just become whatever it is that suits you best. Have you got any idea of what he's going to be?'

He knew. 'It's a wolf. He's going to be a wolf.'

'There is a thing, where you get stuck as an animal, and you forget what you were. Is that what's happened to him?'

'No,' said Dalip. He thought about the conversation he'd had, about wolves and sheep. 'I think he's got stuck halfway. A wolfman, who's actually part-wolf, part-man.'

'A werewolf. Fucking hell. How the fuck do we deal with that?'

'Silver,' said Luiza. 'We need silver.'

Dalip's mouth had gone dry. 'We don't have any silver, whether or not we can make weapons out of it, and anyway, if he's just like Mary or Bell, they don't need anything special to hurt them. But I should be able to talk him down. He'll listen to me.'

'You're kidding yourself, right? Dalip, he's gone crazy. This isn't like telling a mate not to do something stupid. He's gone way beyond that.'

'She is right, Dalip. He is a danger to everyone.' Luiza poked him in the chest. 'Especially you.'

'Why me?'

'Because you will not treat him with care. You will remember him as he was, not as he is. In that moment, he will kill you.'

'He's not going to kill me,' said Dalip, and realised he was lying to himself. Loyalty again; misplaced loyalty. 'Okay. Maybe he'll try. We – I – have to find him first. Go back upstairs. I'll do—'

He was at a loss. What was he supposed to do? Warn the remaining guards for certain. Track Stanislav down and confront him in whatever form he'd taken, and stop him from killing his way through the castle's inhabitants. He'd have to keep him at bay while he talked to him. He could do that. Stanislav had, ironically, taught him well. And if that didn't work, if it came down to a fight: he'd been taught how to do that, too.

'I can help,' said Mary. 'I'll be able to spot him, if he's outside, and if you're right about him being a wolf, I can just fly out of reach. Luiza, go and tell the others what we're doing. Don't leave the room until one of us tells you it's safe.'

'What if he comes for us?'

'You throw everything you have at him. Including Bell if you have to.' Mary moved uncomfortably, her wounds raw.

Luiza left them the lantern and scurried up the last few turns of the stairs, leaving Dalip and Mary not staring at each other.

'Do you,' he said, 'want me to find you a pair of trousers, or something?'

'Because running around in my pants makes me feel like a fucking superhero, right?' She blew out a breath, long and heartfelt. 'If you're hiding a pair of jeans somewhere, then yes. Otherwise, we're just wasting time.'

Under normal circumstances, he'd have found it distracting. He was used to women covering up. These weren't normal circumstances, and she wasn't a Sikh. 'I can cope if you can.'

'This is fucking stupid, you know that? We're just kids, and we're hunting an actual werewolf.'

'It would be even more stupid if you couldn't turn into a giant bird of prey.'

'That's actually a good point. We can do this, can't we?'

Dalip pulled a face. 'No one else is up for it, so I'm game if you are.'

'You really are a posh kid.' But she smiled as she said it.

'Doesn't mean I'm bad or wrong.'

'You're all right really. What first?'

'Let's find the guards. They don't deserve this.'

They dismantled the rest of the barricade and checked the whole of the downstairs area. There were more store rooms off the main kitchen, and each one involved a sweaty-palmed grip of the latch and a flinging wide of the door, expecting to be attacked in a flurry of fur and teeth, and gratefully disappointed when it didn't happen.

'Outside, then,' said Dalip. The doorway, with its broken door on the floor was full of wind and noise. 'This castle was grown? Seriously?'

'It's weird, but it's true.'

'I should be getting used to that, but I don't think I ever will.' He stuck his head out and remembered to look up and behind him at the wall. The sky, black already, was low and heavy and churning with cloud. The invisible moon was no help, and the unattended fire in the courtyard burned low and fitful.

'You go first,' said Mary. 'You've got the knife.'

He looked at it, its broad blade and short length. 'Something longer would be so much better. My grandfather had a sword, a proper sword: he even used it during the war.'

'He's not here though, is he? You are, and that's what we've got.'

When they both stepped outside, they were surprised at the violence of the weather. The gusty wind took hold of them and shook them hard. To the south, behind the bulk of the mountain, lightning flickered.

'It's only a storm, not like before,' said Mary. She clutched at Dalip's arm. 'Fuck me, it's cold.'

'I did say.'

The grass was sharp and brittle under their feet as they trotted across to the guard house. Lights glimmered from the window slits, and more ominously, from the open door.

Dalip slowed, and he pulled Mary back.

'We don't want to fight them. But they won't be happy. We've turned everything upside down for them.'

'Fuck them.'

'We still need to be careful.'

Dalip crossed the remaining distance, past the fire, to the steps up. The door was sideways in the doorway, deep scratches running against the grain of the wood. He leant it against the wall, and beckoned Mary in.

'This isn't good,' she whispered.

'Worked that out for myself.'

The room inside had a fire in the grate, drawing hard in the draught, crackling hard and burning bright. Chairs and tables were strewed across the floor, overturned, some broken, plates and mugs mixed in with the debris. There was a closed door in each of the far corners.

'Left or right?'

'Both of them, eventually. So it doesn't matter.' He thought of his grandfather, waving his age-spotted sword and screaming his defiance like he was still a young man facing his enemies. Then, the war-cries had been a party piece: now, he was repeating them silently, his tongue and lips finding their way around the syllables and accents of his ancestors. 'Left.'

He picked his way across the floor, trying to be as quiet as possible, though he didn't exactly know why. He put his fingertips against the door, gave it a little shove: it creaked a little, a crack of weak light opening out. He glanced around at Mary, who was busy shoving a fallen crust into her mouth.

'What?' she said, spitting out crumbs. 'I'm fucking starving.'

He rolled his eyes and put the flat of his hand to the wood. The door swung aside.

It took a moment, then a moment longer, then a very long moment that only ended when Mary reached past him, leaning out around him so she didn't have to set foot inside that back room, and pulled the door shut again.

'No,' she said. 'No, no, no, no, no. No.'

She pulled him back, all the way to the entrance, and he let himself be led, unblinking, to where the wind buffeted his clothes and tugged at his loose hair.

Mary looked up at him, and he'd never thought of himself as tall until that moment.

'You said a wolf. A wolf!'

'Yes,' he admitted, 'that's what I said.'

'That, that thing is not a wolf.' Her voice was as tight as a drum, as high as a bat.

'But it is Stanislav. I guess.' He finally did blink, and the fleeting instant of his eyes closing showed him a writhing mass of barbed tentacles, tooth-lined mouths, glistening, dripping spikes, vacuous sucking holes, and eyes. So many eyes, and all of them disturbingly human.

'We can't fight that,' said Mary, pointing back inside.

'I know, I know. But ... it's him.'

'Dalip. He's gone. Whatever he was, has gone.'

'But you, you've changed backwards and forwards. Maybe he still can.'

'I change into a bird. The first couple of times almost broke me. You ever seen him like that before?'

'No,' he said.

'When Crows was showing me how to do magic, I got a bit carried away. This ... thing, like that thing, appeared. It was sort of me, but not me. I told it to fuck right off, and it disappeared. If Stanislav took one look at his true self and gave it a big, wet kiss, then he's finished as a human being. Your mate's come home. That's what he really wants to be.'

Dalip thought about the shifting, pulsating mass, constantly forming and breaking down. A wolf, a werewolf even, would have been reasonable, understandable. Instead, they had unfathomable chaos.

'What should I do?' he asked.

'You cannot go in there. I mean, fuck. Did you see what he's done to the guards?'

Dalip had. There were bits of them everywhere, just rolling around on the floor at the urging of the ever-moving tentacles, and some seemed to be in the process of being absorbed into the main mass.

'There might be part of him I can still talk to.'

'No!' She slapped his arm. Twice. 'No. Your parents – and at least you've got parents – are going to want you back, and I'm not telling them you fed yourself to some monster because you thought you ought to try or some other shit excuse. Just no.'

'So what happens now?'

'I don't fucking know. You're supposed to be the smart one. Think of something … smart.'

Dalip tried, but couldn't. All he could think of were tentacles with teeth like chainsaw blades, turning, always turning.

'Let's go back to the tower,' he said.

'That's an idea I can get behind. And you know what? I'm going to run.'

She did, and Dalip was right behind her.

29

Mary sat herself down in front of Bell and steepled her fingers. 'We have a problem.'

'You have a problem,' said the geomancer.

'No, we have a problem. And it's your fault. So what we're going to do is find a way to fix it, before anything else happens. Stanislav—'

'The man, the one who attacked me—'

'The one you took and put in a cell. That one. Turns out that's the worst thing you could possibly have done. He's got bad memories of some war he fought in, and now it's all spilling out of him like a sewer. So you're going to tell us how we deal with this, one way or another, before he comes for you, and then decides that the rest of us are part of the meal deal as well.'

Bell touched the scab on the end of her nose. 'You can just fly away. So can I.'

'I think I know how this works,' said Mary. 'You get to become what it is you want to be, deep down, but you also don't get much of a choice over it. So the fact that you change into a dragon tells me everything I need to know about you. You're like that whether or not you've wings and a tail. Stop shitting me, because you're not getting away from here.' She leaned closer. 'If it comes down to it, I will throw you to him. And if you're lucky, he'll kill you first.'

'She doesn't mean that,' said Mama quickly.

'I do. I really mean it. Cross my heart. So tell us, what the hell do we do?'

Bell shrugged and looked away. 'I don't know everything. I've been here for twenty years, as far as I can tell, and I know half of what I need to.'

'And we've been here for a week.' It was longer than that, but she wasn't going to split hairs. 'Why don't we start with what's happened to him.'

'You tell me. Some people – the ones most susceptible to change – get the idea that they can turn into a creature. Then they do. That's all there is to it. Some survive. Most don't. At least, this is what I've been told. Down is riddled with beasts that used to be someone, and can't change back. What form is he?'

'Formless,' said Dalip. 'A thing with teeth and claws and arms and eyes.'

'I remember,' said Bell, 'back in the beginning, I found myself in a dream, staring at the void. It tried to suck me in, but I refused to go.'

'I had the same dream,' Mary said. 'If Stanislav did, too, then night after night, locked in a cell, no one to talk him out of it ...'

'Almost as if that's what Down is, its raw essence. It changes everything it comes into contact with.' Bell drifted off with a thoughtful expression, and that wasn't what Mary wanted.

'Enough of the whatever-stuff. He's already killed your guards, those that didn't have the sense to run away, the two servant women you had are missing, your steward bloke, and I don't think he's going to be that worried about adding us to his score. Can we change him back?'

'No,' said Bell.

Mary heard Dalip shift behind her.

'Can we, I don't know, tame him in some way?'

'No. Any more than you or I can be tamed.'

'Can we … lock him in a room somewhere so that he'll never be able to get out?'

Bell snorted. 'If you want to stop him, you'll have to kill him.'

'Can we kill him?'

She shrugged. 'If he's that different from us, he might be impossible to damage him enough to finish him: where's his heart, his brain, how does he bleed? When we change, we have a fixed form. We're beasts, but we're mortal, for the want of a better word.'

'I proved that with you.' Mary sat back and wondered if Bell was telling her the truth. She'd admitted that this was outside her own experience, and perhaps this had never happened before. Perhaps it had, and there'd been no survivors left to tell the tale. It could be that dotted all over Down were dark places, filled with visceral, primal hate, and a monster feeding from it.

'Fire,' said Dalip. 'We're going to have to use fire. If words don't work, of course.'

That made a sort of sense. It was quite clear that if any of them got too close to Stanislav in his changed form, he could deal with them however he wanted, singly or all at once.

'And how the fuck are we supposed to do that?' Mary thought of all the things they didn't have: petrol, empty bottles, lighter fluid, fireworks, tyres, old mattresses and settees, meths, even flaming sambucas.

'There's some bottles of spirit in the store room, and that might burn. Magic? Can you magic up fire?' Dalip turned on the geomancer. 'You can, can't you? In the pit, you light all the candles.'

'That's as much as I can do.'

'And I'm not happy with a plan that involves her in any way. Not happy at all.' Mary got to her feet and looked around her, hands on hips. 'What else?'

'Everything will burn if you try hard enough,' offered Bell. 'Even stone.'

290

'You can just shut up now. Dalip, how big a fire do we need?'

He frowned as he thought, then looked puzzled. 'How am I supposed to work that out? It's not like there are books I can find the answer in.'

'Guess, then.'

'Huge. The bigger the better. If we think we've got enough, we haven't.'

The storm rattled the doors, shaking them free, and Luiza and Elena went to shore them up.

Mama shivered. 'Are we going to make it to morning?'

'We'll be fine, Mama,' said Mary. 'We could leave now if we wanted, and no one would stop us. Right, Bell?'

The doors, flapping in the wind, were tamed again.

'Then why don't we?' Mama wore a hopeful expression. 'Stanislav was a good man, but he's turned into all kinds of wrong now. He's beyond our help, and we're putting ourselves in danger – more danger by staying.'

'How far away is Crows' castle?' asked Dalip.

'A day's walk. Down the river, turn towards the rising sun. Keep going. We can get there no problem, but we can't just leave Stanislav as he is. Can we?'

'You can. You can go. Seriously, that makes sense. Take the others and go to Crows' castle; yes, it's not the best of weather, but it's not like before in London. It's not going to kill us.'

'Don't be too sure of that,' said Bell.

Mary gazed at the ceiling. 'Go on, then. Tell us.'

'The storm, like so many other things on Down, is alive. It's not just wind and rain, thunder and lightning. It's spiteful. It'll change direction just to hunt you down. It'll find you and be fiercest where you are.'

'Terrific. Why the fuck would it want to do that? I thought Down liked us.'

'Do I look like I'm in charge?' Bell shrugged. 'It's having a tantrum. You should know what that's like.'

Thunder rolled down the mountainside, close and loud.

'It's just taking the piss now.' Mary stared at Dalip. 'What do we do?'

'I really don't know.' He held his hands out to show he had nothing. Nothing but a knife, which was all but useless. 'I'm sorry.'

'Anyone? Anything?'

No one had.

'Fuck it,' she said. 'We need a better plan than waiting for Stanislav to come crawling up the stairs and cut us into little bits.'

'You arm yourselves with the bottles. I'm going to try to talk to him,' said Dalip. 'That's all I've got left, and I'd rather do that down there than up here. If it all goes wrong, then we're trapped.'

'We're trapped anyway by a storm that actually hates us and wants us to die. Which means you can't go out.'

'I'll risk it. Take one for the team.' He even smiled as he said it.

'That's just stupid. We have to do better.' Mary balled her fists. 'Come on! This is not how it's supposed to end.'

Any reply he might have made was lost in a deep bass rumble that shook the tower to its foundations.

'Do you want me to come with you?' she asked.

'You might want to put on some more clothes first.'

'I'm not distracting you, am I?'

'I'm just worried you'll catch a cold.' He rolled his eyes. 'I'm starting to sound like my mother.'

'Right, people. Find me something to wear. It might be something I'm going to be seen dead in, so let's make it good.'

After their previous search of the room, Elena knew where the clothes were stored. She heaved open the lid of the trunk and started to hold shirts and skirts up. The choice was poor – closing time at a jumble sale poor – and she was about to settle for a set of cast-offs that had come from the backs of those born centuries earlier, when Elena showed her something different.

It was rich and heavy and long, a bright red shot through with gold thread, like something a Spanish princess would wear while escaping from her evil uncle. It was gloriously impractical, with heavy skirt and laced-up bodice, sleeves that started just below the shoulders and a neckline that would get her arrested back in London.

'That one.'

'Seriously?' said Dalip.

'Oh, come on. It's gorgeous.' She held her arms out wide as Elena held it up against her. 'I'd never be able to afford anything like this, ever. And I can just put it on: it doesn't matter if it fits perfectly, or whose it really is.'

Dalip shook his head, which just made Mary all the more determined.

'Go and find your turban, or something. This might take a while.'

Elena gathered up the skirts, and Mary all but crawled inside. Mama padded the wounds on her back with murmurs of concern and squares of torn-up shirt. Luiza pulled the laces tight to hold everything in place, shortening and lengthening them to fit the curve of her back.

She suddenly had shape and form. She stood up straighter and held her shoulders back, instead of in their customary slouch. She dragged her fingers through her hair and away from her face, the oily spirals slipping across the skin at her knuckles.

She was the Red Queen at last, terrible and beautiful, even with – or because of – the bruises and scrapes and cuts that marked and mottled her.

Dalip had found a plain scarf and fashioned a bandanna-style turban out of it, drawing it tight across his forehead and covering his hair. He, still in the dirty orange boilersuit: she, radiant in her finery. He had to turn away, and she felt ... She didn't know what she felt. Pride? Confidence? Something like that. It wasn't the dress. It wasn't the way he looked at her. They were simply two signposts to the destination. Part of her, which had always been missing, had snapped into place.

'Wish us luck,' she said. Her skirts swished against the floor as she walked to the top of the steps. She'd never had anything that had swished before.

Dalip picked up the knife and followed her. To Mary, the blade seemed hopelessly short for the task, but he clutched at it anyway. It was his strength, and she wasn't going to point out its inadequacies. In order to take the stairs, she had to hold her skirts up, grabbing a handful of cloth at each side and lifting to reveal her bare feet.

Dalip snagged the lantern to hold over her head. The shadows leapt and flowed, and they made her feel less brave with every foot forward. The dark, the noise, the wind: Stanislav could be anywhere in the castle, in any form, hiding deliberately or actively seeking them out.

The stairs unwound to the bottom. The storm howled at the doorway, sucking at the air inside one moment, blustering it back in the next. Lightning crackled, tearing thunder from the clouds and rolling it around the natural bowl of rock that was outside the walls.

'Back to where we saw him before?' she asked – shouted at – Dalip.

'It's where we start.'

The lantern, despite its cover, guttered and died. The liminal light in the sky was insufficient to make out detail, but when the lightning flickered and stabbed at the mountain-top, it was enough to show that the guard house, and part of the wall beyond, had collapsed into ruin.

'Stanislav?'

They approached slowly. Mary's skirts threatened to turn into a sail and carry her away, and Dalip was bent over against the swirling wind that tried to rob the words from their mouths.

The building was blown down, or out. Loose blocks of stone lay in a heap, and wooden beams stuck out of the remains of the sagging roof like broken ribs.

'Do you suppose he's under there?' she said to Dalip's ear.

It took him a moment to parse the words, then put his mouth to her ear. 'We can't dig. Not by ourselves.'

They reversed positions again. 'It'd be easier for us if he was.'

He took a step back, nothing but darker black against the night. When the lightning flashed – close, so close that the concussion was almost simultaneous. 'I owe him,' he said in the silence afterwards.

'So let's keep looking.'

They moved unsteadily towards the partly fallen wall. Debris was both inside and out, and Mary suddenly realised what this was. She beckoned Dalip down to her height.

'The castle is being reburied. With so few people here now, it's sinking back into the ground. It grows, it dies.'

She'd thought that Crows' castle had been a ruin when she'd first arrived. It hadn't: it had been sprouting, new growth despite the appearance of age. There'd been no piles of stones, no ragged beams, no mounds of cracked roofing slates to see. Those were the signs of a dying building, not one rising from the ground. She had so much to learn, and she'd do it, assuming she lived long enough.

Dalip climbed the rocks against the wall, which all but reached the top. He felt his way up, and peered over the edge, out towards the lake. Doing so exposed him to the full fury of the storm, and he ducked down almost immediately. Above them the clouds boiled and the sky flickered, the thunder an almost continuous barrage.

'Come back,' she shouted. 'He won't be out there.'

'How do you know?'

'Because he's after people, right?'

Dalip scrambled back down. 'But there's only us left, I think. The others are either all dead or they've run away.'

'Then where is he?'

They stood against each other, waiting for the lightning, trying to see through the darkness.

'There.' She pointed. A shambling figure was briefly outlined on the bridge from the pit to the tower, only vaguely human shaped. Too many limbs, too many of the wrong sort.

The light failed, and when it came back, he was gone.

They ran, the storm behind them, scourging them with hail. Then they were inside, gasping and panting.

'Should have barred the door again.' Dalip swallowed hard. 'Stanislav? Stanislav! Don't do it.'

He led the way this time, the spiral staircase proper dark now, and though Mary was close behind, it was Dalip who'd come up against Stanislav first.

He stopped suddenly, bracing his outstretched arms against the walls. Mary ran into his back, but the boy was like a rock. He wasn't going any further.

'Is that you, Stanislav? It's me, Dalip.'

There was something ahead and above. She couldn't see it, but she could hear it. A rasping breath, slow and deep, a wet burbling that was almost a voice. They needed light, but she was secretly glad that they didn't have any, because the one thing they needed more than light was to keep their sanity.

'We need to talk, Stanislav. We need to talk about what you're doing. Why don't you come with us and we can sit down and see if we can help you?' Dalip's voice was trembling. When Mary put her hand on Dalip's arm, he was, too.

'Stanislav? It's Mary. Something's happened to you, something that Down caused. Do you understand that this isn't your fault? Come downstairs, and I'll tell you about it, because it happened to me, too.'

She held her breath, and in the silence, there came a sibilant gurgle that might have been 'yes' and probably wasn't a 'no'. She pulled at Dalip, and they backed down the stairs to the bottom room.

Dalip heaved a table upright, and put it on its legs between the end of the stairs and the broken-down door. He stationed himself behind it, and put the knife in the middle of the table. Mary immediately leaned across him and took the knife. She held it, point down, behind her back.

'No,' she said. 'You don't get to decide that.'

He nodded, and then faced the stairs again. Something, some-one was coming.

30

It looked like him. It had the same close-cropped bullet head, the same bull chest with a mat of grey hair, the same muscular arms and short, thick legs. But his own mother would have taken one look and realised that this wasn't her son.

Or rather, it had been, and now wasn't. Something else was wearing his skin, and it fitted badly.

Dalip pulled at his beard. This, this whole thing was a miscalculation. It might remember being Stanislav, but there was no way he could count on it ever being him, on knowing the difference between reason and instinct, right and wrong, friend and enemy.

Still he had to try.

'Stanislav?'

His head came around, slowly. He blinked his blue eyes at Dalip, and tried to get them to focus on him, but they kept wandering. Literally wandering, because they should really have stayed under his prominent brow bone and either side of his nose, but had a tendency to slide in all directions before returning: down the cheek towards his mouth, off towards his ear, up his forehead.

It made Dalip feel nauseous. It was only the lack of food in his stomach that kept him from doubling over and vomiting at his feet.

'I need to talk to Stanislav. Is he in there?'

The face shifted again, like a Picasso portrait. The eyes – suddenly three of them, then back to two – settled, and for the briefest of moments, it was Stanislav. The man even gave an uncertain smile, before his teeth began to dance in his gums.

'I can't do this,' gasped Dalip. 'I can't. I'm sorry.'

Stanislav's demeanour changed, and stubby fat tentacles erupted from his mouth, writhing obscenely, questing in the air for prey. Then they were gone again, swallowed up.

'I think you're going to have to,' said Mary. She stood very close behind Dalip, her bare shoulder touching his arm. 'He doesn't like "no".'

'Right.' The light flickered outside like a broken fluorescent bulb, the electrical storm so intense now that objects were glowing on their own. Stanislav's changing form was still ill-lit but visible. Dalip could see, and how he wished he couldn't.

He tried again to find the person inside.

'Stanislav. I'm talking to Stanislav. You're lost, and you need to find yourself again. What you are isn't what you're supposed to be. You're supposed to remember who you are, and keep hold of that when you change, so that you can turn back into a human. Isn't that right?'

'I can change too,' said Mary, 'into a huge eagle-thing. But I don't think like a bird, not completely. I know who I am. Whatever it is you are, you don't have to be it.'

More eyes floated to the surface of Stanislav's skin, all fixing on Mary. Dalip's dread deepened.

'We may have to run,' he said.

'Why isn't he answering?'

'I don't think he can. I don't think he's got lungs any more, or a voice box, or … anything. It's just a shape, a bag of stuff that can be anything it wants to be.' Dalip took a deep breath, feeling his own skin tingle, flexing his muscles, stretching his tendons and his joints, strangely comforted by the way God had knit his bones together and hung flesh from it.

He thought ... What had he thought? Running through the tunnels with fire at his back, there hadn't been time to consider the future, just the present. And then afterwards, struggling through the surging sea to an unexpected shore, the whole proposition of another world just the other side of a door had been so overwhelming, he hadn't been able to comprehend it. Being captured by the wolfman, becoming a slave who was supposed to fight or die: that was clarity, existence reduced to its barest, meanest form. Everything had been focused on the geomancer – how to frustrate her, how to escape her, and finally how to beat her.

They'd done that. Not easily, but with Mary's intervention, they'd succeeded.

While all the time, the monster in their midst had gone unnoticed.

How many nights, after being herded back into his cell, had Stanislav felt the raw, untamed power of Down unravel successive parts of his body until he became not a person, but a thing. How desperate had he become in the darkness, only to wake and believe it a terrible dream? Dalip had heard nothing, hadn't suspected that a few doors down from his, a strange and awful transformation was gradually taking place.

One last go then, before all hell broke loose.

'Stanislav? Stanislav!' He spoke clearly and firmly. His family had never owned a dog, but it was how he imagined it felt like to call one to heel. 'You need to focus. On me. Listen to my voice, Stanislav. Tell me you're listening.'

There came a sucking sound that sounded less like the intake of breath and more like a moist cavern opening up.

The following exhalation was sigh of regret and loss.

'Look, Stanislav. Look at me. You remember me, don't you?

You remember Dalip Singh, who you taught to fight with a knife, to save his life in the pit? You remember training me, all the hard work you put in, the way we escaped in the end? You remember that? Because that's you, that's the real you. This thing in front of me now, that's not Stanislav. It's not the man I remember. That's—'

The gurgling sucking noise came again, and between the pops and bubbles he could hear distinct words.

'Me. This.'

'You were never that. You were never a killer, never a murderer, never a ...' Dalip's voice dried up. He realised the truth, and put out an arm to reach across in front of Mary, to push her behind him as he stepped back. 'It doesn't have to be this way. We all got a new start, every one of us. Even you. It doesn't matter now what you did then. All that matters is what you do now.'

He could feel Mary press the hilt of the knife into the palm of his hand. His fingers closed around it.

Stanislav seemed to melt in front of them. The effort of keeping human form was no longer required. He slumped, the top of his head sinking and flattening, his legs turning to puddles of wax. Eyes popped out like bubbles, and the skin twisted and rose into ropes.

They were outside. The wind was tearing at them, and the sky was ablaze with ragged streaks of light. Inside, the transformation was almost complete. Stanislav swelled and undulated, but rather than follow them, he started back towards the stairs.

'Hey,' shouted Dalip. 'Not that way. Look at us. Us.'

Stanislav ignored them, and continued his slow advance toward the staircase. The mass that was his torso divided, and divided again: the first of four legs of protoplasmic flesh felt its way to the top of the first step, dragging the body along after it.

'We have to do something.' Mary stood in the doorway and

the debris on the floor rose up at her command. She flung it, piece by piece, at Stanislav's back.

Such was the concentrated barrage that Dalip couldn't get anywhere near, reduced to watching lengths of wood, bottles, and pans snap forward, accelerated into a blur and crash into the figure on the stairs.

Except it had little effect. Stanislav had no bones to break, no muscle to bruise. Everything seemed to bounce off him. Mary tried harder, putting extra effort into each missile, grunting with the effort.

Now that did get them noticed. Stanislav writhed, tentacles bursting out to bat the hurled objects aside. Eyes congregated, blinking wetly in the shine. Mary was throwing everything at him, and he took it all.

It couldn't continue. She only had so much she could give. She sagged against the doorframe, skirt snapping and cracking like a sail at sea, and the few objects still in flight lost their momentum. They tumbled to the floor, rattling and rolling.

Stanislav stared at them, his many eyes reflecting the outline of the woman in the red dress. Then he came for them, faster than was conceivably possible, flooding towards the door in a wave.

Dalip stepped forward, arm extended, and the knife went straight in: up to the hilt, up to the wrist. Warm, cloying wetness engulfed his hand, and it was a shock. He remembered enough not to let go, but to turn the knife with a twist and drag it out sideways.

It would have been enough to kill any man – catastrophic injuries that would have bled out in seconds.

Stanislav was not a man, nor did he care about such calculations.

Dalip was punched harder than he'd ever been punched before. It was like being hit by a bus square in the chest, hard enough to break his ribs and stop his heart. He flew without the aid of wings, ending up on his back in the mud outside, gazing up uncomprehending at the flickering, churning sky.

He should, by rights, be lying still, waiting for the ambulance, reassured by strangers that everything was going to be okay and being asked if there was anyone he needed to call.

Instead he found himself getting to his feet, renewing his death grip on his knife, and taking the first unsteady step forward.

Mary had picked up a broken table leg. Holding it in a two-handed grip, she swung it over her shoulder as she retreated, almost unbalancing herself.

'Dalip? Dalip?'

He could barely breathe to reply.

'This isn't working.'

'If you've got something else we haven't tried, don't hold back.'

Stanislav was in the open with them, now fully visible in his pomp, crowned by an ever-moving halo of tentacles.

And then Dalip shouted to her: 'We have to get him to follow us.'

'Is that it?'

'For now.'

'Fuck,' said Mary, and threw herself at the dark, seething mass, swinging as she came within what she hoped was range. The blow was blocked with such severity that it nearly broke her arms. She was wrenched off her feet, and she fell hard. Her wounds stretched and tore.

Dalip ducked under the flailing suckers as they tried to reel both him and her in. He grabbed her around the waist and pulled her backwards, out of reach for a moment.

'Tell me we've got its attention.'

Stanislav surged towards them.

'Run.'

They ran hand in hand, for no other reason but to help the other up if they fell. Dalip guided them towards the gatehouse.

The gates were, as they always had been, open, but the arch tying the posts together had fallen into ruin.

And above them, the storm gathered itself, ready for its final onslaught.

He glanced behind as they reached the line of tumbled stone. Close, too close.

'Climb,' he said, and swung around.

Stanislav rose above him, and he held out the knife. As inadequate as it seemed, the tentacles reared away from it and tried to come at him from the sides. Dalip slashed at the air to keep them away, and gain time for Mary to get clear.

It was impossible to tell whether Stanislav was actually frightened of the knife, or whether he was simply playing. Dalip didn't think he'd wounded him. But hurt him? Surprised him? Perhaps that.

The creature could simply fall on him, envelop him completely and tear him apart like he'd done to the guards. But it didn't. Because some of its reactions were still human.

That insight might save him yet.

A block of dressed stone whirled past his ear. It was big, spinning, and not particularly fast, but Stanislav was too preoccupied to dodge it. It entered the central mass and disappeared. Then Stanislav was on the ground, surface churning as he tried to rid himself of this sudden cold, hard intrusion.

Dalip scrambled up the fallen arch to the top.

'We can't keep this up all night,' said Mary.

There was blood coming from her mouth, and Dalip instinctively reached up to wipe it away.

She knocked his hand aside. 'Bit my tongue, that's all.'

They jumped down the other side. He was outside the crumbling castle's walls for the first time, and looked back at his prison. He didn't recognise it – it had seemed secure, and now it was a shambles of collapsed buildings and broken masonry.

Also, the rising tentacular creature lit by the burning sky.

'I've got an idea.'

'Is it really stupid?' she asked.

'Very.'

'Okay,' she said, and that was the last thing he heard her say for a while. The storm beat down at them with everything it had. The wind tore at them, strong enough to blast them with small sharp stones, and the lightning became a relentless static discharge above their heads.

Dalip raised his arm to protect his face and leant in hard, heading towards the flank of the mountain, to the edge of the bowl carved in it, and where it would be possible, perhaps, to climb to the summit.

After that, it was one foot in front of the other, the palms of his hands and the soles of his feet bleeding from each new cut as he reached up, pulled hard and dragged himself closer to the top. Mary, wearing the red dress, struggled, and he had to stop for her, wordlessly tell her to trust him, tell her that it would all be worth it in the end.

The mad monster that was Stanislav seemed to be having just as much difficulty. The loose surface slid underneath him, and his tentacles fought to hold on to the shining rock.

Pushing Mary ahead of him, he turned to Stanislav and brandished the knife.

'You want me? You want her? You can't have us. You can't keep up because you're weak. Weak, you hear me? You're just a sheep like the others. A sheep.'

He had no idea if Stanislav had heard him or not. The wind stole his words away the moment they left his mouth. But what was important wasn't whether Stanislav understood, rather that he could see his defiance with all hundred of his eyes.

Taunt him. Goad him. Make him angry and make him careless. Just as long as he followed them up the mountain.

It seemed to be working. He crawled and rolled up the bare rock after them, thrashing and bubbling, extruding tentacles into crevices and joints, slowly, inexorably, coming after them.

Whereas they were nimbler, but less sure-footed. Stanislav wasn't going to get blown over the edge of the cliff; they, with their bloodied fingers and toes, their long limbs and impractical clothing, might.

They kept belly-low, but sometimes it wasn't enough. The wind would whip in between them and their handholds, and bodily lift them into the air, driving in like a crowbar to separate them from their tenuous grip on life.

Whenever it happened, Dalip's stomach lurched and his blood ran cold. He splayed himself out and pressed himself to the rock, and prayed for it to pass so he could keep going. It wasn't far now. If he looked up, craning his neck at an unnatural angle to see the zenith, it glowed with pent-up energy. He could feel the buzzing on his skin, the prickle of electricity dancing in the clouds so close above his head, he could have reached up and touched them.

So close, so very close.

'Come on,' he bellowed to both Mary and Stanislav. 'Come on!'

They were all but at the summit, in the very heart of the storm. Fat lances of light burned the rock, cracking it apart, sending shockwaves through the mountain and a blast of hot air against his back. Mary was just below him, and he hauled her up after him, pressing on her head to keep her low.

Stanislav was right behind, a shifting mass of pseudopods dragging itself over the last ledge to the unforgiving bleakness of the top.

The clouds roiled and seethed, and there was nowhere else to go. Dalip had brought them all up here. It only remained to see who would descend again.

The knife was hot in his hand, glowing with a blue aurora. Bringing metal up here, in the middle of an electrical storm? What was he thinking?

This. He started to run, not away across the broad shoulder of the summit, but towards Stanislav. He jumped, flinging his arms high, and brought them down again as hard as he possibly could, plunging the blade deep into the central mass. He couldn't stop himself from falling on to him, turning his head at the last moment but landing square on.

It was like hitting a balloon full of jelly. Soft, yielding, somehow firm and rubbery. It was vile, and even more so as mouths opened up under him to suck him in, tentacles wrapped around him to feed him into the waiting maws.

Dalip let go of the knife, only to find his arm held tight. He kicked hard, then harder still, and the ropes of flesh gripped hardest of all. Eyes flickered at him, reflecting the bright sky. He needed to get away, and yet there was no way of doing so, no way that Mary could intervene without getting trapped herself.

For a moment, one hand was free, and he gouged at an eye. It tried to sink back into the skin, and his fingers followed it, dragging it up from the depths, pulling it away until it was only attached by a thin cord. That seemed to cause Stanislav discomfort, enough that he was lifted clear, then thrown like a discarded toy.

Towards the cliff. He bounced and rattled. The sheer drop behind him yawned, and he teetered, winded, his legs sliding over the edge as he scrabbled for purchase.

The clouds overhead were almost white.

Mary ran to him, reached over his head to grab his boilersuit at the neck, tried to pull him back on to solid ground. That wasn't what he wanted. Instead, he reached up and fastened his hand on her arm. Her eyes flashed wide and she started to rear away, but he wasn't going to let go.

Stanislav was right behind her, tentacles flailing across the rocks, dragging himself closer. He was almost within reach, his bright eyes fixed on her legs.

Dalip leaned backwards, planted his feet firmly on the cliff edge, and pushed.

He and Mary tumbled out into space together, just as the lightning spat down, drawn by the irresistible lure of the knife.

31

They fell. Mary, blind and deaf from the sudden explosion of light, felt the wind start to tear at her and the one point of contact with Dalip falter and slip away. She could blink, and that was all. Her skirts tangled into her legs and her hair covered her face. She was bent like a bow, hands and feet above her, spine curved so far she could almost touch her toes.

The ground, when it eventually came, would be very hard. Even the storm-tossed surface of the lake would be enough to shatter her into a thousand pieces.

Then she remembered.

The transformation seemed to take both forever and a mere second. She was falling, then she was flying, time stretching out long enough that she could experience her skin erupting in feathers, the constricting clothes melting away, her hood of hair disappear and all her senses become as sharp as her talons.

She wheeled away from the orange figure fluttering below her.

She remembered again. The raggedy twist of limbs was worth catching, but she'd left it very late. Her wings, hard against the updraught, folded against her body and her neck craned forward. Not so much falling as diving, faster than anything in the sky, able to outrun even the lightning.

Here he came, flailing in the roaring air, closer and closer, and though the lake was topped with white foam fingers that were reaching up to embrace him, she was quicker. Her legs swung down and her claws opened like traps.

They closed around him, a black keratin cage. Now they were both going to strike the water together. She unfurled her wings to their furthest reach, and her dive became an arc. All her flight feathers strained, and her tail spread wide.

Her speed became unfathomable. There was the water, and there was air, and it passed her in a single blur of steel grey. She lifted her legs as high as she could, because she was that close to dragging them, and her precious cargo, through the surf.

And finally, the curve turned upwards. There was a hair's breadth between her and the rushing ground. Then a hand's breadth. Then more, but no, here came an obstacle, a wall, Down-made but already ruined by the storm and the vagaries of nature – she soared through the gap and managed to gain enough height to crest the opposite side.

She registered that the top of the tower was on fire, but that was all. Its significance eluded her for a moment, as she dropped down into the valley, speeding up again, standing on one wing to pass through the gorge and up back towards the mountain-top.

Now she slowed, her wings wide as she skipped over the shoulder of rock and into the col behind, down towards the lake shore. She flapped once, twice, to kill her forward movement, then fluttered gently as she lowered Dalip to the ground.

He didn't move. He lay just as he was placed, flopped, boneless, lifeless, amongst the shale rocks at the water's edge. She might have killed him, but the blame wouldn't be hers. He was the one who'd thrown himself backwards over the edge of a cliff, knowing that only one of them could fly. It wasn't like he'd discussed his plans with her beforehand: if he'd died, it would have been only because she hadn't quite managed to save him, and with the smallest chance of success at that. He'd known the risks

– or at least, decided that using the storm to get rid of Stanislav took priority over his own life.

She turned her head left and right, examining him. Then she reached down and nudged him with her beak. It wasn't the most sensitive of tools, designed for ripping and tearing: her tongue – what was she supposed to do, tell how he was by licking him? She could smell nothing off him but stale sweat and fear, and he looked ... dead.

She changed back. Where had the dress gone? Where did it reappear from? No matter, for she now had hands to wrestle it back under control as the storm crackled its last above her.

'Dalip? Dalip?'

The tower was properly alight now, burning brightly enough to cast shadows. She felt anxious, but she could only deal with one thing at a time.

She pressed her hand against his cheek. He felt cool, but not cold; that wasn't a definitive sign of either life or death. She knew there was such a thing as a pulse, but not how to confidently feel for it. His heart was in his chest: she gathered her hair to one side and awkwardly knelt down next to him, pressing her ear to him.

It took her a moment – longer than that, because she held her breath until she struggled to contain it. There was the faint, rhythmic, welcome thud of valves opening and closing. All well and good, but she couldn't carry him to shelter, out of the wind and the noise.

'Dalip, you fucking idiot. Wake up.'

She'd seen how it was done on the telly. Her first slap was pathetic, weak and tentative. Her second was barely better, but she didn't want to be out there all night, so she gave enough to make her palm sting.

His eyes opened, and he caught her wrist before she could backhand him too.

'You hit me.'

'You pulled me backwards off a fucking mountain.'

He blinked. 'Did it work?'

'How the fuck should I know? If I go back up there to check, I'm going to get fried by the storm too, right?'

Dalip screwed his face up. 'Everything hurts.'

'The tower's on fire. I don't know what that means.'

'The geomancer?'

'I don't know! This isn't exactly flying weather, is it?'

He reached up and hooked her neck. He did two things, at the same time: pull her down, and twist his body on top of her.

Claws raked the stones beside them, raising a shower of flinty sparks. Then they were gone, away and into the night.

'Bell disagrees,' he said, searching the sky for her.

Mary threw him off, and he was too weak to stop her.

'It was always going to come to this, wasn't it?' A flash of movement on the cliff face caught her attention. A long neck, a long tail, broad leathery wings against the rock, then out again into clear air. 'Fuck. She's coming back.'

'What, precisely, do you want me to do about that?' He raised himself to a half-crouch, but seemed to lack the strength to go any further.

'Run?'

'Where? How?'

She couldn't spot Bell any more. Dalip was right: he couldn't do anything, but she could. She coiled her legs under her and leapt. With a strong sweep of her wings, she was aloft in amongst the turbulence. Her sight, pin-sharp, spotted her quarry immediately. Out over the castle and heading straight for her.

She flapped hard, building momentum. Someone was playing chicken with an East End girl, and she was determined not to flinch. They closed on each other, and at the last moment, she drew in her wings and turned her whole body. For the brief second of contact, they slashed at each other, and then they were apart, the distance between them widening.

Mary turned the right way up and banked hard, wheeling

around the blazing tower and heading back towards the lake.

Here came Bell again, dead ahead, jaws wide, feet raised to strike. And again, Mary flipped over and tried to close her claws on something substantial. Missed. Gone.

They could do this all night until one of them made a mistake, this passing joust. Most likely, because she was less familiar with her skin, it would be Mary who would fall. So she had to change the game. What could she do better than a dragon?

Rather than fly at her – she could see Bell lining up her next pass – she started to climb. The dragon tried to match her, but flew harmlessly underneath.

Mary dipped a wing and gave chase.

The shallow dive she put herself in took her to within touching distance of Bell's scaly back. Bell's serpentine head twisted around and a slight adjustment left Mary with nothing beneath her but the speeding ground. She pulled up, turned in a tight circle and set off after her again.

Now this, this was what she was good at, the dive and strike. She was faster and more manoeuvrable, and the dragon's drum-taut wings, already ragged and lacy at the edges from the previous battle they'd had, were particularly vulnerable. As long as she could stay away from those teeth and keep the fight in the air, she might even win.

She flapped hard, drawing up behind. Bell put some effort into jinking left and right, and Mary overshot. She angled her wings and rose almost effortlessly up again. The dragon stayed closer to the ground than her. Perhaps she was afraid of the lightning. With good reason, too, but the storm seemed to have blown itself out against the twin mountains and was grumbling away over the plains behind. Having claimed one victim, perhaps it was sated. Mary risked a little more, and a little more than that.

Bell looped the tower and started back towards the lake, earnestly pushing air with great beats of her wings. Mary angled her flight and began her descent.

Dalip, doggedly crawling back towards the castle, was directly in the dragon's path.

Mary folded her wings and dove down.

There was a moment when she thought she'd be too late, that the dragon would get Dalip because he had nowhere to hide. That moment passed because her approach was both furious and unnoticed. She dipped down with her claws even as Bell did with hers, but it was the bird's talons that struck first, tightening around the bat-like forelimb, puncturing the leathery membrane and dragging the great beast off-course.

She let go and skimmed the lake to kill her speed. Behind her, the dragon pinwheeled into the ground, bouncing once, twice, and skipping into the water like a spinning stone. The ruined wings spread out over the surface, the sinuous body thrashed, and then it began to sink.

Mary was flying directly at the cliff. She had no room to bank left or right: instead, she flew up, almost to the top, before flipping over and circling back around. Dalip was still struggling over the loose rocks towards the collapsed gatehouse, but he stopped for a moment as she flew overhead and raised his hand to her.

She turned at the tower, taking a good long look at it. The upper floor was burning – all the wood was alight, with fire jetting out of not just the windows, but gaps in the roof where supporting beams had collapsed underneath. The balcony was simply a forest of flame, and nothing in the room beyond was going to survive. Whether Mama, Elena and Luiza had escaped was something to find out soon, but it was going to have to wait for just a moment longer.

Mary flew back down to the lake, settling her huge clawed feet into the damp grit at its edge. She waited, and was rewarded by the crown of blonde hair surfacing just beyond the shallows. Bell coughed and choked, her tattered dress rising up around her like a pale moon. Mary changed too, confident that, if it was needed, she could call on the rocks around her to defend her.

'I knew I hadn't killed you.'

Bell slowly waded towards the shore. Her left arm hung uselessly by her side, a kink in her forearm the reason why.

'You bitch,' said Bell. 'You've ruined everything.'

It wasn't what Mary expected to hear. She had a right to be angry, but to be so resolutely, stupidly, stubborn? 'I don't get it, and I don't get you. Why won't you just give up?'

'It would have worked.' Bell kept coming. The splashing water was up to Bell's knees, then her shins, now her ankles. 'It would have worked if it hadn't been for you.'

'Your plan? To scare open a door back to London? Fucking hell, mate: we've had the shit scared out of us so many times tonight, it's pretty obvious it's never going to work.'

Bell was getting uncomfortably close, her feet slipping on the loose rock just under the surface.

'Everything had to be just right. And it was, until you showed up.' She was a miserable sight, her dress all but falling off her, rags held together by a few stitches. White and gold cloth, once rich, like her, just dropping away, piece by piece.

'Was that ... Was that a wedding dress?'

They were face to face.

Bell wiped the water out of her eyes. 'Yes. It was mine.'

'You just happened to be wearing it, when, what? You were attacked by bears or something?'

'Don't pretend to understand. Don't pretend to know what it's like, to be married off, like some prize cow.'

'Okay. I don't know what that's like. But fucking hell, whatever happened to you, why can't you just leave us alone? You've done all this – all this, everything – to yourself. By behaving like a, a ...'

'A dragon.'

Crows was a snake, sneaky and slippery. Stanislav had been whatever he'd become, that primal chaos she'd first witnessed down by the lake that lay at the heart of everyone. Bell was a dragon, cruel and hard. And she, she was an eagle. What did that say about her?

'Sounds like some bloke had a lucky escape.'

'If I could, I'd—'

'What? Hit me? Is that it? Is that all you have?' Mary leaned in. 'It's your answer to everything, and you've got nothing left.'

'I have everything,' said Bell. 'I still have everything.'

'You can't keep us here. Your guards are gone, you've lost all your maps and all your weird cog-machines. You've got what you stand up in, and that's even less than me.'

'You thought you'd beaten me on the mountain, and then in the tower, and now, here. You're wrong. You're so very wrong.'

Mary shrugged and rather than using her fists again, she turned away. 'It doesn't matter what you think, I don't have to do this any more. We've won the right to walk away from the crazy girl.'

'Come back. Come back here. I order you.'

Mary raised her middle finger.

The air behind her puffed out, like something huge was suddenly present.

She knew what it was. She raised her hands and dragged the darkness out of the sky so that when she confronted the dragon, it had no idea of where she was. Its wounded wing dragged across the ground, the wing-tip claw scraping up the stones into a ridge. Mary should have been in plain sight; there was nothing sophisticated about her hiding, yet the dragon couldn't see her. It turned its smooth scaled head this way and that, in darting movements, and it tasted the air with its forked tongue.

Mary stepped forward, reached up and took hold of the broken wing beyond the fracture. She gave it a tug, and found herself holding a pale, limp arm. Bell staggered and fell, barking her knees on the stones, putting her good hand down in amongst the shale. She retched and heaved. The pain had to be overwhelming.

'I'm sorry,' said Mary. She was, too. 'This brought her no

pleasure, and though it was necessary, she felt ashamed for having to do it. 'You have to stop.'

'I will not.' Bell hissed through clenched teeth. She tried to get up, shivering through the cold and pain. 'I win. I win every time. I take what I want. I'm born to rule. This is my destiny. I decide what happens, not some grubby half-caste whore.'

Mary spun Bell around so she was facing the lake again and, letting go of the arm, she shoved her hands into the woman's back. She stumbled forward and into the water, the splash closing over her head before she half-heartedly raised herself again.

Mary walked into the water after her, and kicked her backside hard enough to send her sprawling again.

'Is that it? You can't stand being beaten by some common street-kid? If I talked posh and was dripping with diamonds, it wouldn't be so bad? You think I should be kissing your arse instead of kicking it? Or are you just fucking nuts because you know you should have stayed in London and told your parents to fuck off? When did it happen? Before or after the wedding?'

She forced Bell out, deeper and deeper, until only the woman's head and shoulders were visible.

'During. It was during. I was supposed to go through and sign the register, and the door opened and there was Down.' For the first and only time, the tears were no longer an act. 'I ran.'

Mary remembered her own escape. The terrible fire, the heat and the smoke, followed by the unexpected, delicious coldness of the sea. Down had decided, for reasons of its own, that the two situations were equally awful, and she relented.

'What am I going to do with you? Do you want me to kill you? Do you want me to hold you under until it's over? Is that what you want? Do you hate yourself that much?'

'Why?' said Bell, her voice reduced to a childish whine. 'Why won't you let me win?'

'Because you did a bad thing to us, and you need to be punished for it. Your punishment is all around you. It's your dead guards, your burnt castle, your broken arm, your bruises, your messed-up plans and your missing maps. You need to learn that you don't fuck around with people's lives. Okay, you get away with it sometimes. But not this time. Just … just stay out of our way. We'll go in the morning. You don't follow us, you don't try and stop us. That's it. That's all we want.'

Mary waded ashore and set off after Dalip. There was no pursuit, not this time.

32

He was only a man, and he was spent like the empty bullet cases that had belonged to his grandfather, and now, in another world, belonged to him.

She was not only a woman, and perhaps that was how she was able to catch him up and pull him to his feet, look hard and deep into his face, then drag his arm over her shoulder so that she could take some of his weight.

He was grateful, and not a little confused. It wasn't how it was supposed to be – not how he'd been taught it was supposed to be – but perhaps he'd left all that behind along with so much else.

'Thanks,' he said.

'Stupid bitch,' she said, not at him. 'I don't know: she's got her reasons, but not her excuses.' She growled deep in her throat.

'You all right?'

'Just ... you learn stuff about someone, and it makes it more difficult to hate them despite what they've done.' She told him about Bell's interrupted wedding. He listened carefully, and when she was done, he twisted his head around to look at the lake.

'She's gone.'

'Do you think I'm going to regret it?' she asked.

'What?'

'Not, you know: not killing her.'

He shrugged, not that he had much strength left to do even that. 'Ask me if I regret killing Stanislav.'

'The storm killed him.'

'Oh, come on. I knew what I was doing, luring him to the top of the mountain, using the knife to attract the lightning. He was human just enough to feel hate, but not enough to realise the danger. I killed him for certain.'

'Do you regret it?'

'Not now. Not today, and probably not tomorrow. Ask me next week, next month, next year if either of us is still around by then. My grandfather – have I told you about my grandfather?'

'A bit, but go on.'

'He was too young to join the army in the Second World War, but he did it anyway, lied about his age, fought for six years against the Japanese, got a chestful of medals, came home and ...' Communal violence, neighbour turning on neighbour. Partition, fleeing in the dark with his parents, aunts and uncles, nephews and nieces, brothers and sisters, and when the light of that first day dawned, it rose on fewer of them than had left. Refugees, relying on the kindness of strangers. Immigrants, in what should have been the Mother Country, but it was a cold love. 'Eventually I happened. I remember him as this fiercely proud, deeply religious, honourable, dependable man, that even when it took all his strength to get up out of his wheelchair, he'd stand to attention as if he was still a child playing at soldiers.'

'He sounds like a right handful.'

'He was – drove my mum mad. If you'd asked him if it had all been worth it, he would have said yes. But he would have said it while remembering all the friends he'd lost, all the men he'd killed, all the suffering, all the fear, all the cruelty and callousness. I never said anything to him, but I did used to wonder if he really thought it had been worth it. He had nightmares, not every night; enough of them, though, that I knew about them. Stanislav? It was a thing that had to be done. Bell? Better leave it undone and make a mistake. We're talking about killing: you can't take it back.'

When his grandfather had died, those few of his compatriots left, who'd served with him and who'd also made their homes in Britain, gathered together at his house. They'd made a curious group, telling their stories, moustaches bristling, beards white as snow, turbans bright and tall. For brief moments, they shifted from little old men, coloured ribbons signifying past battles, to lions, fierce and terrifying, kirpans like claws, banners held high. The little children running around their legs knew nothing of war but its glamour and finery, even though they were both war's legacy and its future combatants.

'Bell's going to hate me, that's for sure.' They'd reached the collapsed gatehouse, and together they slowly, carefully, climbed up the broken blocks to the top. He noticed the way she unselfconsciously waited for him to raise his foot to the next step before helping him up.

The tower was burning itself out. The roof had collapsed into the room below – whatever had been there, be it treasure or merely mundane, was lost for certain.

'Do you think they made it out?'

'Mama's a tough old girl,' said Mary. 'She doesn't take any messing, and it's not like we don't know how to run from fire.'

Flames were flickering behind the slits in the next storey down. It would all burn by morning, leaving nothing but a fragile, baked shell. The guardhouse? No. Not there. The only other substantial building still standing was the prison and the adjacent pit. As long as a stray spark didn't carry, it was as safe as anywhere.

It had looked so substantial as to be timelessly permanent. Yet it had grown from the ground, and to the ground it would return. Down was capriciously generous, its gifts more often than not coming with a double edge.

Mary squinted against the brightness of the fire, peering into the shadows. 'I can't see them.'

The tower rumbled, and a fresh halo of smoke puffed out. The flames shifted and rose higher.

'Try there.' He indicated the door he'd once run out of, in the hope of escape. 'We barred it before we got into the tower, but if they're there, they can unblock it.'

'The guards broke it down,' she said. 'Getting in shouldn't be too hard.'

'If not—' He stopped himself. If the others were dead, and it was just him and Mary, then he was never going to be able to climb up to the bridge. He'd have to – again – leave it to Mary: she could fly up to the parapet, fearlessly navigate the unfamiliar dark, drag the furniture away from the door and finally appear smiling at the opening.

They started the slow descent from the gatehouse to the court-yard below. The wind was blowing north, chasing the storm away, and the pit lay to the south and west of the tower, so that even though the fire was intense, its worst effects were kept away from the squat building's roof: scorched, yes, but not quite hot enough to cause ignition.

Dalip could feel the heat on his skin, though, as hot as it had been on the Underground. He knew that she felt it too, in her slowly increasing unwillingness to get closer. The guard-house door had been splintered and the pieces pushed back together again hard against the frame. There was hope.

He raised his fist and banged it ineffectually against the wood.

'That's not going to get anyone's attention,' she said, and used her own hand to batter at it. 'Hey! Hey, it's Mary and Dalip. Open up. Mama? Elena? Luiza?'

She propped Dalip against the doorstep, and moved back to shout into the night.

'Mama? Mama?'

Then he thought he heard something from inside, close by

rather than the cracking and roaring of burning.

'Dalip?'

'We're here,' he called. 'Let us in.'

After a while, when he felt as baked as a bread, the door edged back.

'Are you sure it's you?' asked Mama's voice.

'As sure as I can be,' said Dalip, and Mary scowled at the opening.

'Just open the fucking door.'

'You have a bad mouth on you, girl,' said Mama. She reached out and caught Dalip as he started to slide around the opening, resting him against her for a moment and beckoning for a chair.

It was mercifully cool inside, protected from the heat by the thick stone walls. Though it was dark, reflected red light shifted through the narrow window openings.

'What happened to Stanislav?' Luiza waited for Mary, then pushed the door closed. She started to shift the furniture back across the gap.

'It's … We dealt with it.' He was very tired, very bruised, and felt as if his skeleton had been liquidised.

'Did you kill him?' She was very direct, and he did her the courtesy of doing the same.

'Yes. Or at least, if he's not, then it's beyond me and probably anyone else.'

'And Bell? Did you see her?'

'Yes, we saw her. She attacked us, tried to kill us.'

'So she is dead too?'

He looked at Mary, who turned instead to stare intently around the room.

'No. But she won't trouble us again. She knows she can't beat—' Us, he was about to say, but it wasn't him Bell was afraid of. 'Not while we have Mary.'

Luiza glanced at her, started to form an objection, then shrugged. 'Just as long as we are safe.'

It was a strange kind of safe: sheltering in his former prison, while the tower next door burnt to the ground, the dead lying both inside and out while the castle collapsed around them. But safe nevertheless: they weren't going to come to any further harm, at least for that night.

'Bell,' said Mary. 'We could have done without her. You were supposed to keep an eye on her.'

'Oh hush, girl,' said Mama. 'She changed, right there in that room. How were we supposed to stop her from just flying away? One moment, she's this tattered princess, the next she's a dragon, all claws and teeth, knocking things over and sending us running. Dalip's right: we can't fight her – but you can.'

She thought about that for a while, finally concluding, 'Whatever.'

'So what do we do now?' said Elena quietly. 'We still cannot go back.'

'What were we going to do?' Dalip found enough strength to scrub his face with his fingers. 'Find the geomancer and ask her to tell us more about the world. You can't say we haven't learnt more, more than we wanted to. We've lost Grace, we've … lost Stanislav.' Lost was the appropriate word to use: they'd lost her because she'd gone on alone, without them, and they'd lost him because he'd lost himself, given himself up to his base instincts. 'We know that the door we came through has gone, possibly destroyed by the fire that pushed us here in the first place. But there are other doors, which still work, and there are people this side trying to open them. We need to find out where they are, and maybe try something different. We know we can't really trust anyone else, so we have to trust each other.'

He lost steam. He'd done enough for today: they were no longer slaves, the castle had fallen, their gaolers had been killed or they'd run away, the threat of the dragon had been neutralised. He was wearing a sort of patka, he'd used his kirpan to protect his friends. His bangles and his comb – that would have to wait, but he felt that the gurus would be pleased with his efforts: he'd lived up to their ideal of the warrior-priest. All he wanted to do now was sleep, and see what the next day brought. Hopefully, it'd be quieter. Bell was still out there, and he hadn't forgotten about the wolfman. But if they all stuck together, it wasn't beyond them to cope with Down.

'We cannot stay here.' Elena gestured at the darkened room. 'This is not ours. Nothing here is.'

'We can go to the White City,' said Mary.

'Do you even know where that is?'

'I know a man who does. And that's what we're going to do: find him, and we'll get not just my map, but his maps and Bell's maps too. That'll make us rich, at least here in Down.'

'And just how are we going to find this Crows?' Mama raised her gaze to the ceiling. 'He'll be long gone, Mary, and even if you can fly now, which is all kinds of preposterous, you're not going to see him again.'

'The clue's in the name,' said Mary, and Dalip, tired even of this slight bickering, told her plainly.

'The wolfman has wolves in the same way Crows has crows. They're not real crows, they're parts of him; he uses them to see where he isn't and they have senses that he doesn't. Find a flock of crows, and that might well be him. Mary can search from the sky, and we'll follow on foot. He can't both carry his maps and get away from us.'

'And his maps are what we need, not him.' Mary snorted, but even if everyone else was fooled, Dalip wasn't. He could tell she liked this Crows, even though he'd stolen what was hers and had abandoned her to her fate.

'We leave in the morning, then,' said Luiza, as if the matter was settled, and by saying, settled it herself. 'We sleep here together. It will be safer.' She didn't want to venture further inside, any more than any of the others did. Pigface was dead in the corridor, and his colleague in one of the cells. She walked over to the fireplace, to see if she could coax some life out of it, even though it was perfectly warm.

A fire, one of human beings' most primal enemies was also one of their most primal needs.

They agreed that someone should keep watch at all times, just because they didn't want to be seen as stupid. The five of them would split up the remaining night easily enough, and Mama was worried about Dalip so suggested taking his shift too.

Even though he insisted, he suspected that they wouldn't wake him when it came to his turn. There was beer in the room, weak but it still made his head spin. There was bread, from which he seemed to have the largest piece, but arguing over that seemed pointless. He ate, and he drank, and curled up in an uncomfortable corner to sleep.

Despite everything, he dropped off, and despite everything, he woke again.

It was still dark – no, it was now properly dark. The firelight glow from the burning tower had gone, and only the faint red smear of their own hearth showed. Mary sat in a chair facing it, her back bent and her elbows on her knees. Her spring-coils of hair curtained her face, and she didn't move, didn't even acknowledge his presence until he'd settled into a chair next to her, grunting with the effort of motion.

'You all right?' she asked. She spoke softly, and the three other figures in the room didn't stir.

'I'll live.' He was bruised and battered, but actually, he felt like he'd earned his stripes. Each welt was his by right.

'You should get some more kip. We don't know how far we'll have to cover in the morning, and catching Crows isn't going to be easy. You can walk right past him and not even see him, though that might only be at night. I don't know what we'll do if he wants to make a fight of it.'

'Do you think he will?' He looked at her carefully, judging her mood by how tense her body was as he couldn't see her expression.

'He doesn't fight. He avoids fights. That's what probably got him here, Down: he ran away until he couldn't run any further. He's got scars from when they caught him. I think he's as scared of Down as we are, he just hides it better.'

'Is that what we are? Scared?'

She dragged her hair out of the way and tilted her head towards him.

'I don't know what's happening to me. I can do stuff like you can only do in films, except this is real.'

'I used to be scared of heights,' he admitted. 'I couldn't even climb ladders.'

'Fuck off,' she said. 'You threw yourself off a fucking cliff. You expected me to catch you.'

'I climbed up the outside of Bell's tower and through a window. Just hanging there, in space, only my fingers and toes in the gaps between the stones. I should've been terrified. I wasn't.' He stared into the embers. 'You're not the only one who's changed.'

'Look, Dalip. Everyone's asleep but us. I wanted to … I …' She couldn't manage it, whatever it was she was trying to say. 'Forget it.'

He genuinely didn't know what she wanted to tell him. What if she said she liked him? Romantically? He had no experience of that sort of thing, at all, ever. Perhaps just the once, then, and he'd been too scared to act on it, even to talk to the girl in question. What would he have said to his parents afterwards? Easier by far to keep silent and not bring shame on himself or his family.

'Go on.' The words formed by themselves. He didn't know where they came from.

She struggled on. 'I've never had a friend that I haven't let down. You know, badly, so they dump me like I'm a sack of shit.' She was shaking, despite the warmth of the room. 'When you jumped, and pulled me after you, you were going to die, and I wasn't. But you knew I was going to catch you, even before I did.

I've never had anyone trust me with as much as you did. I don't ... understand that.'

Dalip felt the low heat from the fire on his face, almost as warm as the embarrassment coming from Mary.

'That's what friends do. What they're supposed to do anyway. In an ideal world.'

'This isn't, though, is it? This world is fucked-up big-time.'

'It's certainly different,' he said, starting to smile. 'When I jumped, I wasn't scared. I thought you'd try and catch me, at least, but if you hadn't? I'd still have done something brave. I fought a monster, and there were no guarantees that I'd win, let alone live. That was my choice. That I'm here to say all this is great, but it's a bit unexpected. I heard my grandfather while I was falling.'

'What did he say?'

'*Bole So Nihal, Sat Sri Akal.*' He looked down at his hands, which had plunged the dagger into Stanislav's inconstant flesh. 'It means, "He who cries 'God is Truth' is ever victorious." It's a war cry, but he's been gone for years. I suppose I thought that meant I was already dead.'

They looked at each other, and she reached over and squeezed his arm. 'You look pretty alive to me.'

'I should say thank you.'

'You should shut the fuck up, Dalip.'

They sat like that for a while, and he slept again.

33

Down was vast: the White City lay in some uncertain direction to the west where all there appeared to be was ocean, the distance to it unknown, the way unmarked by roads. What else were they going to do? Where else should they go? It wasn't as if they had anything better to do, had any pressing appointments, or knew of anywhere particular for them to be. If it was five miles or five hundred, it didn't really matter. Down was all there was, and they had to start somewhere.

Mary flew above them, so high she was barely a speck in the rain-washed sky, wheeling in slow, lazy circles. Dalip had drawn a diagram in soot on the guard-room wall, describing the search patterns she needed to make, covering the maximum area with the minimum effort. She nodded like she'd understood – which she had, she wasn't stupid – but the idea of flying in lines, back and forth, blocking off one grid square before moving on to the other, didn't appeal.

Crows, she guessed, wasn't going to be trying to hide from them. He didn't know anyone was trying to track him down.

The wolfman had been in the south, but he hadn't made it back to the castle by that morning. While he was conceivably on his way, his power over them had been broken at the same time as Bell's. Having tied his fortunes to the geomancer, he'd find himself adrift soon enough. Mary had seen it before, in the bear-pit of children's homes. The ringleader would be moved on, and the operation they'd left behind would fall apart in recrimination and violence. New alliances and loyalties might emerge, but it all took time.

Bell had gone. There was no sign of her around the castle, and no sign of her setting off after Crows herself. He'd been her lover, and Mary didn't know what to make of that. Neither of them seemed the sort of people to show any of the weakness that came with love. Perhaps it had just been a mutual abusing of each other's power. She'd seen that before too.

Now, it came down to her eyesight against Crows' cunning. She couldn't see through the canopy of trees that stretched from the castle to the coast, but she didn't need to. Crows would – sooner or later – send his flock up into the open air as his eyes and ears, to help him find the most direct route to the White City.

If he didn't do it today, then he'd do it tomorrow. If not then, some day. She'd wait, and he'd give himself away. She held that it was inevitable that they would find him and catch him.

She dipped a wing, relished the feeling of air tearing by, and watched for movement across the landscape below. The tail-end of the storm blew the crowns of leaves into swaying soldiers, marching over the hills down to the sea, a great curved bay that was itself divided again with headlands and inlets. Lines of waves moved white across the water, and seagulls folded and dove on shoals of fish.

Looking for movement, she found it everywhere. Down was alive: it seethed and boiled with life, but none of it was what she wanted.

The morning passed, and the sun rose high in the south. Something else, too. A darkly luminous disc chasing it across the heavens. It took her more than a moment to realise what it was. It was the moon, huge and hidden against the bright blue and cotton-wool white.

She spiralled down, flying low over the trees until she spotted a flash of orange boilersuit. It was Mama. Then she had to look for a clearing, where last night's, or last year's, storm had blown a hole in the dense mat of trees to let the sunlight flood in to the under-storey.

She landed on the fallen trunk, already crumbling under her tightening claws, and transformed herself into a girl in a red dress.

'Dalip,' she said when she'd found him. 'That thing that happens when the moon goes in front of the sun.'

'Eclipse,' he said. Perhaps some who were that smart would have judged her for not knowing the proper word, but she didn't feel it.

'That. It's happening, now.'

They all walked with her back to the clearing, and peered up at the sky with their hands across their brows.

'There,' said Elena, pointing at the ghostly curve of a crater's edge as it was illuminated briefly, bright enough to cut through the glare. 'What will happen?'

'It'll go dark, and not for minutes, but for hours.'

'Do we stop, or do we go on?' Mary asked.

'Of course we'll have to stop.' Mama had already sat down, facing the warmth of the sun while she still had it. 'We can't go chasing round in the dark. Besides, my feet are pretty sore, girl, and I could do with a rest.'

'And there's no sign of Crows?' Dalip frowned, looking at the drift of insects turn about the clearing.

'No. Not yet.'

'You all right flying further?'

'Why?'

'Because Crows has been here a while. He'll know when the eclipses are due. He might even be waiting for it to send his spies up.'

She was gone almost before he'd finished speaking, up into the air, gaining as much height as she could. As she climbed she could see the black shadow in the distance, its edge defined by a sharp line on the ground that seemed to be rushing towards her like a riot.

Above her, she could feel the weight of rock rolling above her, threatening to crush her. The sun was consumed, piece by piece, by flashes and haloes, until all that was left was a nail-clipping of light.

Gone.

The black disc was overhead, and she felt so light, so giddy, that she thought she could just keep rising until she joined it in its path around Down. In the distance, the western horizon dimmed as the shadow consumed more. Behind her, the east was aglimmer as day returned.

She could see it, the outline of the moon, pale and golden. And when she looked again, the forest had fallen silent. The wind held its breath.

There, in the next valley over, a sudden disturbance as bright-eyed black specks lifted themselves into the clear still air, and spread out like a fan to the north and west and south. She spotted the clearing again where the others rested, and flew low over it, once, twice, three times, reluctant to land even for a moment in case she lose sight of her quarry.

Someone got the idea, and the four of them started off in the direction of her flight.

She rose again and glided high and stealthily, watching the crows as they came and went, their paths seemingly random but always centred on one slowly moving point.

She kept ahead of her friends on the ground, doubling back occasionally and swooping over their heads to keep them on the right track. Slowly, they began to close the distance between them and Crows.

Another dilemma. soon It would impossible for her to hide

from the crows, or use her flight as a navigation aid. Crows would melt into the dark, and she would be blind to him, passing within touching distance of him and never seeing him.

Daylight, and the trailing edge of the shadow, was some distance away. Once it arrived, Crows would call his birds back, and that would be that. It had to be now, then. And it had to be her.

She was right above where she thought Crows was. She beat her wings to stall her forward flight, then folded them back against her flanks. She dropped, the air roaring in her ears. She struck the twigs first, shattering them with her outstretched feet, but then came the branches and finally the ground. It was undignified, but it was quick.

She ended up at his feet, sprawled in the leaf litter, with torn leaves and split greenwood pattering down around her.

Crows cried out in alarm, something high-pitched and wailing, then he jumped back.

When she raised herself to her hands and knees, she could see almost nothing: her human eyes were defeated where her hawk's eyes had been so clear. The vague outlines of trees, the fluttering of birds, their warning-caws urgent – and a boxy wooden crate the size of a suitcase.

That was it. That was what they'd come for. She crawled her way to it and lay over the top, scratched and torn.

'Hey,' she remembered to call. 'Hey, I'm over here. I've got them. I've got the maps.'

Crows had vanished. Of course he had. He also wouldn't have gone far. He'd be crouched in the deepest shadow, watching to see whether she was bluffing, waiting for a chance to get his maps back.

There came an answering shout, and she yelled all the louder. Crows might try something in the seconds it would take for them to find her, and he'd be desperate.

Nothing. No attempt to knock her aside, open the chest,

grab a handful of maps and run. She thought she could feel the shadows around her shift and swim, but they did that wherever she looked.

Luiza burst into view first, out of breath, hair ragged. 'Where is he?'

'He's here, hiding.'

She turned around, and around again.

'You won't see him until he wants you to,' said Mary. 'Careful.'

Then Mama and Elena appeared, and it looked like they might actually get away with this. Crows wasn't going to fight them all, was he?

'Where's Dalip?'

'He's coming. Slowly, but he's coming.' Mama put her hand to her chest. 'The Lord knows I'm not made for running, girl, but he's like a wet rag.'

Because she was watching for it, Mary could see part of the shadow beside the tree Mama was leaning on split away and move on its own, back in the direction they'd all come.

'I see you, Crows,' she said. She levered herself up off the map box and pointed. 'If I can see you, I can stop you.'

The shadow hesitated. Dalip was visible in the distance between the trees, uncertain of which way to go.

'We're over here,' she waved. 'We're all over here.'

The shadow fell away, although Crows was scarcely more visible without his cloak of night. His nervous, uncertain smile was his only discernible feature. Above them, the moon still dominated the dark sky.

'You appear to have the advantage, Mary,' he said.

'Too fucking right.' She waited for the crows to settle in the branches above their heads, their glassy black eyes watching everything that happened. 'You stole my map,' she said.

'A moment of weakness on my part. I would be glad to return it to you.'

'Not so fast, you bastard. That map is mine, and you don't get to decide whether you give it back or not. But we're taking all these maps: Bell's and yours too.'

Crows gasped like a thwarted pantomime villain. 'Would you beggar me, Mary? Would you leave me poor in this world?'

'You left me to fight Bell on the mountain, while you ran back to the castle and stole my map.' She could feel her fingers twitch, and the leaves and sticks around her grow light. 'Yes. Yes, I would leave you with nothing.'

'I saved you on the mountain. I gave you the chance to escape. I taught you to fly. Your harsh treatment of me does not repay my good deeds, Mary.'

Dalip came up behind Crows and stood at his shoulder.

'Is this him?'

'I'd introduce you, but he doesn't have many reasons to stick around any more. Right, Crows?'

Crows seemed to realise that he was in trouble. He spread his hands wide. 'Perhaps, then, we can come to an arrangement? My maps can be part of any deal.'

'You mean our maps,' said Dalip and went to sit on the roughly finished wooden crate.

'You see,' said Mary. 'We can take it from here. We don't need you.'

She listened to her own words, and saw how Crows' smile slipped and faded, an eclipse of his own making.

'How much – how many maps – are in the box?'

'Wealth unimaginable,' said Crows.

'I can imagine a lot,' she said, thinking back to the jeweller's window with its bright lights and pretty stones. She watched Crows' own fingers flex. Would he fight her now? Did she care enough to want to avoid that?

'Is it enough for six?' she asked.

'More than enough,' said Crows. 'But ...'

'Mary,' said Luiza, 'we cannot trust this man.'

'I know, I know. I know what it's like to pitch up in an

unfamiliar place with no friends. Better make them quick or you'll get thrown to the wolves. In our case, that's literally what happened. What we should do is ditch him and find someone who won't screw us over the first opportunity they get. The problem is, where do we get them from? Everyone here is on the make, or working for someone who is.'

'If it will help, I apologise for my past actions, and look to make amends in the future.' Crows bowed low to them all.

'You serious, girl?' said Mama, stepping forward to examine the man minutely. 'This weasel? He hung you out to dry, and we don't know exactly what happened between him and that woman Bell, either, that let him get her maps too. Something shifty, I don't doubt. Isn't that right, Mr Crows?'

'Madam, I want to explain.'

'Oh, save your explanations. I don't believe a single word that comes out of your mouth, and neither should anyone else.' She jabbed him in the chest, just in case there was any doubt who she was referring to.

Crows stayed silent as Mama circled him, grunting with disapproval.

'So what do we do?' asked Dalip. 'We've got his maps. Do we need him too?'

Mary gnawed at her knuckle. If only Crows wasn't such an inconstant bastard. She liked him despite that, despite everything, but it wasn't up to her. Crows could be useful to them, if they could tame him and stop him from trying to steal the maps back at every opportunity.

'Okay,' she said. 'Where are we going now?'

'This White City,' said Luiza. 'The maps, and your sight, will tell us which direction to take. We do not need him.'

'Crows: where were you going?'

'The White City,' he said.

Mary pursed her lips. If they were all going in the same direction, then why not travel together? There were still five of them to one of him.

Dalip sat up and drummed his heel on the side of the crate. 'It's not any of us who are really going to White City. It's the maps that are going: we're just accompanying them. Who actually owns them is … Look, if we can get paper and ink we can copy them, as many times as we want.'

'No, no, no,' started Crows.

'Shut up,' said Mama. 'Go on, Dalip.'

'Granted that their value goes down with every copy that we make, but we're not primarily interested in selling them and using them as wealth. What we want is the information the maps contain, and whether we can use it to get back home. That doesn't degrade, no matter how many times we copy the maps, and if we can make a bigger, better map that contains all the details from the smaller maps, then we might even make it more valuable.' He shrugged. 'If Crows wants the originals after that, then he can take them, and it won't bother us at all. How does that sound?'

Crows sounded incredulous. 'You would give me the maps? All of them?'

'After we'd made copies and checked them, why not? Like I said, we don't want to spend them. We want to use them to find our way. In the meantime, you can make sure we're not mugged by some other bunch of thieves.'

'Why not copy the maps here?' asked Elena.

'It's not like we can pop to the shops for a pad of A4 and a packet of biros,' said Dalip. 'Paper-making is going to happen in only a very few places here. We may as well go to one of them.'

She nodded, satisfied with his explanation, and his plan. 'Okay. I trust you, and if you say he comes, he comes.'

'I do not trust him,' said Luiza. 'At all. Leave him here to rot.'

'I don't trust him either,' said Dalip. 'But I still think we can work together.'

Mama humphed and put her hands on her hips. 'Fool me

once, shame on you. Fool me twice, shame on me. And I'm figuring that you've been doing a lot of fooling, Mr Crows, and you don't know when to stop. Oh, I'm sure you're full of stories and helpful advice, and who knows, some of it, even most of it, may be true. But at heart, you're a liar and a thief. You're not going to change that any time soon, and being so close to so much treasure is going to be such a temptation, that apple Eve offered Adam is going to look like wormwood after a while. Mark my words, this man is not to be trusted with anything important.'

Crows looked sourly at the ground. 'That is harsh, to have all your faults laid out before you. But, good lady, I cannot deny that you are right. My nature is to betray those who trust me, eventually, when it will do them most damage. I will leave you now, and wish you well. Perhaps we will meet again, under different circumstances.'

Head still down, he started to walk away, and only stopped when Mary started her slow hand-clap.

'Brilliant. I know they don't have telly here, but you'd get some sort of top award for that speech.'

'I do not know what you mean, Mary.'

'Course you don't. Come back, Crows.'

'Are you sure?'

'You'll follow us every step of the way, no matter what we want. So the only way to stop you is to break your legs. What we have are two votes for, and two against. You need to convince me you're worth the bother.'

He scratched at his chin. 'I do not think I can,' he said eventually. 'Your friend was most eloquent and perceptive. I am all that she says I am.'

'It's me you hurt the most. But it's me you helped the most. I'm not going to say I'll trust you, but I am prepared to have you along. A deal's a deal, right? You can have the maps after we've finished with them, and not before.'

'I do not know what to say. I do not deserve such kindness, such mercy.'

'No. No, you don't. Just try not to get us all killed.'

'I will make every effort to deliver you safe to the White City.'

'Which probably is as good an offer as we're going to get.'

The sky above the trees began to lighten, and the crows chattered to each other. The eclipse was almost over. Colour flooded the forest. What had been shades of grey were now greens and browns, the orange of the others' overalls, and the red of her dress. Crows' skin glowed.

'Why don't we see what everyone's been fighting over?' Dalip slid off the crate, and pulled at the stiff metal hasp on the lid. 'Wouldn't it be funny if it was empty?'

'No,' said Mary and Crows simultaneously, urgently.

'It was just a joke.'

The hinges creaked, and they all peered in. It was stuffed with rolls and folded squares of parchment.

'That's ...' said Mary. 'Even I know that's a fuck-load of maps. Where do we even start with them?'

She reached in and picked out the top leaf. When she opened it up, she saw that it was hers. She flattened it out on top of the pile. The others, not knowing that she'd drawn it, pointed out the features that they thought they recognised.

Dalip put his finger on the symbol she'd used for the door to Down Station.

'There,' he said. 'We know where that is, and where it led. Everything else has to fit around that fixed point. So that's where we have to start.'

She folded the map back up, and closed the lid. They'd come with nothing. Now they were rich. Powerful, even. She wasn't used to the idea of that. She was someone, even if she wasn't a queen. Not yet, anyway.

The box had a rope handle on each end. She lifted one, and waited for someone to take the other. It was Crows.

'Which way?'

The birds above them exploded outwards in a flurry of beating black wings, and after a moment, Crows nodded.

'That way.'

They set off, as if they did this all the time: a man who could turn into a serpent, a girl who could turn into a hawk, and a boy who slew monsters.

'This White City,' asked Dalip. 'Why do they call it that?'

'It is made of white stone, cut and dressed by men. It is the only place I know of which is not a gift of Down. Eventually, everyone goes to the White City. They seek answers.'

'Do they find them?'

'Mostly no. And that is why they eventually leave again.'

Mary looked around at Crows. 'So tell me why we're going again?'

'Because this time, we might be the ones with the answers.'

Crows was serious. At least, he was faking serious really well.

'Portals do not close, Mary. If they do, then it is not this world which is ending. It is London and the world we left. What can we learn, and what can we do? Who knows?' He shrugged. 'We will find out when we reach the White City.'

Turn the page for an excerpt from the next thrilling book
in the series:

THE WHITE CITY

1

The moon was overhead, and Mary was on her back, staring up at its vast ivory seas.

'Do you think,' she said idly, 'do you think I could fly there?'

'No.' Dalip, lying nearby, sounded definite, but she wasn't so sure. She could see the shadows cast by the lunar mountains shift as they passed overhead, and if she reached up, she thought she might touch them.

She raised her hand, extending her fingers, stretching out. But all she felt was cool air, not the dry granularity of another world. She traced the curves of the craters, the lines of the rilles, and wondered.

'Why not?' She let her arm fall back and rested her wrist across her forehead.

'The atmosphere's only, what, eighty kilometres thick, and for almost nine-tenths of that it's too thin to sustain life. The moon's further away from Down than that. A lot further.'

'Sure?'

'Positive. Our moon is four hundred thousand kilometres away.'

'Okay.' She batted away a tiny flying thing that seemed intent on hovering between her nose and her top lip. 'But what if it's not like that here? What if, you know, magic?'

'This moon doesn't have an atmosphere. If it did, it'd have weather, and we'd be able to see clouds. The shadows are too sharp, too. Light scatters in air – that's why the sky's blue – and there's no evidence for that. So, yes. Magic. But you can't fly to the moon. Not even here.'

His voice grew increasingly exasperated, and she tutted. The silence between them dragged out.

'I . . .' said Dalip finally. She heard him turn on his side to face her. 'I'm worried.'

There was a lot to be worried about. They had control of the biggest cache of maps that Down had ever seen – at least according to Crows, but he was an inveterate bullshitter – and that level of wealth was going to draw the wrong kind of attention. And in Down, almost all attention seemed to be the wrong kind.

She twisted her head to see Dalip. She was on one side of the rough wooden trunk containing the maps, and he was the other. Though it wasn't big, the size of a large suitcase, the trunk obscured him from shoulders to knees. She touched the planks to remind her of the riches and danger inside.

'So what are you worried about?' she asked. 'Apart from thieves, assassins, monsters, the weather, Crows, the portals, the journey and this city we're supposed to be heading for? Tell me if I've left something out.'

'Tides,' said Dalip.

'Fuck off.'

'No, I'm serious. A moon that huge should create tides higher than mountains, and that's without thinking about the earthquakes it should be causing. It doesn't make sense.'

'I can turn into a giant fucking eagle-thing, and you're saying the tide doesn't do what it should?'

The pale light from above cast deep shadows on Dalip's face. One eye was bright and glittering; the other, dark and hidden.

'Down has to follow rules, even if they're different to what we're used to.'

'Does it?'

'Yes. And we know most of them are similar, because if they weren't, we wouldn't even be able to exist here. Gravity—'

'Gravity?'

'—is an intrinsic property of mass. We don't feel any heavier or lighter, so it must be about the same here, and yet the moon doesn't behave like it is.'

He was lecturing her, so she took her revenge and shook her fist at the sky. 'Fuck you, moon,' she called.

He rolled back and drew his lips into a thin line. She'd offended him again, something she didn't mean to do yet managed almost as often as he pissed her off by parading his education. To her, his quest for order amongst the chaos – a chaos as woven through Down as a silver thread through a banknote – seemed pointless. As far as she could tell, Down did as it pleased: it gave and took away, capricious as a gang leader. Sometimes it was generous, sometimes it was searingly violent, but it was never predictable.

'I'm sorry,' she said, 'that Down doesn't do what you want it to do. It doesn't do some of the things that I want it to. But unlike you, I don't expect it to.'

He groaned, 'I know. It's . . . I want it to be logical. And there are patterns. The thing with the portals, the lines of power, the villages and castles, the instruments Bell used – they had to be measuring something, or she wouldn't have had so many of them. Down orbits its sun, and moon goes round Down predictably. There are rules—'

'Even to magic?'

'Even that. If we can understand them, then we can start to predict events, and then maybe control them.'

'But what if it isn't like that? Bell was batshit crazy. I've got scars on my back to prove that.'

'Then,' he said, 'this box of maps is worthless, and we may as well cut them up for toilet paper.'

He had a point. Everyone, but especially Crows and Bell,

whose opinions about this were the only ones that really counted, thought like Dalip: given enough information, an answer would fall out and give them control of the portals. That was pretty much what being a geomancer was all about. Mary had her doubts, though. Down was more like the kids' homes she'd been brought up in than the schools that had tried to educate her. Lots of rules; almost all of them broken, almost all of the time.

Mary put her hand in front of her face again and looked at the moon through the bars of her fingers. One side of them was silvered. The side closest to her were black shadow. She concentrated on that darkness and dragged it like ribbons through the air, five ragged lines whose edges trembled in time with her fingertips.

She stared at what she'd done, at what she could do. It was simple enough now she knew how. Crows had showed her, and she'd practised. And yet, when the others – Dalip, Elena, Luiza, Mama – had tried, none of them could emulate her. It was a gift to her, and her alone. As far as she knew, science didn't work like that. It didn't prefer one person over another.

So if there were patterns, they were fucking weird. Easier perhaps to believe that she was Down's favourite: unlike poor, mad Stanislav, who had been blessed in an entirely different way. She could still see the eyes and the teeth in her dreams. So many eyes, so many teeth.

She blinked the image away, or at least tried to, because it seemed to be burned on her retinas like a bright light.

'I remember toilet paper,' she said to distract herself. 'I remember the first fag of the day, and leaning out the window to blow the smoke away. I remember the traffic on the street below, and the people on the pavement. I miss the toilet paper.'

'Oh, come on. You were made for Down,' said Dalip, and he sat up, leaf-litter clinging to the back of his orange work overalls. He pushed himself up using the box until he was kneeling, hands on the lid. 'But I don't know about the rest of us.'

The moon, still vast and close, passed with uncanny silence. In her mind, it rumbled and growled past like a huge truck. The trees, the ground, the air itself, should be shaking.

'I don't know why I don't miss those things. Okay, it was all a bit shit, and I was in fuck-ton of trouble, but I was getting it together. I even had a job, for fuck's sake, a crappy cleaning job, but I wasn't going to do that forever. I didn't ask for London to burn down, and I didn't ask to come here. But now we're here . . .'

'. . . we have to decide what we're going to do.' Dalip leaned heavily on the trunk, making it creak, and when he got up, he did so carefully, stiffly.

Mary had given him those injuries, nearly killing him in order to save him from smearing himself against the iron-hard surface of a lake. She still felt guilty. She watched him stretch, and squeeze a finger between his scalp and the band of cloth he wore instead of his turban. He scratched and sagged, and she looked up at him, looking down at her. Her red dress, long to her ankles, bare to her shoulders, was less vibrant than when she'd first worn it to go Stanislav-hunting, but it was still more than serviceable. She'd put on the mantle of the Red Queen. Maybe one day she'd actually be that person: she'd sit on a throne, and let all the responsibility that title brought settle on her proud head.

The presumably airless moon had drifted in the direction of her feet, affording her an oblique look at the ring of mountains surrounding one crater. The sunward slopes were bright, those in the shade utterly dark. Beyond it, the sky was blank, like a wall of night. No stars, no other planets, nothing. Down, its moon and its sun, was all there was.

'What do you think happened?' she asked. 'To London.'

'There's a thing called a firestorm.' Dalip shrugged and sat down on the trunk. 'Learnt about it in history. If enough stuff burns – and we're talking about a city-sized amount of stuff – all the hot air rising causes a hurricane-force wind to suck in fresh air from all around. It feeds the fire with fresh oxygen, and it gets hotter and hotter until there's nothing left to burn. We made it happen in World War Two, dropping incendiaries on German cities. Killed tens of thousands of people. Not soldiers, either. Just civilians, hiding in their cellars from the bombing, roasted alive by the heat. Like we almost were.'

'Fucking hell,' she said.

But they'd escaped. They'd opened the door to the street, caught a fleeting glimpse of an inferno, then been in Down in all its baffling majesty.

'Nuclear bombs can do the same sort of thing. It doesn't take a thousand bombers any more. Only one. But,' and he clenched his teeth, showing them white in the darkness, 'you're right. That's not what happened. We would have felt the bomb go off; it would have been like an earthquake. Unmistakable.'

'There were bangs and other noises first. Like thunder, in the distance sometimes, then closer. I thought it was actually thunder. Then I went underground, and I couldn't hear it any more.'

'And an hour, an hour and a half later, the whole of London was burning down.' Dalip stood again and raised himself up on tip-toe. 'If it wasn't a bomb, then I don't know. London just caught fire, everywhere, all at once. If we made it out, then maybe other people did, if there are other portals attached to our time. They'd all be starting off at different points on Down, and they'd all be as clueless as us. And assuming we stay alive, we might bump into them one day.'

'That'd be weird.'

'No weirder than meeting a whole bunch of people from the sixties, or the thirties. When did Crows say he crossed over?'

'Thirty . . . six? They cut him. Badly. If he hadn't found Down, they would have killed him.'

'That doesn't make him a decent man. Or rather, it didn't. Let's face it, none of us deserved to be saved. None of us are wiser, smarter, stronger or prettier than all those we watched die.

Whatever criteria Down uses, how worthy we are doesn't come into it.'

She climbed to her feet and brushed her skirts free of leaf-litter. 'So what if it was just luck? I didn't want to die, and I still don't. I wanted to live, which is what I can do now. Don't tell me you don't feel the same?'

Dalip looked at the ground, then at the trees around the edge of the small clearing they'd co-opted for their camp.

'It's not just the lack of tides that scares me,' he finally said. 'I'm not very . . . I just . . . Look, I have to face up to the fact that I'm comfortable being told what to do. I know where I am with that. I'm safe.'

'You were nails taking on Stanislav. Fucking nails, man. You threw us off a mountain to finish him off.'

'And where did that get me?'

'Here. Alive. What the fuck are you complaining about?'

'My own choices nearly killed me. When I sleep, I dream I'm falling. Sometimes I don't wake up in time. Sometimes, you don't catch me, and you know what? It hurts. I hit that water so hard, it's bits of me that sink.'

She regarded his shadow. 'Why didn't you say before?'

'Because you're so obviously enjoying yourself, there didn't seem any point in, you know. Raining on your parade.'

'I thought we were mates. Proper friends who told each other stuff.'

'I'm,' he said quietly, 'I'm not supposed to be weak. I'm supposed to be a lion. It's even my name. One of our gaolers called me "Little lion man", but not in a good way. He knew. He knew I was weak.'

'So what happened to him?' she asked Dalip.

'Stanislav killed him. Stabbed him a dozen times in the guts.'

He shrugged again, and she didn't know what to say. She was used to the empty posturing of street kids, posing for shaky-cam videos while brandishing kitchen knives and ball-bearing catapults, where weakness was the one thing you didn't dare show, let alone tell anyone else. It didn't matter whether they were cowards, or too stupid to run when it all went down: it was the act, and that was the one thing that Dalip's tightly-controlled world had never taught him.

If she wasn't careful – if he wasn't careful – Down would eat him alive. It might have already started, and she couldn't tell.

The others were on the opposite side of the fire; four still shapes, curled in various configurations on ground that, no matter how soft it started off, always ended up like concrete.

'That bloke's gone, and you're still here. And you know what? That's what counts. You found it when you needed it, and when you need it again, you can always find it again. I don't know what you think a man is, but I've put up with kids pretending that they're all grown up, all big men, and they can fuck off right off. You don't want that any more than I do. We all know what you did, and none of us think you're weak. Fucking hell, look at you. You were this stringy thing, and now you've got all the muscles and stuff.'

He acknowledged his subtle transformation with a shrug. 'My grandfather—'

'Fought the Japanese when he was still a kid, you told me, like a dozen times. And what a pain in the arse he was to live with.'

For a moment, Dalip's expression darkened and deepened, and he held himself tense and still. Then he let it go, and looked up at the receding moon. 'You sound like my mum.'

'Maybe you should have listened to her.'

'I did. I do. I . . . I'm hanging on to the few certainties I have left.'

Mary walked the few steps to him, and landed a slow, deliberate punch on his shoulder. 'We need you, not your grandfather. The war veteran we had turned into a soup of eyes and teeth, and I don't want you going the same way.'

He nodded, but she could see that he was scared of that, too.

'You're not, are you?' she asked. If he was, there'd be very little she could do, except ask him to leave. Stanislav had hidden his transformation so well that by the time it had taken him completely, he'd been almost impossible to kill. Almost.

'No, that's not happening,' said Dalip. 'At least, not that I know of. Keep an eye, or three, on me.'

'That's not a good joke.'

He shrugged, and the glimmer of his smile shone in the moonlight. 'I was never any good at telling them. Always the serious kid in the corner. I thought I might lighten up a bit.'

'All work and no play, right?'

He shrugged again. 'Something like that. I'm not actually dull, just . . . people tell me what to do, and I do it. It's a habit.'

'No one's going to tell you what to do here. Not now you're free of Bell and her Wolfman.'

'There'll be others. Once they find out what's in the box, it'll be everybody.' Dalip looked at the ground, then at her. 'If we pull this off, we'll be the luckiest people ever.'

'What if that's it? We don't have to be the smartest or the strongest. Just the luckiest. What, if out of all of London, we were the luckiest?'

'Then,' he said, 'everything we ever knew, everyone we ever knew, is ash. My family, Mama's babies: they're all gone, and it doesn't matter what we learn or if we can open the portals: there's nothing to go back to. Perhaps it'd be better to hope we're not lucky at all.'

Mary had forgotten that her escape was his captivity. She burned, and started to walk away.

'It's all a bit academic though, isn't it?' he said at her retreating form. 'We don't know, we won't until we try to find out. And I'd rather know than not.'

'I'm sorry,' she said. She was, too.

'I'll wake Mama and Luiza. It's time.' His bare feet brushed through the grass of the clearing, leaving her with the crate of maps.

She knelt next to it and undogged the hasps that held it closed. She creaked the lid open, just a little way, so she could glimpse the jumble of paper inside. There was so much of it, and they'd barely looked through any of the sheets, let alone tried to work out how, and if, they might fit together.

She lowered the lid again. Crows seemed to be fast asleep, but a single black bird perched on the tree above him, staring down at her, its eyes bright with reflected fire. Mary scowled at it and, with a flutter of dark wings, it was gone.

ABOUT GOLLANCZ

Gollancz is the oldest SF publishing imprint in the world. Since being founded in 1927 Gollancz has continued to publish a focused selection of bestselling and award-winning authors. The front-list includes **Ben Aaronovitch**, **Joe Abercrombie**, **Charlaine Harris**, **Joanne Harris**, **Joe Hill**, **Alastair Reynolds**, **Patrick Rothfuss**, **Nalini Singh** and **Brandon Sanderson**.

As one of the largest Science Fiction and Fantasy imprints in the UK it is no surprise we have one of the most extensive backlists in the world. Find high quality SF on Gateway written by such authors as **Philip K. Dick**, **Ursula Le Guin**, **Connie Willis**, **Sir Arthur C. Clarke**, **Pat Cadigan**, **Michael Moorcock** and **George R.R. Martin**.

We also have a strand of publishing in translation, which includes French, Polish and Russian authors. Gollancz is home to more award-winning authors than any other imprint, with names including **Aliette de Bodard**, **M. John Harrison**, **Paul McAuley**, **Sarah Pinborough**, **Pierre Pevel**, **Justina Robson** and many more.

The SF Gateway
More than 3,000 classic, rare and previously out-of-print SF novels at your fingertips.
www.sfgateway.com

The Gollancz Blog
Bringing you news from our worlds to yours. Stories, interviews, articles and exclusive extracts just for you!
www.gollancz.co.uk

GOLLANCZ
LONDON